SILENT PARTNER

Also by Stephen Frey
in Large Print:

Trust Fund
The Day Trader

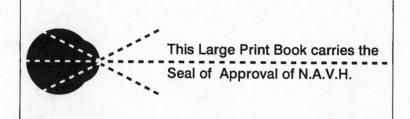

SILENT PARTNER

STEPHEN FREY

Thorndike Press • Waterville, Maine

Published in 2003 by arrangement with The Ballantine Publishing Group, a division of Random House, Inc.

Thorndike Press® Large Print Core Series.

The tree indicium is a trademark of Thorndike Press.

The text of this Large Print edition is unabridged.
Other aspects of the book may vary from the original edition.

Set in 16 pt. Plantin by Christina S. Huff.

Printed in the United States on permanent paper.

ISBN 0-7862-5239-1 (lg. print : hc : alk. paper)

To my daughters, Christina and Ashley.
I love you both so much.
You're growing up too fast.

And to my wife, Lil. I love you too.

ACKNOWLEDGMENTS

A special thanks to all the folks at Ballantine for their continued support, but especially Mark Tavani, Gina Centrello, and Kim Hovey.

A special thanks to my agent, Cynthia Manson.

A special thanks to Matthew Lee, who was tremendously helpful in terms of research and guidance on this book.

And to the others who have consistently supported my efforts: Stephen Watson, Matt Malone, Peter Borland, Jim and Anmarie Galowski, Bob Wieczorek, Kevin "Big Sky" Erdman, Chris Tesoriero, Baron Stewart, Barbara Fertig, Bart Begley, Walter Frey, Scott Andrews, Marvin Bush, and Mike Pocalyko.

PROLOGUE

Angela Day and Sally Chambers had been inseparable for as long as either of them could remember. They'd grown up together in the same trailer park ten miles outside of Asheville, North Carolina. Attended the same public high school. And both had been accepted to the state university where they'd been roommates all four years. Both were strikingly attractive, intelligent, and self-assured despite their modest pedigrees. In fact, there was only one major difference between them. Angela was white, and Sally was black.

Now, only a few weeks from graduation, they realized that the constant closeness they had taken for granted for so many years was almost over. Angela had been accepted to Duke's graduate business school in Durham, and Sally was going home to Asheville — far away from Duke in the western part of North Carolina. She was needed there to care for her ailing mother.

Both assumed they would keep in touch by telephone after graduation, and they would certainly make a point of seeing each other at holidays. But they knew that sooner or later the phone conversations would become less frequent, trips to Asheville would become less appealing to Angela, and, as a result, their lives would probably drift apart. Neither had mentioned the approaching inevitability. They had simply kept to their routine, quietly determined to enjoy their last few weeks together.

"This is it," said Angela, pulling Sally to a stop and pointing up at the large fraternity house looming over them in the darkness of the spring evening. Music blared from inside over muffled shouts and screams. "Tau Kappa Rho."

Sally stepped back. "You didn't tell me we were coming to Tau Kappa."

"What's the big deal?"

"These guys are animals. Aren't they the ones who painted Klan slogans on the freshman dorms last fall?"

"That was just a rumor."

"Well, I heard these guys were responsible. I don't want to go in there," Sally said flatly.

"Oh, come on," Angela pleaded. "It'll be fine. Craig's a member."

"Craig who?"

"He's in our economics class. The one I pointed out to you last week."

"So that's what tonight's hike is all about."

"We've been making eye contact all semester. After class the other day he asked me to stop by the party."

"I'm not going in."

"Oh, please. We'll only stay for a little while. Just long enough for me to find him and say hi."

"No."

"I don't want to go in by myself. I'll look pathetic."

"No."

Angela shook her head. "This isn't like you."

"What do you mean?"

"I've never known you to back down from anything. I've never known you to be scared."

"I'm not scared," Sally said, crossing her arms defiantly.

"Then let's go." Angela grabbed Sally's hand and began pulling her up the cobblestone walkway leading to the fraternity house. "What could happen?"

They climbed the front steps together, moving past several young men tapping a keg in one corner of the raised brick porch that spanned the house's facade. Angela pushed the door open, and, as they slipped into the dimly lit room and a sea of young people, they were hit by rock music blaring from two huge speakers along the far wall. They dodged several couples pretzeling wildly, and skirted small pockets of young men chugging beers.

"This is wild!" Sally shouted, jostled by a woman who had been twisted so recklessly by her dance partner she had lost her grip on his hand and stumbled backward through the crowd.

"This way!" Angela yelled over her shoulder,

leading Sally deeper into the house. "It looks quieter over there."

After pushing their way through the bodies, they made it to another room where things were less chaotic. Around a large table people were playing a game involving cards, dice, and clear plastic cups full of foamy beer. Several of the bleary-eyed participants seemed ready to pass out, swaying as they watched the game and waited for their turn.

"Please, let's leave," Sally begged. "You'll never find the guy in here. This is insane."

"Just a few more minutes. He promised he'd be here."

"He's probably already gone or —"

"Angela!"

They turned at the sound of the voice, and in front of them stood Craig Smythe. He was tall and blond, and he leaned down and gave Angela a quick kiss on the cheek.

Angela smiled at him. "I didn't think I was going to find you!"

"I've been keeping an eye out for you. Glad you could make it."

"This is my friend Sally Chambers," Angela said, pointing.

Craig shook Sally's hand, then leaned down and put his lips to Angela's ear. "Follow me," he said, taking her by the hand and leading her out of the room.

Angela glanced back at Sally, who was doing her best to keep up. A few moments later they reached another room that was less crowded, and far enough away from the bedlam of the dance floor that they didn't have to yell to hear each other.

"This room is off-limits to underclassmen unless they've been given specific permission by a senior to come in," Craig explained.

"This place is out of control," Angela exclaimed.

Craig chuckled. "This is nothing. Just one more Saturday night. Now, what would you two like to drink? How about a little punch?" he suggested. Before either of them could answer, he had motioned to an underclassman loitering outside the room.

The underclassman trotted over to where they stood. "Yes, sir?"

"Go upstairs and get us some grain punch," Craig ordered. "It's in one of the back bedrooms. Tell the guys guarding the tub that I sent you. Use the large cups."

"I can't carry three large cups at once," the underclassman complained.

"That's all right with me," Sally answered. "I don't like that stuff anyway. It's too strong."

Angela managed to catch Sally's eye, and shot her a desperate plea-for-privacy look.

"Oh, all right." Sally sighed, turning to follow the underclassman toward a stairway. "I'll help you," she called to him.

"Sally'll be all right, won't she?" Angela asked, irritated at herself for being so selfish.

"Oh, sure." Craig smiled down at her. "You know, you have incredible eyes," he said, leaning forward. "Has anyone ever told you that?"

Guys told her that constantly, but she never tired of hearing it. *A woman has to be aware of her most outstanding features and never be afraid to use them to her advantage,* her mother had told her many times. She stared at her green eyes in the mirror every morning, trying to understand what they saw. She didn't get it. But they did. *Which,* her mother had counseled her, *is all that matters.*

"I mean it," Craig said. "They're gorgeous."

"Thanks."

Several minutes later the underclassman returned carrying two large cups full of something that looked like Hawaiian Punch. He handed them to Craig and Angela.

"Where's Sally?" Angela asked, taking a sip. Instantly, she closed her eyes and coughed. The alcohol was overpowering.

"Upstairs talking basketball with some guy."

That made sense. Sally had been a star on the girls' basketball team in high school. Though not talented enough to play on the university's intercollegiate team, she excelled in the intramural program.

"So she's okay?" She was still breathless from the grain alcohol.

The young man nodded. "Oh, yeah. She's fine. She seemed to be having a good time showing the guy that she knew more about basketball than he did."

That made sense too. Sally wasn't shy about putting an overconfident male in his place.

"All right, goat," Craig announced, "that's enough. Get out of here. You've served your purpose."

The young man slunk from the room.

"What's a goat?" Angela wanted to know.

"A freshman. The lowest form of life."

Angela rolled her eyes. *Boys would be boys,* she thought.

"Let's dance," Craig suggested, placing their cups aside and whisking Angela toward the dance floor.

When they'd had enough loud music and flying bodies, they retreated once again to the quieter room reserved for seniors.

"That was great," Craig said. "You really know how to move."

"Thanks."

"Here's your drink." He grabbed her cup off the shelf and held it out to her.

"No," she said, looking around for Sally. She hadn't shown up on the dance floor, and Angela had expected her to be waiting here when they returned.

Another young man stumbled up to Craig, clearly drunk. "Hey, Brother Smythe," he said, laughing obnoxiously as he rested his elbow on Craig's shoulder to steady himself. "You should see what's going on up in the launching pad."

"What's the launching pad?" Angela asked.

"A party room on the top floor."

"It's so great," the guy leaning on Craig's shoulder slurred.

"What is?"

Slowly the intoxicated boy looked up, eyes glazed. "They've got some nigger bitch tied to a chair up there. They're forcing her to chug."

For several moments it seemed to Angela that the room had gone deathly silent, and that all things were moving in slow motion. She seemed unable to breathe or move or even think. Then the music was blaring in her ears again and she was racing for the stairway with Craig right behind her.

"Where's the launching pad?" she screamed when they had reached the second floor.

"This way!"

Craig flashed past, and she sprinted after him, up another, steeper flight of steps, then down a long hallway to a closed door. "Open up!" he shouted, banging on the door with both fists. "Open the Goddamn door!"

From inside, Angela could hear whistling and loud voices, and she began to beat on the door too.

"Look out."

Angela darted out of Craig's way as he launched himself at the door, lowering his shoulder and hurling himself against it. It cracked but didn't break. He took three steps back and lunged at it again. This time the lock snapped, the door flew open, and he stumbled into the room.

Sally lay sprawled on a large leather chair in a far corner of the crowded, smoky room, her wrists bound to the arms of the chair. A man was holding her head down so tightly that the veins in her neck rose grotesquely from her skin, and he was pinching her nostrils together so that she had to open her mouth wide to gasp for air.

A second young man stood beside Sally, clenching her chin and sloppily pouring the cherry-colored punch into her mouth so it splashed all over her face and ran down onto her blouse, staining the white cotton a bright red. Sally was struggling, trying to avoid the liquid, but the bindings and the hands were too strong. She tried spitting out the liquid, but they kept pouring, and she was forced to gulp it down in order to breathe.

"That's right. Drink," one of the young men yelled angrily. "Drink it all. Every damn drop."

"Yeah, all of it!" the one holding her head yelled, pulling on her ponytail so hard she screamed in pain.

"Sally!" Angela started toward the chair, but two young men at the edge of the group intercepted her. Through the bodies huddled around Sally, Angela saw her slowly stop struggling, saw her body go limp as the men continued forcing alcohol down her throat.

Craig rushed past Angela, surging into the circle of drunken fraternity brothers. Shouting at them furiously to get away, he reached down

15

and wrenched open the knots binding Sally to the chair. When she was free, he pulled her to her feet and yelled for her to get out.

For a split second Angela locked eyes with Sally across the chaos of the room, and in that instant saw the anguish on her best friend's face. Then Angela was distracted by a fist slamming into Craig's chin. He went down, tumbling backward until he came to rest against a wall, unconscious.

Angela started for Sally again, but the two young men who had intercepted her before easily kept her back. She watched in horror as the young man who had been holding Sally's head while she was tied to the chair shoved her roughly against the wall beside a curtainless window.

"Let me go!" Angela shouted, fighting frantically to free herself. "My God, you can't stand here and let this go on."

"We can do whatever we want," one of them retorted smugly. "And if you aren't careful, you'll be next."

Over his shoulder Angela watched Sally desperately try to break free, scratching and clawing at the face and arms of her attacker. Then he grabbed her by the neck with both hands, choking her and slamming her against the wall over and over. Moving her along the wall until the back of her head hit the wall beside the window, then the molding, then the glass. And then Sally was gone, and the window was smashed, and the young man who had been choking her was staring down into the darkness, his hands outstretched.

For a moment Angela gazed at the smashed window, horror-stricken. Then she raced away, down the hall and the first set of steps, then down the second set of steps and back through the party to the front door. She burst through the door and onto the brick porch, scanning the area to her left. Sally lay there, motionless, one leg pointing away from her body at a horrible, unnatural angle; the bone had snapped like a brittle twig just below the knee.

She rushed to Sally's side and knelt down, cradling Sally's head. "I'm sorry, sweetheart," Angela sobbed, caressing Sally's hair and wiping away blood from her mouth and nose. "You're going to be all right, sweetheart. I promise. You're going to be all right."

CHAPTER ONE

FEBRUARY 2003

Risk versus return. What can be lost versus what can be gained. The essence of *every* critical decision.

Invest in those dependable Treasury bonds yielding a slim but certain return, or throw caution to the wind and snap up shares of the high-tech start-up that could become next week's billion-dollar headline — or, just as easily, a bankrupt memory. Marry the safe, stable person your parents adore, or run away with the lover who ignites body and soul with a single glance — but lives only in the moment. Risk versus return. A simple concept that often imposes difficult choices. And, sometimes, terrible consequences.

Angela Day had chosen well in her business career. It was in her personal life where accepting the risks had proven catastrophic.

Until a few minutes ago the four-hour flight from Virginia had been silky smooth. Zero chop in the dark winter sky, which came as a relief because Angela hated to fly. So many times she'd heard the catchy stat about planes being safer than cars — usually from amused colleagues sitting beside her when she made the sign of the cross over her heart as the aircraft began to roll forward on takeoff. But as the Gulfstream V banked hard left on its final approach into Jackson Hole, Wyoming, and hurtled through a nasty air pocket, the statistical crutch disintegrated — just as it always did.

"Get this thing on the ground," she whispered, her fingernails digging into the arms of the plush leather seat, her stomach starting to churn. "Now."

On the way west a uniformed steward had attended to her every want, serving a delicious crab imperial dinner an hour into the flight and constantly topping off her crystal glass with a dry Chardonnay. She was accustomed to commercial aircraft and economy class, accustomed to flat Coke in plastic cups, stale pretzels, and uncomfortable seats beside infants who screamed at any change in air pressure. So, being the only passenger on a private jet as lavish as a five-star hotel suite was a welcome change, even if the luxury was a one-time-only offer made available for some as-yet-unexplained reason by a reclusive billionaire she'd only read about in the press.

But the pleasurable experience had been ruined somewhere over South Dakota, when one of the pilots had sauntered back to let her know in his gravelly, Chuck Yeager monotone that the landing might get a little dicey. A winter storm had blown in to northwest Wyoming a few hours ahead of schedule, and he wanted to make certain she was buckled in securely. He chuckled at her suggestion that he make a U-turn and beeline it back to the East Coast, then told her he'd see her on the ground. *Hopefully in one piece,* she thought. She tried to convince herself that "a little dicey" wasn't pilot-speak for "imminent disaster." Suddenly she missed economy class and its screaming infants. She glanced out the small window beside her into total darkness. *Probably the side of some mountain we're about to slam into,* she figured grimly.

Then the plane's two engines powered up, landing lights flashed on, and she was hurtling through a wall of white. "Oh, God," she murmured, digging her fingernails even deeper into the leather. A moment later, eerie blue lights appeared through the thick clouds and a snow-covered runway rose up to meet the aircraft. A hard bounce, a softer one, a deafening roar and they were taxiing through a blizzard, apparently under control. She let out an audible sigh.

"Welcome to Wyoming, Ms. Day. I hope you enjoyed the flight."

Angela looked up into the smiling face of the clean-cut attendant who had appeared from a door at the back of the cabin. "Thank you." She thought about telling him the truth — how she wished Orville and Wilbur's mother and father had never met. "Everything was fine."

"Good. Well, it's 11 P.M. here in Jackson Hole. We'll be taxiing for a few minutes, and we'd like you to remain in your seat until the plane comes to a complete stop."

"As opposed to a *partial* stop?" She grinned but he didn't react. "You didn't really have to say all that stuff about me remaining in my seat, did you? After all, I am the only passenger."

"Regulations are regulations," he answered firmly, handing her the small makeup kit she had stowed in an overhead compartment. "The rest of your luggage will be taken care of for you."

"Have you ever met Jake Lawrence?" she asked before the young man moved off.

He hesitated. "I can't say."

She smiled at him. "Does that mean you don't *know* if you've ever met him? That you don't even know what Mr. Lawrence looks like? Or that you know what he looks like, but you aren't allowed to talk about him?"

The young man smiled politely. "I can't say. I hope you enjoy your time here in the Tetons."

Then the young man disappeared through the doorway at the back of the cabin. Angela's favorite meal was crab imperial, accompanied by dry Chardonnay. The movie on the way out — *Erin Brockovich* — was one of her favorites. The books and magazines on board were her favorites, as well. It was all too neatly packaged to be coincidence.

"Sorry about the bumps on the way down,

21

Ms. Day." The pilot helped her slip into her long winter coat as she stood by the cockpit door.

"I'm just glad we're on the ground," she said.

He opened the plane's outer door as a utility truck rolled a metal stairway up to the fuselage. "Well, enjoy your stay."

"I'm sure I will."

A bearded man in orange overalls hustled up the steps toward Angela, open umbrella tilted into the driving snow. "Welcome to Jackson Hole, Ms. Day," he called loudly over the roar of the idling jet engines, holding the umbrella above her head. "Careful," he warned, holding out his arm and helping her down the slick metal stairs. "Over there," he directed when they reached the ground, pointing toward a Ford Expedition that had swung out onto the icy tarmac.

As they neared the SUV, he handed her the umbrella, then jogged ahead and opened the passenger door. A moment later she was inside and the cold, wind, and exhaust smell were gone, replaced by warmth and the soothing aromas of leather, tobacco, and coffee.

"Good evening, Ms. Day. Welcome to Jackson Hole."

Angela took a deep breath, then glanced over at the driver. He was a big man wearing a ten-gallon hat and a leather jacket with a thick wool collar. In the dim dashboard lights she thought she detected friendly eyes. Beneath his full mustache there was a wide smile.

"Is everyone out here always so darn polite?"

"Why wouldn't we be?" he answered as a baggage handler placed her luggage in the back. "After all, this is paradise."

"Sure it is," she said, watching the snow whip past the window.

"Helluva night, huh?"

"Yes," she agreed, "especially when you'd rather crawl across hot coals than fly." She hesitated. "And you can call me Angela. After all the 'Ms. Day this' and 'Ms. Day that' on the way out here, I'm starting to feel like an old maid."

The driver shook his head as he shifted into first gear. "I don't think anybody's going to mistake you for an old maid."

He had a nice voice, she decided. Confident but not cocky. Strong but not overwhelming. Soothing, almost. "What's that supposed to mean?"

"Nuthin'," he said, guiding the SUV out of the small airport and onto a deserted main road already covered by two inches of fresh powder. "I don't want to get into any hot water."

"Tell me what you meant. I'll have to mention your remark to Mr. Lawrence if you don't."

"That wouldn't be very nice," he protested, picking up a coffee mug sitting in the console between them and taking a swallow.

She grinned. "Oh, I'm only kidding." She searched for a place on the dashboard to put her makeup kit down.

"Let me move all that for you." He put the

mug back down, then reached in front of her and slid two revolvers and several boxes of ammunition out of her way.

"That's quite an arsenal you've got there."

"Hey, you never know what you're gonna run into in Wyoming. Yellowstone's only thirty miles north of here and every once in a while the grizzlies come down out of the park to see what's what. I have no desire to end up bear chow. That's not how I picture myself going out."

"Which would explain the .44 Magnum," she agreed, eyeing the larger gun now resting on the dash in front of the steering wheel. "Even though I assume most bears are hibernating, given that it's the middle of February."

"Well —"

"But what about the long-barreled .22?"

"You sure know your guns."

"I've had some experience."

"Interesting. Well, the .22's for rattlesnakes. And before you say anything, no, there aren't any of them around this time of year, either." He hesitated. "The guns are my security blanket, just in case."

"Just in case what?"

"Just in case."

She glanced over at him, trying to see beneath the brim of his ten-gallon. "You didn't tell me your name."

"John Tucker," he answered, reaching across the console without taking his eyes off the road. "Nice to meet you."

"Nice to meet you, too." She could tell he was trying to be gentle, but she still felt immense strength in his grip. "So, what did you mean?"

Tucker smiled. "You're like a dog on a bone, aren't you?"

"That's one way to put it." She'd never been accused of lacking persistence.

"Uh-oh. Now I've gone and done it."

"Tell me what you meant."

"Jesus, just that you're an attractive woman. At least, what I can see of you. But saying something like that can get a man in a lot of trouble these days."

"It won't get you in trouble with me," she assured him. "At my age I welcome all compliments."

"Your age? I bet you aren't more than twenty-five, right?"

"I'm thirty-one."

"Really?" Tucker pushed out his lower lip and raised his eyebrows.

"Does that surprise you?"

"A bit," he admitted.

"It shouldn't. Jake Lawrence is one of the wealthiest men in the world. Would you really expect him to waste time on a business meeting with someone who's just a few years out of college?"

Tucker took another sip of coffee. "Right," he murmured softly. *"A business meeting."*

For a while Angela watched the snow falling in front of the headlights. "Have you worked for

25

Mr. Lawrence very long?" she finally asked.

"Almost twenty years. I manage the working ranch where you'll be staying."

"Working ranch?"

"Yeah. We have about three thousand head of cattle here in Jackson."

"How big is the ranch?"

"Four hundred thousand acres."

Angela whistled. "My God."

"And Mr. Lawrence won't ever see more than a small part of it from the ground. Which is a shame, because some of the scenery is spectacular. He's been all over it in a chopper, but you can't really appreciate it from the air. You have to immerse yourself in something to truly appreciate its beauty." Tucker shrugged. "But Mr. Lawrence is a busy man. I suppose he doesn't have time for that."

Angela looked over at him again. "Are you from Wyoming, Mr. Tucker?"

"No. My father was in the military, so I moved around quite a bit when I was young. I'm from a lot of places. And please call me John."

"I bet you don't have many women come out here on business, do you, John?"

"More than you'd think," he said quietly.

"What did you say?"

"Oh, nothing. Just reminding myself of something I need to take care of in the morning."

"Uh-huh." Angela relaxed into the seat. "So, what's the reclusive Jake Lawrence really like?"

"Can't say," Tucker replied.

Almost as if he'd been coached, Angela thought. "What is it with you people? Is everyone scared to death of him, or does he have all of you drinking some kind of secret punch? Cherry Kool-Aid with a kick?"

"Mr. Lawrence protects his privacy. I respect that."

Angela unbuttoned her coat. It was warm inside the Expedition. "He's worth more than most small countries, and I couldn't find a picture of him anywhere. Not even on the Internet. He's been linked romantically to some of the world's most beautiful women, travels constantly, owns many companies, and probably has thousands of employees. But no photos ever surfaced. According to a couple of Web sites I checked out, the *National Enquirer* is offering a million-dollar reward for any credible photograph of him, but they haven't had to pay out yet. I would think one of you would snap a picture of him and get rich quick."

Tucker turned down the SUV's heat. "People are loyal to him."

"Loyalty usually fades at the prospect of collecting a million dollars."

"I don't know what to tell you."

"What does Mr. Lawrence look like?" she asked.

Tucker bit his lip.

"Have you ever seen him?"

Again, there was no answer.

She shook her head in disbelief. "You don't

27

actually know what he looks like, do you?"

"Heads up!"

Tucker's arm shot across Angela's chest, pinning her to the seat as he slammed on the brakes. The tires grabbed the snow-covered road for a moment, then the SUV began to slide. In the high beams a hulking form materialized out of the storm, standing in the middle of the road like a statue, mesmerized by the bright lights bearing down on it. Then the tires caught and the SUV skidded to a stop ten feet short of the form.

"Is that an elk?" Angela asked, breathless.

"Yup. A big male."

"A male? But it doesn't have any antlers."

"The males lose their antlers every winter and grow new ones in the spring. All deer species males do that. Antelope keep their antlers year-round."

"Then how do you know it's a male?"

"The shoulders. Look how broad they are."

"If you say so." After Tucker's arm slid from her body, Angela reached around and buckled her seat belt. "Thanks for catching me."

"I should have reminded you to buckle up at the airport," he apologized, dousing the headlights and leaning on the horn. When he turned the lights back on thirty seconds later, the elk was gone, the only proof of its presence a disturbed line in the snow leading off into the darkness. "Like I said, you never know what you'll run into out here."

She hadn't come close to hitting the dashboard or the windshield despite the sudden stop. John Tucker was a powerful man.

A few minutes later they turned off the main road and the snowy surface quickly gave way to clear, wet blacktop. "How is that possible?" Angela asked, leaning forward and pointing at the pavement as they approached a guard station. "Where's the snow?"

"Welcome to Jake Lawrence's world."

"What do you mean?"

"There are steam pipes buried beneath the road that prevent the surface from freezing," he explained, slowing to a stop as he waited for the guards inside the station to electronically open the gate that spanned the roadway.

"You're kidding."

He nodded to one of the guards as they passed the station. "No, I'm not. When your father is the original financial backer of the young genius who invents the software running 90 percent of all the personal computers in the world and leaves 40 percent of the company to you when he dies, you can do just about anything you want. No more worrying about the monthly mortgage. Instead of looking for ways to save, you start looking for ways to *spend.*"

Several hundred yards past the guard station, the road turned steep, snaking back and forth through a thick pine forest as it climbed a mountain. Then bright lights appeared through the snow. Moments later Tucker pulled the Expedition to a halt beneath the porte cochere of the ranch's main lodge — a four-story log structure brightly illuminated by powerful spotlights affixed to the eaves.

"Well, I hope you enjoy yourself here, Angela." Tucker held out his hand as a man who had emerged from the lodge opened her door, then retrieved her luggage from the back.

"Thank you." She took his hand, noticing this time how tough the skin of his palm was. It was the palm of a man who worked hard for a living. "Will I see you again?"

He shrugged. "Maybe. That's not up to me."

And then he leaned subtly toward her, and she knew what had happened. The light from the lodge had caught her eyes just so, giving him his first good look at them. She'd seen that same double take many times before.

"Well, good night, Angela," he said quietly.

"Good night."

She stepped out of the Expedition and followed the attendant into the lodge's foyer and down a long hallway into a huge room. The massive area was sixty feet square beneath a twenty-five-foot-high ceiling. The far wall was dominated by dramatic floor-to-ceiling windows, and the other three split-log walls were covered with stuffed animal heads, including those of several species not native to North America.

"So he kills for sport," she murmured. The words echoed in the stillness of the room.

30

As her words dissipated, a young woman wearing a maid uniform appeared from a side doorway and took Angela's makeup kit.

"Oh, thank you."

"This way, Ms. Day," the young man called over his shoulder, motioning toward a wide winding staircase that seemed to tumble into a far corner of the room like a rocky waterfall.

But, as Angela took a deep breath and prepared to climb, the attendant stopped beside the first step, pulled back a hinged picture mounted on the wall, and pressed a button. Moments later, he opened a door beside the button and ushered her and the maid into a small elevator. When the elevator opened on the fourth floor, he led Angela down another long hall to a cozy room dominated by a queen-size sleigh bed that seemed to be calling her name. It was almost midnight, which meant it was two o'clock in the morning back East. She hadn't realized until now just how exhausted she was.

"The bathroom is in there," the attendant explained, placing her bag down on a stand beneath a window, then moving to the bathroom doorway and flicking on a light. "If you need anything, simply pick up the phone on the table by your bed and wait for the operator. The kitchen is open twenty-four hours a day for your convenience," he said, moving back to the hall doorway. "Will there be anything else?"

"What about tomorrow?" she asked, watching the maid disappear into the bathroom with her

31

makeup kit, then reappear empty-handed. The woman then moved to the bed and began turning down the covers. "What time should I be ready for Mr. Lawrence?"

"Your meeting with him is at three o'clock. We have instructions to allow you to sleep until noon. If you wake up earlier, call us and we'll serve you breakfast here or downstairs, whichever you prefer."

"Which do you suggest?"

"Downstairs. The view from the dining area off the great room is fabulous."

"Unless it's still snowing."

"The storm should be past us by mid-morning. It's moving quickly."

"How many other people are staying in the lodge tonight?" Angela asked.

"You are the only guest."

"I see." Somehow she wished there were at least a few other occupants on the floor.

"Good night, Ms. Day," the attendant said, ushering the maid out ahead of him.

"Good night."

When they were gone, Angela slid the deadbolt across the door, then walked into the bathroom. After removing her clothes she stood before the large mirror above the double sink, gazing at herself. She was tired but she wanted to shower before curling up in the sleigh bed. Flying always made her want to take a shower. It was as if she needed to cleanse herself of the fear she'd endured.

She put her hands on the sink, and gazed at the face she had inherited from her parents. The wavy, jet-black hair of her Sicilian mother. The gold-specked green eyes of her Irish father and the long, thick eyelashes of her mother. Her mother's full lips below her father's thin nose. Her high cheekbones, slender face, and delicate chin.

She leaned forward until her lips almost touched the mirror, trying to be objective as she scanned her face for any signs of age lines or wrinkles. There was nothing, but she knew it wouldn't be that way for long. The physical signs of age were just around the corner.

She took two steps back and rose to her full, five-foot-eight-inch height. She was slim-waisted, and her thin upper body was dominated by large, firm breasts. She pivoted, took one of her buttocks in her fingers and squeezed. No dimples at all was an absolute impossibility under this stress, but there weren't many, and none at all when she stopped squeezing.

Her eyes focused on the tiny tattoo high on her hip. It was an etching of a colorful butterfly, its yellow and orange wings no more than an inch across. She'd gotten it near the end of her second year at Duke, at her future husband's urging and despite her own reluctance. He had taken her to a tiny parlor in downtown Durham one Saturday himself, trying to convince her to have the tattoo etched in a more prominent spot on her body as they'd driven from his apartment. On her shoulder, he kept saying, so he could see it when they went swimming or when she wore something strapless. But she had refused. Ultimately, she was glad she had kept the butterfly in a spot that even a skimpy bathing suit could hide.

Angela ran her finger slowly across the butterfly's wings. Despite everything that had happened, despite all the emotional pain she'd endured because of him, she didn't regret getting it because it reminded her of those times with him that had been good. So good. The best she'd ever known.

She turned back around so she was facing the mirror. She might be thirty-one, but by sticking religiously to a demanding exercise regimen and a healthy diet, she'd kept herself looking pretty darned good. She leaned forward again and grimaced at the faint stretch marks on her lower belly. They were small, almost invisible, unless you knew they were there. But they were there, all right. And they were impossible to get rid of. She shook her head and moved toward the shower. Pregnancy had left an indelible scar.

The man on the other side of the bathroom's two-way mirror eased back in his chair and let out a long, slow breath as Angela Day disappeared into the shower. The pictures of her he'd been provided with a few hours ago hadn't done her justice. She was even prettier with nothing left to the imagination, her body only inches from his eyes. He ran his hands through his hair, still picturing the butterfly tattoo. One way or another, he would get what he wanted.

CHAPTER TWO

As promised, the view from the small dining area off the great room was spectacular. Less than a hundred yards from where Angela sat, a deep gorge fell away from the lodge, and in the distance she could see soaring peaks iced by a fresh layer of pristine snow. She shielded her eyes as the early afternoon sun momentarily broke through the storm's lingering clouds and a brilliant glare burst upon the landscape.

"Let me fix that, Ms. Day." The same woman who had taken Angela's breakfast order a few minutes ago closed the blinds over the window beside the table.

"Thank you."

"More coffee?"

"Please."

Angela watched as the woman freshened her cup with more of the delicious Brazilian blend, thinking about how easily she could get used to this life. After her midnight shower she'd slipped between the flannel sheets and fallen asleep right away. Next thing she'd known, it was nine o'clock in the morning. She'd tried to get up but the sheets had seemed to pull her back onto the comfortable mattress, and she'd fallen asleep again. Just before eleven she'd been able to get her feet to the floor, take another shower, and dress for her three o'clock appointment with Jake Lawrence. Now it was almost one, and the anticipation of meeting one of the world's wealthiest men was intensifying.

When the woman was gone, an elderly black man shuffled into the dining room carrying a tray ladened with plates. After setting the tray down on a highboy along one wall, he moved to the table and picked up the white linen napkin folded before her, preparing to place it in her lap.

"You don't need to do that." Angela caught his hand. "Let me have it."

"I really don't mind."

"No," she said firmly, slipping the linen from his fingers.

"As you wish." He moved back to the highboy and returned a moment later with a plate of blueberry pancakes and a small pitcher of maple syrup. His second trip from the highboy brought scrambled eggs and bacon, and the third a bowl of fresh fruit and a basket of warm biscuits. "Would you like anything else?" he asked with a wide grin.

"No, thank you. God, I'll explode if I make it through even half of all this."

The man picked up Angela's fork and handed it to her.

She shook her head. "Please don't —"

"I'm not bitter, Ms. Day," he said. "So don't you feel guilty. It doesn't do anybody any good."

Angela looked up. "What do you mean?"

"If I were white, would you have allowed me to put the napkin in your lap?"

She hesitated. "No."

"You sure?"

"Yes."

He nodded slowly. "Well, don't hesitate to ring me if you need anything," he instructed, tapping a small bell on a far corner of the table as he headed back toward the kitchen.

"Hey, sleepyhead."

Angela looked up to see John Tucker standing in the doorway of the great room, pulling off dusty leather work gloves. She rolled her eyes, embarrassed by the forkful of blueberry pancakes she'd just put in her mouth and the strip of bacon she was holding.

"How in the world do you keep that slim figure of yours eating pancakes and bacon?" he wanted to know, sitting in the chair opposite hers and shaking his head as he surveyed the food. "Taking Mr. Lawrence up on his generosity, I see."

"This is a rare treat for me, I assure you." She'd been right last night in the SUV. Tucker did have friendly eyes. And in the light of day she could see a hint of mischief in them as well. "I usually start the day with half a bowl of oatmeal and two egg whites but, given all of the luxury around me, I decided to make an exception."

"I'll bet you don't eat your first meal of the day at one in the afternoon very often either." Tucker dropped his gloves and his grimy tan ten-gallon down on the white tablecloth. "I heard they were about to send someone up to your room to wake you."

"Someone?" Angela asked coyly.

She'd thought about Tucker while getting dressed this morning, hoping this might happen. He would never grace the cover of *GQ* magazine, but he was attractive in a rugged way. He had wavy, dirty blond hair that fell to the bottom of the wool collar of the leather jacket he'd been wearing last night. His eyes were large and brown, and his face was broad and ruddy beneath a three-day growth of stubble — a hint of gray rippling through the whiskers on his chin. He was a big man, too. Six three, she guessed, with wide shoulders and thick-fingered hands. He appeared to be in his midthirties, but she wasn't sure. Maybe he was older if he'd been Jake Lawrence's employee for twenty years.

Tucker had a natural swagger about him she liked, too. He'd ambled into the room with one hand in the back pocket of his jeans, pulled the chair out with the toe of his muddy boot, and sat down like he owned the place. It was a swagger that told her he was confident he could handle whatever came his way. A swagger she was drawn to, as she had been drawn to another man's once before.

"Yeah, someone," he repeated with a slight smile.

"Not you?"

"Nope."

"Sure, cowboy," she said quietly so the help wouldn't hear, slowly raising one long, thin eyebrow at him. "I bet you wouldn't mind finding out what I wear to bed." It was a forward thing for her to say, but she already felt very comfortable with him, as if they'd known each other for a long time. She prided herself on being a quick and accurate judge of character, and he seemed honest and sincere. A man who wore his heart on his sleeve. "Come on. Tell me the truth."

He tried to hold back, but then chuckled and looked down. "No, I'm sure I wouldn't. But I'm not allowed upstairs without an escort."

"I thought you *ran* this place."

"I run the ranch, but not the lodge. The lodge manager is very careful about all that. Particularly with female guests."

"Oh," she said, thinking back on how the maid had appeared last night and accompanied her to the room with the male attendant.

Tucker dug into the basket of biscuits, grabbed one, and polished off half of it in a single bite. "So, how'd you sleep?" he asked through the mouthful.

"Like a baby. It's been a while since I slept eleven hours in one night. Usually I get six or seven. But it was as if someone had glued my eyelids shut."

"Happens to people all the time when they visit from back east. It's the elevation," he explained, shoving the rest of the biscuit into his mouth. "And all that wine you drank on the plane."

"I didn't drink that much. And, anyway, how would you know?"

"I have my sources."

"Well, it was the flight attendant's fault. He kept refilling my glass and thank God he did, because if he hadn't, I might not have survived the landing. It felt like I was on the space shuttle and we were re-entering the earth's atmosphere." She watched Tucker rummage through the bacon. "Do you treat everything as tenderly as you do your food?"

"Most of the time," he answered, finding a large, particularly crisp piece. He smiled suggestively. "But I can get rough when I need to."

"I'll bet." Something caught her eye and Angela leaned across the table to get a better look. "How'd you get that?" she asked, touching a long scar on the back of his wrist.

"I was wrassling a stray steer a few years ago," Tucker explained, holding up his hand. "I've got this thing by the neck and all of a sudden he turns and gores me."

"Jesus," Angela whispered.

Tucker chuckled. "I was the lucky one."

"What do you mean?"

"Cow killed the horse."

Angela shook her head as she reached for the

fruit, filling a small bowl with wedges of fresh melon. "So what are you doing here? Why aren't you out roping steers?"

"Well, I —"

"Couldn't wait to see me again?" she interrupted. "Even if you couldn't come upstairs to wake me."

Tucker slowly wiped biscuit crumbs from his mustache with the back of his hand. "That's a nice dress you've got on, Ms. Day," he said, avoiding her question. "*Very* chic. I'm sure Mr. Lawrence would approve."

"Thank you," she said, impressed that he'd noticed. He didn't seem like the type who would. "I bought it especially for the trip."

"It's nice, all right," he continued, "but you're gonna have to change."

"Why?"

"Your meeting with Mr. Lawrence is at the ranch's upper cabin, and there's only one way up to it other than by helicopter, which we don't have."

"How's that?"

"Horseback. And that dress would make the ride mighty uncomfortable, maybe even dangerous."

"I'm not getting on a horse," she said flatly. "No way."

Tucker shrugged. "Suit yourself. But if you don't, you won't be meeting Mr. Lawrence."

An hour later, Tucker hauled himself up into a Western saddle strapped to the back of a huge black stallion, then leaned down and held out his hand. "Put your left foot in the stirrup and take my arm," he ordered. "And swing your right leg over the horse's ass on the way up."

"Lord," Angela murmured, careful to avoid the butt end of a rifle protruding from a saddle holster. Then she was behind Tucker and they were moving ahead when he dug his heels into the animal's flanks. Instinctively, she grabbed his wide shoulders. "This is no fun," she called nervously, swaying from side to side.

"What's your problem?" he asked with a smile, guiding the animal away from the lodge and out over an open field of pristine snow.

"I've never been on a horse before," she admitted, resting her face on his broad back. Again she became aware of that soothing leather smell. "It seems higher when you're up here than it does from the ground."

He laughed loudly. "You'll be all right. Just make sure you throw yourself clear if we go down."

She moaned.

"I'm only kidding. We'll be fine."

"Hey!" she yelled.

"What?"

Angela pointed at two men near one corner of the lodge who had just pulled up in snowmobiles. "I thought you said there was only one way to get around without a helicopter."

"Snowmobiles wouldn't do us any good."

"Why not?"

"You'll see."

Soon the open field stretching away from the lodge was behind them and the horse was climbing a trail that twisted through the thick pine forest covering the mountain. The trail grew steadily steeper and the trees sparser until they broke into the open. Then the trail quickly turned into a narrow, rocky path that seemed barely etched into the side of a vertical wall.

The view from the private dining room had been nothing compared to this. To her left Angela could reach out and touch the rock face soaring above them — it made her dizzy when she looked up. To her right, the mountain fell five hundred feet straight down to the bottom of a canyon. Her heart rose into her throat once when the horse stumbled going over a large stone, but Tucker skillfully brought the stallion back under control. Now she understood why a snowmobile wasn't an option. It wouldn't have been able to negotiate this stretch of the trip.

As they moved ahead she watched her breath rise in front of her. She was glad Tucker had ordered her back up to her room to change into the clothes a maid had scrounged up for her at the last minute — jeans, a wool sweater, a ski jacket, warm socks, and insulated boots. The sky had turned overcast again, and it was windy and much colder up here.

"So what *do* you wear to bed?" Tucker called

over his shoulder when the path widened and became less treacherous.

She'd been lost in thought, enjoying the view despite the danger. It was as if they were on top of the world. "Depends," she answered, playfully tilting his ten-gallon forward.

"On what?" he asked, pushing the brim back up.

"I'll let you figure that out."

Tucker sighed, then laughed. "You're killing me, Angela."

"Uh-huh."

"Where did you fly in from?" he asked.

"Richmond, Virginia."

"Is that where you're from?"

"No. I grew up in North Carolina, near Asheville. That's in the western part of the state."

"How'd you end up in Richmond?"

The series of events that had led her to Virginia flashed through her mind. "A man," she answered curtly.

"I'm not one to muck around where I'm not wanted, but it doesn't sound like this guy ended up being your knight in shining armor."

"No, he didn't, and I like your rule about not mucking around where you aren't wanted." She hesitated. One reason she'd hoped to see Tucker again was to have the opportunity to ask him this question. "Why were you so skeptical last night about my meeting with Mr. Lawrence being legit?"

"What are you talking about?" he asked innocently.

"Come on, John. I heard that sarcastic comment you muttered under your breath when we were driving from the airport to the ranch. You thought I didn't, but I did."

He didn't answer for a moment. "Look, Mr. Lawrence is one of the world's most eligible bachelors, and he likes the company of attractive young women. I'm not violating any deep dark secrets here. I've made this trip to the cabin before with a woman behind me."

Angela's pulse quickened and her cheeks began to burn. Though he had provided few details, her boss in Richmond had promised that this meeting was on the up-and-up, and that it could prove to be a tremendous opportunity for the bank and for her personally. "I assure you that's not what's going on here," she said stiffly. Ahead Angela saw that the mountain was flattening out into a high meadow ringed by rock ledges. At the far end of the meadow was a small cabin, and beside it a helicopter, blades still slowly rotating. "I'm not that kind of woman, and I resent your assuming that I am."

"Then I sincerely apologize."

Angela noticed several men milling around the front of the cabin. Most of them carried rifles slung over their shoulders, barrels pointing to the sky. "Apology tentatively accepted."

Tucker pulled back on the reins. They were still fifty yards from the cabin, but one of the men was trudging through the snow toward them. "Be careful, Angela," Tucker warned, his tone turning serious. "Jake Lawrence is a powerful man. He's used to getting his way."

"I can handle myself."

"You're late, John," the man called out in a heavy British accent.

"It's wonderful to see you, too, Billy boy," Tucker replied. "This guy's a real prick," he muttered over his shoulder.

"Ms. Day, I'm William Colby," the man announced as he neared them, looking past Tucker. "Please get down from the horse. We're behind schedule."

Colby had closely set eyes, and a wide, hooked nose that seemed out of place on his thin face. He was completely bald. Unlike the other men milling about the cabin, he wasn't wearing a blue knit ski cap — or shouldering a gun.

"He's Secret Service via Scotland Yard," Tucker whispered. "Very British, very stuffy, and very —"

"Very efficient," Colby finished, his aristocratic accent knifing through the cold air. "I'm very good at what I do, Ms. Day, which is why I run global security for Mr. Lawrence and Mr. Tucker runs a ranch."

"Confident chap, wouldn't you say?" Tucker grunted, helping Angela slide down from the horse.

She nodded subtly at Tucker from the ground. But, despite his slight build, there was an unmistakable aura of competence about Colby. A sense of purpose.

"Please take ten paces toward the cabin, Ms. Day," Colby ordered, signaling to one of his men.

"There's no need for all of that," Tucker assured Colby, swinging his right leg over the horse and dropping down into the snow. "She's clean. I checked."

"Stop right there, Ms. Day," Colby demanded as Angela completed her tenth pace.

Angela stopped and waited as the man Colby had motioned to pulled the weapon from his shoulder, handed it to another man, and jogged toward her.

"Hands behind your head and spread your legs," the guard ordered gruffly.

"What?"

Tucker rolled his eyes. "Billy, don't —"

"Do as you are told, Ms. Day," Colby directed, cutting Tucker off.

When Angela complied, the guard frisked her, starting with her shoulders then moving down her arms.

Tucker shook his head. "You're an asshole, Billy."

"And you are a cowboy, *Johnny*," Colby retorted. "But we each have a job to do. So I won't tell you how to shovel pig slop, and you won't tell me how to protect Mr. Lawrence." The man frisking Angela had halted his search and Colby pointed at him. "Finish!"

"Easy," Angela warned when the man squatted in front of her. "Dammit!" she shouted, stepping back quickly when he placed his hands on her knees, then began moving them up her inner thighs.

"She's not carrying a weapon, sir," the man reported to Colby.

"All right," he acknowledged. "Please proceed to the cabin, Ms. Day. Mr. Lawrence is waiting for you inside."

"Who's responsible for getting her back down the mountain?" Tucker wanted to know.

"You are," Colby snapped.

"Can't you give her a ride to the airport in the chopper, Billy? I'll have somebody from the lodge take her luggage out there."

"We aren't going directly to the airport when Mr. Lawrence is finished with Ms. Day."

"I'm waiting inside, then."

"You'll wait out here," Colby declared, "where I can keep an eye an you."

Tucker let out a frustrated breath. "Then I suppose I'll have to resort to other means of warmth." He pulled a flask from a saddle bag, unscrewed the top, and brought it to his lips.

"Go on, Ms. Day," Colby ordered, watching Tucker take several healthy gulps from the flask.

"I'll be here," Tucker called after her, wiping his mouth with the sleeve of his jacket. "Don't worry."

Angela followed the man who had frisked her

to the cabin, then skirted around him as he held open the door and gestured for her to proceed. The door closed behind her and for a moment she could see little as her eyes adjusted to the dim light. Despite the overcast sky, it had been bright outside with the snow cover, and the only light inside the cabin came from the glow of a low fire.

"Hello, Ms. Day."

Angela's eyes flashed in the direction of the voice. She could barely discern the outline of someone sitting in a large chair in a corner of the room away from the fireplace.

"I'm Jake Lawrence." The figure stood up and came toward her out of the darkness. "Let me help you off with your coat. You'll melt in here if you keep it on."

He was right. It was warm inside the cabin. Very warm. She'd noticed the heat as soon as she'd stepped through the door. Her thoughts flashed to Tucker's cynical view of this meeting. Perhaps there was a reason the room was so warm.

"It's nice to meet you," Lawrence continued, taking her hand.

Lawrence's hand was as smooth as Tucker's had been rough. "It's an honor to meet you, Mr. Lawrence."

"I appreciate your coming all the way out here from the East Coast on such short notice, Ms. Day. I know it was inconvenient, but this arrangement worked out best for me. And I wanted to get together with you as soon as possible. So, thank you."

"Certainly," she replied. She'd promised herself she wouldn't be impressed with Jake Lawrence, but now, in his presence, she found it difficult not to be in awe of him. He was one of the wealthiest and most powerful men in the world. Earning interest on interest faster than he could spend it, and influencing the decisions of world leaders from behind the scenes. She'd grown up digging for nickels and dimes beneath the cushions of the double-wide's ratty sofa. "I appreciate all the hospitality your staff has shown me, especially John Tucker's." She felt Lawrence's hand subtly contract around hers at the mention of Tucker's name. "I like John," she continued. "He's one of those people you trust right away, you know?"

"John is a good man," Lawrence agreed quietly, his demeanor chilling slightly. "A dedicated employee."

"I have to tell you I was nervous coming up here on horseback, particularly when we got to the narrow part of the trail. But it was no problem for John. I get the feeling he could handle almost —"

"Yes," Lawrence cut in curtly, "we are fortunate to have a man like Mr. Tucker managing the ranch."

For a moment there was no sound in the room except the crackle of fire.

Angela cleared her throat. "Well, I just want

you to know that I've been treated like a princess since boarding your plane in Richmond yesterday," Angela said.

"Standard operating procedure." Lawrence slowly allowed her fingers to slip from his. "Especially for a creature as lovely as you."

"Thank you," she murmured self-consciously, glancing up. Lawrence was about the same height as Tucker, but he was slimmer, so he seemed taller. Instead of a flannel shirt, dusty wool-collared jacket, frayed jeans, and muddy boots, Lawrence wore a stylish white turtleneck sweater, pressed, pleated pants, spit-shined brown boots, and a sharp, fawn-colored Stetson. His face was intricately sculpted and, when he smiled, small lines formed at the corners of his mouth and a distinct dimple appeared in each cheek. His smile was warm, but his dark, dead eyes were decidedly not. Though she didn't get a long look at them, she saw instantly in the large black pupils that he was a man who expected immediate compliance with his orders, was accustomed to and comfortable with wielding power, and had little tolerance for opposing opinions. She found herself pulling down the zipper of the borrowed jacket. He was used to getting his way, Tucker had warned.

"Let me take that for you," Lawrence offered, slipping the jacket off her arms from behind. "If you don't mind, please remove those wet boots, as well." He hung up her coat in a nearby closet.

"Leave them by the door," he suggested, returning to his chair.

She slipped out of the boots, then followed his gesture and padded to a couch along the wall near his chair.

"Have some coffee," Lawrence offered, nodding at the pot and cups arranged on a long, low table in front of the couch.

"Thanks. I will." She poured herself a cup, then sat back. After the cold ride up the mountain, the coffee tasted delicious.

"I'm sorry if Bill Colby and his deputies offended you in any way. I asked him not to put you through the standard inspection routine, but he's very thorough."

"Thorough would certainly be an accurate description," Angela agreed.

"The thing is I have to be very careful," Lawrence explained, his voice measured. "You must understand my situation. It's difficult for me to trust anyone. There are people who, for various reasons, wouldn't mind seeing me dead."

"I'm sure you're safe here with that personal army of yours camped outside."

"I'm never completely safe, Ms. Day."

It sounded paranoid but maybe when you had more money than God — as the *Wall Street Journal* had once described his multibillion-dollar net worth — there really was such danger. "Of course, all that money allows you to own a place like this."

"Money does provide me certain luxuries

others don't enjoy," Lawrence replied evenly.

For the first time Angela thought she detected irritation in his voice, and it occurred to her that few people probably ever challenged Jake Lawrence. After all, what would be the point? There could be no upside in making an enemy of him. Perhaps now wasn't the time to let her trailer park bitterness rear its ugly head. Or allow her penchant for putting a poor little rich boy in his place boil to the surface either. "I'm sure you deal with circumstances and pressures I could never understand, Mr. Lawrence."

"There's nothing I can't handle." He waved, as though swatting at a fly. "But enough about me," he said. "Let me hear about your background."

Angela ran her tongue along her upper lip. She'd noticed a strange flavor to the coffee, not an unpleasant taste, but one she didn't recognize. She glanced over into Lawrence's dark eyes, barely visible beneath the brim of his Stetson. She was thinking again about Tucker's inference that this wasn't a legitimate business meeting. That Lawrence had other motivations.

"Something wrong?" Lawrence asked, watching Angela place the cup down on the table.

"No."

Lawrence grinned. "It's Irish whiskey. My staff knows that I always take Irish whiskey in my coffee. I should have warned you."

"No, no, it tastes good." A remote cabin. Heat turned way up. Whiskey in the coffee. An army

54

of men outside. John Tucker had known Lawrence for twenty years. How could she have doubted his judgment? She crossed her arms tightly over her chest. *Well, if that's what Jake Lawrence has in mind, he's going to be very disappointed.*

"*Please* tell me about yourself, Ms. Day."

"Do you mind explaining why I'm here?"

"We'll get to all of that," he assured her. "But I want to hear about you first."

At eight thousand feet even this small amount of alcohol in the coffee was affecting her. She could feel it seeping into her system. "I'm a vice president at Sumter Bank, which is headquartered in Richmond, Virginia," she began. "I make loans to Old Economy manufacturing and retail companies mostly in Georgia and Alabama. That's my territory, so I travel down there quite a bit. Sumter isn't as big as the New York banks but, with thirty billion in assets, we're not small either. We certainly wouldn't have been able to get that big just making loans to companies in Virginia. I've been with the bank for almost six years, and in my current position for four." She watched Lawrence pick up a glass resting on a small table beside his chair. "But you already know all of that."

He froze, the glass just short of his lips. "What do you mean?"

"A man like you wouldn't fly a nobody like me across the country without a purpose. And purpose implies a certain level of knowledge."

"You're starting to sound more like a lawyer than a banker, Ms. Day."

"The flight out here was obviously arranged with me in mind. Crab imperial for dinner, *Erin Brockovich* for me to watch, the books, the magazines: all my favorites. Same with my room at the lodge: my favorite shampoo, my favorite soap, little Brach's peppermint candies by my bed instead of the standard hotel chocolates. You researched me. Candidly, it was a little unnerving."

"Of course I researched you," he answered. "Actually, it was a woman on my staff who did all the legwork," he admitted. "She prepares me for all my meetings. Preparation is one of the most important success drivers. Wars are won or lost before they're ever fought, and the deciding factor is always preparation."

"I didn't know we were talking about war."

"Don't kid yourself," he replied quickly, nodding at the door. "Every day there's an economic war going on out there. Everybody is constantly battling for their piece of the pie."

"Yes, and some people have bigger forks."

Lawrence smiled. "Keep taking me through your background, Ms. Day. You said you worked for Sumter Bank in Richmond."

"Yes, a bank you own 8 percent of, Mr. Lawrence. Which, I have to believe, has something to do with why I'm here." She saw that he was about to speak up. "I checked Free Edgar and the 13-d filings," she explained, anticipating his

56

question. "The 13-d is the report that requires investors like you to inform the Securities and Exchange Commission that he or she has acquired 5 percent or more of a public company. There were a couple on file. You're up from owning 6 percent of Sumter two months ago." She shook her head. "I did a rough calculation. As near as I can tell, you've got about $450 million tied up in Sumter stock."

"Actually, it's closer to $490 million. Almost five hundred."

"Wow." Angela couldn't help reacting aloud. It wasn't just the amount of the investment that impressed her. It was the fact that Lawrence would invest that much in *one* stock. She assumed his financial advisors would keep him widely diversified, so even the liquid portion of his net worth had to be huge if he could devote almost half a billion dollars to a single investment. Even if he was using margin.

"I've spent $490 million so far," he continued, "but you are correct in that my investment is only worth $450 million. The stock has dropped a few points over the last couple of months, even as I've been buying. Usually, the price of a stock rises as word gets out that I'm accumulating. The press calls it the 'Lawrence Effect.' My investment bankers are curious about why the Lawrence Effect isn't kicking in this time. I always said hell would freeze over the day an investment banker didn't have an explanation for something. Maybe it has. I don't

57

know. I hope I never find out. But I do know I'm down $40 million."

Down forty million. The amount was mind-boggling.

"I don't like losses, Ms. Day. In fact, I *hate* them. Even small ones like forty million."

"Do you mind if I ask why you're so interested in Sumter Bank?"

"Not at all. Sumter has a strong market position in the Southeast, and the Southeast is one of the fastest-growing regions of the country. Its earnings, and therefore its share price, have a lot of room on the upside."

"But Sumter's shares already trade at almost two times book value, even with the recent decline in the stock price you mentioned. Isn't that pretty good for a bank? I mean, it's not as if we're going to discover a cure for cancer or invent the next white-hot wireless device. When you get right down to it, bank stocks are pretty boring."

"You have your opinion," he replied stonily, "and I have mine."

Angela cleared her throat, realizing how arrogant she must have sounded. Jake Lawrence and his people were probably in and out of world stock markets on a minute-by-minute basis, trading millions of dollars worth of securities every day. She executed a couple of transactions a year in her tiny portfolio. "I'm sorry, Mr. Lawrence. I —"

"Don't ever be sorry, Ms. Day. It's a certain sign of weakness."

58

She looked up and saw that he was smiling.

"By the way, do you mind if I call you Angela?"

"Of course not."

"Good. And I want you to call me Jake. All right?"

"Sure." But she wasn't. "Mr. Lawrence" seemed more appropriate, and she didn't want him thinking she was getting comfortable.

"So, Angela, where did you grow up?"

"Asheville, North Carolina."

Lawrence snapped his fingers. "I remember now. And you are the product of an Italian-Irish marriage, correct?"

Angela bit her lip. "The product." He made it sound so clinical, as if she'd been born on an assembly line. "That's right."

"It seems like there are so many of those marriages," Lawrence observed, as if he found the combination odd.

"It's the Catholic commonality."

"You're probably right, but I —"

"And the overpowering sex appeal of the Italian woman," she continued. "The poor Irish guys don't stand a chance when they see a woman as beautiful as my mother."

Lawrence chuckled. "Yes, I can see how that might happen." He paused. "You were . . . *poor* growing up."

"We were." Her gaze dropped into her lap. "We didn't have many extras, but we had each other. And that was enough."

"Your father couldn't hold a job for very long."

"My father was a decent man."

"He was an alcoholic."

"Mr. Lawrence, I don't think you have the right to —"

"You earned your undergraduate degree in political science," he continued quickly, not giving her a chance to object. "Yes?"

"Yes."

"And I think I remember from my information that you worked two jobs while you were in college. Night shift during the week at a convenience store near the dorms and as a counselor at a school for underprivileged kids on weekends. Very impressive. From what I understand, you've carried that solid work ethic with you into the business world. You are proof of what can be achieved with hard work and determination, even without a slew of high-level, blue-blooded connections."

Her annual salary at Sumter was forty-eight thousand dollars. Decent, but hardly worth jumping up and down about. So she wasn't certain she was proof of any great achievement. However, there weren't many employment options in Richmond, Virginia, and she *had* to be in Richmond. "The woman on your staff did her research very well, but my world must seem pretty unexciting to a man like you, Mr. Lawrence."

"Please, Angela. Call me *Jake*."

"Okay."

"Were you ever robbed while you were working at the convenience store?" he wanted to know.

They were thorough, she thought to herself. *They must have found the police report.* "Yes. Once."

"What happened?"

She hesitated, replaying the horrible events of that night in her mind. "It's three in the morning and there's no one in the store except me and a stock boy. I'm sitting behind the cash register reading a book and he's in the back. I come to the end of a chapter, look up, and I'm staring down the barrel of a .357 Magnum. On the other side of the gun is a green ski mask. The guy inside the mask grabs the cash from the register, then he forces me into the back behind the cold drinks and ties me up." She shut her eyes, remembering those awful seconds. "While I'm lying there on the floor with my wrists tied to my ankles, he makes the stock boy, who's black, get down on his knees and beg for his life, yells at the kid that 'every nigger ought to beg for his life at least once.' When the kid refuses, the guy in the ski mask shoots him in the face. Kills him instantly. Then he kneels down next to me, puts the gun to my head, and tells me he's gonna kill me 'just for working with a nigger.'" She swallowed hard. "He pulls the trigger, but it only clicks. I guess the chamber was empty, or the gun misfired."

"Or he was just trying to scare you."

"Maybe. But I'll remember that sound for the rest of my life. And I'll remember what he said to the kid before he killed him."

"Did the police find the guy?"

"Of course not."

"Did you show up for your next shift?"

"I was there the next night," she said. "I needed to buy textbooks. I needed to live." It had been the longest night of her life. She hadn't taken her eye off the door the entire time.

Lawrence took another sip of his drink. "You graduated cum laude from college, yes?"

"Yes."

"Then you got your M.B.A. from Duke."

"That's right."

"Which is where you met Samuel Reese, your then *future* and now *former* husband. You were divorced from him six years ago after only a year of marriage." He hesitated. "What happened?"

"Mr. Lawrence, that's a very personal question, and I don't —"

"Angela, if you help me, I'll help you."

She glanced over at him, trying again to see beneath the brim of the Stetson. But he tilted his head forward slightly, blocking her view. "What does that mean?"

"I told you. We'll get to that," Lawrence said, standing up. "Your ex-husband is from a wealthy family?"

"Yes," she replied uneasily as Lawrence walked around the table and sat down on the couch beside her. She was relieved when he kept his distance. He had turned toward her, putting his right arm on the back of the couch and resting his right ankle on his left knee. He was several feet away, but her entire body was tense. It had not occurred to her when her boss had told her to make this trip that Lawrence might want something not of a business nature, that in some way she was a pawn in a $500 million investment. "Based on their lifestyle, I believe my husband's family had a great deal of money, but I was never allowed to know how much." If Lawrence did make a move, what was she supposed to do? Scream? Tucker was out there, but he'd worked for Lawrence for twenty years. What was his incentive to help *her?* Besides, the men with the guns would keep him at bay, even if he did try to come to her aid.

"His last name is Reese, but yours is —"

"I retook my maiden name after the divorce was final," she explained, anticipating his question again.

"I see." Lawrence hesitated. "Are you okay, Angela?" he asked, reaching over and patting her hand.

"I'm fine." They stared at each other for the first time at close range, but he didn't dwell on her eyes as most men did. There hadn't been that subtle double take. And she realized that Jake Lawrence wasn't impressed as easily as most men. Attractive women didn't faze him, probably because he rarely dealt with any who weren't. "Why?"

"You seem a little nervous."

"Not at all," she lied, uncertain of whether or not to insist that he take his hand from hers. He could say it was simply a friendly gesture, and then she'd look foolish. She let out a low breath when he removed it from her lap.

"I like your accent." He took another sip from his glass. "I've always enjoyed a slight Southern drawl. It sounds so nice. Especially in a woman."

"Thank you."

Lawrence stroked his chin with his thumb and forefinger. "So you want to know why you're here."

"I am curious," she admitted. "It seems odd to be whisked all the way out here to Wyoming in a private jet without any explanation. Don't you agree?"

He smiled at her through the dim light. "I like a little mystery. Don't you?"

"Not necessarily."

"So you're one of those people who doesn't like surprises."

"I didn't say that."

"You didn't have to." His smile turned smug. "You probably wondered if I was going to make a pass at you."

"No, I didn't," she replied, trying to act as though his suggestion was silly. "That thought never crossed my mind. My boss said this was a legitimate business meeting, but that the subject matter had to remain confidential so he couldn't tell me anything. My boss and I have a good relationship. I trust him."

"Do you now?"

Angela glanced up. "Yes. Why?"

"Just wondered." Lawrence tapped the back of the sofa. "Well, here's the deal. I'm working on a project and I want your help."

"A project?" she asked, leaning forward.

"Yes. I'm considering taking a run at a public company. At acquiring it. And I want your assistance."

Her anxiety vanished, replaced by a surge of anticipation. It would be a tremendous experience to work directly with a man like Jake Lawrence on the acquisition of a business. It would be something she could tell her son about years from now. Even if she ultimately ended up dealing with one of Lawrence's aides most of the time, she'd still be the envy of some powerful people on Wall Street. "What kind of help?" John Tucker had been wrong about this meeting after all, and she couldn't wait to tell him so.

"I want you to perform due diligence on the company before I actually make a public tender offer. I want you to meet with the company's senior management on my behalf, prior to my making a final decision. I want you to carefully review their financial condition and gather a little market intel so we've got information others don't. See, I always like to have an advantage, Angela. I'll put you in touch with people who can help you there. Then you report back to me, and we'll see what's what."

Even as the thrill coursed through her body at the prospect of developing a direct business relationship with one of the world's richest men, she glanced down, disappointed. This was hard to say, but she had to be honest. "I think your staff may have given you misinformation about me. As I told you, I lend money. I'm not a merger and acquisition advisory specialist."

Lawrence nodded. "I know that."

"But —"

"Angela, you have a certain way about you I think may influence this company's CEO to do the right thing. To do what I want him to do, which is to let me acquire his business without a messy public war. That wouldn't do anyone but the lawyers any good. My aides recommended you for the job, but I wanted to make certain you're the woman for the job, which is why I flew you all the way out here. If I didn't make the appropriate advances before announcing the public tender, odds are the company's CEO would try to repel me. Senior executives always panic when their company is threatened with a takeover. They think the first thing the raider will do is fire their sorry asses for keeping dividends low so they can pay themselves huge salaries and bonuses. And most of the time they're right. And, if I fire them, then how the hell would they pay for their country club memberships or the love nests they maintain for the trophy girlfriends they hide from their age-spotted wives?"

Having to pay country club dues was something she'd never worried about, but a cheating husband struck a chord. "I don't know."

"Besides," Lawrence continued, "when you make a loan to a company, you have to perform the same kind of due diligence I'm asking you to perform. You have to make certain it's a solid business, right?"

"Yes."

"And consider this. I'll certainly want to borrow a good deal of money to pay for the acquisition." He pointed at her. "Always use someone else's money when you can. Even if you do have a lot of your own."

"I've heard that before."

"I'm sure you have."

"I'm still curious about why you want me to do these things for you." Angela had learned that understanding a person's true motivation — not the one they might be guiding you toward — was vital if you didn't want to be hurt, if you wanted to correctly assess the risks and returns. "Why not ask one of those Wall Street investment bankers you work with to help you?"

"I want to keep publicity to a minimum," he explained. "They'd leak it to their friends and the press before I hung up the phone. If there's one thing I've learned about Wall Streeters, they can't keep a secret."

"That still doesn't explain why you want *me*."

"But your persistence does. Exactly what you're doing right now is why I want you to work for me. My aides, who analyzed my investment in Sumter, heard about you, and, after they did some background work on you, they recommended you highly."

She smiled despite herself. Then it hit her, and her enthusiasm faded. "I'm your mole," she whispered.

"What?"

She grimaced, wishing she hadn't said anything.

"What did you mean by that?" he demanded.

She glanced up into his eyes. They were burning beneath the brim of the Stetson. "I, I —"

"You think what I'm really planning is the takeover of Sumter? That I want to use you as some kind of undercover agent?"

"I just thought —"

"Well, you thought wrong," Lawrence snapped. "Although," he said, his tone turning to one of amusement, "from what I understand, Sumter's chairman is extremely concerned about my creeping ownership stake in his beloved bank." He laughed harshly, as if that discomfort gave him a great deal of pleasure. "Hey, if I buy enough shares, I might be able to find out about the girlfriends he's got stashed away." He laughed again, even louder this time. "Then what would his wife think?"

"I don't know," she murmured, glancing down. Maybe Jake Lawrence didn't just kill big game for sport. Maybe he enjoyed destroying people's lives, too. Maybe that was why he needed a personal army.

"That man will not be comfortable about the fact that you and I have talked."

Angela glanced up. "Which man?"

"The chairman of Sumter Bank. Bob Dudley."

She shook her head. "I'm just a vice president, Mr. Lawrence —"

"Jake," he interrupted. "Please."

"Jake," she repeated. It didn't sound right, and she wondered if that was because she didn't feel she could trust him. "There are hundreds of vice presidents at Sumter," she said. "I'm so far down the corporate ladder the senior people don't even know who I am." She'd met the chairman and president of the bank briefly at last year's Christmas party, and each of them had given her nothing but a limp handshake and a fake smile before quickly moving on. "I don't think you have to worry about that."

"Bob Dudley will grill you at length about our conversation as soon as you return to Richmond. Count on it."

"I doubt he even knows I came out here."

"Oh, he knows."

"If you say so," she answered skeptically.

"Don't tell him anything specific when he asks," Lawrence added. "Tell him only that we talked in general about a project I want you to work on for me. Don't mention anything about a public tender offer."

"All right," Angela agreed. "But, assuming you're right and he does want to grill me about our conversation, won't my lack of details make him even more curious? And he may not appreciate the fact that all of a sudden I'm working for you when the bank is the one cutting my paycheck twice a month."

Lawrence nodded. "You might be right. Okay. Tell him I'm thinking about leveraging one of my companies, and that the company operates in an industry you already have experience with. That you'd lead the debt financing and make lots of money for Sumter in the process. That ought to make him feel better. All right?"

"All right."

Lawrence turned his glass upside down and finished what little remained. "So, will you help me?"

"I'd like to talk about the situation with my boss first. But if it involves potential loan business for Sumter, I don't think he'll have a problem with me working on it."

"I can guarantee you he won't have a problem with it," Lawrence replied confidently. "As you pointed out, I own 8 percent of the bank."

70

"That's true." The senior executives had to pay attention to Lawrence, whether they wanted to or not. For a public company as big as Sumter, 8 percent was a meaningful stake. "So what company are you thinking about buying?" she asked.

"I'll let you know in a few days," Lawrence answered cautiously. "I've still got a bit more preliminary information to gather before we go live on this one."

"Oh." *Then why did you bother flying me all the way across the country?* she wondered. She cursed herself silently. Maybe she shouldn't question people's motivations so often. "Is that all?"

"What do you mean?"

"I know you're a busy man."

"Stay awhile," he urged, reaching across the couch and putting a hand on her knee. "I've still got a few minutes before Colby bangs on the door to tell me it's time to go."

"Okay," she agreed hesitantly, easing back onto the couch.

"I like to get to know the people I work with," he explained, sliding subtly closer. "All right with you?"

"Sure, fine." Her instinct was to move away or stand up, but she didn't want to irritate him.

"I think I remember from my notes that you have a son."

Her body went rigid. Apparently nothing was sacred. "That's right."

"Sam Reese's son?"

"Yes," she answered stiffly.

"What's his name?"

"Hunter."

"I like that name. How old is Hunter?"

"Six."

"I assume you got custody of him after the divorce."

Angela glanced down. "No, I didn't."

"What?" Lawrence asked.

"Hunter lives with his father," she explained quietly, wondering why Lawrence was playing this game. Or maybe he just hadn't paid close enough attention to the information his assistant had prepared.

"How often do you see Hunter?"

"One weekend a month and two weeks in the summer."

"Really? Well, I'm no expert when it comes to divorce and child custody, but don't mothers usually get custody?"

"Usually."

"What happened?"

Angela took a deep breath. "I was fighting a machine. My former father-in-law is an influential man in Richmond and he hates me. He hired a legion of lawyers from the best firm in town, and I only had enough money to hire a one-woman shop. I can't prove it, but I think he paid off the judge, too. He doesn't leave much to chance."

"Why does he hate you so much?"

"Because my family was dirt poor," she replied bitterly.

"But you graduated from one of the best business schools in the country. You pulled yourself up by your bootstraps."

"Didn't matter to him. He didn't want me in his beautiful world, or his son's. He wanted Sam married to a blue-blooded debutante from Richmond's West End who grew up knowing all the right people from the day she was born. Not some nobody from a trailer park outside Asheville, North Carolina."

"That's terrible," Lawrence said gently. He was quiet for a few moments. "Who filed for the divorce?"

Angela folded her hands tightly in her lap. "Sam did," she answered.

"On what grounds?"

She hesitated, knowing how this would sound. She could refuse to answer or lie, but chances were good that Lawrence already knew, and all of this was just a test to see if she'd tell him the truth. "Adultery."

"I'm assuming that accusation wasn't true. Just a trumped-up charge for the lawyers to use."

"That's right," she said. The truth was exactly the opposite. She'd caught Sam in bed with a woman one day when she'd come home early from a trip. "But the judge believed it," she added, her eyes starting to burn. Angela thought it was mostly because two of Sam's closest bachelor buddies had lied in court about having sexual relations with her while she was married to Sam. Lied about how she had seduced them, then went into lurid details concerning the alleged trysts in front of a courtroom packed with Reese's family and friends. And the lawyers had coached her accusers expertly. One of the men had even broken down on the stand, begging for Sam's forgiveness across the courtroom. She could only imagine how much they'd been paid to perjure themselves. Probably six figures. Sam's father hated her that much. He had hated her right from the start. But she'd believed all along that Sam was strong enough to be his own man. She'd misjudged the risks and paid a terrible price. "And that was all that mattered," she murmured.

"I'm sorry, Angela," Lawrence offered quietly. "Perhaps I can assist you there."

She glanced up. "If you help me, I'll help you" had been Lawrence's words at the beginning of the meeting. "How?"

"A man in my position can wield a certain amount of influence. And often these things come down to who's got the bigger gun."

He didn't have to tell her that.

"Candidly," Lawrence continued, "there aren't many guns bigger than mine."

"Mr. Lawrence . . . I mean, Jake," Angela interrupted herself, turning to face him. "That would mean a great deal to me," she admitted, grasping the incredible opportunity that lay before her. "I miss Hunter so badly sometimes." She hated begging but, when it came to her son, pride ran a distant second.

"Let me talk to my people." He patted her knee again and smiled.

This time she smiled back, and slipped her hand into his. She hated herself for what she was doing, but Hunter needed her. And she needed him. "Thank you, Jake."

"I can't promise anything. Just that I'll look into it."

"I appreciate that so much."

"There's another thing," he said, sliding his hand up her leg a few inches.

"What's that?" She forced herself not to pull away.

"Why haven't you been promoted to director yet?"

"Excuse me?"

"You told me earlier that you were a vice president at Sumter Bank."

"Yes?"

"Isn't director the next title above vice president?"

"Director, yes. After that it's managing director, then senior managing director."

"Well, I've taken a look at your personnel record at Sumter, and it's outstanding. You've generated a significant amount of business for the bank, and you've never been a discipline problem. Shouldn't a woman with that kind of record have been promoted to director by now? My aides tell me that several of your peers who haven't performed anywhere near as well as you have, including two women, are directors earning a good deal more income than you are."

Angela shrugged, trying not to show emotion. That issue was a constant and bitter source of frustration.

"Did you know that human resources has put you up for that promotion twice?"

She glanced up.

"And," Lawrence continued, "your boss has stonewalled the process both times."

Angela stared at Lawrence, trying not to show emotion.

"Why do you think that is?" Lawrence asked.

"I don't know," she replied, her voice raspy. She'd always considered her boss, Ken Booker, a friend. He'd always blamed her not getting promoted on human resources. Now Lawrence was telling her it was the other way around.

"Could your background be a factor?" he asked directly.

"I suppose anything is possible."

Lawrence hesitated, gently caressing her thigh. "But that explanation doesn't seem entirely plausible. I mean, if you're performing well, wouldn't they be afraid to lose you to another bank?"

"They don't seem to be."

"Could your not getting the promotion have anything to do with the fact that senior executives at Sumter Bank perceive you as a trouble-maker? Even though there's nothing on your record to indicate that."

Angela's eyes flashed to Lawrence's. "What are you talking about?"

"Any possibility that they suspect you are a certain newspaper reporter's source of some very negative information regarding the bank's poor record of service to minorities in its market areas? In the last few months the *Richmond Tribune* has turned up the heat on Sumter Bank about that poor record." Lawrence hesitated. "There was one particularly damaging article written by a reporter named Olivia Jefferson that came out last week. That article led people to believe she might have a source inside Sumter."

Angela said nothing.

"Do you know Ms. Jefferson?"

"I think I may know of her."

"I'm not asking if you know *of* her," Lawrence said, his voice rising, "I'm asking if you *know* her."

"I, um, yes. I've met her at a couple of business functions. She covers local business for the *Tribune*, and Richmond is a pretty small city."

Lawrence's eyes narrowed as he moved his hand higher on Angela's thigh. "Those Wall Street investment bankers I mentioned do have one theory about the decline of Sumter's stock price."

"Oh?"

"Yes. As you probably know, the entire banking industry has been going through a massive consolidation over the past ten years. Small ones and big ones are gobbling each other up every day, making shareholders very wealthy in the process."

"I do know that."

"But what you may not know is that the Federal Reserve and other regulators closely monitor a bank's performance with respect to serving low-income and minority communities. That they review those records before approving any merger or acquisition, and that these regulators can hold up profitable mergers if they aren't satisfied with a bank's record regarding the issue. My investment bankers believe that might be the case with Sumter. They believe that all of this bad press about Sumter in the *Richmond Trib* may have made it less attractive as an acquisition target to the big boys in New York, North Carolina, and on the West Coast because those entities fear that any bid they make would be held up by the regulators. My people think that the decline in Sumter's stock price is directly related to that nasty information, which, by the way, other newspapers seem to be picking up on. My sources tell me the *Wall Street Journal* is considering the possibility of conducting its own investigation into what's going on at Sumter."

Angela swallowed hard. In fact, she was intimately aware of how the government monitored the country's largest banks in terms of how well they were serving low-income people. Perhaps she and Lawrence were getting to the real reason he had flown her all the way out here. He'd spent almost $500 million on Sumter stock. Now it was worth forty million less. If the *Wall Street Journal* decided to investigate Sumter and found anything negative, his investment might be worth *far* less.

"Are you getting my drift, Angela?" he asked, reaching up and stroking her hair.

She closed her eyes tightly, managing not to flinch. "I —"

"One more question."

"Yes?"

"Who's Sally Chambers?"

Angela pulled back with a start, as though she'd touched a live wire. "What?"

"Sally Chambers," Lawrence repeated. "Who is she?"

Angela swallowed hard. "Why are you doing this to me?" she whispered.

"Answer me."

"You have no right to —"

"I will help you, if you help me," he interrupted. "But if you don't, I won't help you. And helping me includes answering each of my questions."

Angela could feel herself shaking. Fear, anger, regret, and guilt were all coming together to form a hurricane of emotion. "Sally was my best friend."

"Was?"

"You know what happened." The awful image of blood pouring from Sally's mouth and nose came flashing back, and she could feel herself losing control. "Why are you doing this to me?"

"Sally died, didn't she?"

"Yes. In my arms."

"That's awful," Lawrence said softly. "You know, there's so much we could do together, so many important problems we could solve. Yours and mine. I'd hate to see anything get in the way of those possibilities." He smiled, then leaned forward and kissed her gently on the lips. "You're a beautiful woman, Angela Day," he whispered, running his fingers up the inside of her leg to her belt. "I'm looking forward to working with you."

CHAPTER THREE

"So, how did it go?"

Angela was gazing at the snow-covered peaks in the distance as she swayed atop the stallion behind Tucker. She was thinking about that night on the fraternity house porch nine years ago. Lawrence had brought it all screaming back to her. "What?"

"Did he lay the Jake Lawrence charm on you?" Tucker wanted to know.

She could still feel Lawrence's hot breath as he'd leaned forward to kiss her. Still remember that look in his dark, dead eyes. The touch of his fingers running up her inner thigh. "I don't know what you're talking about."

"Try to get you to have a little drink with him, then move in?"

She smelled whiskey on Tucker's breath as he turned in the saddle. Hopefully, the flask was still relatively full. He seemed steady enough, and it wasn't as if she had any other way of getting down the mountain. "I told you, John," she said, "it was a *business* meeting."

"Excuse me for living. I just know how Lawrence is." Tucker pushed the brim of his hat back as they neared the point where the trail turned tricky. "He's seduced other pretty young things in less time than it took him to get you into and out of that cabin."

"I thought you told me last night you respected Mr. Lawrence's desire to protect his privacy."

"So?"

"So here you are talking about his sexual exploits with an outsider."

"Ah, the hell with him," Tucker grumbled after a long pause. "Maybe this is the whiskey talking, and maybe I'll be sorry I said anything tomorrow, but Jake Lawrence can be a real prick."

"What do you mean?"

"He makes a lot of promises, but he'll never be mistaken for a postman."

"I don't —"

"He doesn't deliver," Tucker said, clarifying.

"Oh." Angela glanced down into the canyon to her left. "What kind of promises does he make?"

"Money, jobs, relationships. He does his research, finds the opportunity or the weakness, then makes the appropriate pledge." Tucker laughed harshly. "I've heard it all on this trail. Young women can be amazingly naive."

"How do you know he doesn't deliver?"

"I have my ways."

Angela hesitated. "Mr. Lawrence asked me to work on a project with him. I believe you can tell a great deal about how a person will conduct themselves in business by the way they lead their personal lives."

"You aren't going to like what you hear."

"Explain what you — Oh, God!" She wrapped her arms around Tucker's waist as the stallion slid unexpectedly on a patch of ice, then reared up on its hind legs. She pressed her face into Tucker's jacket and shut her eyes tightly. "John!"

"Whoa!" Tucker called, making a soothing, clicking sound with his tongue and cheek. "Steady, boy!" The horse dropped its hooves back to the snow, then snorted loudly and sidled quickly to the left, within a few feet of the cliff. Immediately Tucker kicked hard with his left heel, pulled the right rein toward the rock face and the horse bolted away from danger. When they had stopped short beside the rock face, Tucker reached into his jacket, leaned forward in the stirrups, and fed the animal a carrot. "Thata good boy," he said calmly, patting the stallion's neck as it chomped loudly on the snack. "What a ride, huh, Angela? Like a roller coaster, but better."

Tucker wasn't even fazed, Angela realized. They'd come a few inches from certain death, and for him it was as if nothing had happened.

"You okay?"

"Yeah, sure," she gasped.

Tucker gently urged the horse ahead when it had finished the carrot. "What were you asking me about?"

She took a deep breath to calm herself. Her heart was still pounding. "How do you know Jake Lawrence doesn't deliver on his promises?" she asked again.

"Oh, that's right," he remembered, nodding. "Simple. I checked. There was this one girl who told me on the ride back to the lodge all about how Mr. Lawrence was going to take care of her sick mother. Lawrence convinced her of that while the two of them were sitting on the cabin's couch in front of a fire drinking Irish coffees. She was still pretty drunk and she wasn't holding back. She told me what went on, and she told me what he'd promised before, during, and after he took her back to the cabin's master bedroom. I called her a couple of months later, and Lawrence hadn't done a damn thing for her."

"How did you know where to find her?"

"I drove her to the airport after taking her back down the mountain, and right before I put her on Lawrence's plane, I jotted down her telephone number. I told her I was his right-hand man, and that I might need to get in touch with her to follow up. She bought it."

"And Lawrence hadn't done anything for her when you called?"

Tucker waved his hand. "Hadn't even contacted her."

"What was wrong with her mother?"

"Lung cancer."

"That's terrible," she murmured.

"Exactly what I thought. So I called Lawrence's accounting sharks in New York and told them we needed fifty grand for a new barn out here. They wired it to me the next day, and I sent it on to the girl." He patted the horse's neck again. "Her mother died, but at least she was comfortable during her last few weeks. And the girl didn't have a pile of medical bills to deal with when her mother was gone."

"Is all of that really true?" she asked. There was her natural instinct not to believe, not to fully trust even someone she felt comfortable with. The risks had outweighed the rewards too many times.

"You think I'm lying?"

"What if the accounting guys drop by to check up on the new barn? What will you do when they find out what you really did with the money?"

"They won't. At least, they haven't yet. And if they do, I'll get a message to Mr. Lawrence telling him to call off the dogs. If he ignores me, then I'll call the *National Enquirer* and make a million bucks."

She didn't ask, but the implication was that he had protected himself by sneaking a photograph. "What you did for that girl seems like a big risk to take for someone you don't even know."

Tucker glanced over his shoulder. "You are a tough broad. I guess I oughta believe that your meeting with Mr. Lawrence was just business after all."

"Yes, you should." She shivered. It was getting colder as the sun dropped toward the horizon. "How many times have you brought a woman up here for Jake Lawrence?"

"You sound like a reporter."

"Answer me."

"More than twice, but that's all I'll say."

"How do you know he's made promises to those other women?"

"The story I told you isn't the only one I've heard. And she wasn't the only one I checked up on. And now you sound like a lawyer."

It was the second time in the last few hours she'd been accused of being a lawyer, which wasn't unusual. Her father had always encouraged her to be an attorney because he said she never stopped asking how and why. "How can you be so sure Jake Lawrence makes all kinds of promises when you aren't actually there?"

"I can't," Tucker replied, guiding the horse around a sharp rock protruding from the snow. "Are you defending him?"

"No, I . . ." Her voice trailed off.

"What's this big project Lawrence wants you to work on?" Tucker asked.

"I can't say."

"Oh, I get it. I share a little inside information with you, but now you don't return the favor. I see how it works."

"It has to do with a corporate takeover."

"What company is being taken over?"

"I really can't tell you that." She didn't want

to let on that she didn't know herself. She didn't want Tucker to doubt the legitimacy of the meeting. "If I did, I'd be violating about twenty securities laws, which could get us both in a boatload of trouble."

Tucker snorted loudly. For a moment she wasn't certain if it was him or the horse.

"Here's a chance for me to make a little money," he grumbled, "and you're holding back. I'm not as much of a cowboy as you think. I've got a stock portfolio. It ain't big, but I've got one. Come on, Angela, give me a tip."

"I'm sorry, John, but I really can't say anything."

"Yeah, sure."

"Bill Colby's a scary guy," Angela commented, trying to change the subject.

"Yeah, I don't like him much. But he knows what he's doing," Tucker admitted grudgingly. "Being head of security for Jake Lawrence is no picnic."

"Why is Jake Lawrence tougher to guard than any other wealthy person?" she asked, glad Tucker had taken the bait.

"First of all, Mr. Lawrence isn't just any other wealthy person. He's probably one of the top ten wealthiest people in the world. One of the accountants in New York told me that if he's ever kidnapped, Colby has a standing order to pay up to $100 million just on proof of life."

Angela shook her head. "Lord."

"That's why you can't find pictures of him anywhere. Colby won't allow it. No pictures makes it tougher on anybody who's thinking about kidnapping or killing him." Tucker nodded back over his shoulder in the direction of the cabin. "The army Colby surrounds Lawrence with makes it tougher, too. So do the decoy teams."

"Decoy teams?"

The horse strayed slightly toward the cliff. Tucker steered the animal closer to the rock face. "Yeah. As I understand it, there are three imposter Jake Lawrences running around the world posing as him. They've had plastic surgery to make them look as much like the real McCoy as possible, and they travel with a personal army just like Mr. Lawrence does. Sometimes they're with him and sometimes they aren't."

It was fascinating, the lengths to which Lawrence went to protect himself. "Why would the teams ever be with Lawrence?"

"If he absolutely has to go somewhere, and it's an area that Colby determines is 'hot' or high-risk, especially if the trip is last minute, Colby may send one of the decoy teams in first."

"To test the waters."

"Exactly. Even if the first one makes it to the destination safely, Colby might send a second decoy in while he's slipping the genuine article into the area in an old pickup truck."

"Have any of the teams ever been —"

"Attacked?" Tucker interrupted, anticipating her question.

"Yes."

"Yup. Colby tries to keep all information dealing with Mr. Lawrence's security very hush-hush, but I understand that we lost a decoy two years ago." Tucker's eyes narrowed. "It was a car bomb, and there wasn't much left. I just hope we took care of the son of a bitch's family," he said softly.

"Do you know where the incident occurred?"

"Algeria, I think."

"Algeria? What in the world would Mr. Lawrence be doing in Algeria?"

"I'm sure I don't know."

"I don't remember reading anything about that."

"Of course not. Jake Lawrence has influential friends in high places, including the press. The incident never made it into the newspaper columns."

Angela nodded to herself, thinking about how Jake Lawrence seemed to know that the *Wall Street Journal* was considering a follow-up on Liv Jefferson's articles. "Then based on what you're telling me, I can't be certain that was the real Jake Lawrence I just met."

"That's true," Tucker acknowledged, "except for one thing."

"What?"

"Bill Colby is a control freak. If Colby is

89

around, there's a good chance the real Jake Lawrence is in the area, too. I've tried to tell Bill that unfriendlies may pick up on that, but he doesn't seem to want to take advice from a cowboy."

"So I noticed," Angela said quietly.

"The second reason it's tough to guard Lawrence," Tucker continued, "is that he tends to piss people off. He sticks his nose into sensitive issues, according to one of those in-house New York accountants I shared a flight with last year, into situations where he isn't wanted. Maybe that's what somebody was doing in Algeria."

Angela peered over Tucker's shoulder and saw that they were nearing the end of the narrow section of the trail. Only a hundred yards and they'd be back on safe ground. "What do you mean?"

"Well, he —"

She barely heard the bullet as it ricocheted off a ledge a few feet above their heads. It sounded like nothing more than a hornet buzzing past as it caromed off a rock with an angry whine. Tucker pushed her roughly to the ground, jumped down after her, grabbed his rifle from the saddle holster, and dragged her behind a small rock, barking at her to lie as flat as she could.

A split second later the next bullet came, striking the stallion in its massive black neck, destroying its windpipe and blowing a softball-sized hole out the other side. The huge animal staggered backward and to the left, frothing blood, then collapsed in front of them and tumbled off the side of the cliff.

"Oh, my God!" Angela shouted, trying to burrow into the snow. "Where are the bullets coming from?"

"Ahead!" Tucker lay beside her, aiming the rifle in the direction they'd been going. "Whoever's up there probably wanted us to be on the horse when it went off the cliff."

"What are we going to do?"

"Stay put for now. I don't think they can get a clean shot at us if we stay low."

For five excruciating minutes they waited, pressed to the ground, but there were no more shots. Just the sound of the late afternoon wind wailing eerily through the canyon.

"Follow me," Tucker ordered in a low voice.

"What?"

"We're going back the way we came. There's a cave about fifty yards back. I'm gonna put you in it, then make certain whoever was shooting at us is gone."

"It'll be dark in thirty minutes. Let's wait until then," she suggested, still breathing hard.

"No good. Whoever it is might have night vision capability. We don't. I've got to get you to safety." Tucker motioned to her as he began crawling along the ground. "Come on."

"What am I doing here?" she whispered as she followed him across the snow, wondering if the next moment might be her last. She'd had a front row view of the last bullet tearing out the horse's neck, and she didn't want the same view of the next one tearing through John Tucker. Or her. Suddenly Jake Lawrence didn't seem so paranoid.

When they reached the cave, they scrambled inside, protected for the moment. The cave stretched thirty feet back into the mountain. It was no more than ten feet wide and six feet high at any point.

"You'll be safe in here," Tucker assured her as they hunched down against the wall.

"You're not leaving me," she said, anticipating what he was about to say.

"Look, whoever shot at us probably took off, but I'm going to make sure. I don't want you with me if he didn't and I run into him," he replied, reaching inside his jacket and pulling out the long-barreled .22 that had been on the Expedition's dashboard last night. "Take this. If anybody approaches, shoot them. Don't ask questions. Just aim and start pulling the trigger."

Angela took the revolver. Her father had taught her how to handle a gun when she was young. Before he had run off the road one night on his way home to the trailer park from an Asheville bar and killed himself in the spring of her senior year in high school. "I don't like this."

"You'll be fine," Tucker said, checking the ammunition in the rifle. "Stay back in the cave, but keep checking both sides of the path, too.

Like I said, you see anybody other than me, you start shooting. Here's some extra ammo." He reached into his coat and tossed a box of ammunition on the cave floor in front of her.

"How will I know if someone on the trail is the person who shot at us?"

"Believe me, no one else besides you and me ought to be up here right now. Anybody else is fair game." He stuck his head out of the cave and peered both ways. "I won't be gone long. If I'm not back in a half hour, get out of here. Go left out of the cave. Opposite the way I go. Back toward the cabin. When you get to the end of the narrow part of the path, get into the woods and down off the mountain any way you can." He hesitated. "By the way, who are you?"

"Huh?"

"I haven't pissed anybody off enough to make them shoot at me. Least, I don't think I have. So you must have."

"No, I haven't. I'm a nobody, for God's sake."

Tucker stared intently at her for a few moments, then shook his head. "Sure you are," he mumbled. Then he was gone, moving along the path in the same direction they'd been headed before the shots were fired.

Angela crouched just inside the mouth of the cave, watching Tucker as he moved along the trail, sprinting ten to fifteen yards at a time, bent over at the waist, then flattening himself behind a section of the rock face that jutted out into the path. In this way he provided himself at least a small measure of protection from whomever had shot at them. "Come on, John," she whispered as he neared the trees. "Come on."

When he'd raced the last few yards and disappeared into the woods, she heaved a sigh of relief. At least he wasn't out in the open anymore. At least he had some cover.

For the next thirty minutes, Angela constantly checked both sides of the trail but saw nothing suspicious. "Get back here, John," she muttered, gritting her teeth. "Don't leave me out here alone." The sky was darkening and the temperature was falling. There wasn't even any wind down in the canyon anymore, for which she was thankful. The low moan had been unnerving.

She let out another sigh, then swallowed hard as it hit her. Maybe this whole thing was a setup. Maybe Lawrence was angry at the way their meeting had ended, and Tucker had been ordered to leave her alone to face whoever was shooting. She shook her head. That was silly. She was letting her imagination run wild.

She poked her head out of the cave once more and caught her breath. Through the fading light she saw something. A slight movement down the trail in the direction they'd been coming from before the first shot. Back in the direction of the cabin where the path widened and turned less treacherous. "Oh, God," she muttered. The .22 began trembling in her gloved hand as she saw the movement again.

She retreated inside the cave, sitting against the rock wall, head tilted back, eyes closed, fingers wrapped tightly around the wooden handle of the revolver, shivering. Maybe it was Tucker. Maybe somehow he had made it all the way around to that side of the mountain without finding anyone and now he was coming back for her. *Please let it be him,* she prayed.

She leaned out so she could see down the trail again, one eye barely beyond the cave's entrance. Through the fading light she could see someone walking on the trail toward her. He wore a long coat that fell almost to his ankles and nothing on his head. Definitely not Tucker. She ducked back inside the cave entrance and took three short breaths.

"Dammit!"

The man was walking deliberately, not trying to hide his presence. Not approaching as if he intended harm. If he'd been sprinting or moving along the rock face as though trying to protect himself, as Tucker had, her decision would have been easier. She would have been prepared to aggressively defend herself, as Tucker had instructed. But this guy might have had nothing to do with the shooting. She took another quick look. He was fifty yards away now and still coming. She hadn't seen a gun, but he could be hiding a cannon beneath that long coat.

With a low groan she stood up, hunched over at the waist so she wouldn't hit her head on the low ceiling, and scrambled to the back of the cave. There, she sat back down and wedged herself into a corner that afforded at least some protection, then aimed the .22 at the entrance. She was trying to remember what her father had taught her in the field that day as they'd fired his snub-nosed .38 at an array of labelless tin cans perched atop a rail fence. *Hold the pistol firmly with both hands but don't strangle it, keep your elbows slightly bent, take a deep breath, then fire.* The barrel of the gun shook in front of her, and she clenched her teeth. The next time she saw her boss, she was going to tell him exactly what she thought of him sending her to Wyoming.

Maybe the man who was approaching would stay outside the cave to protect himself, then reach around with one hand and start shooting randomly, hoping to hit her without making himself a target. Or maybe he'd continue past the cave without even bothering to investigate. Maybe he hadn't seen her. She squinted. The low light was playing tricks on her eyes, making her think someone had passed by the entrance. She could hear herself breathing hard. Hadn't it been long enough for the guy to cover those fifty yards? Maybe he'd turned back.

"Hello!"

Angela froze.

"I know you're in there." The voice came again, echoing inside the cave. "I saw you watching me. Don't shoot."

Why would he suspect she might even have a gun, let alone shoot? But why would he walk along the trail without protecting himself if he meant her harm and thought she might shoot him? The possibilities churned through her mind.

"I'm going to move out so you can see me," the man called. "Here I come."

A dark silhouette appeared at the cave entrance. He was holding his arms out away from his body, trying to convince her he wasn't a threat. Friend or foe? Risk versus return. She was breathing as if she'd just run a marathon. She could feel perspiration soaking her back.

She rose cautiously to her knees, the .22 trained on the man's chest. *If you ever have to fire in self-defense,* she remembered her father saying when they had finished target practice that first time, *assume you will only get one shot. Aim at the heart, then squeeze the trigger smoothly. If you pull back too quickly, you will jerk the gun to one side or the other and you will miss. And shoot to kill, never to wound.*

"Stay where you are!" she yelled. "Don't move."

"Don't worry, ma'am," he answered smoothly, keeping his arms out away from his body. "My job is just to get you down off the mountain."

Angela inched toward him, making certain she didn't stumble on the cave's jagged floor. She kept her finger on the trigger the whole time. "Who sent you?" she demanded, stopping five feet away. She couldn't see much. Just a full curly beard and a shaggy head of hair.

"People at the lodge. They were worried. They said you were supposed to be back a while ago."

That seemed odd. They hadn't been gone that long. Of course, it was almost dark. Maybe that was what had them worried. But wouldn't he have come from the other direction if the lodge had sent him?

"Anybody else in there?" The man glanced past her into the cave.

"No," she answered hesitantly. Shouldn't he know that John Tucker was supposed to be with her? Wouldn't people at the lodge have told him that?

"Wasn't there supposed to be someone with you? That's what they told me."

"There was, but he went to scout around."

"Scout around?"

"We had some trouble."

"Trouble?"

"Yeah."

The man glanced down at the pistol. "Ma'am, I'd feel a whole lot better if you'd point that thing in another direction."

Could I really shoot him? Could I really end another human being's life, even if he means me harm? she asked herself. "Who owns this ranch?" she demanded.

"Jake Lawrence," the man answered.

She could tell he knew he was being tested. "Who *runs* the ranch?"

The man chuckled. "John Tucker, the son of a bitch."

Angela let out a long breath, then lowered the gun slightly and blinked.

In that moment the man lunged, knocking her to the ground as she screamed and pulled the trigger twice. The bullets whined as they caromed about the cave, and then he was on top of her, slamming her hand against the rock floor fiercely until the gun skittered away. He grabbed her by the throat and lifted her to her feet. She could feel herself starting to go dizzy as her air supply was cut off. *Never trust. Never trust.* She clawed at his beard as he slammed her back against the wall, then spun her around.

"Where's Lawrence?" he hissed, lips to her ear as he pressed her cheek hard against the rough rock wall.

"At a cabin further up the mountain," she moaned, grimacing in pain.

"What?"

She could feel his hot breath on her face. "At the cabin."

"But you're supposed to be with him."

"Our meeting is over. He's probably gone." She didn't know what else to say. "Please stop hurting me."

"This isn't right!" the man roared. "Not right at all. Goddamnit, you're supposed to be with him!"

"I don't know what to tell you."

"Tell me where —"

She thrust her heel into the man's shin, and he groaned loudly. For a split second she was free and she broke for the back of the cave and the revolver. But he managed to trip her and fall on top of her heavily, knocking the wind from her lungs as they fell. She reached desperately for the gun, just inches from her fingertips, but his hand darted past hers and he tossed it further back into the darkness.

Suddenly she was being pulled to her feet again, her hands forced together behind her back, and he was pushing her toward the cave entrance, the cliff, and five hundred feet straight down. She fought desperately, struggling to dig her toes into the ground, but he was too powerful and she closed her eyes, trying to prepare herself for the terror of the plunge and the horrible impact. Perhaps this was why she had hated heights since childhood. Perhaps somehow she had known she would die this way.

She opened her eyes wide as they burst from the cave and screamed wildly as the man propelled her the last few feet. The canyon stretched out before her, sheer walls falling to a frozen river. This had to be a nightmare. She was going to wake up in her room at the lodge, on the edge of the sleigh bed, about to tumble to the floor. This couldn't be happening. "No! My God, no!"

And then they were both down on the trail, faces buried in the snow after a powerful impact. Angela could feel her head and shoulders hanging over the edge of the cliff, nothing but air beneath her. Her attacker was trying desperately to push her over, and she clawed wildly at the snow, digging for anything to hold on to. For an instant she found a rock, but it popped from the ground as she grabbed it and she was sliding further over oblivion.

Then strong hands clamped down on her ankles, then her legs, and she was being dragged away from danger and pulled to her feet. Lawrence's personal army had turned into her personal cavalry and suddenly she was safe. There were four of them around her, brushing the snow from her clothes and asking her if she was all right. She nodded, unable to speak, catching glimpses of her attacker being pummeled by four more of the guards a few feet away. He was shouting at them in a foreign language she didn't recognize.

Two of the men who had rescued her stepped in front of her, blocking her view of the scuffle. She strained to see, but once more they moved to block her view. When she was able to see again, her attacker was gone. For a few moments she didn't understand what had happened, then the realization set in. He was off the cliff into the abyss. Dead. She stared at the empty space where he'd just been, dazed.

Then she glanced to her right, between two of the men who had rescued her, and directly into the burning eyes of William Colby.

★ ★ ★

It was almost midnight, and he was tired of trying to pick up the woman. She was with two female friends who'd made it clear with their withering looks across the bar that they weren't going to let her go home with him. Besides, he had an important sales call in the morning, and he didn't want to have to drive her back to her car when they were done. She wasn't *that* good looking.

So he downed the rest of his beer, tossed his business card at her as a courtesy, and headed out the tavern door across a deserted parking lot toward his Lexus. As he neared the car, he thought he could see a man leaning against it through the darkness.

"Hey, off the car, hemorrhoid." No reaction, and now he could see two of them. "I said, off the —" He swallowed his words when they broke from the car and raced toward him. He tried to run and at the same time pull his cell phone from his pocket. But they were on him quickly, pushing him to the ground roughly and snatching the phone. "What's going on?" he stammered as one of the men grabbed him by his collar and yanked him to his feet. The attacker was the size of a double door refrigerator. "There's been some mistake."

"There's been no mistake."

"What do you want?"

"You're gonna get a call tomorrow."

"A call?"

"You'll do what the caller tells you to do. *Exactly* what he tells you to do."

"All right," he gasped.

The refrigerator tightened his grip. "You understand?"

"Yes."

"Good. You don't do what you're told, and you'll see us again. And next time it'll be a lot worse," the refrigerator growled, slamming his huge fist into the man's midsection.

The other one dropped the man's phone on top of him, and then they were gone, faded into the night, leaving the man to try to figure out what had just happened as he clutched his stomach and gasped for air.

CHAPTER FOUR

Daytime temperatures rarely dropped below freezing in Richmond, even in the middle of February. But today, beneath ominous gray clouds, the brisk morning gusts of central Virginia were bitter cold.

Angela pulled the tapered ends of the collar of her long wool coat tightly around her neck and shivered as she hurried up Ninth Street toward Main, bent over against the wind and the incline of the steep sidewalk. It seemed colder here in Richmond than it had in Wyoming.

As she turned the corner on to Main, Sumter Bank's headquarters came into view. The Sumter Tower was a fifty-story glass-encased monolith that soared above the rest of Richmond's skyline. The city's next tallest building was forty stories, and the rumor was that the city wouldn't grant a building permit for anything over that, not as long as Bob Dudley, Sumter's chairman of the board, was around. He'd commissioned the Sumter Tower ten years ago — at the beginning of his tenure as chairman — as a monument to himself.

"Hey, there," called a short black woman. She

was clasping a notepad and a pen in one hand as she descended the steps from the Sumter Tower courtyard and quickly covered the last few yards between them. She was surprisingly agile for her stocky build.

"Hello, Liv." Olivia Jefferson was the *Richmond Tribune* reporter Jake Lawrence had referred to, the woman who was taking Sumter to task for what she perceived as its poor service to the city's minority community. Jefferson was a tough-talking, middle-aged woman who'd grown up on the city's rough east side, but now lived in the Fan, a desirable neighborhood west of downtown.

"Where have you been, Angela?" Liv asked. "I tried calling you three times yesterday."

"Traveling. I told you I was going out of town on business."

"But I thought you were supposed to be back yesterday."

The original itinerary had Angela returning to Richmond on one of Jake Lawrence's Gulfstream jets as soon as their meeting was over. But after she had come within inches of being hurled off the mountain, Lawrence's armed guards had escorted her back to the lodge where she'd taken a warm shower, relaxed for a few hours, then eaten a late dinner alone with William Colby.

John Tucker had made no further appearances. During dinner, Colby volunteered that Tucker had made it down the mountain safely.

However, Tucker had not shown up to say good-bye that evening, nor did she see him the next morning before Colby drove her to the airport. She was disappointed. She had wanted to see Tucker again. If only to convince herself that he really was all right. As much as she trusted John, she did not trust Colby.

Over dessert Colby had informed her that his men had recovered the body of her attacker from the canyon and determined that he was a recently hired ranch hand. A drifter, Colby had been advised by local authorities only a few minutes before sitting down to dinner, who had an assault record. He had apologized stiffly — Angela could tell it was something he was not accustomed to doing — criticizing Tucker several times for not doing a more thorough job of screening applicants. Then he'd requested that she not speak of the incident with anyone in return for a cash payment of ten thousand dollars, which she hadn't accepted. She'd flown back to Richmond yesterday, arriving in the late afternoon.

There was only one question Angela had really wanted to ask Colby during dinner. Had her attacker fallen from the cliff — or been pushed? But she hadn't asked because she didn't want to provoke him, particularly with another night alone on the lodge's fourth floor ahead of her. It was clear Colby hadn't wanted to discuss the incident in any detail, and that she wouldn't have been given a straight answer anyway. Besides, given several of Colby's remarks, she was fairly certain by the end of dinner that she had her answer. The question had then become *why* had the man been thrown off the cliff? But she wasn't prepared to ask that question either. Perhaps that was simply the standard way Colby dealt with anyone who threatened Jake Lawrence. Perhaps he was as cold as he seemed.

"My trip went a day longer than I expected," Angela answered, glancing past Olivia at a dozen warmly bundled people walking in a slow circle in front of the Sumter Bank main entrance. Each of them carried a homemade sign accusing Sumter of discriminatory banking practices, and each was doing his or her best to subtly get in the way of anyone trying to gain access to the building. They were also shouting insults at employees as they darted toward one of the entrance's three revolving doors. Two Richmond policemen drinking coffee from 7-Eleven cups kept a casual eye on the protesters from inside the bank's main lobby. "Is that all right with you?"

"Well, you certainly came back from your trip stretched tighter than a drum."

"Yeah, well." Angela caught sight of a man coming down Main Street, head bowed against the gusts. It was Ken Booker, her boss, and she turned away, hoping he wouldn't see her.

"Your meeting must have been pretty rough," Olivia commented.

"Why do you say that?"

The older woman reached out and touched Angela's face gently. "Your cheek is all scratched up."

"Oh, I fell in my bathroom last night," Angela explained, pulling back from Olivia's fingers and glancing after Booker to make certain he'd gone inside. "I slipped stepping out of the shower." She could still feel the cave's gritty rock wall scraping her face, and the incredible terror as her attacker had propelled her toward the edge of the cliff. She hadn't told Colby at dinner that the man had mentioned Lawrence, indicating to her that his attack wasn't the result of some psychotic vendetta against women, that he wasn't just some mindless drifter. "I hit my cheek against the sink when I fell."

"That's more of a scrape than a bruise."

"I'm late, Liv."

"Wait a minute. We need to talk."

"Not here," Angela answered, glancing around furtively. "Not now."

"What's gotten into you?"

"Nothing." She brushed past Liv and headed toward the protesters. "I'll talk to you this afternoon," she called over her shoulder, moving around the human circle without incident when Liv motioned to them that Angela shouldn't be harassed.

Five minutes later, Angela reached her workstation in the middle of the fourteenth floor, remaining there only long enough to place her briefcase down on her desk and lay her coat over the back of her chair. Then she headed for Ken Booker's office at the far corner of the large room.

"I'm back from Wyoming," Angela announced, walking briskly through Booker's doorway.

He glanced up from behind his desk. "So I see." He was a senior managing director, in charge of all of Sumter's corporate lending and a man not far from the corporate ladder's top rung. He was preppy looking, with thinning blond hair and tortoiseshell glasses, and he always wore a heavily starched, white Oxford button-down shirt. "Angela, I'm busy right now. We'll have to talk later."

"This can't wait." Booker was the one who had approached her about the meeting with Jake Lawrence. "Who contacted you, Ken?"

"What?"

"How did Jake Lawrence's people get in touch with you? How did they get you to send me to Wyoming?"

Booker placed the gold Cross pen he'd been making notes with down on the legal pad in front of him. "Is there a problem?"

"Just tell me." She wanted to ask him why he had gotten in the way of her promotion twice, but that would be risky. Maybe Lawrence really had no idea about that. Maybe he was plying her with misinformation because he had his own agenda. She wasn't certain who or what to believe at this point, and she was going to be very careful about what she conveyed to anyone.

Booker eased back in his chair, a puzzled expression on his face. "You okay?"

"Fine."

"All right. Well, Lawrence's New York office called. It was one of his financial people. In fact, I'd met the guy before. I'd called on him in the past to try to get business from some of Lawrence's portfolio companies, but they've always stuck with the big New York banks. The guy called to tell me that Lawrence wanted to speak with *you.* Frankly, I was a little put off by his attitude and the fact that he didn't want to meet with me, but —"

"Ken, I —"

"Mr. Booker." Booker's assistant stood in the office doorway. "I'm sorry to interrupt, sir."

"That's all right, Jean. Look," he said, glancing back at Angela, "I don't know what the problem is but this is a conference call with some very important people in Washington that I've had scheduled for some time and I've got to —"

"No, actually it isn't," the stern-looking woman at the door interrupted. "Angela, the chairman has requested that you come up to his office on the fiftieth floor right away. He and the president are waiting for you."

For a moment the office fell silent, then Booker looked up at Angela and shrugged. "Better go see what they want."

She nodded slowly. Jake Lawrence's prediction had been eerily accurate. She hadn't been back in the building for ten minutes and already Bob Dudley was looking for her.

"By the way, Angela," Booker called after her, "I wouldn't mention to the men on fifty that you were talking to Liv Jefferson this morning." He nodded at Angela's startled reaction. "Yeah, I saw you."

"I wasn't *talking* to her."

"Don't get so defensive."

"I'm not."

"Could have fooled me."

"Look, Ken, she asked me for a comment on that little protest going on downstairs, but I wouldn't give her one."

Booker nodded. "That was smart. You know we have a policy here at Sumter about talking to the press without senior management's authorization. It's a policy we take very seriously."

The elevator ride from fourteen to fifty was quick. *Too quick,* Angela thought to herself when the doors opened. Nothing good could come of this. She was about to meet with Sumter's two most senior executives, and they weren't summoning her to the top of the tower to congratulate her on closing a profitable transaction. They wanted to grill her about her meeting with Jake Lawrence. There could be no other reason for their sudden need to speak to her.

"Hi, I'm here to see Mr. Dudley," she informed the receptionist.

"Your name?"

"Angela Day. Mr. Dudley is expecting me."

The woman looked Angela up and down, then pointed to a plush sofa behind an antique coffee table. "You can have a seat over there."

"Thank you."

As she walked across the room's huge Oriental rug, she gazed steadily at the long row of dark oil paintings stretching the length of the wall behind the sofa. These were paintings of the men who had run Sumter Bank since its founding in the early 1860s, their tenures inscribed on small gold plaques affixed to the bottom of each ornate frame: 1917–1926, 1926–1932, and so on. In their portraits, hung on the wall in chronological order from left to right, the men looked strikingly similar. All were white, silver-haired, and strong-jawed. They were all clad in dark suit jackets, conservative ties, and white shirts. And they all wore stony expressions. There were no smiles on the wall.

"The chairman is ready for you, Ms. Day," the receptionist called. "Over there."

Angela nodded and headed toward the door the receptionist had pointed to. Behind the door was an anteroom and another woman seated behind a desk, a gray-haired woman with half-lens spectacles who seemed friendly enough at first but who gave Angela the same up-and-down the receptionist had. Without a word the woman waved Angela toward a large door at the back of the anteroom.

Angela hesitated at the door, then turned the large brass knob and pushed.

"Come in, Ms. Day."

She looked across the large office in the direction of the voice. The chairman and president were on the far side of the room, near a wide window, posed almost exactly as they had been in last year's glossy annual report to the bank's shareholders. The chairman sat in a huge leather wing chair, legs crossed at the knees, hands folded in his lap — a picture of cool control. The president stood behind him, arms folded across his chest.

"Please, come in," the president called, beckoning as he moved out from behind the chairman and met her halfway across the room. "I'm Carter Hill, and I'm sure you recognize our chairman, Bob Dudley."

"Of course," Angela said, aware of the fact that Hill hadn't offered his hand in greeting, as many men still didn't, even in business settings. They'd shake hands with her male counterparts, but not her. "Hello, Mr. Dudley."

Dudley nodded, almost imperceptibly, but said nothing.

"We appreciate your being available to see us so quickly," Hill continued politely.

"It's my pleasure." She was struck by how much Dudley and Hill resembled the men in the paintings along the lobby wall. "I want to help you in any way I can."

"Yes, I'm sure you do." Hill gave her a quick, forced smile. "Would you care for anything to drink? Coffee? Coke?"

"No, thanks, I'm fine," she replied, following him past a large desk to the area by the window where Dudley waited.

"Please have a seat." Hill directed her to a wooden chair by the window. He sat in another large leather wing chair beside the chairman's.

Angela glanced out the window at a panoramic view of Richmond and the wide James River at the base of the steep hill the city was built on, then looked away and sat down. God, she hated heights.

"Everything all right, Ms. Day?" Hill asked.

"Fine." There was a table beside the chair that caught her eye. On it was a collection of toy soldiers, each only a few inches high. They were Confederate soldiers, she noted, one of which, at the front of the unit, was bearing a small Rebel flag. "Just fine," she repeated, smoothing out her dress.

"Angela, you have a fine record of performance here at Sumter," Hill began. "The chairman and I were just reviewing it. Several years of very strong production in Ken Booker's division. Lots of income, including fees, and no loan write-offs. We appreciate your fine service."

"Thank you."

"Which is why we were a little surprised —"

"What did Jake Lawrence want?" Dudley interrupted gruffly.

"Easy, Bob," Hill urged, "let's take it slowly. We don't want to —"

"What did Lawrence want?" Dudley repeated.

Angela and Dudley locked eyes. "Mr. Lawrence asked me to come to Wyoming to discuss one of his portfolio companies," she explained. Dudley's eyes were cold and dark, just like Lawrence's. "He wants to leverage the company with long-term debt, and he wants Sumter to be the lead bank in terms of providing the loans." Angela sniffed, as though she wasn't enthusiastic about the opportunity. "Of course, he intends to pay himself a huge dividend with the cash we lend to his company."

"Why did he call *you*, Ms. Day?" Dudley continued.

"He didn't."

"What do you mean?" Hill asked quickly.

"First of all, Jake Lawrence didn't make the initial contact. It was a person out of his New York office that called. Second, that individual initially called Ken Booker, who then relayed the message to me. I want to be very clear on all of that because New York isn't my territory, and I don't want to step on any toes. My territory is Georgia and Alabama."

"Ken didn't tell me about it happening that way when I spoke to him," Dudley hissed. "He seemed to think you were acting on your own."

"Well, I don't know why he would have told you that, Mr. Dudley, because I —"

"You've had such a stellar employment record here at Sumter, Ms. Day," Hill cut in, "up until now, anyway. You should have run your meeting with Jake Lawrence up the chain of command before accepting his invitation. You should have —"

"Excuse me, sir, but, as I said, Ken Booker took the initial call from Lawrence's people, then approached me." She wasn't going to give Dudley or Hill any opportunity to scar her record. "You can check with him."

"Why did Lawrence want to talk to you and not Booker?" Dudley inquired.

"Because I have specific industry experience related to the portfolio company Mr. Lawrence wants to leverage," she answered, repeating what Lawrence had told her to say. "So he thinks I'm best suited to guide the transaction through the bank and to convince other banks to join us." She glanced down at the toy soldiers marching toward her on the small table, wondering if Dudley and Hill understood how hateful she found all the display represented. Perhaps the soldiers had been put there on purpose, she realized. Just for her. Perhaps they knew that she had friends who were black. One in particular. "From what Lawrence was saying, it will be a significant transaction. About a billion dollars in total, so we'll need a broad syndicate of other lenders."

"What's the name of the company he wants to leverage?" Dudley asked.

Angela hesitated, knowing how this would sound. "I'm not certain. He didn't want to go into detail yet."

"Why not?"

"I'm not sure."

"What industry does the company operate in?" Dudley pressed. "He must have mentioned the industry if that was why he wanted to speak with you and not Booker."

She hesitated again. "He didn't tell me that either."

Dudley pounded the arm of the chair with his fist. "Well, what *did* he tell you?"

"Only what I've related."

"You expect me to believe that Jake Lawrence flew you all the way out to Wyoming just for that?" Dudley's cheeks were becoming flushed. "Ms. Day, you'd better come up with more —"

"He made a pass at me," she snapped, glaring at Dudley. "He made a pass at me," she repeated softly, gritting her teeth and glancing down at her lap, feeling the heat rush to her eyes. "I think that's why he flew me all the way out to Wyoming."

Carter Hill rose quickly from his chair, pulled a clean white handkerchief from the top pocket of his suit jacket and held it out for her. "Here," he offered gently.

"I'm fine," she said, holding up her hand.

She wanted Jake Lawrence's help in getting custody of her son, but there were limits to how far she'd go to get it. She had found that out as Lawrence's physical advances on the cabin's couch had turned into a short but scary struggle. "Look, I didn't want to say anything. I know Mr. Lawrence is a powerful man, and I don't want any trouble. Not for Sumter Bank or for me personally. I just want to forget I ever went out there. I want to forget it happened."

"The guy's a bastard," Hill muttered to Dudley, stalking back to his chair. "I've heard how aggressive he can be with women. People I know in New York have told me. Jake Lawrence seems to think all that money gives him carte blanche to do whatever he wants. It's the God complex."

Angela glanced at Dudley who was staring straight back, no sympathy in his expression. "Do you really believe Jake Lawrence flew you to Wyoming to make a pass at you under the guise of a big transaction about which he gave you no details? That makes no sense." Dudley shook his head. "No offense, Ms. Day, but I'm certain Jake Lawrence could find more willing partners, women who would be willing to look at what he wanted simply as a business transaction. If you get my drift."

"What are you saying, Bob?" Hill asked after a long pause.

"I think Jake Lawrence had another agenda,"

Dudley answered, not taking his eyes off of Angela.

"Such as?"

Dudley's eyes narrowed. "I'm sure you did a little background work on Mr. Lawrence before you went to see him, right, Ms. Day?"

Angela stared back at Dudley, wondering where he was headed with this question.

"At least that's what the network management people reported after studying their server records," Dudley continued when she didn't respond. "In the days before you went to Wyoming, you visited several Web sites looking for information on Jake Lawrence. And you accessed Free Edgar and probably discovered in a 13-d filing that he owns 8 percent of Sumter Bank. Isn't that right, Ms. Day?"

"Is that a problem?" she asked quietly, shocked by the fact that Bob Dudley had directed the bank's information technology specialists to spy on her. "Wouldn't you expect me to do background work before meeting with one of the world's wealthiest men?"

"Yes, I would." Dudley looked out the window over downtown Richmond, then back at her. "Did he bring up the fact that he owned all of that Sumter stock?"

"No, *I* brought it up, Mr. Dudley. I told Lawrence I had found out about his large position in Sumter stock. I told him I had calculated that he had spent four hundred and fifty million so far on Sumter stock, and he corrected me and told me that it was actually closer to half a billion. And he was down forty million so far on his purchase."

Dudley was gazing at her intently, hanging on her every word. And as she looked closely, she could see a trace of fear hiding in his intensity, a tiny sliver of anxiety, working its way into Dudley's fiercely proud expression. Jake Lawrence and his army of analysts were at the Sumter gate, and Dudley understood as well as any financial expert that the bottom line in a business war was money. Who had more of it, and who was willing to risk it. If Jake Lawrence offered a significant premium for Sumter shares, the market would sell to him, and all the value Dudley had created for the bank's shareholders during his ten years at the helm as chairman would be forgotten in the time it took them to endorse their stock certificates. And once Lawrence owned the bank, if that were his ultimate objective, Dudley's grip on the office of chairman would turn tenuous at best. Because, as the new owner, Lawrence could do whatever he wanted. Including replacing any senior executive he chose to.

"I asked Mr. Lawrence why he was so interested in Sumter," Angela continued. "I made the point that he couldn't view an investment in a bank as a high-return proposition, that we weren't going to find a cure for cancer or invent the next white-hot wireless device. I made the point that the bank's stock is trading around two times its book value, which I told him I thought was pretty high."

"And?"

Bob Dudley had a reputation as one of the toughest senior executives in the entire banking business. During his ten years as chairman, through a series of expertly planned and smoothly executed acquisitions, he had propelled Sumter from its position as a sleepy Virginia retail institution — little more than a corner savings and loan operation — to an aggressive, superregional bank with a massive mortgage portfolio that had caught Wall Street's attention. After several large, high-profile acquisitions in North Carolina and Tennessee, Dudley had been ruthless, summarily firing the acquisitions' existing senior management and replacing them with his lieutenants — after initially promising that there would be no blood once the deal was done. But Dudley had made billions for Sumter stockholders, and the defeated men had slunk silently away, unable to get anyone to listen to the fact that Dudley had lied to them.

But now Dudley was on the defensive, uncertain of Lawrence's motives. Now he was the hunted.

"What was his response, Ms. Day?" Dudley demanded.

A week ago she'd been a nobody. Now this. Suddenly she wished she could go back and decline the opportunity to meet Jake Lawrence.

121

"He said he thought the bank's shares still had a good deal of room on the upside. He said he thought that the bank was very well positioned as a strong player in one of the hottest regions in the country. The Southeast."

"Did he say anything about acquiring Sumter?" Hill spoke up. "Or wanting a board seat? Did he mention anything like that?"

Angela shook her head. "No."

"Did he say he was viewing Sumter as simply another investment in his liquid portfolio? Did he talk about buying more shares?"

She knew where Hill was going with this. He was trying to read the tea leaves to figure out Lawrence's true intentions. Searching for buzz-words in anything Lawrence might have said for clues as to whether Lawrence would buy more shares and ultimately announce what would be a hostile takeover attempt or remain passive, which was what she knew they hoped.

"No," she answered.

"Dammit," Dudley cursed under his breath.

"Easy, Bob," Hill said soothingly. "I don't think you need to —"

"Shut up, Carter," he snapped, glaring at Angela. "Ms. Day, don't you find it odd that out of all the banks in this country and all the lending officers working at those banks, Jake Lawrence would secretly contact you to discuss a transaction about which he ended up giving you no real information? While at the same time he's accumulating shares of *my* bank. Don't you get the picture? He could have called any of the big New York banks he works with all the time to help him leverage his portfolio company." Dudley gritted his teeth. "They'd fall all over themselves to do a deal like that with him, but he called you."

"I told you," Angela said evenly. "Nobody *secretly* contacted me. The contact was made through Ken Booker. You can check with him. He'll tell you what happened."

Dudley continued staring at her for a few moments, then eased back in his chair and forced a calm smile to his face. "How did you leave things with Jake Lawrence?"

"I told him not to contact me again, Mr. Dudley. The man made a pass at me. Didn't you hear me? My God!"

Dudley's eyes narrowed. "What did he say to that?"

"Say?" she asked.

"Did he tell you he still wanted you to be involved in this supposed transaction? Did he still want you to lead it, even when you wouldn't let him have what he wanted?"

"Even?"

"If you're so damned angry about him copping a feel, why didn't you call the police?"

"The police?" she asked incredulously. "Do you think they would have believed me?" The world took the word of a rich man over that of a girl from a trailer park. She knew that from personal experience. "Or done anything even if they had believed me? We're talking about Jake Lawrence here."

"So how did Lawrence leave it with you?" Dudley demanded. "What did he say when you told him no?"

"I didn't give him a chance to say anything. I got out of there as fast as I could."

Dudley pointed at her with a gnarled finger, the way he always did when he really wanted someone's attention. "If Jake Lawrence or one of his people contacts you again, I want to know immediately." He hesitated. "And I don't want you to tell him to go to hell either, Ms. Day."

"I don't understand."

"I want to know what Jake Lawrence's intentions are. I want you to be loyal to Sumter Bank and to me," Dudley said firmly. "I don't want you to mention what he did to you in that cabin if he calls. I want you to act as if nothing out of the ordinary happened in Wyoming. You are to continue working on this transaction, if that is what he asks of you."

"But, I —"

"Bob, we ought to think this through," Hill cut in. "I mean, we don't want to put ourselves in a difficult position." He flashed a nervous smile at Angela. "We don't want to put Ms. Day in a difficult position either."

"I'm not asking Ms. Day to put herself in a difficult position," Dudley snapped, peering at Angela. "I'm simply asking her to be a loyal employee, loyal to the bank and loyal to me. Jake

124

Lawrence is a bad man. And he has no idea how to run a bank like mine. I've devoted too much of myself to this organization and its shareholders to let a slimy son of a bitch like him ooze his way through the crack beneath the front door just because he's got so much money. None of which he earned himself," Dudley added snidely. "Do you understand what I'm saying, Ms. Day?"

She nodded slowly, appalled by what the chairman was saying, appalled by what he was asking of her.

Dudley nodded back. "Good. If you hear from Jake Lawrence, you are to contact Mr. Hill or his assistant immediately," he instructed, gesturing at the president, "and arrange an appointment with Mr. Hill using the project name Snake. Mr. Hill's assistant will understand what that means and what to do. Are we clear on all of that?"

Adrenaline surged through Angela. The bastard didn't give a damn what Jake Lawrence had done to her on that couch in Wyoming. To Dudley she was nothing but a readily expendable foot soldier in his personal war to maintain total control of Sumter Bank.

"Ms. Day?"

"Yes," she said curtly. "We're clear."

"Good. That will be all for now."

Angela stood up and headed for the door, feeling Dudley's glare boring into her back. When she'd made it through the anteroom and the lobby, and the elevator doors had closed in front of the receptionist who had watched her walk all the way across the lobby, Angela allowed her head to fall back against the car wall and closed her eyes as it began to descend. The risks in her life had suddenly risen immeasurably. She hoped Jake Lawrence would leave her alone.

"What do you think, Carter?" Dudley stood in front of the window, hands clasped tightly behind his back, gazing out at the snow falling on Richmond. "What did you think of Angela Day's performance?"

"Performance?"

"What was truth and what was for our benefit?"

Hill shook his head. "I don't know, Bob. If any of that was acting, she should win an Oscar."

"Do you think Jake Lawrence really assaulted her?"

"Yes," Hill answered thoughtfully. "I'm convinced. I saw sincere emotion in her expression."

As Dudley watched, the snow began to fall more heavily. The James River, only a quarter of a mile away, was all but obscured. "But why would he do that, Carter? What was his motive?"

"I don't think there was any motive, other than getting some action. It's as simple as that." Hill shrugged. "After all, she is pretty."

Dudley pivoted slowly away from the window. "What did you say?" he asked coldly. "That she's pretty?"

Hill shook his head. "Don't get me wrong. I was just making a point about how Lawrence —"

"First of all, according to the preliminary information your people dug up, she's a Wop from a trailer park."

"Well, yes, but —"

Dudley's lip curled. "Worse, she's a nigger lover. She hangs around with that reporter bitch Olivia Jefferson from the *Tribune*."

Hill grimaced.

"She's one of those bleeding hearts who feels sorry for savages whose ancestors ran around spearing water buffalo and running from lions, whose cousins still do."

"Jesus, Bob, you've got to be careful about that kind of stuff. One of these days you're going to do that in public. Then there will be hell to pay."

"I don't care about the public," he muttered. "What I care about is figuring out what Lawrence is up to."

Hill glanced at the ceiling and groaned quietly. "I think it was simply as she described. He was looking for a little action."

"You're being naive, Carter."

"Bob, people I know in New York have told me that he's got a helluva sex drive. It borders on addiction."

"What people?" Dudley hissed. "Have you

spoken to any woman who's ever actually been assaulted by Jake Lawrence?"

"Well, no," Hill answered slowly. "The people I spoke to said they'd heard about him from others. But they weren't rumormongers."

"Everyone's a rumormonger. Remember that."

"These were senior people at several of the large investment banks I'm talking about."

"And we all know how ethical and honest they can be."

"Well . . ."

"So you didn't press them on how they acquired their information concerning Jake Lawrence?"

"No," Hill admitted.

"Well, I suggest you do, Carter. I have. And when you really drill down there is no hard evidence of anything concerning Jake Lawrence. And I'm not talking about silly sexual dalliances that you, I, Jake Lawrence, and the rest of the male galaxy are guilty of. I'm talking about any hard information at all. I can't even find a picture of him." Dudley turned back toward the window. Only the closest building was still visible through the snow at this point. "From now on, Carter, we will monitor Angela Day very closely."

"Are you worried that Lawrence might try to use her as some kind of information source? Inside information?"

"Of course I am."

"But how could she help him? What kind of

information could she possibly have access to that would help him take over Sumter?"

Dudley shook his head, gazing into the storm settling down onto the city. "I don't know. But by five o'clock this afternoon I want your people to get us a second, much more detailed report on Ms. Day. Not just the easy and obvious stuff this time. I want to know exactly what time she gets up in the morning, what she eats for breakfast, who her friends are, who she's screwing, and how he's doing it to her. I want to know what drawer she keeps her damn panties in!" Dudley paused to catch his breath. "Do you understand?"

Hill nodded and turned to go. He'd made a career out of doing Bob Dudley's dirty work. This was simply another filthy example.

"One more thing, Carter."

Hill sighed quietly and stopped. "Yes?" he asked, trying to mask his irritation.

"Do you think any of this could be related to that article Liv Jefferson wrote?"

"Sir?"

Dudley moved away from the window to his desk. "*The* article," he said loudly, frustrated that Hill didn't understand exactly what he was talking about right away. "The one accusing me of shutting down our branches in minority-dominated areas of the city, of orchestrating a conspiracy to deny mortgages and other services to minorities across the state."

"I suppose, but I don't think it's likely."

Dudley clenched his hands more tightly. "I called the *Trib*'s publisher the day that article came out, and I told him I was going to sue the paper. He told me he would welcome that. He told me he had evidence supporting Liv Jefferson's claims. A memo or something." Dudley stared at Hill. "Do you think that's possible?"

Hill shrugged. "I have no idea."

Dudley pursed his lips, then nodded. "You've been tasked, Carter. Get to work."

Angela slowly replaced her office phone in its cradle after listening to her voice mail. The last message had been from Kate Charboneau, the attorney who had represented Angela in her divorce from Sam Reese six years ago. And in Angela's failed attempt to win custody of Hunter. She and Kate hadn't spoken in two years, and now Kate wanted to get together for a drink after work. One of the men who had lied in court about having sexual relations with Angela during her marriage to Sam Reese had contacted Kate late yesterday and there was an important development to report.

Angela gazed across the large room at Ken Booker, who was staring back at her from his doorway. Jake Lawrence had promised to talk to his people about helping her. Perhaps, despite Tucker's skepticism, Lawrence had come through after all. But why this time? What made this situation so special?

She moved out from behind her desk and

headed quickly toward Booker's office. "I need to talk to you," she said angrily as she neared him. This was risky, but she wanted answers. And she felt she deserved them.

"All right."

"Inside." She didn't want Booker's assistant to hear this.

He shrugged, moved back to his chair, and sat. "What is it?"

"Why did you tell Bob Dudley I was acting on my own when I went out to meet with Jake Lawrence in Wyoming?"

Booker shook his head. "What are you talking about? Bob Dudley and I never spoke about you going to meet with Jake Lawrence. I haven't spoken to Bob Dudley in six months. I report to Carter Hill."

CHAPTER FIVE

The sharp rap on the oak door came exactly at five o'clock, as ordered. And that was what Bob Dudley liked most about Carter Hill: his precision. He did what he was told to do exactly when he was told to do it.

Carter would never be Sumter's chairman. Dudley had come to that conclusion two years ago, disclosing to a confidant on the bank's board of directors that Hill was too much of a consensus builder. In essence, Hill didn't understand enough about manipulation, coercion, and ruthlessness to run an organization as large and complex as Sumter. Worst of all, Hill cared too much about people's feelings. But, like everyone else in Dudley's life, Hill served a purpose.

"Come in," Dudley called from the same chair he'd been sitting in this morning when he'd met with Angela Day.

"Hello, Bob," Hill said pleasantly, closing the office door.

"Come on, Carter, let's get going. I've got a dinner meeting. Thank God the snow stopped," he muttered under his breath. He enjoyed the luxury of his limousine and hadn't been looking forward to climbing into an SUV to get to the young woman's apartment through the storm. His wife was vacationing in Palm Beach for February, and he wasn't about to miss a single evening of pleasure with the young woman while nights away from his West End home didn't have to be explained.

Hill hustled across the office and sat down in the chair beside Dudley's.

"So, Carter, what did you find out about Angela Day?"

Hill glanced down at the pad of white pages on which he had scribbled his notes. For the last six months Bob Dudley hadn't allowed the bank's purchasing managers to order any other paper color than white: no yellow, no accountant's faded green, not even pastels or neons for Post-its. "Angela Day is a divorced mother of one." Hill hesitated and looked up at the chairman. "Her ex-husband is Sam Reese."

Dudley's eyes flashed from the small LCD screen of his Blackberry to Hill. His plan had been to riffle through e-mails while Carter gave his report, multitasking as his dictatorial father had taught him to do from an early age. "*Chuck Reese*'s son?"

Charles "Chuck" Reese was the senior and managing partner of Albemarle Capital, a private investment management firm that had handled most of Richmond's stock market money since the War between the States. Sumter Bank and Albemarle Capital were the city's most prominent financial institutions, and Dudley and Reese her most prominent business leaders. They had trained in finance together at Sumter after rooming together at the University of Virginia. And they'd been best friends until Reese had left Sumter in his midthirties to join Albemarle Capital, where his meteoric rise to the top of that institution had been rivaled only by Dudley's at Sumter. Over the years their relationship had deteriorated. They'd gone from friends to rivals to enemies, competing aggressively in everything from the number of articles written about them in the national press to an annual head-to-head golf match held at the Country Club of Virginia. They played the match under the guise of good-natured charity, but it could not have been fought more intensely if their lives had depended on the outcome.

After Dudley had successfully constructed his fifty-story downtown monument, Chuck Reese had tried to get zoning for a *sixty*-story building that would have blocked the Sumter Tower's panoramic view of the James River. But the zoning application had bogged down in city red tape, and it had become very clear who Richmond's alpha dog was. However, Reese had won their golf match each of the last three years, and the losses gnawed at Dudley. Last year it had come down to a five-foot putt on the eighteenth green in front of a gallery numbering in the thousands. Dudley had missed the putt, and Reese had been crowing about the victory — and Dudley's choke — for six months. Since that day Dudley had been working with a pro three times a week. He was determined to win this year.

"Yes, Chuck Reese," Hill confirmed. "Your favorite person."

"Bastard." Dudley rose from his chair and grabbed a putter leaning against the wall. "I remember that now." He snickered as he hunched over a dimpled Titleist, aiming it toward an automatic ball-return device on the floor a few feet away. "It was a messy divorce. Happened about . . ." Dudley's voice trailed off as he swung the putter back and forth, then tapped the shiny white ball and watched it roll smoothly across the carpet directly into the target. "Damn. That should have happened last summer."

"You were saying, Bob?"

"The divorce was four or five years ago."

"Six, actually."

Dudley chuckled, thinking about the embarrassment the situation must have caused Reese. "The divorce actually went to court, right?"

"Yes. Two men, acquaintances of Sam Reese, testified that they had engaged in sexual intercourse with Ms. Day during the time she was married to Reese. The judge found her guilty of adultery and refused to grant her alimony."

Dudley putted again — with the same result. "I'm sure Chuck didn't want his son married to

135

some poor Italian from a trailer park. I bet he didn't leave anything to chance during the proceedings." Dudley laughed loudly. "The only thing worse for Chuck would have been if Angela were black. Too bad she isn't," he muttered. "I wonder if she ever brought any of her nigger friends home. That would have killed him."

Hill winced. "Bob, this behind-closed-doors racism's got to stop. It's going to get you in real trouble. I can't emphasize —"

"Enough, Carter."

Hill bit his tongue. "Bob, I haven't been able to confirm that Chuck Reese paid off the two men who testified in court."

"Stop trying," Dudley advised Hill. "You're wasting your time. As much as I'd like to have that kind of information on the prick," he added. "You and I both know he bribed the men, but we'll never be able to prove it. Chuck's too careful. He has too many ways of covering his financial tracks. Besides, it doesn't matter. I'm focused on Ms. Day right now." He lined up the golf ball with the device once more. Once more the ball found the target. He smiled, satisfied on several counts. "So our own Angela Day was Chuck Reese's daughter-in-law. I'll have to remind him of that just before we tee off on the first hole next summer."

"Good idea," Hill agreed. "That ought to distract him."

"You said Ms. Day has a child?"

"Yes. A boy named Hunter."

"Sam Reese's?"

"Of course."

"Hey, I had to ask. Could have been anybody's kid. She's probably been screwing like a rabbit since she was ten. What else is there to do in a trailer park?" Dudley chuckled as he looked out the window at the city lights beneath him. "Don't tell me; let me guess."

"Don't tell you what?"

"Whether Chuck Reese allowed Ms. Day to keep the little boy or took him away, too. When Chuck goes to war, he doesn't go halfway. He goes for everything." For a moment Dudley relived the miss on the eighteenth green last summer. The ball had been headed straight for the cup, then hit a spike mark at the last second and darted left, lipping out. He could still hear the loud groan of the crowd as if it were yesterday. "I bet Chuck took Ms. Day aside when Sam brought her home the first time and forbid her to marry his son. Probably warned her that if she went through with the wedding, she'd ultimately lose. That in the end he'd drive her away and take everything." He looked over at Hill. "Is Ms. Day originally from Richmond?"

"No."

"Where is she from?"

"Asheville, North Carolina."

Dudley nodded. "Well, Carter, my guess is that Ms. Day lost custody of her son in the divorce. I bet the judge found her unstable and incapable of caring for a child, probably citing her promiscuous lifestyle before and during her marriage to Sam Reese as evidence."

Hill nodded, impressed. "That's right."

"Of course it is. Otherwise Ms. Day would have been on the first train out of town right after the divorce. Too many nasty memories here. Women are weak and associate physical places with memories. But her maternal instinct is stronger than her desire to leave a place she has terrible memories of, so it keeps her here." Dudley stroked his chin for a moment. "What kind of visitation rights did she get?"

"A weekend a month and two weeks in the summer."

Dudley whistled. "Jesus. Chuck didn't screw around. The judge on the case was probably able to buy himself a nice new beach house on the Outer Banks after coming down with that decision."

"Brutal, huh?"

"So that's an important piece of information for us," Dudley commented, propping the putter back up against the wall and sitting down again. "She needs this job. How much do we pay her, Carter?"

"A little under fifty grand."

Dudley burst out laughing. "Can you believe anybody actually *survives* on that kind of salary? Christ, that's minimum wage."

"It's not that bad, Bob. It isn't the three million you pulled down last year, but she's able to

138

live comfortably. She rents a two-bedroom apartment in the Fan for twelve hundred a month, drives a Saab convertible she bought new a year ago, and vacations in the Caribbean twice a year. She was in Saint Bart's a few weeks ago, and she'll go again in the fall if she follows her pattern of the last four years. She doesn't live extravagantly, and she doesn't have any real expenses as far as her son is concerned. The Reese family takes care of all that." He paused. "Oh, and by the way, it's the top drawer."

Dudley looked up. "Huh? What is?"

"The drawer she keeps her panties in."

Dudley flashed a quick smile.

Hill shook his head. "I know what you're thinking, Bob. If she doesn't work with us on this Jake Lawrence thing, we could threaten her. But she's a talented banker. With her contacts, she'd get another job."

"Not in Richmond," Dudley replied confidently. "There aren't any other big banks with corporate lending operations here in the city anymore now that the Carolina banks have acquired all the other big Richmond houses except us. All the important positions have been moved out of town. Mostly just administration stuff here now. And I could make certain no one in Baltimore, Washington, or Charlotte would hire her either. Especially if I let people know that she was fired because she was screwing married men in the bank. Everybody from tellers to Ken Booker."

Hill gazed at the chairman, then chuckled. "Bob, I think you might actually give Jake Lawrence a run for his money if the bastard does decide to launch a hostile bid. I don't think he understands what he's up against, the lengths to which you'll go."

"I'll take that as a compliment. I'm sure that's how it was intended."

"Of course —"

"Back to Angela Day."

"Okay."

"You see, Carter, she *has* to live in or near Richmond," Dudley said. "Chuck probably had the judge insert some tough language into the custody order about that. Like if Ms. Day misses more than three consecutive visits with her son, she has constructively abandoned the boy and automatically relinquishes any further rights to visitation unless the Reeses give her specific permission to see the boy — which, of course, they wouldn't." Dudley smiled, pleased with himself. "So, we've figured out how to manipulate Ms. Day. Now she'll have to be loyal to me if she was telling us the truth this morning and Jake Lawrence really did try to get into her pants. Even if she can't stand the sight of him, she'll have to do what I want." Dudley pointed at Hill. "Next week you will have a conversation with Ms. Day and deliver the gist of what we've just discussed."

"Bob, I don't think that's necessary. She got the message this morning. If Lawrence contacts her, she'll let us know right away. She seems levelheaded. She knows where her bread is buttered."

"I'm sure Jake Lawrence can be very persuasive," Dudley said. "I want Ms. Day to understand exactly how vulnerable she is."

"Bob, she seems plenty smart. I'm sure she gets it. I don't think we need to get into the intimidation racket."

"Carter," Dudley snapped, frustrated with Hill's passive nature, furious with his penchant to search for a middle ground. "I don't want to hear any of your Good Samaritan bullshit. Do as you're told."

"I'm sure if I didn't, you'd make it as tough for me to get a job as you would Ms. Day," Hill muttered under his breath.

"What was that?"

"Nothing."

"On second thought, you have your chat with Ms. Day tomorrow," Dudley decided. "There's no need to put it off until next week."

Hill nodded obediently. "All right," he agreed, standing up. "I'll do as you wish."

"Good boy. Oh, one more thing, Carter."

"Yes?"

"I noticed in the internal second-quarter operating report that the growth of our on-line mortgage portfolio was off." One of the ways Dudley had grown Sumter so quickly was to implement an aggressive Web-enabled mortgage offering.

"Year-to-year we were still up 14 percent," Hill protested.

"That's not enough, Carter. I want at least twenty."

"Okay, I'll talk to Russ Thompson about it tomorrow."

"Call him tonight at home."

"All right," Hill agreed stiffly.

The intercom on Dudley's desk buzzed.

"What is it, Betty?" Dudley called to his assistant in the anteroom.

"Ken Booker is here to see you."

Dudley glanced up as Hill's eyes flashed to his. "Tell him it will be another few minutes. I'm just finishing up my meeting with Mr. Hill now."

"Yes, sir."

"Do you want me to stay?" Hill asked.

"No."

"Why do you need to see Ken?"

"I haven't had a chance to speak with him one-on-one for a while. I think it's a good idea for me to keep in touch with the men a rung below you." Dudley's only direct report was Carter Hill. He'd turned over all other reporting responsibilities to Hill several years ago to free himself up to focus on strategic initiatives, mostly acquisitions. "Don't you?"

"I suppose," Hill agreed tepidly.

Dudley suppressed a smile, aware of the stress the other man was feeling. He had deliberately arranged the Booker meeting right after this one so Hill would know. It was an effective management technique to keep a direct report back on his heels, wondering. "Good."

"You sure you don't want me to stay? Ken and I have been working on several important projects together, but he isn't up to speed on all of the developments. It might help if I were here to fill in the gaps."

"No need," Dudley replied brusquely. "This will be mostly social." That would make Hill feel even worse. "We're done, Carter."

Chuck Reese leaned back in his office chair and gazed out into the darkness at the lights of the Sumter Tower a quarter of a mile away, visible again now that the snowstorm had let up. Bob Dudley was up there at the apex of that tower, twenty stories above the top of the building Albemarle Capital leased. Probably looking down here right now with smug satisfaction, Reese thought to himself glumly, catching his reflection in the glass. Winning the golf grudge match wasn't enough any longer. There had to be more.

Reese turned to the side, checking his profile: still no spare tire and not even the hint of double chin, still a full head of blond hair, still in pretty damn good shape for sixty-two years old. He took great pride in the fact that, late last year, the *Wall Street Journal* had run an extensive article on him, describing him as "a high-energy executive who looks and acts half his age.

A man who turns one day into four because he accomplishes twice as much as others do in half the time." The reporter had documented the fact that Reese was a natural-born risk-taker, parachuting from airplanes, driving his collection of Porsches in a southern road-race circuit, and, last summer, sailing from Newport News to England solo.

Which was why he was completely at ease in the ulcer-inducing equity markets and Bob Dudley had chosen banking. Bob Dudley had no appetite for risk. He was a bully when he had the odds in his favor, but he never took a chance without them. He'd never go for that long shot over water with a fairway wood. He'd always lay up, which was why he would always lose.

Reese turned away from the window and punched up a couple of stock tickers on his computer, wondering how he and Dudley had become such bitter rivals. They'd been close in college and during the first few years at Sumter. But somewhere along the way, the relationship had soured.

"Chuck."

"Yeah, come on in, Andy," Reese called, looking up from the computer screen.

Andy Phillips was Albemarle's head of equity research. Only six years out of Harvard Business School, Phillips already had a growing reputation on Wall Street as a superb stock picker. "Had another idea, Chuck."

Everyone was on a first-name basis at

Albemarle, no matter the age or seniority of position. And dress was business casual every day. Reese liked all of that. Being comfortable made for a better working environment. He knew full well how staid and stiff things were at Sumter. "What's that, young gun? What's your next billion-dollar idea?"

"I think we oughta short General Datacom in a big way. It's a —"

"A storage device company out in San Jose," Reese interrupted. "About six hundred million in revenues and they've suffered delays getting their next-generation device to market. So what?"

Phillips chuckled. Of course, Chuck Reese knew that. Chuck Reese knew everything. "They're about to report bad results for the last quarter."

"The market already seems to know that," Reese said, punching up a chart of the company's stock. "The share price is off 10 percent in the last two weeks."

"Right, but what the market doesn't know is that the senior managers out there are about to mutiny. They can't stand the CEO. The stock's probably going to fall 30 to 40 percent when the shit hits the fan in a couple of weeks."

"How do you know this?"

"A friend. He says the product is ready, but the problem is that there's infighting among senior management."

Reese held up his hand. "Andy, never attribute to malice what can be explained by ineptitude. Hold off on that one. They'll end up getting it right out there. But I liked your ideas earlier today concerning the health-care sector. Go for it there."

"Right."

"That'll be all."

"Thanks, Chuck."

"Sure." Reese watched the young man exit the office, then turned back to the window and glanced up at the Sumter Tower again. Everything else in his life was good. If only he could look *down* on the Sumter Tower.

CHAPTER SIX

The Fan — named for the way its main avenues spread west from Richmond's downtown like the spokes of a lady's fan — is an eclectic neighborhood nestled between the outskirts of center city and the upscale, old-money residential area of the West End. The antebellum homes overlooking the Fan's tree-lined streets are large but built close together, with small yards taken up mostly by flower gardens. Over the years many of the old homes have been divided into apartments, so the Fan is densely populated. Health food stores, art galleries, and offbeat boutiques dot the main avenues, and, unlike other areas of the city, backgrounds, creeds, and colors are as diverse as the residents' interests. Blacks and whites. Young and old. Hippies, professionals, creative types, and students. It's the city's melting pot.

Angela slid into a wooden booth in Castro's, named not for Fidel but for a rhythm and blues band, Skip Castro, that had gained a measure of fame in Virginia during the seventies and eighties, but never quite made it onto the national scene. On the other side of the scratched table sat Kate Charboneau, a slim woman in her early forties. Kate had long blonde hair that cascaded past her shoulders in unruly waves, penetrating hazel eyes, thin features, and fair skin.

They hadn't spoken in two years. Not since a last-ditch appeal to win Hunter back had ended in an emotionally painful defeat, and now Angela found herself wishing they had kept in touch. Kate was always optimistic, even when the situation seemed bleak. She had pledged to Angela that someday they would win Hunter back. Maybe she'd been right after all.

"Sorry I'm late," Angela apologized. It was quarter to seven and she'd promised to be at Castro's by 6:30. She hated to keep people waiting. "Traffic was terrible because of what's leftover of the snow. The streets coming out of downtown are pretty icy." Kate's office was in the basement of a four-story mansion a few blocks away, so she would have gotten to Castro's without much trouble.

Kate smiled. "No problem. Was it hard to find a place to park?" she asked in her heavy Southern accent. She had come to Richmond from New Orleans for law school and never left.

"I got lucky. Someone was leaving just as I pulled up in front of my apartment."

"So you still live out here?"

"Yes, same place as before. It's just a few blocks away." Angela spotted Kate's half-empty glass of white wine as she placed her coat down beside her on the bench seat. "How've you been? Practice going OK?"

"I'm finding a way to make ends meet." Kate practiced mostly family law, mostly by herself. She'd had several partners over the years, but only for short periods of time. They inevitably became frustrated with her penchant for giving away her services to the poor. "Same as always."

Angela motioned to a waiter that she wanted a glass of wine, too. She'd hired Kate six years ago because she seemed determined. Plus, she was affordable. If money hadn't been a problem, she would have hired the other prominent law firm in town — the one Chuck Reese hadn't hired. But the partner Angela had spoken to there wanted five hundred dollars an hour and a ten-thousand-dollar retainer just for starters. And he'd given her a condescending look that had told her he didn't really want the case.

"You look great."

Kate laughed. "You're always so nice, Angela. The truth is I look three years older, and I ought to start using more makeup. You're the one who looks great." She reached across the table and touched Angela's hand. "I don't know how you do it. I think you're prettier now than the first time I saw you. You really ought to give up all the banking stuff and go into modeling."

Angela scoffed. "I wish you'd been in charge of the agencies I talked to in college."

Most of the fashion people who had visited campus had used phrases like "so close" and "just on the edge of what we're looking for" when Angela had interviewed with them in her freshman year. It hadn't helped that she didn't have a portfolio — she couldn't afford the expense — but one firm had invited her to their main offices in New York City anyway. They'd put her up overnight in the Plaza Hotel, wined and dined her, and told her that she had a real future in the business. But, after returning to campus, she'd never heard from the agency again, despite her repeated attempts to contact the people she'd interviewed with. She'd always wondered if the silence had anything to do with her background. The other girls visiting the agency that day were from places like East Hampton on Long Island, Darien, Connecticut, and the Main Line in Philadelphia.

"Unfortunately, the decision makers didn't share your enthusiasm for my prospects in the industry. And that was almost fifteen years ago."

"Well, they were wrong," Kate replied adamantly.

Angela shrugged. "So what's up?" she asked. "You sounded so mysterious on the phone this morning."

"Danny Ford's lawyer called me late yesterday afternoon."

Danny Ford was one of the two men who had accused Angela of adultery in divorce court, one of the men who had helped ruin her life. "And?" she asked, picking up the glass of wine the waiter had just delivered.

"It seems Danny has some things on his mind he wants to talk about."

Angela's heart skipped a beat. Jake Lawrence must have made good on his promise. That was the only explanation for Danny's sudden desire to talk. The timing was too convenient. "What does he have to say after all this time?"

"I don't know yet. His lawyer wouldn't be specific on the phone. He just said that they wanted to get together. I've arranged a meeting with them this coming Monday afternoon in my office." Kate hesitated. "I think it would be best if you let me handle this one myself. Ford might not be as forthcoming if you're there staring him down. He knows what he did to you."

Angela nodded, gazing into her wineglass. She was certain of what Danny was going to say. He was going to say that he'd lied about the affair. Jake Lawrence had pulled some very powerful strings. God, the things money could do. "Let's assume for a second Danny admits to you that he lied on the stand during the divorce proceedings," Angela said.

"Don't get your hopes up, Angela," Kate was quick to warn. "You never know. He might just be —"

"I'm not getting my hopes up," Angela interrupted. "I just want to make certain we anticipate all the possibilities, then react accordingly. As quickly as possible. What if Danny looks across the table at you on Monday and admits that he committed perjury six years ago? That he lied about having sex with me. That, other than in photographs, he'd never even laid eyes on me before the first day of the proceedings. What then?"

Kate thought for a second. "We might be able to get you some alimony, and —"

"I don't care about alimony. All I care about is —"

"Getting Hunter back. Yes, I know that. I was going to say that we might be able to reopen the custody case as well." She glanced away. "I wouldn't be so confident except that . . ."

Angela couldn't hear the rest. It was Thursday night and the bar was becoming crowded. Kate's voice had faded into the growing hum of conversation and music. "What did you say?" she asked, leaning over the table.

Kate pushed her blonde bangs out of her eyes. "It's so strange."

"What is?"

"Remember you told me that you had once caught Sam in bed with another woman while you were married?"

Angela nodded slowly, the awful memory of the woman's naked body wrapped around Sam's flashing back to her. She had realized at that moment that her world was falling apart, that the risks had turned out to be too great after all, and that the choice she had made had been terribly wrong. "Yes," she answered, her voice hoarse.

"I had a private investigator friend approach

the woman before the trial, but she refused to testify. She told him that she would simply deny everything. That there were no objective witnesses, and we'd never be able to prove anything, which my friend confirmed."

"Of course I remember."

Kate swirled the wine in her glass. "That woman called me today, too. After you and I spoke this morning."

Angela glanced up, a shiver crawling slowly up her spine. What was Jake Lawrence's agenda? Why was he going to such great lengths to help? "And?" she asked, anticipating what Kate would say next.

"She admitted to having an eighteen-month affair with Sam that started a few months after you and he were married." Kate shook her head, as if the timing of the two phone calls was hard to fathom. "She's considering testifying to that."

"Did you ask her why, after all this time, she would suddenly be willing to come forward?"

"I did, and she just said that her conscience had gotten the better of her. That and the fact Sam had promised her marriage and children and cars and homes and he hadn't come through on any of it. I sensed there was a little bit of guilt and a lot of revenge in her motivation." Kate finished what was left in her glass and nodded to the waiter that she wanted another. "Is there anything you're not telling me, Angela?" she asked suspiciously.

"What do you mean?"

"I'm half expecting the other guy who accused you of screwing him behind Sam's back to call me tomorrow."

Angela shook her head. "I can promise you that won't happen."

"How?"

"The guy's dead."

"Really? How'd you do away with him?"

"That's not funny."

"Sorry. What happened?"

"He died in a car accident. He had a blood alcohol level of .23 and drove his BMW straight into a telephone pole at ninety miles an hour."

"How do you know?"

"I saw an article in the Metro Section of the *Richmond Trib* two years ago. There was a picture of the accident, and his name was in the caption beneath. The name jumped out at me right away. I called a friend of mine at the paper, and she confirmed that it was the same guy." Angela paused. "I suppose I shouldn't have been happy, but I was," she admitted quietly. "I guess I'm human."

"We all are, honey." Kate hesitated. "So?"

"So what?"

"So, is there anything you aren't telling me?"

Angela didn't answer until the waiter bringing Kate's second glass of wine had come and gone. "No. Of course not."

"You sure?" Kate gazed at Angela for several moments, her smile slowly turning into a frown. "I didn't do very well in math class so I never

154

understood much about statistics or probability, but the odds of getting those two calls within a twenty-four-hour period seem pretty remote. Especially after all this time."

Angela shrugged and looked down. "I don't know what to say."

Kate nodded deliberately, as if Angela's caginess told her everything. "You know what I always found so disturbing about the judge in your divorce case?"

Angela glanced up. "What?"

"The fact that he could believe you had affairs with two men while you were pregnant."

Hunter had been born seven months after her wedding to Sam Reese, a wedding held before a justice of the peace in a small town just outside Durham with one of their business school classmates as the only witness. She hadn't told Sam until after the wedding that she was pregnant because she hadn't wanted to forever wonder about his motivation for marrying her. But in the end, it hadn't mattered anyway. In the end, the two men who had testified to affairs with her had been able to convince the judge that they'd slept with her while she was as much as eight months pregnant, based on their testimony, based on the days they claimed to have been with her. Days, it turned out, Sam could conveniently prove he'd been out of town.

Kate had argued that there was no way the affairs could have taken place, that Angela loved Sam, and that no one could bring any credible evidence to bear of physical contact between either man and Angela. And that the notion that Angela would sleep with two men while she was eight months' pregnant made the accusations categorically absurd.

The elderly male judge had stared down from his bench and, when Kate had finished her closing argument, awarded custody of five-month-old Hunter to the Reeses. Angela had simply stared at the man in his flowing black robe as he'd disappeared into his chambers after announcing the decision, which had been greeted with loud cheers from the Reese camp. Stared after the first person in her life she'd actually wanted to see endure horrible pain.

"That was despicable," Kate continued, glancing toward the bar. "I have to tell you that there is one very large fly in the ointment here."

"What's that?"

"The judge doesn't have to listen to any of this."

Angela shrugged. "We'll just have to see what happens." She watched Kate take a long look at an attractive young man at the bar.

As Kate's eyes drifted back to Angela's, her expression brightened. "So what's your deal these days? I figured you'd be remarried by now, but I don't see a wedding band." She tapped Angela's ring finger.

"I'm still single."

"You must be beating the men away with a stick."

"No, I've been focused on my career lately."

"Have you sworn off men because of your Sam Reese experience? Which would be understandable. I've seen it happen before."

"No, nothing like that. I'm dating someone, but it isn't serious. I doubt it'll go anywhere." She wasn't really dating anyone, but this explanation seemed more convenient. "What about you?"

"Still playing the field." Kate pushed the bangs from her eyes once more. "What are you doing?" she asked as Angela gathered her things.

"I apologize," she said, taking a twenty out of her wallet and placing it down on the table by her empty glass, "but I've got to go."

"I was hoping we could have dinner."

"I'd love to, but I can't tonight." Angela stood up and slipped into her coat. "How about next week after you meet with Danny Ford and his lawyer?"

Kate nodded. "Great. I'll look forward to it. I'll call you Monday after I've met with them."

"Call me the minute you finish," Angela urged her.

"I will. I promise."

A moment later Angela was out of Castro's and into the quiet, cold Richmond evening. Most of the sidewalks had been shoveled, but the trees and buildings were still covered, and the Fan was a glistening winter wonderland in the faint rays of the streetlights. For a moment she took it all in — Richmond didn't get snow very often. Then she pulled her collar up and walked briskly down a dark side street away from the wide avenue on which Castro's was located.

In the middle of the block Angela stopped and turned around, convinced someone on the other side of the street was pacing her. She peered into the darkness but saw nothing except an unbroken string of snow-covered cars on both sides of the narrow lane. She began walking again, checking over her shoulder every few steps as she headed toward the next avenue, the Fan's next spoke. There she stopped again, expecting someone to appear on the other side of the street. But no one did. She hurried a few more paces, reached the next avenue and the next tavern, walked into the crowded establishment, and moved directly to the back of the smoky room. She'd been to this place several times and knew there was a back door she could slip out of.

When she reached the narrow hall outside the restrooms, she glanced back through the crowd at the front door. Again she saw nothing suspicious, no lone wolf with a baseball cap pulled low over his eyes and probably a pistol beneath his coat. She sighed at her paranoia as she sidestepped a young man coming out of the men's room. Then she exited the tavern through the back door and headed down the alley toward Tortelli's, an Italian restaurant a few blocks away, where she was meeting Liv Jefferson for dinner.

At the restaurant door she hesitated, moving back a few steps after touching the handle. Maybe she needed to back off on her friendship with Liv Jefferson, she thought. At least for a while. Or perhaps not be so obvious about it. Ken Booker had warned her about speaking to the press. Even Jake Lawrence had accused her of being Liv's source for the negative articles about Sumter. How could he have known that?

She'd chosen Tortelli's because it was off the beaten track. It was not a place any of Sumter's senior executives were likely to frequent. But maybe at this point she needed to worry less about chance encounters, and more about other possibilities. She glanced around the area in front of the restaurant, then up and down the avenue. She shook her head. What had happened in Wyoming was affecting her. And screw the bank's policy about talking to the press. Liv had been a loyal friend for years. They couldn't tell her whom to talk to, much less whom to be friends with. She reached for the handle, pulled the door open, and stepped inside.

Liv Jefferson sat at a table in the back of the quiet restaurant. There was only one other occupied table in the place, and the couple seated at it appeared too young to be served alcohol. Neither of them bothered to look up when Angela entered.

"Hello, there," Liv called, waving as Angela

159

handed her coat and briefcase to a white-aproned waiter.

"Hi." Angela sat down across the red and white checked tablecloth and smiled. Liv was mercurial. Elated or irate, but never mellow. "How are you?"

"A little put off," Liv said.

"What's wrong? Man trouble again?" Angela asked. Liv had cycled through three husbands in the last fifteen years. Fortunately, as she often said, none of them had stuck around long enough to get her pregnant. "Is that it?"

"Honey, I don't let men be trouble for me anymore," she answered, shaking her head emphatically and wagging a finger. "I've become trouble for them. You know that. Mmm, mmm, mmm. They see this fine body and they just have to have it."

Angela recognized a glint in the other woman's eye. There was a nugget of wisdom on the way.

"Want to hear my new motto?" Liv asked.

Angela rolled her eyes good-naturedly. "I can't wait."

"I *tease* but I do not *please*."

Angela laughed loudly. Typical Liv. In the years since they'd met, Liv had become the older sister Angela had never had. She often sought Liv's advice on difficult issues, both personal and work related. And Liv always made a point of inviting Angela to dinner on those Sunday nights when she had to drop Hunter off at the Reese estate after her paltry forty-eight

160

hours a month had expired. Somehow Liv could always raise her spirits when she was down. Or calm her when her world seemed to be falling apart.

She glanced across the table, thinking back on Jake Lawrence's reference to Sally Chambers. Liv was a lot like Sally: self-assured and confident. A lot like Sally should have been.

"What is it then?" Angela asked. "What's wrong?"

"Well, I was irritated that you walked right past me this morning in front of the Sumter Tower," Liv explained, picking up an open bottle of Merlot standing on one corner of the table and pouring each of them a glass. "That wasn't very nice."

"I'm sorry."

"No way to treat someone who's —"

"I said I was sorry," Angela repeated, glancing around at the couple a few tables away. They were holding hands and gazing into one another's eyes, oblivious to what was going on around them. "Lord."

"Well, what's the matter? First you don't return my calls, then you ignore me on the street this morning."

"I told you. I was away a day longer on business than I anticipated, and, besides, I didn't *ignore* you."

"Pretty close."

"I was late for a meeting," Angela explained lamely.

"Isn't that convenient?" Liv asked sarcastically, her expression turning serious. "Are they starting to get to you?"

"What do you mean?"

"Have the senior executives at the bank started telling you to stay away from me?"

"Why do you ask?"

"It's happened before. A company's senior management not wanting employees to talk to me after I write something negative about them or their firm. As long as I'm saying good things, everybody's my best friend. But as soon as I say something nasty, as soon as I write the truth, they all —"

"And that comes as a surprise to you after being a reporter for twenty years?" Angela interrupted. "Less than two weeks ago you might as well have called Sumter Bank's most senior executive the grand imperial wizard of the KKK."

"What are you talking about?"

"The article you wrote about him. The one accusing him of shutting down branches in black areas of the city. About him arbitrarily denying mortgages to blacks. 'A carefully planned strategy to keep blacks imprisoned in undesirable areas of the city, to keep them out of traditionally white neighborhoods that offer safe streets and good schools.' Wasn't that what you wrote? 'An atrocious sixties-style strategy formulated and carried out by the highest levels of Sumter Bank management.' Do you really expect Bob Dudley to encourage employees to speak freely with you after reading that?"

A satisfied smile spread across Liv's round face. "No, but he could nominate me for a Pulitzer. That was one of the best pieces of my career."

"Uh-huh. But you made some assumptions you shouldn't have."

"I just wish I could have been there the first time Dudley read that column," Liv said, ignoring Angela's rebuke, "when that ass-kissing Carter Hill brought the morning newspaper to Dudley like the yapping little lapdog he is. I'd have paid a lot of money to see Dudley's reaction."

Angela hesitated, wondering once more if she should have come tonight. "You'd better watch out," she warned. "You'd better keep your eyes open and your head down."

Liv waved as if she wasn't afraid. "I'm not worried about Bob Dudley. We've hated each other for a while. I told you that story, right?"

Six months ago, Angela remembered Liv telling her, the University of Richmond business school had convened a panel of important local business leaders — including, as the most senior business reporter in Richmond, Liv Jefferson — to discuss the effects of the Internet on the Richmond economy. The program had turned out to be so popular that the university's auditorium was filled to capacity an hour before it was to start. At one point Liv had stated that the Internet's positive effect had been less pronounced on low-income families because they needed to spend what little money they had on essentials — as opposed to computers and Internet access. That, in effect, the Internet was actually broadening the divide between rich and poor.

Dudley had quickly remarked that low-income people needed to work harder and not constantly seek handouts from those who were successful. The exchange had turned heated, and quickly intensified until the program's moderator had imposed a ten-minute, unscheduled intermission. After the break Dudley had not reappeared on stage due to a "sudden pressing engagement."

"Yes, you did," Angela answered.

"Did I tell you that he called the owners of the *Trib* and tried to have me fired for writing the article?"

Angela looked up. "No."

"He tried, but it didn't work. The owners know what kind of man he really is." Liv took a large swallow of Merlot. "Of course, I wouldn't have been able to print that story without a copy of the memo," she added, her voice low. "Thanks again."

Angela gazed across the table. She'd thought long and hard about giving the memo she'd found behind the shredder in Ken Booker's office to Liv. It had been late one night a month ago — past ten and she'd been the only one left on the floor. She'd been looking for a client file

Booker had taken from her workstation earlier in the day, a file she needed to process a time-sensitive loan she was trying to get through the bank's credit committee. Angela had stood there in Booker's office, shaking as she read the memo. It had come from "The Chairman" to Booker, Russ Thompson, senior managing director for all Sumter funding and security trading activity, and Glenn Abbott, senior managing director in charge of all Sumter retail banking activity. Booker, Thompson, and Abbott comprised Sumter's executive committee, or ExecCom, as it was nicknamed. They were the men who ran the bank on a day-to-day basis.

The strange thing about the memo was that it had been sent directly from Bob Dudley to the members of ExecCom. But ExecCom reported to Carter Hill, not Dudley, as Booker had pointed out to Angela this morning. Dudley had announced the reporting change to all employees with an e-mail. The e-mail had cited Dudley's need to focus on external matters — primarily new acquisitions — as his reason for handing over ExecCom reporting responsibility to Hill. But Hill's name hadn't been anywhere on the memo Angela had stumbled on in Booker's office.

The chairman's recommendation in the memo had been clear. Sumter needed to make it as difficult as possible for people in low-income areas to get loans, whether the loans be in the form of mortgages, credit cards, or small business loans. And mortgage applications needed to be carefully scrutinized to stop "certain" people from moving into "certain" areas of the city.

She'd hustled back to her desk with the evidence tucked into a pocket of her blazer, aware that she had unearthed a stick of dynamite and, perhaps, the tip of an iceberg. Aware that she would have been fired immediately if anyone found out that she had passed the memo on to Liv. But she'd been so damn insulted that a man as important as Bob Dudley would use his influence to manipulate the poor, too damn insulted just to let it go in order to protect her career. It made her furious that Dudley's kind still existed in what was supposed to be an enlightened society, and so she'd handed the memo over to Liv.

"You went too far in your article, Liv."

"How?"

"You shouldn't have turned the article into a race issue."

"Why not?" Liv snapped indignantly. "That's what it was."

"The memo I gave you didn't mention race."

"Not specifically, but we both know what was really going on there. Low-income areas in this city are populated by blacks and Hispanics. 'Certain' people mean minorities to Bob Dudley. You know it. I know it. You're sounding naive, and I know you aren't. You know the deal."

Liv was right. That was the deal. "Still, I —"

"Look, what are you worried about anyway? It's my neck on the line. No one will ever find out you were the one who gave me the memo."

Angela played with her napkin nervously, regretting what she had done for the first time. Jake Lawrence had scared her. The article Liv had written might make the big New York and West Coast banks think twice about acquiring Sumter. Maybe keep anyone from making a high-priced acquisition offer for the bank. Then Lawrence would lose out on hundreds of millions, maybe even billions, in profits. Maybe even lose money, which could easily cause his interest in helping her win back Hunter to wane. "I hope not."

"Angela, they could jam toothpicks under my fingernails and I still wouldn't tell them how I got the memo. I'm good for my word."

"I know," Angela said slowly, thinking how so many dollars might actually cause people to resort to torture. Worried Liv's giving her word could come back to haunt her friend.

"It makes me so mad that my article didn't get more attention," Liv continued. "And I'm not talking about personal attention."

"What are you talking about?"

"The fact that Bob Dudley still has his job. He still sits on top of Sumter Bank."

"He denied your accusations. He pointed to all of the charities he's involved with that help minorities."

"Bob Dudley is a racist."

"Maybe, but most of Richmond considers him a pillar of the community. People don't believe he would ever endorse anything like what your article accused the bank of. Other than that incident with you at that business forum, he's never had any problems in public." Angela took a sip of wine. "And from what I read, the spin from the forum was that you were trying to bait him. That you came off as the aggressor."

"A spin crafted by the white contingent of reporters in town who constantly kiss Dudley's ass." Liv shook her head. "Sometimes I want to tear my hair out it makes me so mad. That article should have turned people's heads, but it didn't. How can people not even care? Not even notice?"

"People noticed," Angela murmured. Jake Lawrence might have termed the forty-million-dollar paper loss on his Sumter Bank investment "small," but it had been important enough for him to mention the article, and to mention that the *Wall Street Journal* was thinking about picking up on it. Angela considered telling Liv that but didn't. Once again she couldn't be sure if Lawrence was telling the truth, or trying to manipulate her. "You organized that protest outside the bank's entrance this morning, right?"

Liv grinned. "You figured that out, huh?"

"It wasn't hard." If Liv really got things stirred up, Jake Lawrence probably wouldn't be as calm about the situation next time they talked — if there was a next time.

"If I'm going to bring Bob Dudley down, it's going to have to be with a grassroots effort. The black community is going to have to rise up against him, with a little help from their friends."

Angela stared across the table at Liv. "Is that what this is all about?" she asked. "Bringing Bob Dudley down?"

"I told you. He's a racist," Liv said angrily. "He'll do whatever he can to keep minorities from making any progress in the world. All the way from keeping me out of his country club to keeping my brother in a hovel on the east side. You know, I'd love to see Dudley hanging from a tree the way my —" Liv held her tongue when the waiter arrived at the table to describe the evening's specials. When he was gone, she pursed her full lips as if she wanted to say something very important. Then she relaxed and shook her head. "Dinner's on me tonight."

"That's all right. We'll —"

"No, no. I invited you, and I'm going to pay," Liv said firmly. "But I am going to make you work for it."

"Work for it?"

"Last time we were together you started to tell me how I could check on Sumter Bank's record of serving the minority community, but you had to leave before we were able to go into detail."

"Oh, right."

Angela and Liv had run into each other at a city chamber of commerce luncheon a few weeks ago, but Angela had had to leave before dessert to make a meeting.

"You were talking about statistical areas or something."

"Metropolitan statistical areas: M.S.A.'s."

"That was it," Liv confirmed, reaching down and pulling a notepad and pen from a large leather pocketbook at her feet. "What are M.S.A.'s?"

"The federal government's Office of Management and Budget —"

"The OMB," Liv cut in.

"Right, the OMB. The OMB has diced the country into M.S.A.'s. The city of Richmond, the town of Crozet, the county of Henrico, and so on are M.S.A.'s. Most banks, especially big ones, operate in lots of M.S.A.'s. And the M.S.A.'s are further broken down into census tracks."

"Go on."

"The OMB segments individuals and households within the M.S.A.'s and the census tracks them by income. Those income categories are broadly defined as low, moderate, middle, and upper."

The waiter returned to take their order, but Liv shooed him away, telling him they hadn't even looked at their menus. "How does OMB define those income levels?" she asked when he was gone. "What are the ranges?"

Angela closed her eyes, trying to remember her research. "I think low is below 50 percent of the specific M.S.A.'s median income," she said slowly. "Moderate is like 50 to 75 or 80 percent of median. Middle is 80 to 120 percent, and high is over 120 percent."

Liv crossed her arms over her chest, a puzzled look on her face. "So it's a *relative* measure."

"That's right."

"The absolute level of median income in one M.S.A. might be different from that in another M.S.A."

"Not might be, probably is."

"But to be able to calculate a median income level for an M.S.A., the OMB has to know what everyone in that M.S.A. is making."

"True."

"How can the OMB possibly know everybody's income?" Liv asked bluntly.

"They could use census information."

"Do you think people are truthful about their incomes on that form?"

Angela shook her head. "No. I think most people don't even fill in that box. I don't."

"Then how —"

"Liv," Angela interrupted, "let's say you could have any resource in the federal government available to you. And let's say you wanted to know what my income was for last year. Where would you go?"

Liv thought for a second, then her eyes widened. "The IRS?"

"Right. Now don't quote me on that. In fact, you can't quote me on anything we discuss tonight. That's my one condition for helping you."

"Fine," Liv agreed as she scribbled on her notepad. "But you're saying that the OMB has access to IRS records?"

"I'm saying it wouldn't surprise me."

"But the OMB isn't part of the Treasury Department," Liv pointed out.

"That's true."

"Isn't that interesting?" Liv muttered to herself. "Government departments sharing information about our income levels." She looked up. "God, I'm so rude. You must be starving."

Angela smiled. She was hungry and the aromas coming from the kitchen were enticing. "I am, but I doubt our waiter will come back to the table unless we beg. You almost bit his head off a few minutes ago."

"I just get so wrapped up in all of this. Let's eat."

When they had both decided what they wanted, Liv waved to the small, mustachioed waiter, who hurried to the table.

As soon as he was gone, Liv started up again. "Okay, so the OMB designates areas and pegs relative income levels within the areas. Then what?"

"Then they can calculate a bank's record in each of the M.S.A.'s in which it operates. So many loans to low-income individuals, so many to moderate-income individuals, and so on. Banks are required to report certain loans they make, and certain loans they don't make, so the government can see what percentage of low-income applications are being approved and what percentage are being denied. Then they can compare that ratio to the ratio for other levels." Angela watched Liv write feverishly. When the pen hesitated, Angela continued. "By the way, it's only the big banks that have to report to the government: banks with more than $250 million in assets, or bank holding companies with more than a billion. That's about two thousand entities in the United States. Banks below those levels don't have to report."

"Why only the big guys?"

"The government claims the small banks don't have enough market share or clout to really make a difference, which is totally wrong. There's ten thousand of them, for God's sake. The real reason they don't require those entities to report is that they simply don't have the manpower to monitor all of them."

Liv nodded. "It all makes sense now. It's against the law for banks to take an individual's race into account when making a loan. They probably can't even collect that kind of information, right? But, of course, you have to know someone's income because you have to try to assess their ability to repay the loan. That's only fair."

"Which are two very different issues."

Liv looked up. "What do you mean?"

"It's definitely against the law for banks to take race into account when determining whether or not to make a loan. But, in fact, the federal government *requires* banks to identify the applicant's race when it comes to mortgages."

Liv stared at Angela skeptically. "You're kidding, right?"

"I'm dead serious. Go to any bank and ask for a standard mortgage application. You'll see that the applicant's race is one of the last questions on the form. It's the Race/National Origin box." Angela held up her hand. "Now, the applicant doesn't *have* to respond."

"Of course not," Liv agreed emphatically. "If you were black, you'd have to be an idiot to check that box."

"Why?" Angela was fairly certain she knew how Liv was going to respond, but she wanted to hear her say it.

"*Why?* Come on, Angela. Don't be silly."

"I want you to tell me."

"Because then everybody in the bank who's involved in approving your loan knows you're black."

"So?"

"So? So maybe some white person who's involved in the process lives in a nice neighborhood with good schools and safe streets. The same neighborhood the black man applying for the mortgage is trying to move his family to." Liv chuckled grimly. "Just for kicks, let's call our black man Leroy *Jefferson,*" she suggested. "Anyway, that white person in the bank sees from the application that Leroy is black, and that Leroy is about to move in next door. He figures Leroy will have at least fifteen children, throw wild parties, and probably sell heroin and crack as his primary source of income. Maybe even sell those drugs to the white man's kids. So the white man steps in and denies the loan. He keeps the black man out."

"Well, I —"

"With a name like Leroy Jefferson," Liv interrupted, "every white guy out there will assume the applicant is black. But what if his name is John Smith? That name wouldn't catch anybody's attention. Everybody assumes John is white, and he slips into the neighborhood. But by identifying himself on the application as black, everybody knows what's going on." She pointed at Angela. "Or maybe it goes even deeper than that at some organizations. Maybe it isn't just one person who happens to see a black man applying for a mortgage on a house in a traditionally white neighborhood and denies the application because he happens to live in that neighborhood. Maybe there's a policy at the bank to deny black people loans in certain sections of cities or in certain M.S.A.'s. Maybe the policy isn't written down anywhere, but everybody knows about it just the same. That kind of thing goes on in the residential real estate business. You read all the time about agents not showing houses in certain highly desirable sections of town to black families. A bank might do the same thing. A bank like Sumter."

Angela shrugged. "So the solution is simple, right? Don't check the box."

"Exactly."

"Just one problem with that."

"What?"

"If the applicant opts not to answer the race question on the form, the bank employee who accepts the application must do it instead. I'll repeat that. That bank employee *must* fill in the box if the applicant doesn't. It's required by law."

Liv shook her head in disbelief. "What?"

"Yes. It says that right on the application."

"So they fill in the box just by sight?"

"Or by reviewing the surname if the race isn't clear by looking at the applicant, which, of course, can be a very inaccurate way of gathering data."

"My God."

Angela nodded. "Shocking, huh? Now that's only for mortgages. When it comes to small business loans or credit cards, the race question isn't on the application. In fact, with respect to small business loans and consumer credit, it's illegal for a lending entity to ask what race you are."

"Why would the federal government have banks require blacks to identify themselves on a mortgage application? That bothers me."

"They do it so they can compile information. So they can monitor a bank's performance on minority lending."

Liv raised her eyebrows, then nodded.

"It's actually intended to help *prevent* the problem," Angela continued.

They were quiet for a while until Liv finally spoke up. "So what?" she asked bluntly.

"I don't understand."

"So the government compiles all this data. So what? What do they do with it?"

"It really only comes into play when banks want to merge."

"How does it come into play then?"

"The government can disallow a merger of two banks if one of them has a bad record regarding service to low-income individuals in a particular M.S.A., or a bad record of serving minorities." Angela shook her head. "I should emphasize the word 'might.' The government hasn't taken exception very often, despite the fact that some very big banks who have merged in the last few years have had atrocious records when it comes to serving low-income M.S.A.'s."

Liv sneered. "How would we know what a bank's records indicate, anyway? I'm sure the government keeps all that data hidden away where the public can't get at it."

"Not true. There's a Web site where you can check the record of any bank that has to report."

"Really?"

"Yep. Take the Web address down and check it out tomorrow when you get to your office. It's fascinating to go to it and play around."

Liv picked up her pen. She'd put it down to take another swallow of wine.

"The address is *www.ffiec.gov/cra*."

"What does f-f-i-e-c stand for?" Liv asked.

"Federal Financial Institutions Examination Council. That's the agency tasked with monitoring the information banks are required to report. The F.F.I.E.C. is an umbrella group with reporting responsibility to regulatory bodies, including the Federal Reserve, the Office of the Comptroller of the Currency, the FDIC, and a couple of others."

"So I can check out a bank's record myself?"

"Sure. Not that it makes much difference."

"But I don't understand. If regulators go to all of that trouble to amass information, why don't they act against banks with bad records more often? Banks like Sumter."

Angela sighed. "You said it yourself a few minutes ago."

"I did?"

"You pointed out that a bank needs to know what someone's income is so they can determine that person's ability to repay a loan, that having that piece of information is only fair."

Liv rolled her eyes.

"That's the crux of the problem, Liv. Banks hide behind the fact that, while, by law, they are supposed to serve everyone in the communities in which they operate, they end up being monitored by the exact same regulators who monitor them for the quality of their loan portfolios as well. The FDIC guarantees everybody's deposits up to $100,000 per bank. And you'd better believe politicians don't want to have to answer to taxpayers about bank failures and bailouts, because it's their constituents who pick up the tab. So when regulators and examiners start warning banks that they aren't properly serving low-income communities, they whine about having to keep their loan portfolios clean. That being forced to lend to low-income borrowers will jeopardize the quality of their assets. That usually gets the regulators to back right off."

"So, essentially, all of this reporting doesn't do any good."

Angela nodded. "Unfortunately not. By the way, when you look at Sumter's record on the government Web site I told you about, you'll notice that while the record isn't good, there are others that are worse."

"How's that possible?"

"First of all, other banks really are that bad. Second, of the four categories in the bank-rating system with respect to what's called the Community Reinvestment Act — the categories being outstanding, satisfactory, need for improvement, and substantial noncompliance — about 98 percent of all banks receive an outstanding or satisfactory rating."

Liv shook her head. "Please tell me you're joking."

"No. I'm not."

"That's incredible."

"It's pathetic," Angela agreed. "And it's due in part to the old garbage in, garbage out problem."

"You mean banks lie to the government?"

"We have a division with 140 people at Sumter dedicated to reporting under the Community Reinvestment Act. Are you telling me that one or two bank examiners, which is what the government sends to audit us, are going to outsmart us?" She glanced around. "Throw on top of that the fact that most of the examiners ultimately want a job with the bank they're regulating. The government doesn't pay well, and the bank promises a nice salary when their gig with the government is up. So what's an examiner's incentive to be tough?"

Liv sat back in her seat, no longer writing, astounded by what she had heard. "How do you know all of this?"

Angela's eyes narrowed. "Last year, an old friend of mine's father was denied a loan he needed to purchase a small house in North Carolina, near where I grew up. He had the down payment and had held the same job for seven years, but five different banks refused to offer him a loan. So I did some research. What I've just told you is what I found out."

The old friend had been Sally Chambers. Her father, Willie, had managed to save what he thought was enough to buy a small home in a decent neighborhood and get himself out of the trailer park. But he hadn't been able to get a mortgage. So she'd helped him, finally finding him a lender who agreed to provide him with a mortgage, but only after she'd traveled to

180

Asheville personally and gone into the bank with him, threatening to bring discrimination charges against the institution if they didn't reconsider.

She'd never told Liv about Sally. She had often wanted to but never had. Maybe now was the time.

Liv reached across the table and touched Angela's hand. "What's wrong, honey?"

"What do you mean?" Angela asked.

"There's something on your mind. I can always tell."

Angela stared back at Liv. She wanted to talk about that night. To tell Liv about the guilt she'd endured for so many years. But then Liv might think less of her, or, worse, begin to wonder why they had become such good friends over the past few years. She might begin to wonder if Angela had darker motivations for being in this friendship.

"Just some issues with my boss," Angela answered. "Nothing I can't handle."

CHAPTER SEVEN

His orders were to stick to Angela Day like green on grass, because eventually she'd lead them to Jake Lawrence. Eventually, in the rich man's dog-in-heat desire to see the woman again, the reclusive billionaire would put himself at risk, put himself in a vulnerable spot they could take advantage of. At least, that was the word from the source on the inside.

In his coat pocket the man carried three photographs, three blurry head shots of an individual he'd been told was Jake Lawrence. He'd studied the photographs for hours, committing them to memory. His assignment was to kill anyone who showed up on Angela Day's doorstep looking even remotely like the face in the photographs. But he was to take the ultimate action only if he was *certain* he had a kill shot. That wasn't going to be easy. Apparently there had been an "incident" on the Wyoming ranch, and the people who had retained his services didn't want Lawrence so alarmed by a second failed attack that he went completely underground where no one could get to him for months, even years.

The man had also received a stern warning not to arouse Angela Day's suspicions, not to let her think for a moment that she was under surveillance.

Of course, he snickered, chewing on a Milky Way bar. He was watching Tortelli's from behind a minivan parked fifty yards down the street from the restaurant's front door. That was always a component of the directive. "Do not arouse the mark's suspicion." Why did they even need to communicate that? He was a professional, trained by the world's elite spy agency before deciding to make a *real* living, as opposed to a paltry government stipend, a stipend that didn't come close to compensating him for the mortal danger they put him in time after time in countries so tiny and far from home they hardly seemed capable of causing any real damage to the homeland. He'd never had that zealous God-and-country attitude that drove most of his associates. He was driven by economics, so he'd taken a different tack and disappeared during a mission in South America, supposedly captured by insurgents and supposedly dead.

Now, after several highly profitable private assignments, he ought to have had some jingle-juice in the bank, he thought to himself grimly, allowing the candy bar wrapper to flutter to the snow. But somehow he always seemed to spend everything within six months of the payoff.

This time would be different, he promised

himself. This time he was going to stash the big payday away, then retire. He'd been in this game too long. Sooner or later, probably sooner, he was going to slip up — it was inevitable in this line of work — and he didn't want to think about what would happen then. He'd been on the delivery side of those torture sessions. He'd seen firsthand what it meant to endure incredible physical pain: all thirty-two teeth extracted one by one, back to front, with needle-nosed pliers; eyes slowly gouged out over two hours with a ballpoint pen; intestine pulled out inch by inch through an incision in the subject's belly until it lay coiled on the floor like a garden hose.

The door to Tortelli's opened and the man leaned forward, one hand on the minivan's passenger door side mirror as he watched Angela Day hug a woman in the dim light streaming down from a bulb above the front door, then head off toward her third-floor apartment a few blocks away. He waited until the other woman had climbed into a cab, then moved slowly out from behind the vehicle. He was careful to skirt the glow from the streetlights as he followed from a safe distance.

Angela Day had seemed uneasy from the moment he'd begun his surveillance. Constantly checking over her shoulder, as if she felt his presence. Even taking the trouble to go through that second tavern and emerge from the back door. She was nervous all right, and that wasn't good. It made things much more difficult. But he was confident she hadn't seen him. He could turn into a ghost when he wanted to.

The snow made things more difficult as he moved furtively through front yards. He was leaving a trail, which he wasn't pleased about. But the temperature in Richmond was supposed to warm tomorrow — into the fifties — and the tracks would quickly melt, taking with them the proof of his presence. He probably didn't have to follow her so closely. He probably could have waited for her down the street from her apartment, but he took pride in his work, and you never knew when or how someone like Jake Lawrence was going to make contact. He'd learned to expect the unexpected, and he couldn't afford to screw up this assignment. The more he thought about it, the more he wanted this one to be his last. He'd take the million he'd been guaranteed, open a bar in Tahiti, and get out of this racket forever.

He nimbly negotiated the waist-high picket fence surrounding the house across the street from Angela's apartment, then knelt down behind a small white pine to watch her climb the building's snowy steps to the top floor. She lived on the third story of a mansion that had been converted into floor-through apartments. Hers was a spacious two-bedroom place, and he'd rigged the door while she was away so that he could easily get inside once she was asleep. He was going to make certain Jake Lawrence didn't slip quietly into her bed right under his nose.

In the glow of an outside light, he watched her hesitate on the landing in front of her door. The next moment he was facedown on the ground, snow filling his eyes, nose, and mouth, wrists forced roughly behind his back. He was a powerful man and, based upon his inability to so much as move his legs, he was guessing that he had been attacked by at least three people, maybe even four. He cursed himself as they lifted him roughly to his feet, yanked a hood over his head, and informed him he would be killed instantly if he made so much as a sound. He nodded his assent, wondering how and when he would be executed. He'd had a bad feeling about this assignment right from the start.

An hour later he was removed from whatever vehicle he'd been tossed into. With the musty hood still covering his face, and his wrists now tied together in front of him, he was led down into a basement. He assumed it was a basement from the room's deep chill and mildew smell, and the way the muffled voices of his captors echoed off the walls.

"Sit down," said someone with a deep voice and a thick British accent.

Strong hands pushed him down into a hard wooden chair. The hood was yanked from his head, and he blinked several times, the bright light from the single bulb burning his eyes. Two men towered over him.

"Why were you following the woman?"

The man glanced up into the intense eyes of the skinny bald captor who had asked the question. "What are you talking about?"

"We know you were watching her."

The man's eyes flashed to the other one, a brute wearing a leather jacket with a wool collar. "You're out of your mind. I wasn't watching anybody."

"Then what were you doing in the yard across the street from her apartment?" the Brit demanded.

The man could see others in the background. There were at least four of them. They all appeared to be brandishing weapons. "Hanging Christmas ornaments."

"Christmas was six weeks ago."

"Okay, then I was taking them down."

The big one in the leather jacket grabbed him by the throat and squeezed, until his vision began to dim. But there was no point struggling. The men in the background were aiming their hardware directly at him. With just his wrists tied in front of him, he could have made short work of the one grabbing his throat — and probably the Brit too — but he wouldn't have been able to dodge the bullets.

"Talk, you stupid shit."

The man's gaze dropped when the big one removed the hand from his throat, his eyes narrowing even as he gasped for precious air. There was a large scar on the back of the big one's left

187

wrist. It was the mark he'd been told to look for. He glanced up and saw a speck of reassurance in the expression.

The Brit reached into the pocket of his black trousers for something, but the big one interrupted the move, grabbing his arm.

"No, Billy. We're not going to get anything out of him so quickly. Why don't we let him think about it for a while? Let him stew on his situation."

The Brit hesitated. "All right," he agreed quietly, motioning over his shoulder to the men behind them. "Take this guy away," he ordered. "No food or water."

After the man had been dragged into another area of the secluded farmhouse's dank basement, he was stripped to the waist and hung by his wrists from the ceiling so that his toes barely touched the cold floor.

"Let him stay there for a while," Tucker suggested. "That'll tenderize him. That'll make it easier for you to break him down. Don't worry. You'll get the information you want."

"Yes, I will, Johnny," Colby agreed confidently, staring back, wondering if he'd get the chance to break Tucker down one day, too. "You know, I still can't figure out why Mr. Lawrence wanted me to bring you east."

"Because Angela Day trusts me. After what he did to her at the cabin, he needs me to help him get back in contact with her."

"You're probably right," Colby agreed, nodding slowly. "And God help her for it," he whispered under his breath.

Typically, ExecCom didn't meet like this. Typically, Booker, Abbott, and Thompson met to discuss operational strategy in a Sumter conference room, not in a cramped basement room of a West End church. But this wasn't a typical meeting.

The church was a convenient location because each of the men lived within two miles of it. Ken Booker's wife managed the church choir, so she had a key. As instructed, they had parked their cars on quiet side streets well away from the church, then walked the rest of the way to a back door, making absolutely certain they weren't being followed.

"Anybody else read the *Washington Post* today?" Russ Thompson wanted to know. They were seated in folding metal chairs that Booker had arranged around a card table usually used by blue-haired ladies for Tuesday afternoon bridge games. Thompson was responsible for all of the bank's liability management and trading operations. Each day his people made certain that Sumter's thirty billion dollars in loans and investments were funded, as well as bought and sold everything from Treasury bonds to Japanese yen to interest rate swaps and shares of General Motors. "Helluv an article about this slavery lawsuit in it this morning."

"What are you talking about?" Glenn Abbott asked, blowing his nose with a handkerchief. Abbott ran Sumter's retail network, which now stretched from Virginia to Florida, thanks to the many acquisitions Bob Dudley had made. Over a thousand branches throughout the Southeast. "God, it's dusty in here," he muttered.

"A class action lawsuit a couple of high-profile black lawyers are trying to get off the ground," Thompson explained. "They're going to file a civil suit against the federal government demanding compensation for slavery."

Booker clasped his hands behind his head, then leaned back and put his feet up on another metal chair. "Well, we all know they deserve the money," he said sarcastically. "They've suffered so much."

"At least a trillion dollars' worth," Thompson said.

"A trillion dollars?" Abbott thundered.

"That's what they're demanding as restitution," Thompson explained. "And if they win and are awarded the money, they plan to give it to blacks here *and* in Africa."

Abbott shook his head. "The scary thing is that there are enough bleeding heart assholes in positions of authority in this country to allow a ridiculous thing like that to actually get legs. Then, watch out."

Thompson removed a cigar from his shirt pocket and lit up. "Let me tell you something," he said, pointing the smoldering tip at Abbott

190

after taking several puffs. "A suit like that gets so much as a little toe, and we'll have an all-out civil war on our hands. What happened in the 1860s will seem trivial compared to what will erupt if some court actually grants every black in this country his or her share of a trillion dollars."

"About thirty grand per," Booker chimed in.

"We all know plenty of people who would take matters into their own hands if every nigger in this country got thirty grand out of our pockets," Thompson said. "There aren't enough trees to hang 'em all from."

"It'll never happen," Booker said confidently. "It'll get some press, and a few senators will pay attention to it for a little while just to get votes. But nothing will ever come of it."

"I think you're wrong," Abbott argued. "The Nazis are paying off the Jews for Christ's sake. Why is it a stretch to think the pansies in Washington would buckle to the Nation of Islam?"

"Amen, my brother," Thompson agreed.

Abbott shook his head. "Let me tell you guys something. If that lawsuit does get momentum, I'll be one of those people Russ mentioned. People willing to take justice into their own hands. I've got shotguns at home, and I'll use them." He stashed the handkerchief in his pants pocket. "I was in that mall out Three Chopt Road last weekend. Took my boys to a sporting goods store there to buy a couple of things. Anyway, we're walking down the main corridor and here comes this gang of black teenagers the other way. All of them looked —"

"Like they'd just broken out of jail," Booker interjected. "Do-rags, big jackets, pants hanging way down off their asses, and big suede boots. Right?"

"Exactly."

"Screaming and yelling."

"Like fucking savages."

Booker shrugged. "Well, that's what they are. Savages. We all know that."

Abbott snorted. "One of the bastards flipped the baseball cap off my younger boy's head as he walked past. There were seven of them and one of me. They had everybody in the mall petrified, including a security guard. What the hell was I supposed to do?"

Thompson took another puff from his cigar. "You continue doing exactly what you're doing. Exactly what we're all doing. Making it as hard as we can for them to come into our neighborhoods and our schools. We do everything we can to keep them on their side of the fence."

"That's easy for you to say," Abbott snapped. "You run trading, Russ. I'm the one in charge of retail operations. I'm the one who's going to take the heat if this thing ever sees the light of day."

Thompson's eyes narrowed. "Hey, I'm fighting the good fight."

"What are you talking about?" Abbott shot

back. "How are you fighting the fight?"

"First of all," Thompson said evenly, "you won't see a nigger on any trading floor of mine. Okay, maybe a secretary or two, but you've got to have a token here and there. But not in any position of authority. Second, who handles on-line mortgages?" he asked, pounding his own chest. "I do."

Booker nodded. "That's right, Glenn. Russ is in charge of all that."

"Which ain't easy," Thompson said. "Especially when Carter Hill calls me at home tonight and tells me he's not happy with 14 percent growth. Fourteen percent growth on a mortgage portfolio the size of ours is damn good, especially when it has to be clean."

The three of them exchanged knowing glances. "Clean" was the operative word.

"And when that *Trib* reporter keeps writing those damn articles," Thompson continued. "What's her name?" he asked, looking around.

"Liv Jefferson," Abbott answered.

"Which reminds me," Booker piped up, "as a result of those articles she's writing, there will be no further written communication among us. No notes, no e-mails, no nothing. We can't risk it. Seems that, somehow, Ms. Jefferson got hold of something substantive. We know the *Trib* is run by some of those bleeding hearts we were talking about before, but we also know they wouldn't have printed that article without some kind of evidence."

"Somebody ought to teach Liv Jefferson a lesson," Thompson said quietly.

Booker glanced over at Thompson. "Maybe somebody will."

CHAPTER EIGHT

"What you have to understand is that Bob Dudley has dedicated his entire working life to Sumter Bank and its shareholders. That's almost forty years, the last ten of those as the bank's chairman. During his decade at the top of this institution, he has created a vast amount of wealth for the shareholders. When he took over as chairman, the bank was only worth a few hundred million dollars. Today, Sumter's stock market value is almost ten billion dollars. *Ten billion*, Angela. It's incredible.

"But that success hasn't come without huge risks and a great deal of personal sacrifice. Now, just as Bob Dudley ought to be relaxing and enjoying the fruits of his labor, he sees a potential raider at Sumter's front door. A raider seeking to take advantage of his hard work and devotion. And it makes him furious. Can you understand that?"

Angela gazed up at Carter Hill from the chair in front of his desk. Hill was leaning back against the desk, arms folded across his chest, red tie falling down over the rolled-up sleeves of his white shirt.

"Angela?"

This was getting ridiculous. When she had arrived at her desk this morning there had been a message on her voice mail from Hill's executive assistant requesting that she come to his office on the fiftieth floor at nine o'clock sharp. Hill had something of high importance he needed to discuss with her. There had been no mention of what that something was, but she'd had a pretty good idea. And she'd been right.

"Of course I can understand that," she answered quietly. "You and Mr. Dudley made it crystal clear yesterday morning in his office that you didn't appreciate the fact that Jake Lawrence was accumulating Sumter shares."

"Yes, we did." Hill nodded. "It's not right for him to do that."

Angela hesitated. She ought to just let it go. But it was against her nature just to let something go when she knew she was being manipulated. "Why isn't it right for him to do that?"

"What?" Hill snapped.

"Shouldn't Jake Lawrence be allowed to buy shares of any public company he wants to, just like anyone else can?"

"Not without making his intentions clear."

"Intentions?"

"If he's buying our shares as a passive investment, that's fine. We welcome his participation in our business. But if he intends to take over the bank, if he intends to make a hostile offer to buy 100 percent of the outstanding shares, well, that would be totally unacceptable."

"If he intends to take over the bank, won't he have to send out information about his intentions to the shareholders in his tender offer documents? Won't he ultimately offer a share price that's at least 20 or 30 percent above the current market price? Isn't that typical in a public takeover?"

Hill didn't answer immediately.

"Mr. Hill?"

"Yes," he finally admitted.

"Doesn't that create a lot of value for the shareholders too? And that kind of value is created overnight, as opposed to over years."

Hill's eyes narrowed. "Jake Lawrence did convey something to you about acquiring Sumter when you and he met in Jackson Hole. Didn't he, Angela?"

"No, he did not. I told both of you that yesterday."

"He is going to take a run at Bob Dudley, isn't he?"

"I have no idea," Angela answered politely but firmly. "I just don't understand how Mr. Dudley can arbitrarily decide it isn't acceptable for Jake Lawrence, or anyone else, to buy as many shares in Sumter Bank as they want. If Lawrence is buying, then someone has to be selling. And the person who's selling doesn't have a gun pointed at his or her head. Lawrence isn't forcing them to hand over their shares. If they accept his offer, they must figure the price he's willing to pay makes it worth it. Otherwise they wouldn't sell."

"Sometimes shareholders don't have all the information," Hill muttered.

He hadn't been prepared for these questions. That was clear to Angela. He'd probably assumed that she would meekly agree to everything he was saying and leave his office completely shaken. And maybe she should have left without questioning him. Maybe that would have been the smart thing to do.

"I, and many others, believe that, ultimately, Bob Dudley will create the most value for the shareholders," Hill said. "If you're holding back information about Mr. Lawrence's intentions, you'd better tell me now. It'll be much easier for you that way."

"I don't know how else to convince you, Mr. Hill. I've told you —"

"Has Lawrence tried to contact you since you visited him?"

"No."

"Bob Dudley demands your loyalty here, Angela. He could make things very difficult for you if he found out you were assisting Jake Lawrence in any way," Hill warned, his voice rising. "If you were somehow secretly acting as Lawrence's agent in this whole thing."

She stared at Hill for several moments. "What are you saying?"

"We know about your need to be in Richmond. We know about your son, Hunter, and how you lost custody of him after your divorce from Sam Reese."

Angela felt her anger beginning to burn. How could these men be so cruel?

"Let me remind you," Hill continued, "Bob Dudley is Richmond's most influential business leader. People all over the mid-Atlantic region owe him favors. He is prepared to call in those favors if he needs to." He paused. "As soon as you hear from Jake Lawrence you are to contact us immediately. And I mean *immediately*. If we find out you have communicated with him and not reported that to us, even if it's five minutes after you and he talk, you'll be fired. On the spot, no questions asked. The *moment* you finish speaking to Lawrence, or anyone you suspect is working for him, the very next thing you do is call me or my assistant. If it's after hours, leave a message on her machine and call me at this number." He handed Angela a piece of paper with his cell phone number on it. "Now you have no excuses."

"Fired?" she asked, reluctantly taking the piece of paper.

"Fired," Hill repeated.

"You can't be serious," Angela said, her voice betraying her emotion.

"I'm very serious."

"I've worked hard for this bank. I haven't done anything to deserve this."

With her fear building, Angela could see that Hill was relieved. Perhaps he'd been worried she might do something drastic. Or that she might be capable of things Dudley and he hadn't anticipated. "Just cooperate with us," Hill advised, his voice softening as he moved back behind the desk and relaxed into his chair. "That's all we want, Angela. Your full cooperation. If you give us that, I promise you will be safe."

Angela stared into Hill's eyes. "Safe?"

He looked away, then rubbed his eyes. "Your *job*, Angela. Your *job* will be safe." She was still afraid. "Work with me, Angela. Please. I want to help you. I really do."

"Mr. Lawrence?"

Jake Lawrence looked up from the report he was reading and motioned for Colby to enter the small room he was using as his temporary study. "Sit down."

Colby eased himself into the rickety chair Lawrence had pointed to.

"What's on your mind, Bill?"

Colby frowned as he cased the room. After so many years, he did this automatically every time he entered new surroundings. "No disrespect, Mr. Lawrence," he said, nodding at the window behind his boss, "but I wish you would help make my job easier."

"What are you talking about?"

"The window, sir. It's a straightforward kill shot for anyone with a rifle and a half-decent scope. Dark outside, light in here. No curtains covering a second-story window. You are terribly vulnerable to attack right now."

"We're in a farmhouse in the middle of the

Virginia countryside, Bill," said Lawrence, not even attempting to hide his annoyance. "In the middle of two hundred acres. The closest house is half a mile away. There are huge oak trees all around the house, making it impossible for anyone to see this window from more than fifty yards away. That's one of the reasons I bought this place, and not the one closer to Richmond. It was your recommendation. Remember? And I'm sure you have men patrolling the perimeter beyond the trees." Lawrence sighed. "Let me send some comfort your way, Bill. No one's going to get me tonight. Now, why are you bothering me?"

Colby checked the window once more, giving it a disdainful look. "I wanted to let you know that we have almost completed preparations for your entrance into the city. The target will be contacted later this evening."

"By 'the target,' " Lawrence said deliberately, tossing the report onto a table, "I assume you mean Angela Day."

"Yes."

"Good."

"Yes, sir."

Lawrence waited for additional information, but there wasn't any. "Is that why you came up here, Bill? To chastise me about sitting in front of a window, and to tell me that Angela would be contacted later this evening? If it is, I have to be honest. I'm not sure I needed to be interrupted for that."

Lawrence's brusqueness didn't bother Colby. He had protected other wealthy individuals and celebrities, and he was immune to their arrogance. Besides, he was the best in the business, and he knew it. His job was secure. "I came up here to ask you to reconsider."

"Reconsider?" Lawrence asked curiously. "Reconsider what?"

"I'd rather you not meet with Angela Day again."

"Oh, really?"

"That's right."

"Why not?"

"Several reasons," Colby replied.

Lawrence nodded. "Go on."

"First of all, there was an attack on one of our teams today."

Lawrence sat up in his chair and leaned forward, his smug expression becoming one of intense concern. "Was anyone hurt?"

"One of the men in the unit protecting your decoy lost an arm. Your decoy is fine. He was never in danger."

"Jesus." Lawrence grimaced. "Make certain the man gets his benefit."

Colby nodded. The man would receive five million dollars as compensation for his injury — a practice Colby didn't approve of. At least, he didn't approve of making the men aware of it. The prospect of receiving five million dollars might cause certain individuals to act irresponsibly. To shoot themselves in the foot — or in the arm, as it were. "I'll make the arrangements."

"Which team was it?" Lawrence wanted to know.

"Team two."

"The one currently in Israel?"

Colby nodded.

"What happened?"

"A bomb exploded in the lobby of the Tel Aviv hotel your decoy was staying in. It was just a crude device filled with nails and screws for shrapnel. No one has taken responsibility yet. Unfortunately, one of our plainclothes people was in the lobby at the time. He'll survive, but, as I said, his arm had to be amputated at the elbow."

Lawrence nodded gravely. "That's terrible."

"So perhaps I can convince you to let us bring Ms. Day to you," he suggested. "As we did in Wyoming."

Lawrence shook his head. "No. I don't want Angela thinking she has to go through something so involved every time I want to see her."

"I can easily arrange to bring a woman out here who would present much less of a security risk. A woman who would also be a much more willing companion."

"What's that supposed to mean?" Lawrence snapped.

"Forgive me for saying this but, from what I understand, your last meeting with Ms. Day didn't go exactly as planned."

"How the hell do you know how my meeting

203

with her went? Or how it was *planned* to go? You aren't privy to everything, Bill." Lawrence slammed his hand on the table. "Do you have that cabin bugged?"

"No, sir."

"Well, where'd you get your information?"

"One of the boys informed me that the bed wasn't used. The sheets were still perfectly tucked in at the corners." Colby shrugged. "Perhaps I'm wrong."

"I need to get back to work," Lawrence said coldly. "That will be all for the evening."

Colby nodded, rising from the rickety chair and heading for the hall. At the doorway he turned back. "One more thing, Mr. Lawrence."

"What?"

"I hadn't informed you of this before now because I didn't want to alarm you in case it turned out to be inconsequential."

"Go on."

"Angela Day and John Tucker were attacked on their way back down to the lodge after your meeting with her at the upper cabin."

Lawrence glanced up. "Attacked?"

"Yes, sir. They were fired on while they were on that narrow section of the trail."

"My God, why didn't you tell me all of this before?"

"It appeared at first that the man who perpetrated the attack was nothing more than a drifter, a nobody John Tucker had hired to work on the ranch."

"Do you have the man in custody?"

Colby shook his head. "No. He was killed as we attempted to apprehend him."

"Killed? How should I take that, Bill? Did your people help him die?"

"No, sir. Just the opposite. We were trying to keep him alive so we could question him. In fact, his actions at the point we were about to apprehend him were what caused me to dig more deeply into his past. Past the initial findings."

"What actions were those?"

"He committed suicide. He threw himself off the mountain rather than allow us to take him alive." Colby's eyes narrowed. "He was very committed to what he was trying to do, and I have not been able to track down his true identity. Even with all of the resources available to us."

"What are you saying?"

"I'm concerned that somehow Angela Day poses more of a security risk to you than either of us understands."

Lawrence shook his head. "No, you're way off base with that."

"I've been working in the crime and protection businesses far too long to completely dismiss any possibility out of hand. But, don't misunderstand me. I'm not trying to convince you that she's involved in some kind of plot to harm you."

"What then?"

"I believe that the individual who shot at Ms. Day and Mr. Tucker on the mountain was working with someone inside our camp."

"Why do you say that?"

"Just a sense." Colby wasn't yet prepared to tell anyone about the silent communication he thought he had detected between Tucker and the man who was still hanging from the basement ceiling of the farmhouse, the man who had been watching Angela Day. He needed more proof before he would do that. "But my instincts are pretty good. Though I haven't figured out how yet, I'm concerned that Ms. Day's presence somehow compromises your safety." He'd figured it out all right. Tucker was getting close to Lawrence because Lawrence believed that Angela trusted Tucker. What Colby hadn't figured out was why Tucker would want Angela Day dead. Why he would leave her in that cave alone. Colby's eyes narrowed. "Mr. Lawrence, my job is never to allow your safety to be compromised. And I never will."

Once a month she had this opportunity. Just once a month for two short days, and an additional two weeks in the summer. She had thirty-eight days a year to see her son. Otherwise, except for a once-a-week half-hour telephone call, Hunter was off-limits. And the judge probably hadn't even given his edict a second thought since the day he'd come down with it. Hadn't ever considered the emotional torment he'd caused. In fact, he'd probably long forgotten the case. Forgotten everything except the bribe Chuck Reese must have paid him.

Angela hurried out of the elevator toward her car, parked in a far corner of the basement garage on Cary Street. Because she wasn't allowed to pick Hunter up until seven o'clock, she had remained at her desk to get some work done. Now she was late.

Late because Ken Booker had stuck around, too. At 5:15 he had asked her to come to his office to talk about a piece of business they were trying to win from an Atlanta bank. At 5:45 she had told him she needed to leave, but he had ignored her. Finally, at six o'clock she had simply gotten up and walked out of his office, even though he was still talking. Booker knew where she was going, and he knew that her time with Hunter was extremely limited. But he had still tried to make her stay. She hurried across the garage, footsteps echoing as she trotted to her car. And he had children of his own. Two of them. Of course he had no idea what it was like to not be able to see them whenever he wanted. He saw them every night when he got home.

As Angela neared her Saab, a huge form stepped from the shadows and moved directly in front of her, blocking her way. "Oh, my God!" she shouted, stepping back and turning to run.

"Angela!"

She recognized the voice instantly and stopped, looking back over her shoulder through the dim light. "John?"

"Yes," Tucker confirmed, moving toward her.

"You scared me," she gasped. "What are you doing here?"

"I have a message from Mr. Lawrence."

She glanced around furtively. There were only a few cars left in the garage, and she saw no one. But she was coming to realize that not seeing anyone didn't mean a thing. "I don't want any messages from Mr. Lawrence. Please," she begged, thinking about Carter Hill. "Just leave me alone."

"Angela —"

"I'm late, John. I'm on my way to pick up my son. Please just let me go," she murmured, reaching for the car door.

But Tucker blocked her path. "This won't take long."

"Get out of my way!" she yelled, trying to push him aside.

"Angela."

She thrust her arm past him and grabbed for the door.

This time he took her by the wrists, spun her around, and pushed her back against the cinder block wall. "Dammit, listen to me!"

"I'm going to scream bloody murder, John."

"Lawrence wants to have dinner with you tomorrow night," Tucker said, ignoring her threat. "He told me what happened at the cabin, and he said to tell you that he very much regrets his actions. I can't believe it, but he followed up on a promise this time. I'm sure you know that by now."

"Let me go!"

"Are you really willing to give up your son?"

Angela stared into Tucker's eyes. "What are you talking about?"

"The Lord giveth and the Lord can taketh away."

"Stop speaking in code."

"Jake Lawrence has become involved in your son's situation. In *your* situation." Tucker glanced around, then looked back at her. "You've already received a call from your attorney. One of the men who accused you of adultery six years ago wants to talk all of a sudden. Right?"

She hesitated, the horrible understanding that her life was no longer her own overwhelming her. A horrible feeling that she was being manipulated by forces which she had no chance of controlling. Forces whose motivations were cloaked, so that she could not determine who was friend and who was foe. There seemed no way for her to figure out which side to ally herself with. Perhaps the answer was that there was no side to ally with. Perhaps both sides would ultimately discard her once they'd gotten from her what they needed.

"Angela!"

She dreaded what was coming. She had a

feeling that something was out there, stalking her. Something that meant her terrible harm.

"Jake Lawrence can help you more than you can possibly imagine," Tucker said, holding her wrists tightly. "But he can hurt you too. I've seen him in action for twenty years, admittedly from the cheap seats. But it's still clear to me what kind of man he is. He's a vindictive son of a bitch, Angela. If you're loyal to him, he'll go to the ends of the earth for you. But if you don't play by his rules, he'll destroy you."

"You mean he won't help me get Hunter back," she whispered.

"Worse. Much worse. He'll make certain you never see the boy again. He'll spin a hundred and eighty degrees on you in the time it takes to say 'custody battle.' He'll use all of his power to make certain that judge reopens the case. But not to help you. To *hurt* you. To make certain the judge decides you aren't fit to see the boy at all. Ever."

"He wouldn't."

"Oh, yes, he would. He'd do it and laugh at you when it was done."

Angela searched Tucker's eyes for some sign that he was just trying to intimidate her. Instead, she found an intensity that told her he sincerely believed what he was saying. "What's going on, John?" she asked, her voice wavering slightly. "Why is he doing this to me?"

Tucker shook his head slowly. "How the hell do I know, Angela? I'm just one of his boys, just one of those people who carries out orders. I'm not privy to the big picture."

"Tell him to leave me alone, John. Please. Just leave me alone."

Tucker shook his head. "It wouldn't do any good, even if I did. Once he's got you in his sights, you stay there until he's finished with you. What I say would have no effect on him."

"I've got to go," she blurted, pulling away from Tucker's grip. She climbed in behind the steering wheel and reached for the door.

"There's one more thing," said Tucker, grabbing the door before she could close it.

"John!"

"Something else Mr. Lawrence wanted me to tell you."

"What?" she snapped.

"He said you need to be very careful with Hunter."

"Careful?"

"Yes. The boy could be in danger."

Angela stopped trying to yank the door shut and turned in the seat to look up at Tucker. "Don't threaten my son," she warned. "If Jake Lawrence lays one finger on my son just to protect his precious billions, I swear to God I'll kill him. Even Bill Colby won't be able to stop me with all those men in Wyoming."

"Angela, shut up and listen to me."

She glared at Tucker, her entire body shaking in rage.

"Mr. Lawrence has entered the situation. He

has become engaged in the battle to win your son back. He has chosen a side. Understand that there are those who watch his every move, enemies who might believe that they could manipulate Mr. Lawrence if they control the boy. Mr. Lawrence wants you to understand that his assistance comes with potential consequences."

Jake Lawrence had told her in the cabin that he was never truly safe, that there were those who wanted to see him dead. She'd thought him paranoid. Then she and Tucker had been shot at on the way back down the mountain. Now Tucker was warning her about Hunter. She had to believe what Tucker was saying.

Tucker pulled a small piece of paper from his pocket. "Take this," he ordered, holding out his hand.

"What is it?" she asked, taking the note from his fingers.

"My cell phone number."

She glanced at it, thinking about how everyone was suddenly giving her their phone numbers. Tucker had penned his full name in a looping script, then written the number beneath his name. "Thanks," she said quietly, looking up. He had begun to turn away, but stopped and looked back.

"By the way, Angela," Tucker said. "Mr. Lawrence also wanted you to understand that your former father-in-law is a very bad man." He hesitated. "But I think you already know that."

Then he was gone.

"What are you saying?" Chuck Reese asked.

"I'm saying that Angela Day has managed to restart the custody process for her son."

Reese shifted uncomfortably in the large chair. He had shelled out a significant amount of money to ensure that this would never happen. "That can't be."

"You should know better than anyone that there is no such thing as 'can't.' "

"In this case it would have to be someone with tremendous resources."

"I agree."

"Then I think we can assume we know who's behind the activity."

"You're probably right."

"But you aren't comfortable —"

"Not yet. This thing is like an artichoke. You peel away layer after layer, but you can't get to the core."

CHAPTER NINE

Chuck Reese had two homes in Richmond. A three-story brick colonial on two acres in the heart of the West End and a gray stone mansion on a hundred acres of heavily wooded riverfront property twenty-five miles east of center city. The mansion — fifteen thousand square feet of it — was set atop a small ridge several hundred yards back from the banks of the James. A wide, gardened lawn — lush and meticulously manicured in summer — sloped gently away from the mansion, cutting a swath through the forest until it reached the river and an impressive boathouse. There, Reese's children, grandchildren, and many friends and acquaintances enjoyed his fleet of power boats in the warmer months.

In winter, when the weather turned too cold to enjoy the river, the estate's indoor pool became the center of recreational activity. It was connected to the mansion by a long underground passageway so that no one had to endure the elements to get to it. And so, the landscape wasn't spoiled by an above-ground eyesore. Reese was particularly proud of this

214

feature of his beloved estate, which he had named Rosemary in memory of his wife. She had passed away a decade ago after a series of strokes.

After cutting off the Saab's engine, Angela remained in the car for a few moments, hands clasping the steering wheel. She hated coming to Rosemary because of the inevitable confrontation with Chuck Reese. It happened every time. Reese would appear unexpectedly, as if out of thin air, giving her that smug expression she wanted to smack off his face. The same expression he'd given her across the courtroom when the judge had come down with his final decision, an expression that said, "You only have your son for forty-eight hours a month. Then he's mine again."

Reese had a reputation as a gregarious man who would regale a room full of admirers for hours with stories of his adventures, a man with a kind word for everyone. But he rarely said anything to Angela when she came to the estate, as he had rarely said anything to her when she and Sam were married. He didn't have to. His eyes conveyed his hatred more effectively than words ever could. And when he did deign to say anything to her, the words were far from kind.

Angela reached for the handle, then eased back onto the seat and shut her eyes. She was nervous about seeing Hunter too. He was growing up, his physical and mental development apparent each time she saw him. He was getting to an age when he would appreciate the material things the Reese money provided, nearing an age where going from a palace on the James River to a two-bedroom apartment in the Fan would be noticed — and perhaps resented.

At some point in the not too distant future, Hunter might not want to come with her any longer, might not race toward her the moment he saw her and throw his arms around her neck the way he did now. Angela had already anticipated the scenario. Chuck Reese would tempt Hunter with a fabulous weekend, a get-anything-and-everything-you-want shopping spree at the FAO Schwarz store on Fifth Avenue in New York City, or a VIP trip to a Redskins game, including an autograph session with the star players. Then he'd tell the little boy that all of that was possible except for one thing. His mother was coming to take him away. She couldn't bear the thought of that. In her mind's eye, she would see the crest-fallen look on Hunter's face; the satisfied look on Reese's.

There was something else, too. John Tucker's surprise appearance in the basement garage had unnerved her. It had been almost an hour since she'd seen him and she was still shaking, still an-gered and upset by his warnings, increasingly anxious each minute she didn't log in a call to Carter Hill.

She stepped from the Saab and hurried across the circular driveway toward the mansion's huge front door. She had no doubt that Chuck Reese adored Hunter. That had been obvious from the moment Hunter had been born — the first male grandchild. And she'd seen the way Reese still doted on the boy. But Chuck Reese was a selfish man. Sharing someone as precious as Hunter was something he would avoid at all costs — which was why, Angela knew, he tried making her visits to Rosemary as unpleasant as possible. Perhaps he hoped to make her loathe the visits so much that she would ultimately give up and stay away from his world for good. She gritted her teeth as she pushed the doorbell. That would never happen. No matter what he tried.

A blonde woman opened the door, smiling politely. "Yes?"

Angela glanced down at the foyer's gray slate. This was Caroline Reese, Sam's wife of two years. It was the first time they had ever met, but Angela recognized Caroline immediately from newspaper and magazine photographs. Caroline and Sam had quickly become one of Richmond's most prominent couples. She was from a well-to-do family of Savannah, Georgia, and no charity event or social gala was an A-list affair without the Reeses.

Angela had read about Caroline in the society pages of the *Richmond Tribune* when the engagement was announced. Caroline was the daughter-in-law Chuck Reese had always wanted, a rich debutante from an old-money neighborhood in a stylish southern city. In fact, he'd probably arranged the marriage himself. Rosemary had been his wedding gift to them, according to the newspapers. He still stayed there on weekends, but according to the press, Rosemary had been deeded to Sam.

"I'm Angela Day."

"Oh, *Angela*," Caroline said, her Southern accent becoming more pronounced as she emphasized Angela's name. "I'm Caroline. Sam's wife."

"I know."

"It's nice to meet you after all this time."

"Nice to meet you, too," Angela said coolly.

"You must be here to pick up Hunter."

"Yes."

"Well, please come in." Caroline opened the door wide, beckoning her inside. "It must be cold out there."

"It's not bad." The temperature had turned warm around noon, climbing into the fifties and quickly melting yesterday's snow. But here it was after dark, and Caroline didn't know it had gotten warmer. She probably hadn't been out of the house all day. And, if she had, it would have been through a heated garage and straight into a waiting limousine. Angela was well aware of the charmed life Caroline Reese led.

"I believe Hunter's still at the pool with his father. He's such a wonderful little boy. I really love spending so much time with him."

Angela said nothing.

"Do you want to wait here or would you like

to go out to the pool?" Caroline asked.

"I'd like to go to the pool," Angela replied quickly.

"Of course you would," Caroline agreed, reaching out and patting Angela's hand. "I understand completely. Let me get someone who can take you. I would, but Sam and I are going out later, and I was just headed upstairs to start getting ready when you rang the doorbell. I'll be right back, okay?"

"Okay."

In person, Caroline wasn't as pretty as she was in photographs. She was tall and blonde, but very pale, almost ashen, and not at all exotic. Plain, in fact. So many times Sam had told Angela how he found exotic women — like her — so much more physically alluring. Like the woman she had caught Sam in bed with. Just as often Sam had told her how he could never be attracted to a woman like Caroline. But perhaps that had been a lie, as so many other things he said had turned out to be. Maybe, like most men, he could be physically attracted to almost any woman — at least for a time.

Caroline returned a few moments later with a scowling, middle-aged black woman in tow. "Alice will take you out to the pool, Angela."

"All right." Alice wore a gray and white maid's uniform, complete with a lace bonnet.

"It's been nice to meet you, Angela," Caroline said with a smile.

"Yes, nice to meet you, too."

"Get along, Alice," Caroline ordered, gesturing to her right with a flip of her fingers as she headed toward a staircase and the second floor. "Take Ms. Day to the pool."

"Yes, ma'am," Alice said tersely. "Please come with me, Ms. Day."

Angela followed the woman through a maze of rooms to a long set of steps at the bottom of which lay the underground passageway leading to the pool. The passageway was wide, carpeted, and dimly lit by lamps affixed to its dark green walls. Off the corridor were guest bedrooms and recreational rooms. Some of the rec rooms were furnished with wide-screen televisions surrounded by comfortable sofas and chairs, others with pool tables, Ping-Pong tables, or exercise equipment. Angela shook her head as she walked with the maid. Hunter had all of this available to him twenty-four hours a day. How was she ever going to compete?

The air in the corridor turned warm and humid, and they reached the far end of the corridor and the bottom of another stairway leading up to the pool. As Angela neared the top step, the pool came into view. It was massive, fifty yards long and thirty wide, with a huge sliding board as well as two diving boards at the far end.

Her eyes widened when she spied her son. "Hunter!"

The young boy stood at the end of the pool's high-dive board, poised ten feet above the water's surface. "Mom!" he yelled back, waving excitedly. "Watch this!"

"Hunter, no!" Instinctively Angela began running down the deck toward the high-dive, her hard-soled shoes clicking on the cement as she raced past lounge chairs and tables. "Don't, honey!"

But the boy paid no attention, swinging his arms by his sides three times, then leaping fearlessly from the board, shouting as he fell toward the water.

Her only thought was that Hunter was about to drown. He shouldn't be jumping off a high-dive. He was only six years old, for God's sake. She was going to kill Sam for being so irresponsible.

She watched in horror as Hunter hit the water and disappeared beneath the surface with a splash. But he popped up almost instantly, laughing and whooping as he dog-paddled toward a ladder on the side of the pool.

"Hunter, you scared Mom to death," Angela admonished, relief washing over her as she knelt down and helped him climb up the ladder. "Please don't ever do that again."

"It was easy," he said, throwing his arms around her neck and giving her a loud kiss on the cheek. "How ya doing, Mom?"

Angela closed her eyes, hugging him back and laughing, feeling the water dripping all over her but not minding a bit. "I missed you so much," she whispered.

"I missed you too, Mom. Love you."

She adored those words. Adored the emotion he could evoke so quickly. "I love you too, sweetheart."

"Watch me do it again," he said, pulling back and giving her a smile.

"Hunter."

"What?"

"You lost a front tooth. What happened?"

He giggled and pulled his lip back. "It fell out yesterday," he explained, his words almost unintelligible with the finger in his mouth. "The big tooth is already coming in," he said, tilting his head back. "See?"

"Yes, I can," she said softly, spotting a tiny line of enamel protruding through his upper gum where the baby tooth had been.

Hunter hadn't mentioned the tooth being loose when they had spoken by phone last Sunday evening — the night before she had left for Wyoming — and suddenly she was overwhelmed by how quickly he was growing up, struck by the fact that she hadn't been around for the loss of his first baby tooth. And that, because of the situation, there might be many more of these once-in-a-lifetime events she would miss.

"The Tooth Fairy gave me fifty dollars, Mom. The money was under my pillow when I woke up this morning."

"Fifty dollars?"

"Yup." A puzzled expression spread across the

young boy's face. "Fifty dollars. Is that a lot?"

"I would say so." To her maybe, but not to Chuck Reese. "Too much."

"You know what?" Hunter asked, his voice dropping.

"What?"

"I don't really think it was the Tooth Fairy that gave me the money."

"You don't?"

The boy shook his head deliberately. "No. I think it was Caroline."

"Oh. Why?"

The smile danced back to his face. "Because I was awake when she came into my room," he said, giggling again, pleased with himself. "I peeked when the door opened, and I saw it was her."

"Well, maybe the Tooth Fairy asked Caroline to help her out. Maybe the Tooth Fairy was too busy to get to everybody last night. There are a lot of children who lose teeth every day."

"Santa Claus gets to *everybody* in one night."

"That's true," Angela agreed hesitantly, wondering how to argue with his logic. Aware that she probably wouldn't be around to comfort him when he figured out that Santa Claus had help too.

Hunter shrugged his small shoulders. "I like Caroline. She's nice."

"Mmm." Angela looked away, unable to bring herself to giving the other woman any endorsement at all.

"I'm going off the high-dive again," Hunter announced, pulling away and scampering toward the ladder leading up to the board, the bottoms of his wet bathing trunks sagging down to his knees. "Watch me, Mom."

"Hunter, no!"

"He'll be fine."

Angela glanced down. Sam was hanging on to the edge of the pool a few feet away, submerged in the water up to his neck. She hadn't even noticed him in her panic-induced sprint down the deck. "But he's only six years old."

"Relax." Sam chuckled. "He's growing up. You'll just have to accept that, Angie."

The world blurred before her momentarily. Other than her father, Sam was the only one who had ever called her "Angie." She loved the sound of it, even if it was Sam saying it. Maybe she loved it because it was Sam. She swallowed hard and looked away. She still wasn't over him. Despite all the grief he had caused her, she still couldn't shake him. Perhaps she never would.

Sam hauled himself out of the water without using the ladder, sitting on the side of the pool for a moment, then rising to his feet. "How you been, Angie?" he asked, striding confidently to a lounge chair and grabbing a towel.

"Fine," she answered, still not looking at him.

He wanted her to look at him, she knew. Look at him in just his bathing trunks, his tanned body glistening with drops of water. She'd been attracted to Sam from the first moment she'd seen him across the Duke business school class-room. It had never been that way for her before, or since. Not with anyone else.

When they were introduced two days later — during a coffee break between marketing and finance classes — Sam had had the audacity to gently take her hand, lean forward, kiss her on the cheek, and whisper in her ear that he couldn't take his eyes off her in class. That he'd noticed she couldn't take her eyes off him, either. And that he could think of a much more exciting way to spend an hour and a half than sitting in a classroom listening to a professor drone on about finance.

Had it been any other man, she would have tossed her coffee in his face for saying something forward. But for some reason she'd simply gazed at him as he'd pulled back, marveling at his ability to calmly say what he'd said. He'd said it in the same way he spoke in front of the other eighty students in class when professors asked him to lay out the case they were working on that day. Without a trace of fear or hesitation in his voice. Unlike the nervous tones she and everyone else had spoken in during the first few days.

The most incredible thing was that, even now, she didn't have any regrets about meeting Sam. It wasn't as if she wished they had never been introduced. Or wished that she'd actually thrown the coffee in his face that day, which would have saved her the emotional anguish she'd endured since that day she'd discovered him in bed with another woman and realized he wasn't hers anymore. The thing of it was, she didn't blame Sam. Not for most of what had happened anyway. She blamed Chuck Reese. If he had supported their marriage, they would still be together. She was sure of it.

"You're late, Angie. You're never late to pick up Hunter. What happened?"

"My boss wouldn't let me go."

"Mom!"

Angela glanced up. Hunter had made it to the end of the high-dive again. "Careful, baby," she called, her voice echoing around the huge room.

"Can't call him 'baby' anymore, Angie," Sam chided gently, moving next to her. "He's growing up. Pretty soon you'll be watching him on the football field. He's got a good arm for a six-year-old. You should see him."

Sam's voice was like the gentle purring of a cat: low and smooth and soothing, with a hint of a Southern drawl in his words. The enticing inflections of his voice brought everything hurtling back, the way sounds sometimes stir latent, nearly lost memories more powerfully than sight ever can. "Careful, Hunter." She was trying not to think about the memories, but it was hard.

Sam clapped, urging his son on. "Come on. Make this one a real good one."

Hunter followed the same routine, swinging his arms by his sides three times, then leaping fearlessly into the water.

Angela brought her hands to her mouth as he fell, her heart in her throat. But once again, Hunter popped right to the surface, and was already paddling determinedly toward the ladder before his head had fully emerged.

"Good job, son," said Sam. This time he reached down and helped Hunter up the ladder. "Now you've got to get ready to go with Mom."

"Aw, Dad. One more time. Please."

"No. It's getting late." Sam waved toward the other end of the pool, where the maid stood. "Alice," he called loudly, "please take Hunter to the house and get him dried off and into his clothes."

"Yes, sir."

"Go on, Hunter. Go with the help. Your mom and I will be back over to the house in a minute."

"Oh, all right," Hunter agreed dejectedly, walking head down and shoulders slumped for the first few steps. Then, sneaking a look back, he broke into a trot, then into a full sprint, yelling and shouting as he ran.

"Careful," Sam shouted. "The deck's wet. Watch out."

But Hunter made it to where Alice was waiting without incident, and then they were gone, heads disappearing down the steps leading to the underground passageway, the boy's first, then the maid's.

"I better get going, too," Angela murmured, taking a step in the direction Hunter had just gone. She felt Sam's fingers curl around her wrist.

"Not yet, Angie."

He might as well have glued her shoes to the deck. She tried pulling away, but it was impossible.

Sam chuckled. "It'll take Alice a half hour to get Hunter ready to go. The boy will run her ragged. You know that."

"This isn't right. We shouldn't be here like this."

"Why not?" Sam asked, turning her toward him. "What's so wrong with this?"

She gazed down at the puddles beneath her shoes, wishing he would take his hand from her wrist and, at the same time, hoping he would keep it right where it was. She tried to keep her head down, tried to count the tiny decorative tiles embedded in the deck at the water's edge, but in the end she had to look up, up into the confident eyes of a man she knew lived only in the moment.

She'd known that the first time she'd kissed him — a week after they had met. He was not safe, not stable. Far from it, in fact. But she'd kissed him anyway, trying to resist at first, then just trying to maintain control.

Sam wasn't a physically imposing man. He

wasn't overpowering like John Tucker. And he didn't have Jake Lawrence's pretty-boy looks, either. Sam was lifeguard handsome: blond, slim, and taut. But it was his presence that had caught Angela's attention so long ago, the cool confidence in his light blue eyes and his I-know-something-you-don't smile. The way he could hold a class full of cynical graduate students and professors in the palm of his hand while he calmly presented his solution to the day's case. Somehow, he made even the most boring material seem fascinating as he wove personal stories and anecdotes into his tale so that, when he had finished his presentation, the room was pin-drop quiet until the trance was broken by the professor. Sam was part evangelist and part politician, with a little bit of the devil thrown in somewhere. And he had that swagger too. The one John Tucker had. He'd hooked her in a heartbeat.

"I've got to go."

"No," Sam said firmly, "you don't."

"Sam." He was leading her toward a little room off the pool, a private dining area with a table and chairs where people could take a break from swimming and look back at the mansion through the woods while they ate. "What are you doing?"

"I just want to talk."

"About what?"

Sam backed Angela gently against a wall just inside the door, then moved back a step to reassure her. Keeping his distance for the moment. "We never talk."

"That would be because you divorced me."

Sam shook his head. "My father did that to us. You know that."

"Yes, just the way he made you get into bed with that other woman."

"That was terrible, Angie," Sam admitted, sliding his forefinger beneath her chin and tilting her head back. "I'm guilty as charged there. I was very immature back then. I wish I could take it all back."

Angela looked away. "I met Caroline."

"Oh?"

"She greeted me at the front door."

"You mean she actually opened the front door?" Sam asked sarcastically. "She actually lifted a finger?"

"Yes. Why?"

He laughed. "She must have been going past the door just as you rang the bell."

"That's right. That's what she said."

"Figures. Caroline certainly wouldn't go out of her way to do that — or anything else around here, for that matter." Sam put a hand to his head. "No, wait. I take that back. She might move quickly if it were toward the limousine and an afternoon of shopping."

"She said she was going upstairs to get ready to go out with you tonight."

Sam groaned. "Don't remind me. We've got to go to some damn museum opening to cut a ribbon. Then there will be the requisite party afterward and a night of all the same people and all the same conversations."

"Don't sound so enthusiastic."

"It'll be awful." Sam sighed. "But Caroline will be happy. And that's what's important," he said nodding gravely, then breaking into a smile.

"Poor baby." Angela patted his chest then made a move back toward the pool. "I feel so bad for you. You lead such a difficult life."

"Hey, why are you leaving?" he asked, snagging her wrist again.

"Because you need to start getting ready for your museum party."

"I bet I could think of a more exciting way to spend the evening."

Angela had seen that look on Sam's face many times. His eyes were aflame with lust. "I'm sure you could," she said, surprising herself.

Sex with Sam had been incredible from the first time they'd been together. No initial period of awkwardness as they'd gotten to know each other, as there had been with her only other lover, a boy in college. No having to show Sam her special wants. He'd found them himself so effectively and efficiently she'd bitten his shoulder to keep from screaming. She'd left deep and purple marks, and he'd pointed at them proudly the next morning as proof that she'd experienced intense pleasure.

And it wasn't just the physical part of the act

231

that had brought about such incredible pleasure. As Sam had slowly and tantalizingly inves-
tigated her body that first night, he had
whispered to her, too, gently probing her mind
as well. The college boy had been too inexperi-
enced to understand the psychological component of her need, and turned selfish when
satisfying her became too much of a chore.
She'd accepted it by making him believe he was
satisfying her when he wasn't. That had never
been an issue with Sam. Not once had she ever
had to fake anything with him.

Sam had made her feel as she was convinced
she never could, even during their initial encounter. And it had only become better over
time. He explored her fantasies and desires,
coaxing her into telling him her most private
thoughts. She'd become physically addicted to
him, in so absolute a way that her body had actually ached for months after the divorce. Now
she simply tried to ignore those urges. She
hadn't been with anyone since the divorce,
hadn't even been tempted because she was certain the experience would be so disappointing.

"What did you think of Caroline?" Sam
asked, moving close.

"She seemed nice."

"She isn't. She was being her usual plastic
self, I can assure you. But that's not what I was
talking about."

"Oh?" Sam ran his finger up her forearm and
the feeling raced through her body, the fire

spreading even as she tried desperately to throw water on the flames. "What *were* you talking about?"

"What did you think of her physically?"

"She's attractive."

"She's plain," Sam said. "Not like you."

"Well, I —"

"You are so beautiful." He bent down so they were on the same level, searching her expression. "Those eyes of yours," he said softly. "They're like magnets to men."

Angela looked down.

"Are you seeing anyone?" he asked.

"No."

He put his finger back beneath her chin and lifted it again, forcing her to look at him this time. "Are you telling me the truth?"

"Yes."

"No woman has ever come close to you, Angie."

She ought to hate him for what he had done, and on a rational level she did. But on a deeper plane she couldn't. "Which is, of course, why you felt you needed to cheat on me."

"I said I was sorry for that."

"I don't care about sorry. Sorry doesn't help me."

"You have your skeletons too."

Angela's eyes flashed to his. "You know none of that was true," she said, tight-lipped. "You know your father was responsible for all of that. I was never with either of those men."

There was a long silence. "Let's start seeing each other again," Sam finally suggested.

"No. Not in a million years."

"Why not?"

"For starters, let's try the fact that you're married. I don't do —"

"I don't mean in that way," he interrupted.

She hesitated. "Then what are you talking about?"

"At some point Hunter is going to start asking questions about what happened to us. In fact, he already has. It would be much better for him as he gets older if you and I had a healthier relationship. Don't you think?"

"Maybe," she said slowly. This was just like Sam to throw her a curveball. She'd thought he was trying to seduce her, but he was talking about something platonic. So why was there that twinge of disappointment?

"I see you in Hunter so much, Angie." Sam's voice was subdued. "The way he walks and smiles. That attitude of his. It's all you, Angie. It brings back lots of wonderful memories, I have to admit."

Angela swallowed hard. "What are you suggesting?"

"Let's have lunch sometime. It'll have to be somewhere out of the way. I hope you can understand why. I can't have an innocent lunch getting into the newspapers and being misconstrued, you know?"

She nodded.

"But I can be a good boy. I can keep my hands to myself."

How could he have sat there in that court-room and watched those men testify about having sex with her? If he truly loved her, how could he have allowed them to say the things they'd said? Could he really have believed their stories? "Sam, I —"

"Are you game for it, Angie? Just lunch. Maybe next week. I'll call you at work one day and we'll set it up. You know it would be fun."

That was the problem. It *would* be fun. And, despite his promises, the odds were very good that he'd try to turn it into something more. "I don't know."

"I do. I'm going to call you. I'm going to set it up for —"

"Hello, Angela."

Sam and Angela glanced toward the doorway at the same time. Chuck Reese stood there, peering at his son's fingers wrapped around Angela's wrist.

"What are you doing here?" the elder Reese demanded.

"She's here to pick up Hunter, Dad," Sam explained.

"I see." He took Angela's hand and pulled it away from Sam's. "Son, Bill Morris called a few minutes ago about that property in Atlanta," Chuck Reese informed Sam, handing his son a cordless phone. "He's anxious to talk to you."

Sam managed the family money. He'd never

had any other job. "I'll call him in a little while, Dad."

"I'd appreciate it if you'd get back to him right away. As I said, he was anxious to talk to you."

Slowly, Sam took the phone from his father. "All right."

"I can't remember Bill's number. You'll need to go back to the house to get it. It's on the Rolodex in the study. Say good-bye to Angela."

"I'll be going myself," she said quickly.

"I'd like to speak to you for a moment," Chuck Reese said, blocking her way to the door as Sam headed out. "This won't take long. Promise."

"Bye, Angie."

Then Sam was gone and she was alone with Chuck Reese. "Mr. Reese, I'm not comfortable —"

"How much will it take, Angela?" he growled, his demeanor turning confrontational.

"Take? How much will *what* take?"

"Let me say this as politely as possible. I'm tired of seeing you. Tired of having to deal with you. I want you out of my family for good. I want you out of Hunter's life, and I want you out of Sam's life. I know what was going on here when I walked in. I know my son. God help me, I love Sam, but he has a very hard time controlling himself. He seems to only want what isn't his. I'm just looking out for him, and for Hunter. It'll be best for both of them not to see you anymore. It's best that I take care of them without any influence from you." Reese drew a long breath. "There will have to be consideration for you. I understand that."

Angela stared up at Chuck Reese, unable to believe what she had heard. "You are the most despicable —"

"How much, Angela?" he asked again, a determined tone in his voice. "What's it going to take? Let's start at five hundred thousand in cash. How about that?"

"You would try to buy me?" she asked incredulously. "To buy out my ability to see my son? I'm his mother, for God's sake. He needs me."

"All right a *million* dollars. I can have it to you tomorrow along with a contract that you will sign agreeing to give up all rights to Hunter."

Angela stared at Chuck Reese, hatred coursing through her body. His face blurring before her. "You are the most disgusting man I've ever known," she hissed, pushing past him. At the doorway she stopped and turned back, pointing a trembling finger at him. "You will never be able to buy me off. Not for a million, not for ten million," she said, shaking her head. "I hope you burn in hell."

As she walked quickly along the deck toward the stairway and the underground passage, she could hear him laughing from inside the room. She began to run.

John Tucker nodded to the armed guards posted on the wide porch before the farmhouse's front door. He had also nodded in the same way to the two men at the end of the farmhouse's long driveway, and to the two men halfway down the driveway. Colby was taking absolutely no chances with Lawrence's safety on this trip.

Once inside the house, Tucker moved quickly along the dimly lit hallway toward the basement door. He was thinking back on the fear he'd detected in Angela Day's eyes a little over an hour ago. The dread that had settled into her expression like a palm print in setting cement.

The hall door creaked when it swung open, as did the second step of the rickety basement stairway under Tucker's weight. The muffled groans were becoming louder, and he took the last four steps in a single leap, then hustled toward the closed door at one end of the dank basement.

"What the hell's going on here?" he roared, bursting into the small room.

The man they had apprehended on the lawn across from Angela's apartment was still hanging from a thick beam, chin on his chest. One of Colby's men stood close to the prisoner, a lit cigarette in his fingers. Tucker knew that Colby didn't allow any of his men to smoke or drink. They were in top physical condition, and would have been terminated immediately for violating the rules. The cigarette had another, darker purpose.

"I'm following orders," said the crew cut young man.

Tucker had been introduced to the detail as a "special assistant" to Jake Lawrence on this trip. But during the briefing in Wyoming, Colby had made certain his men understood that Tucker had no authority over them.

The prisoner was naked from the waist up, and Tucker spotted two burn marks — one on the back of the neck, and one on the left shoulder blade. "That'll be all, son."

"I take my orders from Mr. Colby."

Tucker moved a step closer, confident he could overpower the smaller man if necessary. "That will be all," he repeated loudly.

"I'm not going any —"

"Leave us," Colby ordered, striding into the room past Tucker and nodding at the young man. "Now."

"Yes, sir." The man quickly exited the room.

"I thought we agreed that this guy had nothing to tell us," Tucker said when the guard was gone. "What's the deal here?"

Colby moved close, so that their faces were just inches apart. "Why do you care so much, John?"

"I can't wait to see this movie, Mom."

Angela and Hunter were hurrying through a crowded indoor mall, trying to make a nine o'clock showing. She was dead tired, but the next two days would be filled with anything and everything Hunter wanted to do. Before they'd even made it down the estate's driveway, Hunter had told her how his granddad was planning to build a barn at Rosemary for a couple of new ponies.

"Me, too, sweetheart. We're going to have so much fun this weekend," she said.

"We always do."

She smiled down at him as they neared the ticket booth. "Yes, we do."

The theater had six screens and Angela scanned the listings, then reached into her purse for a twenty when they made it to the front of the line. She was thinking that she needed to call Carter Hill to let him know that Jake Lawrence had contacted her. She had no choice.

"Two tickets for . . ." Angela's voice trailed off as she glanced down. Hunter was gone. He'd been right beside her a moment ago. Her eyes snapped up, quickly scanning the theater's crowded lobby. Another movie had just finished and people were pouring out of the theater into the mall. "Hunter!"

"Hey," said the man behind her in line, "are you going to buy tickets or what?"

Tucker had warned her about needing to be careful with Hunter because Jake Lawrence had become involved in the situation with her son.

"Come on, lady."

Angela felt panic setting in. Her heart was thumping in her chest; her brain was beginning to pound. "Hunter!" she yelled, people blurring before her as her eyes flashed around the area. She stepped out of line and staggered ahead,

240

fighting to cross the river of moviegoers passing in front of her. Maybe Hunter had gone to buy candy. He was such an independent child. "Hunter!" She could hear the panic in her own voice, and it unnerved her. "Hunter!" She pushed through a family of five and made it to the food counter, but the little boy was nowhere in sight.

"Are you all right?" asked a woman holding a bag of popcorn.

"It's my son," Angela answered, her voice choking up. "He was right here a second ago. Right with me. Then I looked down, and he was gone."

"Now keep calm," the woman urged. "Everything will be okay. He's probably right here."

Angela shook her head and raced back out toward the mall, looking wildly in both directions, uncertain what to do. Pick one way to run and search every store? But what if that was the wrong way? Or stay right here? But what if he had walked into the mall? Or been taken? She had to do something.

"What does he look like?" The kindly woman had followed Angela. "I'll go this way," she said, pointing to the left, "and you go over there. But you have to tell me what he looks like first."

"He's about this tall," she said quickly, putting a hand at her hip. "He's got medium-length brown hair and blue eyes. He's wearing a green down jacket," she said, trying to think clearly as the words spilled out. "Thank you. Thank you so much." Suddenly Angela felt a hard tug on the bottom of her coat.

"Mom, did you get the tickets?"

She glanced down and her eyes were met by the most beautiful sight she could have imagined. Hunter looking up at her with that wonderful smile. She knelt, tears flowing down her cheeks as relief rushed through her body. "Where were you?"

"I went to the bathroom. I thought you heard me tell you."

"No, honey. No, I didn't." She grabbed him and hugged him tightly. "You have to make sure I hear you, Hunter. Please don't ever do that again."

Hunter nodded obediently as Angela pulled back. "Sorry to scare you," he said, wiping tears from her face.

"It's okay, Hunter. It's okay."

The man standing against a wall outside the movie theater folded the newspaper he had been pretending to read, and moved casually on. What had just happened was bad luck for him. Now it was going to be extremely difficult to get the boy away from her.

Ken Booker took a long puff from a cigar, then, for a second time this evening, read the article in the *Washington Post* about the lawsuit seeking $1.4 trillion. The scary thing about the suit was that someone at the *Post* thought there was enough to it to report on it. "Bastards," he muttered, feeling his blood begin to boil.

He reached for the Jack Daniels highball and took a long drink. Why was he getting so worked up? The man they were supporting was very connected. And he would see to it that this could never happen.

CHAPTER TEN

The weekend with Hunter had flashed by. The way they always did. Her two days were gone, and he was back at Rosemary. It would be another month before she would see him again, and the loneliness was already setting in. It had hurt so deeply to watch him scamper gleefully back into the mansion after giving her a final hug, undoubtedly looking forward to playing with the magical things that millions could buy.

Angela knew now more than ever that there would soon come a day when Hunter wouldn't want to spend the weekend with her, a Friday when he would trudge to her car and get in because he *had* to, not because he wanted to. This very morning he'd mentioned for the first time she could ever remember that he was bored.

Typically, she and Liv would have had dinner tonight — the Sunday night after her weekend with Hunter. Liv had an amazing ability to comfort her, while at the same time making her realize that she couldn't feel sorry for herself, that she alone could effect change. The dinner-with-Liv-routine had been interrupted this evening in the name of doing just that.

"Everything all right?"

Angela nodded slowly, gazing through the candlelight at Jake Lawrence.

Tucker had called yesterday morning, asking again if she would consent to dinner with Lawrence. She had turned down the request for last night, Saturday night, because nothing could make her give up so much as a minute of her precious time with Hunter. She had agreed, however, to meet Lawrence late this evening after dropping the boy off at Rosemary.

But she had agreed with a condition. John Tucker would have to be close by at all times, close enough so that if she felt any uneasiness at all, she could get to him right away. And he could get to her.

Angela glanced at the double door of the hotel suite's tastefully decorated private dining room. Jake Lawrence had agreed to her condition. They were alone in here, but Tucker was on the other side of those doors watching television. She'd already checked twice. William Colby was out there too, along with four of his men, two of whom were carrying weapons — and watching Tucker like a hawk.

"Relax, Angela. Everything is fine," Lawrence said reassuringly, adjusting his black bow tie. "You know John Tucker is out there, right?"

Angela nodded again. Lawrence smiled and the dimples she'd first noticed in Wyoming appeared.

"I learned my lesson last time." His smile faded when Angela didn't respond. "I mean that."

"Okay," she agreed, her steely expression starting to fade.

"Hey, I got all dressed up for you. The last time I wore one of these penguin suits, I was having a private dinner with a head of state." Lawrence held his arms out to show off the sharp black tuxedo. "Give me some credit," he pleaded.

"You look nice." Lawrence looked more than nice. He looked like he ought to be on the cover of a magazine. She had to keep reminding herself of what he had done to her.

"And you look fabulous, Angela."

"Thank you."

She was wearing the dress she'd bought for the trip to Wyoming, though she hadn't been as excited about putting it on this time. Tucker had given her the same compliment when he'd picked her up at her apartment in the Fan. It had meant more coming from him because she felt sure he meant it.

"I like your hair up off your shoulders that way too," Lawrence continued. "It makes you look like a princess."

Angela glanced down, embarrassed.

Lawrence rolled his eyes. "Jesus, I've gone and done it again, haven't I? I'm sorry."

"It's all right," she said, cracking a faint smile for the first time. "Don't try so hard."

"Right." He picked up an open bottle off the table. "Do you mind if I have some wine?"

"You don't need my permission."

"Somehow I think I do."

"It's fine if *you* want some," she said after a few moments, making her glance at the doors obvious.

"Would you like a little?"

She shook her head. "No."

"Okay." Lawrence poured himself a glass, motioning toward the doors when he was finished. "You like John, don't you?"

She shrugged. "I trust him."

"But you barely know him."

"That's true. But I still trust him."

"How can that be?" Lawrence pushed.

"It's a feeling." She wasn't going to tell Lawrence about Tucker's advice in the garage, how his warning had seemed heartfelt, delivered because he cared. She wasn't going to put him in jeopardy that way. "I can't explain it to you."

"Shouldn't you approach something like trust more deliberately? Shouldn't you give it more time?"

"Why do you care so much?"

A tight-lipped expression came to Lawrence's face. "You're right. I don't. That's your business."

"Good."

Lawrence took a sip of wine. "By now, I assume, you are aware that the custody war for your son is back on." His manner turned businesslike. "Your attorney, Ms. Charboneau, will meet tomorrow with one of the men who accused you of having sex with him while you were married to Sam Reese. A Mr. Ford, I believe. The one who is still alive," Lawrence added quietly. "And Ms. Charboneau will be talking further with a woman who had an affair with your ex-husband, the woman you caught Sam Reese in bed with." Lawrence put the glass back down on the linen tablecloth. "I've also made arrangements for my people to speak with the judge in the case. He doesn't have to reopen it, but I believe he will."

"How did you convince these people to change their minds?" Angela asked. "How did you convince Danny Ford?"

"Several of my associates had a chance encounter with Mr. Ford in a parking lot late one evening last week. They reasoned with him."

"You mean they threatened him, don't you? Or did they actually hurt him?"

"In the end, Angela, the slime of our world must pay for their actions," he said coldly. "There must be retribution for acts of evil. Otherwise decent people are left unprotected, and chaos reigns."

"I see," she said quietly.

"Would you rather Mr. Ford be allowed to go through life without ever paying for what he did to you? For helping to take Hunter from you?"

Angela stared at Lawrence through the flickering candlelight. "No."

"Then we're in agree—"

"Why are you doing this for me?" she cut in. "Why are you going to such great lengths to help me?"

"You've agreed to do a favor for me, so I'll do the same for you. You scratch my back, I scratch yours. That's the way the world works."

"What you have asked of me is simply my job. The financing of an acquisition. Just business."

"But I don't think you fully understood the consequences of my request. I don't believe you understood how strongly Bob Dudley would react to your involvement with me."

Angela ran her finger around the base of her empty wineglass. "No, I suppose I didn't."

Lawrence rose from his seat, bottle in hand, and moved to Angela's side of the small table. "Have a little," he urged gently.

She looked up into his dark, dead eyes, reminding herself that Tucker was in the next room. "Half a glass. That's all."

Wine poured, Lawrence returned to his seat.

"Dudley and Hill have ordered me to keep them informed of any contact I have with you," she said. "I'm required to call them as soon as I talk to you or your people. If I don't, and they find out, I face the possibility of being fired on the spot. I left a message for Carter Hill this evening before Tucker picked me up to let him know about this dinner."

"That's fine," he acknowledged. "But they didn't forbid you from seeing me, did they?"

"No. In fact, just the opposite. When I told them about our meeting in Wyoming, and that I never wanted to meet with you again," she said, watching Lawrence's reaction, "Dudley didn't bat an eye. He made it clear to me that he didn't care about me one bit, that our relationship was all about him, that I was to be enthusiastic about working with you if you called again."

"Always keep your enemies as close as possible," Lawrence said quietly.

"Excuse me? I didn't hear you."

"Bob Dudley believes that I'm out to steal his beloved Sumter Bank from him. Because my resources are so much greater than his, he figures his best, perhaps only, chance of stopping me is to anticipate my every move. So he's trying to stay as close to me as he can through you. He doesn't understand that I have no interest in acquiring the damn bank."

"Then why have you increased your ownership stake from 8 to 10 percent?" she asked.

Lawrence peered intently at Angela from across the table but said nothing.

"I checked the 13-d filings again on Friday afternoon," she explained. "You spent another $110 million for an additional 2 percent of the bank's shares. If you have no interest in acquiring Sumter, why do you keep buying more shares?"

"I told you," Lawrence replied evenly. "I believe it's a good long-term investment."

"No chance it's really the other way around here? That I'm the one keeping Bob Dudley close to you?" she pressed.

"No chance at all," he said firmly.

"Then describe this company you are so interested in acquiring."

"Certainly. That *was* why I wanted to meet with you tonight."

Angela eased back into her chair, slightly surprised at his amiable reaction. She'd expected him to stall once more. She was certain that there wasn't any acquisition transaction — other than the acquisition of Sumter — and that tonight's dinner would turn out to be nothing more than a debriefing session, with Lawrence trying to determine Dudley's level of resolve for a fight to keep Sumter out of Lawrence's hands. And Lawrence giving her instructions for her next meeting with Dudley and Hill, which, she assumed, would occur first thing tomorrow morning.

She was resigned to the role of pawn, tonight's dinner being just another move on the board. It wasn't a game she was proud to participate in, but, with Lawrence's help, there seemed to be the very real possibility of winning Hunter back. Or at least seeing him a great deal more. For that possibility, she was willing to be put in play.

"The firm I want to buy is an IT group based in Reston, Virginia, which is about twenty miles west of Washington, D.C."

"You mean, information technology?" she asked.

"Yes. The firm helps large, multinational companies install and integrate state-of-the-art software systems into their existing legacy networks. Their engineers design and build custom software systems in certain situations, as well."

"IT is a tough business right now, isn't it?" Angela asked. "I don't have much experience with companies like that, but I've read that those professional-service models are difficult to scale. And that corporate America isn't spending as much on those kinds of services as they were a while ago. Lots of IT companies have seen their stock prices hit the skids lately, haven't they?"

"Which makes it an excellent time to buy. A year ago the firm I'm looking at had a stock market value of almost a billion dollars. Now, with the share price trading in single digits, the total value of the firm is down to around two hundred million."

"What's the name of the company?"

"Proxmire Consulting."

Angela didn't recognize the name. "What's so special about Proxmire? As I understand it, there are lots of IT companies that do what you've described. Why are you so hot on these guys?"

Lawrence smiled approvingly. "Very good, Angela."

"Thank you, Mr. Lawrence, but —"

"Jake," he interrupted quickly. "I've asked you to call me Jake several times. I don't want to ask again."

"Sorry." She hesitated. "Jake."

"So why these guys? An excellent question." He nodded at her glass. "You haven't touched your wine. It really is delicious. Don't waste it."

"Why Proxmire?" she repeated firmly.

Lawrence nodded, resigned to her cautiousness. "Two years ago Proxmire acquired a company named ESP Technologies in a stock swap. ESP designs and develops cutting-edge predictive software systems."

"Predictive software? You mean the kind of application where a user inputs historical data and the software provides most likely outcomes."

"Yes."

"Forgive me for being so blunt, but that isn't cutting edge. There are lots of other companies doing that."

"Believe me, these people are light-years ahead of the competition. Their proprietary logarithms are incredible. With only a few variables their predictions are more dependable than the competition's by a factor of ten. Maybe more. And this firm has huge data banks to cross the incoming historical data with, which further refines the predicted outcomes."

"How do you know?"

"One of my portfolio companies licensed ESP's software six months ago and the results have been spectacular."

"I'm listening," she said, picking up her wine-glass for the first time.

Lawrence watched as she drank. "I own a chain of convenience stores in the South."

"Really? Which one?"

"Cubbies."

"You're kidding. You own Cubbies?"

"Yes, I bought it three years ago from the founder. It was a private transaction. We kept the deal extremely quiet."

"There was a Cubbies near the trailer park I grew up in. They used to have this great Italian Ice machine at the back of the store."

"They still do. Thanks to the ESP technology, we've moved those machines closer to the potato chips at most of our two hundred locations. Same-store sales increased 14 percent last quarter without any increase in advertising dollars."

"Because of ESP?"

"Absolutely. They researched the demographics for each store, then analyzed specific historical item volumes, pricing, and merchandising across the chain, and developed a new store setup profile for every location. One of the software's recommendations was to relocate that machine at a lot of sites. The results have been immediate and measurable. No question ESP has had a profound effect on the business. Cash flow has doubled."

"So you're impressed enough to buy the entire company just to get to ESP?"

"I believe ESP could ultimately be worth billions by itself. The problem is that Proxmire, the parent company, hasn't had the marketing dollars to spend on rolling out ESP's software through the appropriate distribution channels. As you mentioned earlier, they've had their own cash flow challenges over the last twelve months, and they seem focused on simply keeping themselves afloat."

Suddenly things were beginning to sound interesting again, and she took another swallow of wine. Lawrence was right. The wine was delicious. Of course, why would she have expected anything else? The bottle probably came from some special stock. A stock the hotel reserved for the few guests who could afford this suite.

For a moment she allowed herself to wonder what it would be like to have no monetary concerns, to do anything and everything she wanted, whenever she wanted. Would total financial freedom be worth the need to have armed guards and decoy teams, to live life always looking over her shoulder? She couldn't convince herself it would be. In some ways Lawrence was a prisoner of his own wealth. In a gilded cell, for sure, but a prisoner nonetheless.

"Do you intend to make a public tender offer for Proxmire?" she asked.

"Yes."

"But, if I'm remembering our conversation in Wyoming correctly, you were worried that

Proxmire's senior management wouldn't be enthusiastic about your intentions."

"Right. Look at Bob Dudley's reaction to his *perception* that I'm stalking Sumter," Lawrence scoffed. "Imagine a CEO's reaction when he *knows* I'm coming after his company. These men enjoy running the show, Angela. It's all about ego for most of them, not about what's best for the stockholders. As I told you, senior executives worry that, once I gain control, I'll come in and change everything, and, at a minimum, hold them accountable for their performance, or the lack thereof. Maybe even fire them if I wake up on the wrong side of the bed one morning when they aren't hitting their numbers. That's where you come in."

Angela licked a drop of wine from the corner of her mouth. This might turn out to be fun after all. "You want me to meet with Proxmire's senior executives? By myself?"

"Yes," said Lawrence. "I want you to lay out the entire scenario for Walter Fogel, their CEO. Explain to him that I'm willing to pay a reasonable premium for Proxmire shares if he and his board accept my offer without a messy proxy battle. Explain that I want to work with them to develop a plan for a major rollout of ESP's primary products. That I will commit additional capital over and above what I pay the public stockholders for their shares to enable management to accomplish that rollout." He smiled. "Then use your considerable charm and beauty

256

to persuade Walter to embrace my offer."

Angela put a hand on her chest. "You are going to let me negotiate the deal?"

"Absolutely. And lead the due diligence effort, focusing almost exclusively on ESP. I really don't care what you find at the rest of Proxmire. I care only that everything checks out at ESP. You have to scrub that part of the deal squeaky clean. Find out everything there is to find out at ESP. Make certain there aren't any skeletons in the closet."

"Why so much focus there?"

"My ultimate strategy is to take ESP public out of Proxmire. I want to make certain the investment bankers I use don't find anything that would get in the way of the IPO. And, as long as you are diligent, they won't."

Angela's eyes narrowed. "Tell me the truth, Jake. No more screwing around. Why me? Why not one of your high-priced Wall Street suits who does this for a living?"

"I told you. I'm very focused on keeping this project confidential. I-bankers can't seem to keep their mouths shut. They'll whisper the information to their friends, and before you know it the price will jump ten bucks before we even announce our offer to purchase. I'll end up paying the price."

"I'm not buying it. There's more to it than that."

Lawrence nodded approvingly once more. "You're a sharp lady. My people were right."

"I'm very happy for them and I hope you give them all big bonuses for being so perceptive. What's the real answer?"

Lawrence looked away for a moment, then stared directly into her eyes. "The CEO of Proxmire is single and black. Walter Fogel is from a small town in the South, and he's lifted himself out of poverty by his bootstraps with nothing but brains and determination. No old boy network was on his side. In fact, he's had just the opposite. That network has been working against him all of his life. You will connect with him immediately because you understand exactly what a man like Walter has gone through to get where he is today. And because you connect with him, he will connect with you, making everything a great deal easier." Lawrence paused, trying to gauge her reaction. "It's as simple as that."

"How can you be so sure I understand what a man like Walter Fogel has gone through?"

"You've been exposed to racism since you were a child," Lawrence replied confidently. "You've seen firsthand how white store owners follow black customers down the aisles to make certain they aren't shoplifting, but don't do the same to whites. You've been with blacks when they've had to sit in certain sections of restaurants. You've held a black woman in your arms as she died after what a gang of white frat boys did to her." He nodded as her face went ashen. "I told you my people were thorough."

Angela sat back in her chair. "Stop bringing Sally into this," she whispered. "You have no right to do that."

As Angela retreated, Lawrence leaned forward, placing his elbows on the table as he held his glass of wine in both hands. "I have the right to do whatever I want. I know what's best."

"Don't give me that God-speak. Just because you have so much money doesn't give you the right to —"

"Don't let Sally's death hold you back for the rest of your life, Angela. Get past it. You must."

She gazed at him steadily, anger and bitterness raging inside. "Stop it! Stop trying to manipulate me."

"I'm not trying to manipulate you," Lawrence replied quietly. "I just want to make certain I get ESP Technologies, and you get your son." He leaned back. "This is life, Angela. Sometimes it's not pretty, but it is what it is. I need a person who can relate to Walter Fogel, a person who is motivated and someone I have faith in. You fit that description. If you help me, I'll help you. Trust me."

Angela stared at Jake Lawrence for several moments. The only noise was the faint sound of the television coming from the other side of the doors. She reached for her wineglass and took a long swallow.

"Can I take that as a yes?" he asked.

She gritted her teeth. She hated being used, but there was no other way, not if she wanted to accomplish her goal. "Yes," she said quietly. He was right. This was life, and it wasn't pretty. Sometimes it was downright ugly.

"Good. You're making a wise decision, Angela." He put down his wineglass. "I had my people prepare an information package concerning Proxmire. I brought that package with me tonight, and I'll give it to you before you leave. I want you to be intimately familiar with all of the information in the package no later than tomorrow afternoon, and I expect you to attempt initial contact with Walter Fogel no later than Tuesday morning. His curriculum vitae is in the package."

"I won't sleep with him, Jake," she said adamantly. "Not even to get my son back."

"I'm well aware of that, Angela," Lawrence agreed smoothly. "Remember?"

She stared deeper into the dark eyes, trying to find a hint of emotion behind the cool facade.

"Let's talk share price," Lawrence suggested. "Proxmire has been trading in the $8 to $10 range for the past three months. It was as high as $50 at one point, but it's dropped off the table in the last eighteen months. I'm willing to go as high as $25 a share to get the company. Start at $17 with Fogel when you negotiate with him, but go no higher than $25 in the end. Twenty-five bucks a share implies a valuation of almost half a billion dollars. That's very generous."

Angela shook her head. "Why do you care

what you pay? If you're so hot on ESP, why do you need to negotiate? You've got the money."

"First of all, I never overpay, no matter how much money I have. It's the principle of the thing. Second, if I did come in with a bear hug, an offer that Fogel couldn't responsibly refuse, he still might try to sell ESP out from under me. Just to spite me."

The wine was beginning to have its effect. She could feel herself becoming light-headed. She finished what remained in her glass anyway. Tucker was outside and, besides, this was fascinating. They were deciding what to bid for a public company. Once the tender was announced, it would be splashed all over the financial newspapers. It wasn't a huge transaction, but it was big enough. And she'd been so certain that Lawrence had been bluffing about the M&A project, certain there was no Proxmire or ESP, certain there was only Sumter.

"My suggestions as far as target share price and pricing strategy are covered in the package," he explained, standing up and refilling her wineglass despite her halfhearted attempt to stop him. "But I figured I'd provide you with a coming-attraction trailer."

"Thank you," she replied, her voice raspy. They had locked eyes for a moment as he'd towered over her.

Lawrence chuckled as he moved back to his chair. "I wish I could have been a fly on the wall when you met with Dudley and Hill. Pretty upset, were they? Trying to figure out my intentions." He paused. "By the way, what did you tell them?"

Angela glanced up. If Sumter was just an investment, why did Lawrence care? Why did he keep bringing the conversation back to Dudley and Hill? "I told them just what you told me in Wyoming. That you had no intention of entering into a hostile takeover battle with them, that you believed it was a well-run bank in a high-growth market, and that it was nothing more than a passive investment for you."

"I assume Dudley was more aggravated than Hill. I bet Dudley was the one asking most of the questions."

"The tough ones anyway. Hill seems like a decent enough person." She bit her tongue, trying to keep herself from saying too much. But the wine had done its work. "Dudley doesn't."

"Tell me more."

She looked down into her lap. "Bob Dudley is a racist."

"Why do you say that? What has he done to give you that impression?"

"Nothing specific," she answered quietly, thinking about the memo she had discovered in Ken Booker's office.

"Are you Liv Jefferson's informant?" Lawrence asked suddenly. "Are you the one who provided her information so she could write that article about the bank not serving the black community?"

Angela stared back at him. She'd anticipated him asking this question again, and was ready with her answer this time. "Maybe John Tucker needs to join us at this point," she said calmly.

"There's no need for that." Lawrence picked up his menu. "Let's order."

"How do I know you'll follow through on the custody battle?" she demanded, unwilling to let him change the subject. "How do I know that this isn't just a lot of show? How can I be certain that when you get what you want, Kate Charboneau won't call out of the blue to tell me that everyone's memory has turned selective again? I won't have a job either if you abandon me. We both know that. Dudley will kick me out Sumter Bank's front door himself. I need to know that you won't abandon me."

"You have my word," he said, putting down the menu.

"I need more."

"Too bad. The bottom line is that you want your son back more than I want ESP. You know it. I know it."

He was right. If the Proxmire acquisition didn't work out, he'd simply move on to the next deal. But her life would be changed forever. What could be gained versus what could be lost: perhaps seeing her son more, perhaps never seeing him again. The risks and rewards had never been greater.

"You have to trust me, Angela."

"I told Dudley last week that the reason you

contacted me as opposed to other bankers was that I had extensive industry experience," Angela said, wondering how she could ever trust a man like Lawrence. A man who had so many agendas. "That the target company operated in an industry I knew a great deal about. Dudley will figure out very quickly that I don't know much about information technology because I don't have any of those kinds of companies in my loan portfolio. He'll find out from his subordinates that I focus on Old Economy companies. He'll be suspicious about why I'm helping you analyze Proxmire."

"Don't tell him why."

"I have to tell him something."

"Tell him anything you want except the truth. I do not, under any circumstances, want you to tell him that the company you and I are looking at is Proxmire Consulting."

"But —"

"As I'm sure you know," Lawrence interrupted, "the government scrutinizes all public takeovers for possible insider trading activity. I don't want word of my intentions leaking out. I do not want this transaction being held up by federal and state regulators while they review unusual trading patterns in Proxmire shares prior to our takeover announcement. Right now the only people who know about this are you, one assistant of mine, and me. I want to keep it that way as long as I can. At least until you contact Walter Fogel."

She was silent for a few moments. She'd made her deal with the devil. "All right."

Lawrence waved, an irritated expression on his face. "In addition, if Dudley found out what the target was, he might try to use Sumter's resources to get in my way. He might have his trading floor buy up blocks of Proxmire shares to bid up the price. Just to piss me off."

That didn't seem logical. Why would Dudley want to irritate Lawrence? Then Lawrence might come after Sumter just for revenge. "Why aren't there any pictures of you in the family history book?" she asked.

Lawrence blinked, then laughed. "What?"

"The family history book. I found a copy of it on the plane coming back from Wyoming last week. It was stashed in an overhead compartment. There were pictures of your mother and father but none of you."

He shrugged. "I wasn't a very photogenic child."

"I don't believe that."

"Believe what you wish."

"You're an only child, right? That's what the press reports, and what the book said."

"That's right."

"Was it lonely growing up?"

Lawrence chuckled. "I refuse to answer that question on the grounds that it may tend to incriminate me."

She'd struck a chord, but she wouldn't press.

If she did, he might never open up again. And there could come a time when she would have to get beneath his surface to find out something she desperately needed to know. "Your father made it huge in software."

Lawrence took a swallow of wine. "That's right, Angela. Billions and billions and billions from a tiny little investment. Tiny for Dad anyway. All those billions, and he didn't even have to lift a finger. A programming nerd he met at a Harvard symposium took Dad's two hundred grand in return for a big chunk of a fledgling software company, and the rest is history. Literally. Now that fledgling software company is one of the most powerful juggernauts in the world. Its operating systems control almost every personal computer in the world. What a country America is, huh?"

She'd spent two hours perusing the family history book, fascinated. She'd been tempted to take it with her, but in the end, she'd put it back where she'd found it before getting off the plane. "But your family was already wealthy at that point."

Lawrence glanced up. "Very."

She could tell the wine was getting to Lawrence. His dark eyes were developing a glassy sheen. "Your family owned huge timber tracts in the West."

"That's true. Large areas of Montana and Wyoming. The ranch outside Jackson is a leftover piece of one of those tracts."

"But the family's start in the timber business didn't begin in the West."

Lawrence turned his head to one side. "Right," he agreed slowly.

"It actually started in the South," she continued. "In Georgia in the early 1800s. But your great-great-great-grandfather saw the Civil War coming and sold the business, worried that if the North won, he might lose everything. After he sold the business, he took the proceeds and bought all that timberland out West."

"Mmm."

"Or was it Alabama where your family got its start?"

Lawrence reached for his glass.

"Jake?"

"What?"

"I can't remember what the book said, Jake. Was your family originally from Georgia or Alabama?"

"Georgia. Near Atlanta."

"Do you still have family down there?"

"On the Callaghan side, as the book says. My mother's side, God rest her soul." For a moment, Lawrence's eyes took on a distant look.

"Your father was —"

"Do you think Carter Hill could run Sumter Bank?" Lawrence asked. "Would he be an effective chairman?"

She hesitated. "I suppose, but I don't think my opinion is worth much. I've only met the man twice."

"Your opinion is worth a great deal." Lawrence pushed a small button embedded in the edge of the table. "How do the rank and file feel?"

Angela considered the question carefully. "Bob Dudley is feared. People think he's a dictator. It's my impression that most of the bank's employees think the other senior executives are nothing more than puppets. Including Carter Hill. I do think Hill is viewed as much more approachable, more of a consensus builder. But all of that is based on hearsay."

"Perhaps Carter Hill is a man who is better suited to run a bank in this day and age," Lawrence observed. "Particularly a bank with the lion's share of its operations in the South."

"Perhaps, but I don't —"

"Take a look at your menu, Angela," Lawrence suggested. "Please."

Moments later the dining room door opened. One of Colby's men entered first, followed by a nervous-looking waiter dressed in a white dinner jacket and black pants, then Colby. Colby's aide quickly scooped up both silverware settings, then the waiter was allowed to take the dinner order. First Angela's, then Lawrence's. When the waiter had exited, the aide replaced the silverware in front of Angela and Lawrence and also exited the room, just ahead of Colby, who closed the door.

Angela relaxed only when the men were gone, aware that she had been as uneasy as the waiter the entire time the other men were in the room.

She glanced across the table at Lawrence. He was fiddling with his steak knife, tracing tiny circles on the linen tablecloth with it.

"Are you all right?" she asked softly. She wondered if it was difficult to be constantly reminded that you could be a target at any moment, that even a waiter couldn't be trusted.

"Fine," he answered loudly, putting the knife down.

Too loudly, she realized. She smiled at him. "I've read on the Internet that you are supposed to be somewhat of a thrill-seeker. What kinds of things do you do?"

Lawrence finished what was left in his glass, then leaned over the table and smiled a sinister smile back at her. "Angela, I'm like the girl with a tattoo on her ass. I'll do anything."

Just coincidence, or did Jake Lawrence somehow know about her tattoo? As John Tucker guided the Town Car through the deserted downtown streets toward the Fan, she replayed Lawrence's comment. The dead eyes had momentarily come alive as he'd spoken, dancing in the candlelight. She thought about how he'd been wrong about his family being from Atlanta. The book indicated that the Lawrences were originally from Birmingham. But maybe he had been trying to throw her off track for some reason.

"You okay, Angela?" Tucker asked.

"Yeah, sure."

"I have to be honest with you."

"About what?"

"I'm surprised you were willing to meet Lawrence again after what he did to you in Wyoming. Even with me there."

Angela put her elbow on the door and rubbed her forehead. "Everything is so complicated at this point, John."

"Things must be *very* complicated. All of this must have something to do with that takeover you were talking about."

"Well . . ." She stopped herself when Tucker turned off the boulevard onto a side street. They were out of downtown now and getting into the Fan. "You could have just kept going straight there."

"Oh, okay," he said quietly, checking his side mirror again. "These are nice big houses," he commented.

"Yeah, I like it here."

"So are you going to give me a hint about the name of the company?" he asked. "Give me a little heads-up on the takeover?"

"No. I told you in Wyoming. I can't do that."

"Figures," he muttered glumly.

"John, I can't."

"Whatever."

"Telling you anything about that would be against the law. It would constitute insider trading if Jake announced a takeover." She hesitated. "But you will find out what company it is before any transaction is announced, and then you can do what you want. You can make your own decision."

"What do you mean?"

"I told Jake that I wanted you around. You aren't going back to Wyoming — not any time soon anyway."

Tucker glanced over at her. "Really?"

"Really."

He chuckled. "Angela, I don't know what to say. I didn't know you cared."

"I want you around to protect me, John," she replied quickly, watching his expression turn to one of disappointment. "That's all. Don't flatter yourself," she continued, aware that his sad face was probably just a charade. "I took your warning about my son to heart. And I figure that if someone might want to kidnap my son to get to Jake Lawrence, they might do something to me, too."

"Angela, I'm crushed," he said dejectedly. "I thought maybe this was the start of something."

She stole a quick glance at him, trying to see if he was serious. She liked him. There was no denying that. But a relationship with him would be too dangerous. "Nope. Sorry."

Tucker pulled out onto the next boulevard. "How am I going to find out the target company's name if you don't tell me?" he asked.

"Oh, you'll find out all right."

Tucker turned left onto the next side street.

"What are you doing?" Angela asked.

"Heading back to the boulevard we were on

271

before. I thought you said I was supposed to go straight on it."

"Okay, okay. Don't get upset."

"I'm not upset," he muttered. "Just disappointed. You had me on cloud nine for a minute. Now I'm in the basement."

She gazed over at him in the dashboard lights, still wondering if there was any shred of sincerity in the hurt-puppy-dog act, or if he was just having fun. "What happened to you after you left me in the cave up there on the mountain?"

He shrugged. "I went looking for whoever shot at us. I found tracks and two spent cartridge casings but that was it. Whoever it was got out of there."

"You didn't say good-bye. Didn't come to dinner or take me back to the airport the next day."

"Colby's orders. He runs the show unless Lawrence overrides. I guess with everything that happened Colby wanted to be the one to monitor you. See how you were handling it all. I asked to speak with you, but he said no."

"I was disappointed not to see you again," she admitted, watching Tucker check the rearview mirror once more.

"How close are we to your place?"

"Pretty close," she answered, wondering if he had heard her. He wasn't acting as if he had. "A half mile or so."

"Then let's walk," he suggested loudly,

swinging the Town Car into an open spot.

"What? Are you out of your mind? I've got to be at work early tomorrow."

"Ah, you'll be all right." He jumped out of the car and hurried to her side, yanking open the passenger door. "Come on!"

"John!"

Tucker reached down and grabbed her arm, pulling her from her seat. "It'll be nice. It isn't cold."

"But —"

"Hey, I'm a spontaneous guy," he said, laughing. "What can I say?"

She was laughing too as he led her across a yard and toward a waist-high white picket fence. "You're insane."

"You got that right." He picked her up quickly and put her down on the other side of the fence, then hopped over, grabbed her by the hand and took off, leading her through a garden.

"We're going to be arrested." She laughed as they jogged. "I'm going to end up in jail."

"At least you'll be alive," he muttered.

A few minutes later they had made it to Angela's apartment.

"Well, good night," Tucker said, standing on the landing outside her apartment door. They were both still breathing hard from the run.

"Do you want to come in?"

He shuffled his feet. "Well, I —"

"To call a cab, I mean. Or maybe for a glass of water."

Tucker started to say something, then thought better of it. "I'd better not. I mean, no, that's all right."

Angela reached out and took his hand. "I felt safe tonight because I knew you were there, John."

"I know."

"And I'm glad you're going to be around for a while."

"Me, too."

Angela squeezed his thick fingers. "Do you really think someone would go after Hunter?"

"Yes," he said quietly. "I've seen it before when it comes to Mr. Lawrence. You have to be *very* careful."

She took a deep breath and looked out into the darkness. "Well, thanks for getting me home." She tried to pull her hand away, but he held on to it for a moment.

"Angela."

"Yes?"

"There's something you ought to know about . . ." His voice trailed off.

"What is it, John?"

"I just, well, I just want you to understand that I . . ." But once again he didn't finish.

"Tell me."

He shook his head. "I have to go," he said, turning away.

"John!"

"Call when you need me, Angela."

And then he disappeared into the night.

★ ★ ★

Angela never heard about the explosion that incinerated the Town Car minutes after she and Tucker had left it. Lawrence's people were able to keep the incident out of the newspapers. A remotely controlled incendiary device affixed to the underside of the Town Car's chassis had been set off by a button pushed by one of the two men riding in the car that had followed Angela and Tucker from the hotel.

CHAPTER ELEVEN

"You met with him last night?"

"As I communicated to Mr. Hill, we had dinner together."

"Dinner?"

Angela's anticipation of an early morning meeting with Dudley and Hill had been warranted. She had arrived at her desk just before 7:30 and Hill's executive assistant had been waiting. The woman hadn't even given her a chance to get settled, barely allowing her the opportunity to take off her coat before leading her to the elevators and the fiftieth floor. "Yes, dinner."

"Just you and Jake Lawrence."

"Several of his associates were there, but we were the only ones eating. The only ones actually in the room."

"That seems pretty intimate. It's surprising that you would agree to something like that after telling us what he did to you in Wyoming."

"I was careful," she answered.

"Were you now?" Dudley asked. "And did he try anything this time?"

"No. This time he was a gentleman."

Dudley shot Hill a cynical glance. "As if he really tried anything in Wyoming."

Angela gritted her teeth. The faster she was out of Dudley's office the better, but she couldn't allow that comment to go unaddressed. "What is that supposed to mean?"

Dudley's eyes narrowed. "Perhaps you were the one who became physically aggressive with Lawrence in Wyoming. After all, he is one of the wealthiest men in the world. Lots of women probably have Cinderella dreams about him. Perhaps he was the one who rejected you so you made up the whole story to try to save yourself the embarrassment in case he told someone the truth."

"That's ridiculous!"

"Easy, Ms. Day," Hill urged soothingly. "We're all under a lot of pressure. Why don't we get into what you and Mr. Lawrence discussed last night."

Angela stared at Dudley, hoping he might look up so he could see the fire in her eyes. But he didn't. "We focused on the company he wants to acquire," she replied, her voice strained. "The target."

"What's the name of it?" Dudley snapped.

Dudley seemed more on edge than last time they had met, Angela observed, as if he knew the enemy was closing in. "Mr. Lawrence ordered me not to disclose the name of the target to anyone. He wants it kept confidential."

"Bullshit!" Dudley barked.

"Settle down, Bob," Hill pleaded.

"Shut up, Carter. Tell me the name of the company, Ms. Day, or so help me . . ."

Angela saw fury flash cross Carter Hill's face for the first time, as if he'd almost reached the breaking point, as if he couldn't take the role of lapdog any longer. "So help you what?" she demanded, her voice steely. Suddenly she was in the driver's seat. She could feel it. She was Dudley's only direct connection to a man he believed was stalking him. Like it or not, he needed her.

"Perhaps you can tell us what industry the target operates in," Hill suggested when Dudley remained silent. "Would you do that?"

"Retail. Convenience stores, specifically. Lawrence already owns a chain called Cubbies, and he intends to grow it substantially with this acquisition." Hopefully that would throw them off the track long enough for her to meet with Walter Fogel. When they found out she had misled them, she'd blame it on Lawrence by telling them she had only found out at the last moment that the true target was Proxmire.

"Well, there are only a few publicly held convenience store chains," Dudley commented. "I can probably figure that one out on my own."

"I'm sure you can," she agreed. "Now, if that's all, I'm going to go back down —"

"That's not all, Ms. Day," Dudley hissed. "You'll leave when I say you can leave."

"All right," she said evenly, "Mr. Chairman."

"What else did you talk about while you dined with Mr. Lawrence?"

"A number of things."

"Did you discuss the fact that he has now increased his stake in Sumter to 10 percent?"

Dudley was a man on the run, sensing that his pursuer was gaining ground, and his predicament gave Angela immense satisfaction. Deep down she was hoping that Jake really was lying to her, and that his ultimate intention was to take over Sumter, kick Bob Dudley out on his ass, and, at least temporarily, replace him with Carter Hill. "Yes, we did."

"And?"

"And that was all. I was the one who brought up the subject. I told him I had checked the latest 13-d filings and was aware of the fact that he now held 10 percent of the bank."

Dudley scoffed. "I assume he continues to maintain his innocence."

"Innocence?"

"I assume he continues to claim that his purchase of Sumter shares is simply a passive investment and that he has no intention of making a run at my bank."

"That's right."

Dudley passed a hand through his silver hair. "He's a slimy son of a bitch."

"Mr. Lawrence did ask one interesting question," she volunteered.

Both men glanced up quickly.

"What was that, Angela?" Hill prompted.

She'd been waiting since the moment she'd walked into the office to deliver this round from the howitzer. Dudley might keel over from a heart attack when he heard what she was about to say, but she wasn't going to be the one to give him CPR. "He wanted to know if I thought you would make a good chairman, Mr. Hill."

For a moment the room was deathly still, then Dudley exploded. "I'll kill the bastard! I'll kill the fucking bastard!"

Angela glanced out of the Honda Accord's passenger window at the stately homes and beautifully manicured lawns and gardens of Richmond's West End. Liv had picked her up in front of the Sumter Tower for lunch, then headed out to the city's most affluent neighborhood. "Why are you bringing me all the way out here?"

"It's an experiment," Liv answered evasively.

Angela rolled her eyes. It seemed as if there was always a surprise with Liv. "I can't be gone from the office too long. I've got things to do."

"Like what?" Liv wanted to know. "Good God, you work yourself to the bone for that bank. What have the stuffed shirts at the top ever done for you? You can play hooky every once in a while."

Liv was right. The only pressing thing on her plate right now was to keep reviewing the package Jake Lawrence had handed her last night before she left his hotel suite. She'd already been through it once. Unable to sleep much last night, she'd spent time going through the information after Tucker had taken her home. Besides, she was having a difficult time keeping her mind on anything but the fact that Kate Charboneau was about to meet with Danny Ford and his lawyer. Jake had led the horses to water, but he might not be able to make them drink. Perhaps a little distraction wasn't such a bad idea after all.

"You seem preoccupied."

"No, I'm not," Angela protested.

Liv grunted. "I've known you long enough to recognize the signs. You haven't said a word all the way out here. And your fingers couldn't be locked together any tighter," she said, nodding at Angela's lap.

Angela shook her head and smiled. "You think you're so smart."

"You're nervous about that meeting your lawyer is having this afternoon."

She had told Liv about the meeting but hadn't provided many details. Not how or why it had come about. "If the guy recants his testimony, I might get to see Hunter more than two days a month. It's a very important meeting. Of course I'm anxious."

"It's important all right, but worrying about it won't do you any good." Liv gestured out the window at a particularly large home they were just passing. "Look at that place, Angela. It's huge."

"It's beautiful," she agreed.

"This is how the 'haves' live." The boulevard was two lanes wide here and Liv zipped around a car in front of them. "By the way, I had an interesting call last night."

"Oh?"

"Yup. The guy wouldn't tell me his name, but he claimed he had information on Bob Dudley. Information Dudley wouldn't want me to hear."

Angela's eyes flashed from the window to Liv. "You're kidding."

"No, I'm not. He kept asking me if I was committed to bringing down the chairman. Said he'd read my article in the *Trib* about Sumter and Dudley, and he wanted to know if I really had the stomach for a fight. The thing is, I just had my number changed again last week. Seems like I have to do that more and more often these days."

"What information did the guy have?"

"He wouldn't tell me. Said he'd call back in a few days, then he hung up when I started pressing him for specifics." Liv paused. "He was probably just a crackpot, but I had my number changed again this morning just in case."

A chill raced up Angela's spine. Jake Lawrence had the resources to get almost anything. Finding an unlisted number would be child's play for his people. "Did you star 69 him?"

"Yeah. The call was made from a pay phone not far from my place." She laughed. "I didn't even know there were pay phones anymore."

Angela took a deep breath. "How can you be so calm? Did you call the police?"

"No." Liv eased off the accelerator, flicked on the car's turn signal, and entered a Sumter branch parking lot.

"You should have."

"When you've been a reporter as long as I have, you get used to this kind of thing. Calling the police would be a big waste of time," she said, swinging into a parking space next to a large Mercedes sedan. "Here we are," she announced. "Let's go."

Angela stepped out of the car and looked up. The Sumter branch building was a picturesque Colonial structure with a brick facade and white pillars in front. The area around the building was impeccably maintained, and huge trees obscured the building from the surrounding residences.

"What are we doing here?" Angela asked as they headed toward the front door. A white woman coming out of the branch gave Liv a long look, then darted toward her car.

"Conducting our experiment."

A few minutes later Angela and Liv were sitting in the glassed-in cubicle of a young loan officer. He was no more than twenty-four, Angela guessed. In all probability this branch assignment was only temporary for him, a part of the same training program she'd completed in her first six months at the bank. Sooner or later he'd be transferred downtown into the corporate lending department where he could make Sumter some real money. He had the right look. Preppy and monied. She knew what kind of salaries permanent branch loan officers made, and it wasn't enough to pay for the Brooks Brothers suit and the flashy silk tie the young man was wearing. Besides, a young man like this wouldn't be satisfied with a career handling mortgages.

"I'm Trip Bishop," he announced, smoothing his tie. "And you two are?"

"I'm Liv Jefferson and this is my friend Angela," she explained, gesturing at Angela.

Bishop smiled over his desk. "Nice to meet you, Angela. Now, how can I help you, Ms. Jefferson?"

"I need a mortgage," she replied. "I'm buying a house out here in the West End."

Trip's smile faded. "Here in the West End?"

"Yes. Over by Saint Christopher's School. You know, the boys' private school?"

"I know where Saint Chris's is." Trip scrunched up his face. "My parents live over near there. That's expensive territory, Ms. Jefferson. You can't get anything for less than half a million. You sure you can afford that?"

"I'm sure."

"Okay. Well, you'll need to fill out a loan application. You can go over there," he suggested, gesturing at a counter. "When you've completed it, someone else can help you if I'm busy."

"I've already filled one out." Liv pulled a

completed application from her purse and placed it down on the young man's desk. "I stopped by yesterday and picked it up."

"We will be discussing personal items such as income and net worth, Ms. Jefferson," Trip explained as he opened the application. "Would you rather your friend waited in the lobby?"

"You can say anything you want in front of her. She's a good friend," Liv said quietly, patting Angela's hand.

Trip's eyes followed Liv's fingers. "You've checked the unmarried box. Have you ever been married?"

"Yes."

"Divorced?"

"Yup."

"How many times?"

"Why do you need to know that?"

"It's just a standard question."

"No, it's not. The form simply asks if I'm divorced, not how many times." She sniffed. "But I will tell you that I am neither receiving nor paying alimony."

"We'll check that out."

"I'm sure you will."

"If it's even necessary," he added quietly.

"Why wouldn't it be?"

"No reason," Trip answered nonchalantly. "It says here that the house you want to buy is going to cost nine hundred and fifty thousand," he said, scanning the information on the pages.

"Yes, that's right."

"Why would you want to spend that much on a house out here? Wouldn't you be happier in the Fan? We've got a couple of branches down there. I'd be happy to call one of those managers and set you up with an appointment. If the real estate broker you're working with now doesn't cover that area, I'm sure we could help you find another one who does."

"I live there now," Liv answered calmly. "I'm moving out here."

"What broker are you working with at this point?" Trip asked, pulling a notepad from a drawer.

"A friend at one of the bigger firms."

"Which firm?"

"Does that really matter? I'd rather focus on getting this mortgage, if you don't mind."

"Okay, okay," Trip agreed, putting down his pen. He scanned the application. "You claim on here that you are going to be able to put *80* percent down. With closing costs that would amount to more than seven hundred thousand dollars."

"I'm well aware of that."

Trip's eyes flashed to another section of the application. "This says that you currently rent an apartment, so you have no existing home equity. And you've listed savings of under a hundred thousand dollars." He looked up. "How exactly do you plan on coming up with a seven-hundred-thousand-dollar down payment?"

"If you must know, a wealthy relative of mine

died recently. I'll be inheriting close to a million dollars in a few weeks."

"*A million dollars?*" he asked loudly. "Wow. How did your relative come into that kind of money?"

"None of your business," Angela cut in.

Trip gave Angela an irritated glance, then reached for a calculator and punched a few buttons. When he was finished, he grimaced.

"What's wrong?" Liv asked.

Trip smiled stiffly. "Nothing."

Liv smiled too, aware of the young lending officer's dilemma. "I make over a hundred thousand dollars a year," she pointed out, "which you can easily verify. I can handle the monthly mortgage payment, including real estate taxes."

Trip rubbed his eyes as if he were developing a migraine. "Real estate is a tricky asset to invest in, Ms. Jefferson. Are you sure you want to put the majority of your inheritance into property right now? These are uncertain economic times. Why not be safe and invest the money in a more conservative vehicle? Say, a certificate of deposit."

It was clear to Angela that the young man was trying to divert Liv away from the West End. The issue for Angela was whether he was doing it on his own — or if he'd been told to do it. "Why are you trying so hard to get my friend to reconsider purchasing this home? Is there something going on here we should know about?"

Trip stared at Angela for several moments, then shook his head, as if he were reminding himself of a certain part of his training manual. "Not at all," he answered politely, picking up his pen again and checking the rest of the application. "I notice you haven't filled out the 'Race/National Origin' box here on the bottom of page 3."

"I believe that's optional," Liv replied.

"Yes, it is," Angela agreed, "but you'll want to fill it in."

"No, I don't."

"If you don't, he will," Angela reminded Liv. "Right?" she asked, looking at Trip for confirmation.

He nodded. "That's correct."

"Oh. Well, then, let me have your pen."

"Press firmly," Angela encouraged, pointing subtly at the box marked "White, not of Hispanic origin." Liv glanced up, questioning the direction, but Angela tapped it again and Liv checked the box.

When she was finished, Trip took the application and stood up. "Someone will be back to you in a few days, Ms. Jefferson. Thanks for coming in."

A half hour later they were back downtown, almost to the Sumter Tower.

"I still can't believe that guy," Angela said angrily.

"People think the world has changed so much in the last few decades," Liv said, coasting to a stop in front of the bank's plaza. "But it really hasn't."

"You're right. It hasn't."

"Why did you have me fill in the 'white' box?" Liv asked.

"You conducted your experiment, and I'm conducting mine."

"Okay. Well, sorry about not getting anything to eat. But you wanted to get back."

Angela stepped out of the Accord, then turned and leaned back down into the car. "No problem. I'm not that hungry anyway. See you later." She closed the door and waved as Liv drove off.

"Hello, Angie."

Angela spun around at the sound of her name. Sam Reese stood a few feet away. "What are you doing here?" she asked him.

"A little family business," Sam explained, pointing over his shoulder at the bank. "Despite my father's intense dislike for your chairman, he still believes that Sumter is the safest place around for the family's liquid assets." Sam hesitated. "You look great, Angie. Not that you don't always. You do. Just extra special today." He raised one eyebrow and gave her a suggestive smile.

There was that feeling again, the one she always got when Sam looked at her that way. "Thanks."

"Got time for a cup of coffee?" he asked.

Angela shook her head. "Sorry."

"Come on. I want to talk to you about Hunter."

"Talk to me right here."

"All right. How would you like to see him again this weekend?"

Angela's heart jumped. "This weekend? But I just saw him. I mean, of course I want to, but —"

"He had a great time with you last weekend," Sam interrupted. "He was missing you last night. Crying a little."

Angela felt a lump in her throat instantly, and she looked away. "How could you arrange for me to see him, Sam? Your father would be furious."

"You let me worry about my father. The question is, do you want to see Hunter this weekend?"

"Of course I do."

"Then we'll do it. I'll make the arrangements and call you at work later in the week."

"Thank you," she whispered.

"I told you I wanted us to have a better relationship. That starts with your getting to see Hunter more. I understand that."

She looked up at him. "I can't believe you're doing this for me."

Sam shrugged. "I'm not as bad a guy as you think I am, Angie." He leaned forward, took her hand, and kissed her tenderly on the cheek. "Talk to you later."

Angela watched him walk away. He hadn't asked for anything in return. No quid pro quo. Maybe he was right. Maybe he wasn't as bad as she thought he was. Or maybe he just wasn't as bad as he used to be.

When Sam turned the corner, she hurried for the front door. She'd been gone almost two hours. Ken Booker seemed to be watching her closely these days, and he wouldn't be happy about her taking so long a lunch.

As she sat down behind her desk, Booker appeared from his office, headed toward the elevators. He gave her a long look as she answered the telephone that had been ringing as she'd walked on to the floor.

"Hello."

"Ms. Day?"

"Yes," she answered, trying to place the voice.

"This is Carter Hill."

"Oh, hello, Mr. Hill." Angela glanced around quickly, hoping no one else on the floor had heard her say his name. She didn't want people knowing that she was in direct contact with the bank's president. That could generate questions she didn't want to answer right now. "What can I do for you, sir?"

"I'd like to have a quick chat with you. If you don't mind, of course."

"Not at all. I'll come right up to the fiftieth floor. Will we be meeting in your office or Mr. Dudley's?"

Hill hesitated. "Um, let's meet in the lobby on the twenty-seventh floor instead. See you in five minutes."

The phone clicked in Angela's ear. Slowly, she

hung up the receiver, then reached for the bank directory. There were no listings for anyone on twenty-seven.

A few minutes later the elevator door opened on the twenty-seventh floor and Angela stepped cautiously out of the car, glancing back over her shoulder as the doors slid shut behind her. The lobby was dimly lit and quiet, clearly unoccupied. This couldn't be good. She turned around and reached for the elevator button.

"Hello, Angela."

"Oh, God." Angela turned around quickly as Carter Hill emerged from the shadows.

"Sorry to startle you," he apologized.

"No, that's all right."

"I realize this may seem a bit unusual."

"Well, yes, it does."

"I just didn't want Bob Dudley to see us speaking."

"Why not?" she asked suspiciously.

Hill moved closer, until they were only a few feet apart. "I wanted to follow up on something you said this morning when the three of us were together in his office."

"What was that?"

"You said that Jake Lawrence had asked if you thought I would make a good chairman."

"That's right," she agreed hesitantly. "He did."

"What did you say?"

"I told him I thought you were more of a consensus builder than Mr. Dudley. I also told him that my opinion didn't matter much because I didn't know you that well."

"But you're right, Ms. Day," Hill said quickly. "I am a consensus builder. I do care what others think." He locked eyes with her. "I'm not like Bob Dudley."

"That's obvious."

"It pains me to hear him say some of the things he says. I want you to understand that. I do not endorse his view of the world."

"What exactly do you mean, Mr. Hill?"

Hill hesitated. "Bob has certain opinions about minorities and women that simply aren't acceptable."

Angela nodded. Here was secondhand confirmation of the memo she'd found in Booker's office.

"Please communicate that to Mr. Lawrence when you talk to him next."

Her eyes narrowed. "Of course you'll know when that is, Mr. Hill, because if I don't tell you, you'll fire me. Remember?"

Hill held up his hands. "Don't blame me for that. That's Dudley making me say those things. I know how valuable an employee you are. I've checked. In fact, if I were chairman, I could see an expanded role for you here at Sumter Bank."

The tables were turning everywhere. Now she had the power. But that could change quickly, Tucker had warned her. It all hinged on Jake Lawrence. "I appreciate that."

Hill exhaled heavily, as if he'd been holding

his breath for a long time, as if it had been a terrible gamble for him to meet her this way, but now he was glad that he had. "I still think it would be a good idea for you to let me know when you're meeting with Lawrence. If you don't, Dudley will become suspicious. And he is still chairman. He could fire us both. We wouldn't want that."

"No, we wouldn't," she agreed.

Hill opened his arms wide. "There's so much we could do together, Ms. Day. I want to have that chance."

She gazed at him in disbelief. Suddenly everyone wanted to be her partner.

Angela checked her watch: 6:45. Kate Charboneau was supposed to have been here at six. As a rule, Kate was fifteen minutes late, and this was unusual — even for her. Angela motioned to the bartender and nodded down at her glass. The anticipation was too much. She needed another Chardonnay crutch.

A few minutes later Kate appeared, blonde hair streaming behind her as she trotted through the restaurant. "What a day," she said excitedly, placing her briefcase down on a stool and giving Angela a hug.

Kate was so thrilled she was shaking. That had to be a good sign. "What happened?" Angela asked.

"Sorry I'm late, but it was a great day for our team."

"What do you mean? Come on, tell me."

Kate ran her fingers through her hair, then signaled to the bartender that she wanted a glass of wine, too. "I just wish they could all be like this. Then I might even be able to enjoy the law."

"Kate!"

"We batted a thousand today, Angela. Three for three, and it all happened over the last few hours. I met with Danny Ford and his lawyer at four o'clock and Danny couldn't stop talking. His attorney kept trying to interrupt him, you know, kept trying to get him to shut up. But Danny wouldn't stop. He admitted he hadn't laid eyes on you in person before the first day of the divorce proceedings. He admitted that the whole thing about you having sex with him was a lie. Basically, he admitted he'd perjured himself."

"Chuck Reese?" Angela asked, excitement rushing through her. "Did he pay Danny cash to provide the testimony?"

"Danny wouldn't admit to that. He wouldn't go that far. He said he owed Sam's father a favor and testifying to an affair with you was how he was paying the favor off. It doesn't really matter. The important thing is that he's willing to admit to the judge that he lied. Believe me, judges do not take kindly to that."

"What else happened?"

"I spoke to the woman who had the affair with Sam. She's more resolved than ever to go forward, and — this is why I was so late — the judge in the custody case called me back just as I was leaving my office to come over here. He's willing to hear about these new developments. As I told you before, he doesn't really have to. He could refuse to hear anything. But he was open to discussing these new details. In effect, he's willing to reopen the case." Kate picked up the wineglass the bartender had just delivered and took a healthy swallow. "Nothing is ever for certain in the law, but things could be a lot worse. I know I shouldn't say this, but I think there's a good chance that at some point in the future you will be seeing a great deal more of Hunter. We've still got a few mountains to climb, and the other side will try to break our momentum when they hear about it, but, all in all, it's damn good news."

Angela clasped her hands together and brought them to her forehead. Unbelievable.

"Angela," Kate said.

"Yes?"

"What's going on here?"

"What do you mean?"

"Why am I suddenly on such a hot streak? Why are people tripping all over themselves to be so accommodating? I'm not naive enough to think that it was something momentous I said in court six years ago that has people feeling guilty all of a sudden."

The answer to Kate's question was simple. Jake Lawrence and his people had been hard at work over the last several days, influencing those who needed to be influenced. The real question for her centered around Jake's willingness to provide all of that influence. Angela still wasn't satisfied with Jake's answer that he was simply repaying her for her agreement to help him acquire Proxmire, but what was she going to do? Turn him down and lose the chance to get Hunter back? Not in a million years.

"Angela," Kate prompted when Angela hadn't responded.

"How should I know?"

Kate stared at Angela for several moments without saying anything. "Uh-huh."

"How's my big boy?" Chuck Reese stepped into Rosemary's massive second-floor playroom. It contained just about any toy a six-year-old could want.

"Hey, Pops."

"You sound a little down. Everything okay?" he asked, easing himself onto a chair that was at least three times too small for him.

"Yeah, sure," Hunter answered, tinkering with a slot car.

"Come clean, son. Tell me what's bugging you."

"Nothing." But then his tears began to flow, and he rushed into his grandfather's arms. "I miss my mom."

Chuck Reese wrapped his arms around the boy and hugged him tightly. "Don't worry," he said quietly. "Everything will be all right. I know it's hard, but I'm going to take care of your mom. Don't you worry. I promise you, I will take care of her."

CHAPTER TWELVE

Everything about Walter Fogel reminded Angela of Sally's older brother Richard. He was slim, six feet tall, and had tight curly black hair, mahogany skin, a broad face, and large brown eyes. The extensive curriculum vitae Jake Lawrence had provided in the package identified Fogel's age as forty-eight, but he seemed ten years younger. He was cool, almost detached, but she had already noticed flashes of the requisite charisma too. He could turn it on when he wanted to.

"Thank you for seeing me so quickly, Mr. Fogel," Angela began, taking a seat at the head of the Proxmire boardroom's table. They were the only ones at a table that could easily accommodate thirty people, and her voice echoed slightly in the big room. "I appreciate your cooperation."

"It's my duty as CEO to investigate all serious inquiries."

Angela had placed a call to Fogel's office Tuesday afternoon, requesting this meeting. He had responded through his executive assistant the next morning. Yesterday morning.

Wednesday. Now it was early Thursday afternoon. She had driven up from Richmond this morning with Tucker, who was waiting in the parking lot.

"I need to emphasize the word *serious*," said Fogel. "If this turns out to be an unchartered fishing expedition, Ms. Day, I will call your superior, whoever that may be, and let him know what you're doing."

"I assure you that this inquiry is quite serious, Mr. Fogel."

"You can call me Walter."

She nodded. "As long as you'll call me Angela."

He nodded back, flashing a sincere smile for the first time. "All right."

Jake Lawrence knew exactly what he was doing. She could see it in Fogel's expression. Fogel hadn't wanted to connect with her because, for all he knew, she was a Trojan horse, an intriguing emissary running cover for a powerful enemy who might wrest his company from him. But he'd been unable to hold back that smile. And she'd caught him giving her the once-over as they'd walked from the lobby to the boardroom. The short skirt hadn't hurt things. *Men could be so predictable.*

"Do you have a card, Angela?"

"Certainly." She reached into her folder, pulled one out, and placed it in front of him.

Fogel picked it up and a perplexed expression crossed his face. "Sumter Bank?" he asked skeptically. "And, forgive me for being so blunt, but just a vice president?"

"That's right. I'm a lending officer. M&A advisory isn't my specialty. And I don't usually cover this geographic area."

Fogel groaned. "Then why am I wasting my time? I told you I would call your superior if this boat didn't have a captain. I don't appreciate you —"

"I'm representing a man named Jake Lawrence." Fogel clammed up instantly. "I will assume by your reaction that you know who Mr. Lawrence is."

"I read the newspapers," he replied stoically, adjusting a cuff link.

She glanced down. The cuff links were tiny replicas of antique faucets, one designated "hot," the other "cold." "Mr. Lawrence has taken a strong interest in your company. He wants to acquire 100 percent of the stock, but he doesn't want to have to enter into a public proxy fight to do so. No press war. As you might imagine, he abhors publicity. He wants me to negotiate with you so that when the takeover is announced, it's a done deal. So that we've all agreed on a fair price up-front. So that when the transaction is announced, there's nothing left to do but sign documents."

"Why has he taken such an interest in Proxmire?"

"He thinks it's a valuable asset."

"We lost five million dollars last quarter,

301

Angela. Corporate America is spending far less on information technology now than they were a year ago. And our lenders are getting nervous." Fogel paused. "Tell me why Jake Lawrence thinks Proxmire is so valuable."

Jake had instructed her to try to keep the real agenda hidden because he was concerned that Fogel might try to sell ESP before the transaction could be completed. However, she sensed a need to quickly build the relationship, to provide Fogel with a rationale he could hang his hat on. "Mr. Lawrence thinks that your ESP Technologies subsidiary is a winner. ESP did some work for one of his portfolio companies, and the results were impressive. Mr. Lawrence is prepared to purchase all of Proxmire's shares, and, on top of that, invest additional funds into the company so that you can roll out the ESP product on an accelerated basis."

"Really?"

"Yes, and he's also prepared to enter into long-term contracts with you and your executive team in order to provide all of you with personal financial stability — that is, as long as I don't find anything out of the ordinary during the course of my due diligence."

"You won't find anything," Fogel assured her. "We're squeaky clean."

"If you say so."

"On top of the money Mr. Lawrence invests to roll out ESP, he would also have to promise to invest funds to stabilize Proxmire," Fogel said. "My board of directors will require that as a condition of closing."

Angela hadn't discussed this deal point with Jake, but he'd given her the flexibility to agree to whatever she needed to agree to to get to the due diligence stage. As long as it seemed reasonable. "I believe that can be arranged."

Fogel tapped the table. "How much money does Jake Lawrence really have, Angela?"

"Enough to buy Proxmire out of petty cash, and I don't say that out of arrogance. It's just a fact. Call your investment bankers. They'll tell you. He owns 10 percent of Sumter. That alone has cost him more than six hundred million."

Fogel nodded. "So that's the connection. The fact that he owns a big chunk of your bank."

"Yes."

"But that doesn't explain why you are the messenger. *Normal* protocol would have a senior Sumter executive representing Mr. Lawrence in a transaction like this."

"In this case, he felt I was the more appropriate individual to make contact with you."

Fogel smiled. "What Mr. Lawrence felt was that I would be more taken by you than by a silver-haired, fifty-five-year-old WASP. That I would connect with a woman who has probably endured many of the same things I have. I bet, if we were to have a more social conversation, I'd find that our backgrounds are very similar."

Angela gazed at Fogel. "Yes, you would."

His smile faded. "But I will not be a pushover.

I will drive a good deal for my shareholders."

Angela's expression toughened. "I appreciate that. And I hope you will appreciate that Jake will not be a pushover either. He doesn't want a public proxy fight, but he's prepared for one. He doesn't bluff. You can have your investment bankers check his history as far as that goes too. He will go to the mat. You can also have your bankers check on Jake's win-loss record in proxy fights." She paused for effect. "He's undefeated, Walter."

All of this information had been included in the package to provide her with ammunition for just this moment. Jake had coached her over dessert, assuring her that this moment would arise. That this would not be like negotiating a loan agreement. That this was more akin to life and death. That Fogel might seem prepared to accept the terms of surrender, but that she shouldn't be fooled. Nothing would be certain until the documents had been signed and the stock transferred.

"Mr. Lawrence is absolutely prepared to go through that fight," she continued, "but he won't appreciate the extra time, money, and mental aggravation it will cause."

"Is that a threat?"

"There would be consequences."

"That's definitely a threat."

Angela nodded. "Sure. To the extent there's a proxy fight and Jake wins, there will be no man-agement contracts. A new management team will be formed. You can be certain of that."

"I have plenty of stock options. My board has seen to that. I'll be a rich man anyway."

"The strike prices on most of your call options are way out of the money. You won't be as rich as you would like me to believe. You'll still have to work for a living. We've done the analysis." She hadn't wanted to use this next arrow, but Jake had given her permission to if she felt delivering it would push Fogel over the edge. "And you will have irritated one of the richest men in the world. A man who doesn't forget. Is that something you really want to do?"

Fogel leaned back and rubbed his neck. "Probably not," he admitted.

"I'm glad to hear you say that."

"So, let me get this straight. Mr. Lawrence is basically telling me that I'm about to get raped. But instead of fighting it, I might as well lay back and let it happen."

"First of all, I'm not wild about the analogy."

"Sorry, I didn't mean to —"

"Second, I believe that if you work with Mr. Lawrence, you will find him to be a worthy business partner."

Fogel looked down at the table. "When I first met you out in the lobby, I have to admit I wasn't sure what to think. But I guess I misjudged the situation, didn't I?"

"I just want to get a deal done," she answered quietly. She could tell by Fogel's tone that resignation was setting in, and she forced herself to suppress a smile. This was more exhilarating than she had anticipated. For the first time in her life she felt the power that Jake Lawrence felt every day. And it was intoxicating.

"Will Sumter Bank be providing debt for this transaction?" Fogel asked.

"If everything checks out."

Fogel reached for a stack of legal pads in the center of the table. "Let's talk share price, Ms. Day," he suggested.

"All right. Just before we met, Proxmire was trading at $8.75 a share. My thought is that —"

"I won't take less than fifty," Fogel interrupted, pulling his pen out and scribbling on the pad. "That's the stock's all-time high. Mr. Lawrence will have to pay at least that."

Angela shook her head. "Not even close, Mr. Fogel." She found it interesting that last names were being used again now that the conversation had gotten down to brass tacks. "That would value the company at more than a billion dollars. As you pointed out, Proxmire lost five million dollars last quarter. And your lenders are getting nervous. I'm sure cash is in short supply," she said.

"All right. Forty a share."

She was surprised Fogel hadn't immediately referred her to his investment bankers, refusing to enter into a price discussion. That would have been standard operating procedure. The fact that he was willing to negotiate conveyed to her that Proxmire was probably in worse shape than she and Jake had anticipated. That he was searching for a port in the storm. Which gave them a clear advantage. "No."

"Work with me, Ms. Day," he pleaded. "Where are you on price? Make me an offer. I'm not going to sit here and bid against myself."

"Fifteen a share."

"That's absurd!" Fogel shouted, pounding the table.

"Plus we'll offer you an employment contract with an immediate 20 percent raise, as well as a year-end bonus. And your contract will be unconditionally guaranteed by a Jake Lawrence entity unrelated to Proxmire, so that if Proxmire were to ever endure financial distress, you would be paid regardless."

"What kind of bonus are we talking?"

"A minimum of 100 percent of your salary." That would be about three hundred thousand dollars, according to the last proxy statement. A great deal to Fogel, but nothing to Lawrence. "And a maximum of 300 percent." That would be almost a million dollars. "Based upon Proxmire achieving certain preagreed financial goals, of course."

Fogel's eyes widened. "Three hundred percent? Really?"

"Yes."

"What about my other senior executives?" he asked.

"I'm not prepared to talk about their packages at this time."

Fogel held his hands up. "Oh, no, I have to have assurances that —"

"But I am prepared to guarantee both your salary and your minimum bonus for *two* years."

Fogel toyed with his cuff links again. "Make it five years," he said quietly. "And give my stockholders thirty bucks a share."

Angela shook her head. "I'll give your stockholders twenty, but I'm staying firm on the two-year contract guarantee."

"Twenty-five and four."

She hesitated, trying hard not to smile. As they were saying good-bye Sunday night, Jake had bet her that she couldn't rope Fogel for less than twenty-five a share. "Twenty-three and three," she said, "and that's my final offer."

Fogel wrote the numbers twenty-three and three down on the legal pad, stared at them for a few moments, then slowly nodded. "I'll take it to my board of directors. I don't know if they'll approve it, but I will recommend that they do."

"When will you convene that board meeting?"

"Sometime next week."

"Unacceptable, Walter. I need an answer no later than ten o'clock Monday morning."

The blindfold was lifted and he saw two armed men standing ten feet in front of him, rifles pointed directly at his chest. In the moonlight he recognized one of them as his torturer, the young one with the buzz cut who had seared the skin of his shoulder with the cigarette.

He rubbed his wrists. He'd been a prisoner for almost a week, and he'd spent most of that time hanging from a damn beam. Now he was standing in a field beside a dirt road after what had been an hour's drive in a van. The van was parked nearby — lights off, engine idling. So this was how it was going to end. He glanced around for the grave they must have been digging while he was forced to remain on the van floor after the vehicle had stopped.

"You're free to go." The one who had lifted the blindfold over his eyes from behind now moved in front of him and unlocked the silver handcuffs with a small key.

"Free?" he whispered. A moment ago he had been preparing to die. Now they were telling him he could go. Just like that.

"Yes. That's yours as well," the guard said, gesturing down.

The man followed the guard's motion. On the ground was a large briefcase. "What the hell is going on here?" But his captors were already jogging across the field back toward the van. Moments later they were inside, the doors were closed, and the vehicle was moving away down the dirt road. "What in the hell is going on?" he repeated loudly into the night, watching the red taillights disappear.

He glanced down at the briefcase again, this time warily, wondering if he should open it. It might be a bomb, designed to do away with him when they weren't around. But that made no sense. If they were going to kill him, they wouldn't leave clues. They'd shoot him in the head and bury him in a remote field, or tie cinder blocks to his ankles and drop him in the ocean ten miles offshore. A bomb and a blown-up body would give local authorities plenty to go on. And plenty of reason to call in the Feds.

He knelt down slowly beside the briefcase, groaning loudly. His entire body was sore from his having been hung by his wrists for so long. For a few moments he gazed at the dark case, then he flipped the latches and allowed it to fall open. As he surveyed the contents, he began to laugh. A deep hearty laugh that echoed among the trees.

In the moonlight he could see rows of hundred-dollar bills inside the briefcase. Stacked neatly one on top of the other. The original agreement had called for him to be paid a million dollars. As far as he could tell, it was all here.

CHAPTER THIRTEEN

"I don't understand why you have to meet with him in person," Tucker grumbled as he guided the Jeep through the darkness engulfing the isolated country lane. He had to speak loudly over the noise of the engine. "Why couldn't you just send Lawrence a written report?"

"I need to update him on my meeting in Reston this morning," Angela replied, checking the road ahead. She and Tucker were deep into the heavily wooded countryside west of Richmond, and she was well aware of how many deer were out here. Once a week, it seemed, she read in the newspaper about someone hitting one. And, since their brush with the elk in Wyoming, she had become much more aware. "Jake told me that he wants to stay close to this situation, and he wants to meet me in person in case he has questions." Lawrence had called her directly — for the first time — this morning to let her know about tonight.

"Oh, it's *Jake* now," Tucker said smugly. "A week ago the guy assaulted you in Wyoming, and now you and he are best buddies."

"What's your problem?"

"What do you mean?"

"Why do you care so much about my relationship with Jake Lawrence?"

"I don't."

"You certainly seem to."

"Nah."

She smiled over at him. "Maybe a little jealous? Mmm?"

"Not at all. I just hate the way he can manipulate people so easily because he has so much money."

"I'm not being manipulated," Angela replied firmly, her voice rising.

"Yeah, right."

"Well, I'm not."

"I'm sure that without the possibility of changing your son's custody situation, you'd be willing to go through all of this," Tucker said.

She looked out her window into the darkness, wishing Tucker didn't know about that. Wishing Lawrence hadn't relayed that information to him. "What are you complaining about, anyway? So you have to take a little drive. You're going to make money off this deal. I bet you called a stock broker right after you dropped me off in front of the Proxmire building this morning."

Tucker grinned slyly. "No way. I'd never do that."

"Uh-huh."

"Hey, I had to wait outside in the parking lot.

How would I know what company you were talking to?"

"For starters, what about the big letters on top of the building that spell Proxmire?"

"Yeah, well."

Angela punched Tucker's upper arm gently. "Come on, how many shares did you buy?"

"Who did you meet with at Proxmire?" Tucker asked quickly, ignoring her question.

"The chief executive officer."

"Really?"

Angela glanced at Tucker. She could tell he was impressed. "Yes."

"And what did you talk about?"

"Stuff."

Tucker snorted angrily. "Right. The dumb ranch hand wouldn't get it anyway."

"John, it's not —"

"Save it, Angela. I understand."

She gazed at him. He was a good man, and he'd been about the only one in this whole mess who'd dealt with her honestly right from the start. As far as she knew. "We talked about Jake buying Proxmire. How much he was willing to pay and what would happen to the CEO after the transaction. I needed to explain to the guy why Jake is so interested in Proxmire."

Tucker glanced over at her and nodded gratefully. "Big-picture issues, huh?"

"Yes."

There was a short silence. "Why *is* Mr. Lawrence so interested in Proxmire?"

"One of the company's subsidiaries has a technology Jake wants to get his hands on."

"What kind of technology?"

Angela checked her watch. It was almost ten o'clock. "You know, you ask a lot of questions."

Tucker shrugged. "I'm a curious guy. So what?"

Jake had quickly become irritated at dinner when she had conveyed that she trusted John Tucker. She wondered if Jake was right. Perhaps she did need to be more cautious. "It's a software."

"What kind of software?" Tucker pushed.

"I don't know."

Tucker rolled his eyes and groaned. "Here we go again."

"I'm serious."

"Right. You and Mr. Lawrence have a three-hour dinner to discuss this and you expect me to believe that in all of that time you don't ask what the software does? I haven't known you long, Angela, but I've known you long enough to be certain that you'd ask that question."

"I don't know what to —"

"That's all right," Tucker interrupted, holding up one hand. "Don't tell me. Hey, I'm just trying to learn, just trying to better myself. But maybe it's best that I don't know."

"It's not like that."

"Look, I don't blame you for doing a one-eighty on Mr. Lawrence. He's rich and he's good looking. He's got it all. Just don't treat me like a fourth-class citizen. Second-class is fine. Maybe even third. I understand where I fit into the grand scheme, I really do. Just don't treat me like I'm some idiot who can't grasp complicated concepts."

Angela gazed at him for a few moments in the dim light of the dashboard lights, thinking about how different he was from Sam Reese. A simple man. A man who told you what he was thinking when he was thinking it. Not a man who manipulated you. Or used you for entertainment. But they sure shared that swagger. Slowly, she slipped her hand onto Tucker's as he was shifting gears. "I'm sorry, John," she said, squeezing gently.

"Ah, forget it."

"I mean it."

"Okay."

He tried to move his hand away from hers, but she wouldn't release her grip. "Tell me more about your family. You said your father was in the military. Which service?"

"Air Force."

"Was he a pilot?"

"No. Nothing exciting like that. He was a grunt. Just a guy who pushed around spare parts and munitions."

"Where was his longest stay?"

"Alaska."

She could tell he was still irritated. "John, I grew up very poor. I would never treat anyone like they were lower class. I've been treated that

way myself, so I know how it makes you feel."
They were coming to an intersection, and it became quieter as Tucker slowed the Jeep down.
"The reason I can't talk about details of the transaction is that these things must remain confidential. I've told you that." She looked down, then back up at him. "Maybe I do want you to be a little jealous after all." For a few moments they stared at each other, then she leaned toward him, moving her hand up his arm to his face.

But he shook his head. "You have to do something for me at this point," he said quietly, reaching into a coat pocket.

"What do you mean?" She was certain he had been leaning toward her, too, but then pulled back.

Tucker held up a blindfold. "You have to wear this thing until we get to the rendezvous point with Mr. Lawrence. Colby's orders."

"Oh, come on. You can't be serious."

"Unfortunately, I am. You have your secrets, and we have ours." He motioned to her. "Turn around."

Reluctantly she turned her head, then the world was gone behind a soft fabric extending from her forehead to beneath her nose. "Not too tight," she protested.

"Sorry."

"I can't believe I'm doing this," she muttered to herself.

Tucker knotted the blindfold at the back of

her head, then slipped the Jeep into first gear, turned right at the intersection, and gunned the engine.

She gripped the Jeep's door and the console between them tightly, now unable to anticipate the turns of the narrow lane. "Hey, slow down!"

"Okay, okay." Tucker eased off the accelerator. "So, what else is going on in your world?"

Her feelings for him had come from nowhere. Suddenly she'd realized that she cared about him, but, just as she thought the spark was about to ignite and that he felt the same way, he had pulled back. Perhaps he was afraid that Jake would find out. "I'm seeing my son this weekend," she said. "My ex-husband is dropping Hunter off tomorrow evening."

"Didn't you just see Hunter last weekend?"

"Yes."

"But I thought Mr. Lawrence told me you only got to see him once a month."

"That's right."

"Then what's going on?"

"My ex seems to be developing a conscience."

"This would be the guy who brought you to Richmond in the first place, the one who didn't turn out to be your knight in shining armor."

"Yes."

"Be careful, Angela."

"Why?"

"You know why. He wants something."

Angela gripped the Jeep door tightly as they went around a sharp curve. "Maybe he does, but I can handle myself. Besides, any extra time I get to spend with Hunter is worth any risk."

Tucker slowed the Jeep down and they coasted across a narrow bridge spanning a creek. "Why aren't you seeing anyone, Angela?"

At least he was still trying. That was a good sign. "How do you know I'm not?"

"Colby gave me a full rundown on you while you were having dinner with Mr. Lawrence."

Of course they knew. They seemed to know everything. "I've been too busy lately."

"Uh-huh."

"How long until we get there?" she asked, her thoughts turning to the voice mail she'd received from Liv this morning. The man who had claimed to have information concerning Bob Dudley had called back and wanted to meet. She had tried to call Liv to warn her against going — or at least to be very careful — but hadn't been able to reach her.

"Not too long."

Five minutes later Tucker stopped at the first checkpoint. It was another bridge crossing a creek. Two armed men emerged from the woods, pointing a flashlight into Tucker's face and on Angela's blindfold. "Half a mile ahead up on your right," one of them said gruffly. "There's an entrance to a dirt road between two large oak trees. Follow that road until you arrive at the first T. A person there will direct you further."

"Right." Tucker gestured at Angela. "Can she take off the blindfold?"

"Not yet," came the sharp reply. "Now move ahead."

A half a mile down the lane Tucker identified two huge oak trees and a dirt road leading off into the forest. As he turned onto it, two more men appeared from the brush and signaled for him to stop. Once again, Angela and he were inspected, then waved ahead. Once again, Angela was not allowed to remove her blindfold. But at the first T in the road — where they were instructed to go left until they reached the next fork — she was given permission to uncover her eyes. Tucker had convinced the guards that there was no reason to impose such strict precautions at this point. Angela had been blindfolded for fifteen minutes and would never be able to find her way back here again. The guards had relented because they'd been given strict orders to treat her respectfully. She was not to be frisked this time.

"It sure is lonely back here," Angela observed as Tucker guided the Jeep along the rutted dirt path. "Kind of spooky too." Tall, bare oaks and elms rose above them into the winter night. "Why do you think this road is here? It doesn't look like a driveway."

"Probably an old logging access route," Tucker responded. "Doesn't look like it's been used in a while."

Once more, armed men appeared like specters from the woods as Angela and Tucker rounded a bend. This time there were five of them. Once more the Jeep was waved ahead after being closely inspected. Then the road opened up onto the edge of a small field, and Angela spied several other Jeeps as well as what appeared to be about fifteen to twenty men standing around the vehicles in groups of three and four, rifles slung over their shoulders. Then she recognized William Colby striding purposefully toward them in the headlights.

"Hello, Bill," Tucker called, stepping from the vehicle.

"Good evening, John." Colby nodded at the guard following him. The man moved briskly to where Tucker stood and began frisking him.

"What the hell is this?" Tucker bellowed as the guard patted him down.

"Shut up, John." Colby turned toward Angela, who had gotten out of the Jeep and come around to the driver's side. "Hello, Ms. Day. I'm sorry for the inconvenience, but we're on high alert tonight due to some intelligence I've just received. Mr. Lawrence was in New York City today and is flying in by helicopter to meet you. He should be here in no more than ten minutes."

"Thank you," she answered. Colby seemed more polite tonight. Almost civil.

He turned back toward Tucker. "I trust you didn't see anyone following you. Not like the other night," he said quietly so Angela couldn't hear.

"I didn't see anything. Look I'm pissed that

you would have your guys frisk me for Christ —"

"Enough," Colby interrupted, turning his attention to Angela. "I assume after the instructions I gave you last Sunday night, Ms. Day, you didn't tell anyone what you were doing this evening."

Before leaving the hotel, Colby had given her specific instructions not to disclose her meetings with Jake Lawrence to anyone. Just before leaving her apartment, however, she had recorded a message on Carter Hill's cell phone voice mail. "No," she answered hesitantly, "I didn't." She looked away, wondering if he could tell she was lying.

"Good." He motioned for Angela and Tucker to follow him. "Come this way."

With guards surrounding them, Angela had to jog through the knee-high underbrush along the edge of the field to keep up with Colby's quick pace. It was clear and cold, and as she hustled along, she pulled the zipper of her ski jacket up to her neck.

"Here." Colby held up his hand, then signaled for the detail of men to spread out along the edge of the field. "Shouldn't be long."

Angela watched the guards fade into the darkness ahead of them, then glanced up. There was a half-moon low on the horizon and the sky was littered with stars. "It's so quiet out here," she murmured. The wind was absolutely still.

"Here he comes," Colby announced. "Stand

by!" he shouted, then shouted it again, over his shoulder.

Tucker tapped Angela on the shoulder as she scanned the sky and pointed to the northeast. There she caught sight of flashing green lights, then heard the sound of a rotor chopping the air. Within seconds the helicopter was hovering several hundred feet above them, transforming the tranquil evening into a maelstrom. She grabbed her hair to keep it from whipping against her face, then she shielded her eyes with her other hand when the helicopter pilot turned on a spotlight that illuminated an area on the ground fifty feet in diameter as brightly as though it were day.

Angela spread her fingers slightly and peeked through them up at the helicopter as it hovered. Out of the corner of one eye, she was vaguely aware of a sparkling trail of light arcing through the darkness like a comet.

As the searing light reached the helicopter, Angela screamed, aware of what was happening. But her voice was drowned out by a violent explosion as the helicopter disintegrated in a mushrooming fireball. A wave of searing heat blew past her and she was hurled back violently into the underbrush near the trees. She was unable to see, temporarily blinded by the explosion's flash, and she curled up into a ball as fiery pieces of helicopter rained down on the field around her.

A small shard of something clipped her upper

leg and she came out of her tucked position, crawling wildly toward the trees for protection, her sight beginning to return. The trees were ghostly images ahead, illuminated by the intense fire behind. The field was ablaze and she tumbled into the trees, aware that she had to get out of the area. Aware that the fire could quickly race from the field to the woods and ignite the dead leaves covering the forest floor.

She pulled herself to her feet, then glanced back for a moment. Against the flames she spotted the silhouettes of two sprinting guards, then heard a burst of automatic gunfire over the crackling of the flames and saw the guards tumble to the ground. Mowed down by someone up in the trees to the left.

Instinctively, she staggered into the forest, guided by the intense light from the fire. As she moved forward, the light dimmed and she had to slow down for fear of plowing headlong into a tree. Then she was plunged into total darkness, and she was feeling her way along, hands extended in front of her. Slowly, her eyesight improved, but her progress was still slow. And she was certain she could hear footsteps behind her, crashing through the leaves.

She forged ahead, dodging trees that loomed out of the darkness. And then she was down, tumbling over and over until she reached the bottom of a steep ravine and splashed into a creek. She was up instantly, wiping leaves, twigs, and moss from her face and her soaking hair as she stood thigh-deep in water. She had to keep moving. She knew that.

She stepped forward and slipped off an unseen ledge in the stream bed, totally submerged for a moment until she could fight her way back to the surface of the freezing water, the breath ripped from her lungs by the intense cold. Despite her soggy clothes, she was able to make her way to the far bank. She glanced up the ravine, decided it was too steep to climb, and moved further downstream. Finally, she found a spot that seemed scalable, grabbed a thick vine tightly with both hands, and began pulling herself up.

As Angela made it close to the top of the embankment, she heard voices. Quick, muffled commands from the other side of the ravine. And then there was a beam of light playing on the trees to her left. Moving toward the spot where she would emerge from the ravine. She clawed at the soft earth, frantically trying to pull herself the last few feet to the top, but the soil was unstable and gave way. She caught herself on a root, then glanced over her left shoulder and saw the spotlight being aimed down into the stream and quickly scanning the water. There were several dark forms on top of the ravine on the other side. Friends or foes? No way to tell, and finding out was not a risk she was prepared to take right now.

With all her strength, Angela lifted herself the rest of the way up the embankment, tumbled into the woods, then quickly scrambled behind the base of a thick tree, aware that she'd made a good deal of noise crawling through the leaves. Instantly, the light was streaming past her on all sides, reflecting off the trees. She glanced up and saw the animal bearing down on her. It seemed monstrous, but somehow she kept herself from screaming as the massive buck darted past and along the top of the ravine, crashing away into the darkness. Then the light was pointed in another direction, and she heard the people moving off. She waited for several moments, shivering in her wet clothes, then made it to her feet with the help of the tree and jogged deeper into the woods.

Several hundred yards farther into the forest, Angela turned right and walked for a quarter of a mile along the top of a ridge. As best she could tell, she was headed away from the logging road she and Tucker had come in on. Her plan was simple. Keep moving until she reached civilization. If she came upon one of the narrow roads back here, she wouldn't flag down a passing car. There could be no telling who they were or who they represented. Jake Lawrence hadn't been paranoid at all. He was a hunted man. Even his army hadn't been able to protect him this time. No, she would keep going until she reached a major road or a residence. She had learned her lesson.

Angela stopped, turning instantly into a statue. There was a voice in the night. A single speaker, words coming quickly, demands being made. Then another voice in answer. A voice she recognized. As she lowered herself to her hands and knees and began to crawl along the forest floor, she felt her heart pounding. The voices she had heard were close. No more than fifty feet ahead and slightly down the slope to her left. Every sound she made seemed loud, every leaf that crunched beneath her palm and every twig that snapped under her knee amplified by the stillness of the woods. But she kept going.

Her eyes had now become accustomed to the darkness and she could see two people in a small clearing. One man — the one with a rifle — standing behind another who was kneeling, hands clasped behind his head. She was only twenty feet away and they were unaware of her presence. As she focused on the rifle, her instinct was to run, to turn and get away as fast as she could. But that was not an option.

"Tell me!" the man holding the rifle demanded. "I know you have important information."

"You don't know anything," Tucker replied calmly, despite the barrel of the rifle pressed roughly to the base of his neck.

Angela's hand came to rest on a thick branch a foot and a half long.

"Tell me about the network! Tell me how it works. Give me details."

"Piss off."

She was at the edge of the clearing now, just ten feet behind the man pointing the rifle at Tucker.

"I'll kill you right here."

"That wouldn't do you much good."

Angela took a deep breath, tightened her grip on the branch, and rushed from her hiding place, aiming for the man's head. A step before she reached him, he turned. She smacked his forehead with the piece of wood, and he toppled to the ground.

Tucker was on him like a cat, grabbing the rifle and slamming the butt end of it directly into one eye. The man went limp, unconscious.

Tucker stood up, rifle in hand, breathing heavily, staring at Angela. As he gazed at her, he slowly brought the gun down until the barrel was pointed at her chest.

She took a step back, struck by the eerie feeling that she had just made a horrible mistake, that somehow she had misjudged everything, that Lawrence had been right, that in her attempt to help someone she thought was her friend, she had sealed her own fate instead.

Then Tucker smiled. "I'm not a very religious man, but I'll believe in angels from now on." He lowered the rifle. "When your parents decided on a name, they sure picked the right one." He moved to where she stood and took her hand. "Come on. Let's get your little tattooed ass out of here."

CHAPTER FOURTEEN

Colby tapped gently. "Sir?"

"Come in."

He pushed open the door and noticed right away that Jake Lawrence was not sitting in front of the farmhouse window, and that the three-way bulb of the lamp on the desk was illuminated at its lowest setting. "It's time to go. We've got to get you out of here."

When the helicopter carrying Lawrence's decoy had exploded in the field ten miles from the farmhouse, Colby's men had been smuggling the real McCoy to the nest in a rusting, twenty-year-old Torino station wagon. Now it had been two hours since the explosion and Colby was growing increasingly uncomfortable about having Lawrence so close to the hot zone.

"Any word on Angela Day?"

Colby had delivered the latest update ten minutes ago. "Nothing yet."

"Who did this, William?" Lawrence demanded, teeth gritted.

"We don't know yet. But believe me, we'll find out."

"You better."

"The investigation is already under way. We are using every means at our disposal to identify the perpetrator."

Lawrence looked up. "You must locate Angela Day, too."

"We will," Colby said. "One way or the other."

"What does that mean?"

"She may be dead, sir. We have to consider that possibility."

"But you said she was right next to you when the explosion occurred. You're okay."

"Yes, I am."

"Well?"

"Well, she may have died after the explosion. Two of my men were killed by sniper fire."

"But it was pitch-dark!"

"The light from the fire was intense for several minutes after the explosion. Or the enemy may have had night-vision capability."

Lawrence let out a quick, frustrated breath. "I don't understand how individuals armed with surface-to-air missiles could have gotten so close with all of your men around. Don't you sweep the area before I arrive?"

"Of course. Several times."

"Then how in the —"

"I didn't want to have to tell you this."

"Tell me what?"

"That there may have been help from the inside."

Lawrence frowned. "Go on."

"You'll remember that I told you about a man

we apprehended who was following Angela Day. We took him down one evening on a lawn across from her apartment in Richmond."

"Yes." Lawrence's eyes narrowed. "And that man has escaped. You told me that."

"Right. But what I haven't told you is that the guard who was on duty at the time the prisoner escaped is missing."

"You think he helped the prisoner?"

"Yes. And this guard was in the group that thought you were actually coming in by helicopter."

"You're right. That's not good."

"And that's not all."

"My God, what else is there?"

"I believe John Tucker may know something about the prisoner's escape as well."

"What!" Lawrence rose from his seat and moved to where Colby stood. "John Tucker?" he asked incredulously.

"Yes. I believe Tucker may have been involved in the incident on the mountain in Wyoming, and that he may know a great deal about what happened this evening, too. I suspect that John Tucker may have convinced a small cadre of my men to become soldiers of fortune, so to speak. I think Tucker may have been approached by people who don't appreciate the causes you involve yourself in. People who want to see you dead," he said bluntly.

"Angela Day trusts him. Without him close to her I may lose her participation."

Colby cleared his throat. "If you don't mind me asking, sir, participation in what?"

Lawrence gazed silently ahead.

At first, Colby had assumed that Angela Day was simply a physical distraction. Now he knew that wasn't true. But it irritated the hell out of him not to know what was really going on. "Sir?"

"A matter of great importance."

"Sir, I feel in this case that I must have full disclosure if I'm expected to protect you. I insist that you tell me what's really going on here. Otherwise, there could be terrible consequences."

Lawrence shook his head. "I can't tell you any more at this time."

"Well," Colby said after a short pause, "perhaps it's a moot point."

"Tucker hasn't surfaced either?" Lawrence asked, aware of what Colby was implying.

"No."

"Were you able to apprehend any of the men who were involved in the attack on the helicopter?"

"Just one, and he isn't talking."

"But you have ways of getting what you want, William."

Colby nodded. "I do, sir. And I will use those ways." He hesitated. "But the man we've apprehended may not really know much. If the people responsible for tonight's attack are as sophisticated as I believe, the foot soldiers will not be privy to any important information. They may not know who they're really fighting for. In fact, they may have been given misinformation to throw us off track."

"I understand."

Colby placed a hand on Lawrence's shoulder. It was the first time he had ever done so, and he saw the surprise in the other man's expression. "Don't worry, Mr. Lawrence. You'll be fine."

Lawrence nodded. "I trust you, William." He let out a heavy sigh. "Is there any possibility that Angela Day was somehow involved in what happened tonight?"

Colby stared at Lawrence evenly. "I think that's a very real possibility."

It was after two o'clock in the morning, and Angela stood on the landing of her apartment. She and Tucker had hiked through the woods until they'd reached a house at the edge of a field. There they had convinced the elderly couple inside to allow them to dry off and warm up, and to call a cab — neither Angela nor Tucker could get a signal on their cell phones. The cab had taken almost an hour to arrive, and the drive to Richmond had taken another hour.

"Thanks for taking care of the fare."

"No problem," Tucker answered. "It's the least I can do for the woman who saved my life."

"Jake Lawrence is dead," she said quietly.

"Yes."

"That was one of the most awful things I've ever seen."

"Terrible."

"What will happen?"

Tucker shrugged. "I don't know." He looked into her eyes. "I know you were counting on Mr. Lawrence to help you get your son back."

Angela stepped forward, put her arms around Tucker's neck, and hugged him. It felt wonderful when he hugged her back.

"It'll be all right, Angela."

"What was that man talking about?" she whispered, closing her eyes as Tucker moved his hands beneath her ski jacket and caressed her back through her sweater.

"Which man?"

"The one who was holding you captive when I found you."

"What do you mean, what was he talking about?" Tucker asked, leaning back so he could look into her eyes.

"He wanted you to tell him about the 'network.'"

"I have no idea what that was about, Angela. Maybe it was a case of mistaken identity. Or, more likely, he was fishing for something. Look, there are many secrets in the Lawrence world. People assume someone like me knows something important, but it isn't true. When it comes down to it, I really am just a ranch hand." He shook his head sadly. "I guess there'll be a lot fewer secrets in the Lawrence world now."

Angela gazed up at him in the moonlight. He was right. She *had* saved his life. She had acted on instinct. If she'd thought about it at all, she might have hesitated and lost her courage. It was as if something had been guiding her. Communicating to her silently that she had to save this man.

She curled one hand around the back of his neck, and pulled him close. "Kiss me, John."

CHAPTER FIFTEEN

"What's this all about?" Angela demanded, glancing furtively around the parking garage's third level. "Why did you have me walk all the way over here?" she asked, irritated that she'd been called away from the bank so late on a Friday afternoon.

"Because I didn't figure you'd be able to talk from your desk," Liv explained. "And I wanted you to see the exact spot where I met my contact."

"Contact?"

Liv rolled her eyes. As if Angela ought to know instantly what she was talking about. "A few days ago I got an anonymous call from a man who claimed to have sensitive information about Bob Dudley. I told you, remember?"

That sounded familiar, but she was almost too exhausted to think. She'd caught a couple of hours of sleep last night, but had forced herself to get into the bank as close to her usual time as possible. Booker seemed to be monitoring her very closely.

"Information that would help bring Dudley down," Liv prompted impatiently.

"Oh, right," Angela said, remembering. "You told me that Monday on our way out to the West End. The afternoon you submitted that phony mortgage application."

"Which, by the way, I was turned down for."

Incredible, thought Angela. That application should have been approved very quickly. "Really?"

"Yes. Maybe I should have checked the 'Black' box after all."

"No. I guarantee you that kid altered it the minute we left. I told you —"

"Look, it doesn't matter," Liv interrupted. "I want you to hear what this guy relayed to me last night."

"Okay. But first of all, tell me how he contacted you."

"He called me a few minutes after I got home from work last night."

"But didn't you say you were going to have your number changed again?"

"Yes, and the phone company had changed it by Tuesday evening. Somehow he got the new number."

"That's creepy, Liv. Like I said before, I really think you ought to call the police."

Liv shook her head. "No. He's on our side."

"How can you be so sure?"

"Like I told you, I met with him right here last night. He hates Dudley as much as I do. I can assure you of that."

"Well, who was he?"

"He claimed he was a Sumter Bank employee," Liv replied, grinning, "but he looked more like a cowboy than a bank employee."

Angela froze. "A cowboy?"

"Yeah. He was wearing boots, jeans, and this jacket with a wool collar. Like he was right off the range or something."

"Did he have a mustache?" Angela asked quietly, her mouth suddenly bone-dry.

"Yeah, I think so. Honestly, I couldn't see much of his face. He had his hat pulled down low. Why do you ask?"

"No reason." John Tucker. It had to have been him. But why? "What time did you meet this guy?"

"Around 8:30."

"How long were you with him?"

"Five minutes, tops. I could tell he was uneasy. Like he thought we were being watched. He kept looking around. One time I turned my head, and he had just kind of melted into the shadows. That was it."

At that time of the evening it would take no more than fifteen minutes to get from here to her apartment in the Fan, Angela realized. If Tucker had left Liv by 8:35, he would have had plenty of time to get to her apartment by nine to take her to meet Jake Lawrence.

"What did the guy say?"

Liv looked around to make certain they were alone. "He told me that Dudley's family was originally from Birmingham, Alabama, and that

337

they have been involved in Klan activity down there for a hundred years. He also said he's pretty sure Dudley himself is a member."

Angela gazed steadily at Liv's round face. "Bob Dudley is originally from Birmingham, Alabama?"

"That's what this guy said."

That was interesting. A piece of information she would make certain to follow up on. "And how exactly did he know that Dudley's family had been involved with the Klan for so long? And that Dudley was a member now?"

Liv shrugged. "I asked him about that. All he would say was that he had done a great deal of research on his own and that was what he had found. He said it sickened him to think that the man who ran Sumter Bank could be a Klansman, and that he wanted other employees, people in Richmond, and the rest of the world to know about it. That was why he had contacted me. Said he didn't have any way to get the information out, but he knew that I could because I was a reporter."

"You can't be prepared to print something like that on the word of a man you've met once on the third level of a parking garage under the cover of darkness."

"Of course I'm not," Liv snapped.

"But you'd love to."

"Whose side are you on?"

"How do you intend to confirm what he said?" Angela wanted to know, ignoring Liv's angry retort. "Are you going to put on a white sheet and follow him to the next meeting?"

"Maybe I won't have to," Liv replied ominously.

"Why not?"

"The guy gave me some other information as well. Information that might be just as damaging."

"What?"

A satisfied smile spread across Liv's face. "He claimed Dudley was defrauding Sumter Bank. Claimed Dudley was siphoning off millions of depositor dollars into a little company on the side, a company that was supposed to be performing some kind of operational consulting work for Sumter, but was really just a shell. A company Dudley owns. Talk about a conflict of interest," Liv scoffed. "Even if the company was acting in good faith. But the guy said that the whole thing was really a scam. He claimed Dudley himself approved the contract for the work six months ago, but nothing's been generated except some good-for-nothing three-page report. More than ten million dollars has walked out the door straight into Dudley's pockets."

"How does your contact know all this?" Angela asked. The whole thing seemed too easy. "I bet he wouldn't tell you how he got his information about this accusation either."

"Wrong. He said he saw confirmations of outbound wire transfers. He also said he overheard someone very senior at the bank talking about how Dudley controls the consulting company. I think he used the term 'ExecCom.' And he believes that when someone digs deep enough they'll find that the ten million bucks ultimately found its way into a Dudley account. I believe him," Liv declared firmly. "The fact that Dudley approved the contracts and that the company is based in Birmingham is too coincidental. Well, the guy claimed the company was based in Birmingham, anyhow. I haven't had time to follow up yet."

Angela checked her watch. It was after four. Sam was coming by the apartment at six to drop Hunter off for the weekend, and she needed to pick up a couple of things before Hunter arrived. But she needed to go back to the bank, too. There wasn't much time if she was going to be home before Sam and Hunter arrived. "It's still not enough to print any kind of story on."

"I know that," Liv agreed. "There's a lot of work to do before I can approach my editor, and I need your help."

"What kind of help?" Angela asked suspiciously.

"Your enthusiasm is really blowing me away."

"Hey, Liv, I've got other concerns here. What do you think Bob Dudley would do if he found out I was helping you investigate him for fraud?"

"How would he find out?"

Liv didn't know about Jake Lawrence's involvement in the custody battle for Hunter, or how Angela felt as if someone was constantly watching her now. There wasn't any reason to burden Liv with the information in case these people turned out to be cold-blooded. Then it would be better if Liv didn't know. "Bob Dudley is a powerful man, Liv. Don't underestimate him."

"Now you're really sounding paranoid."

"Maybe I have a right to."

Liv grabbed Angela's hands. "Look, if we don't do everything possible to bring down Bob Dudley and expose him for the racist monster he is, the cycle will never be broken. We have to fight him now, because if we don't, there'll be another man just like him when he's gone. Like that little punk who turned down my mortgage application." She took a deep breath. "You know that guy's reaction to me the other day was a result of a directive from the very top of the Sumter organization. He wasn't acting on his own. Somebody told him to keep people like me out of the West End. That's what the memo you found was all about. Why do you think I took you all the way out there to the West End on Monday? I wanted you to see the directive in action."

Angela clenched her jaw. What Liv was saying made sense. "All right," she said quietly. "What do you need from me?"

Liv's expression softened. "I need you to track

341

down the wire transfers going from Sumter to the shell company Dudley has set up. Confirm what the guy told me."

"That'll be difficult without knowing the name of the company. Which I bet your contact didn't tell you because he doesn't really know —"

"Strategy Partners."

Angela stopped short.

"Strategy Partners," Liv repeated. "In Birmingham, Alabama. Track the money transfers and confirm that Bob Dudley controls the company. Please do that for me, Angela."

Fifteen minutes later Angela was back at her desk, tapping commands on her keyboard as she zipped along the Internet. It was almost 4:30, and she needed to get going if she was to have everything ready for Hunter. But she had to confirm several things before leaving. First, that there was a firm named Strategy Partners in Birmingham, Alabama. Second, that Bob Dudley's family was from Birmingham. And, third, that Jake Lawrence had lied to her about his family originally being from Atlanta. That they too originally hailed from Birmingham.

She executed several more commands, closing in on her objective, smiling to herself as images flashed across the screen. In five minutes' time she'd confirmed the answers to her first two questions, and now she was closing in on the answer to the Jake Lawrence question. She clicked "go" and waited.

"Hello, Angela."

Her eyes flashed up from the screen. Ken Booker stood in front of her, arms folded across his chest. Her eyes flickered back to the screen as the information she had been searching for appeared.

"What are you working on so diligently?"

"Just some research," she answered evasively.

"Fascinated by Jake Lawrence, aren't you?" Booker leaned forward over her desk and chuckled. "The information on your screen indicates that his family is originally from Birmingham." Booker's eyes narrowed as he glared down at her. "Isn't that interesting?"

She glared back, tempted to ask him again why he'd already derailed her promotion twice. According to Jake Lawrence, anyway. Tempted to grill him on the memo she'd found in his office. To ask him what he knew of it, and how involved he was in Bob Dudley's plan to segregate the city, and perhaps do more than that. But now wasn't the time. "Yes, it is interesting," she agreed, wondering why Carter Hill hadn't contacted her today.

6:45. Sam was late. And Sam was never late.

Maybe he wasn't coming. Maybe all of his suggestions about the two of them developing a better relationship for Hunter's sake weren't so well-intentioned after all. Perhaps he had simply been raising her hopes just to dash them once again. She sighed dejectedly. Now that she could no longer pin her hopes on Jake Lawrence, she needed Sam's help if she was going to get to see Hunter more.

The box lay on Hunter's bed, wrapped in colorful paper. Inside was a toy truck he had mentioned he wanted last weekend. Somehow Chuck Reese hadn't figured out that Hunter wanted it, and she was planning to preempt him and savor a tiny but sweet victory. Now the prospects of enjoying that victory seemed to be slipping away.

The knock on the apartment door startled her. Her heart rose to her throat as she trotted to the door, opened it, and knelt down. And then Hunter was in her arms, hugging her neck tightly and kissing her cheeks over and over.

"Hi, Mom!"

"Hi, sweetheart." She glanced up over his shoulder. Sam stood in her doorway, smiling down at her. "Hello, Sam."

"Hello, Angie. Sorry I'm late. I had to wait for the right moment to get out of the house, if you get my drift."

She nodded, appreciating that Sam was willing to take such a risk. "There's something in the bedroom for you, Hunter," she whispered in the young boy's ear.

"All right!" he shouted, releasing his grip on her and sprinting toward the bedroom.

"I really appreciate you doing this, Sam," she said, standing up. "I'm sure there's going to be hell to pay when your father realizes what you've done."

"I'm sure you're right, but I don't really care. I'm a big boy. I can handle him. You'd be proud of me these days." Sam gestured toward the bedroom. "Besides, Hunter needs to see you more. No two ways about it."

"I know," she murmured.

Sam pulled her close. "I wouldn't mind seeing you a bit more myself, Angie."

His arms were strong and reassuring, and she allowed herself to hug him back. This was dangerous. She'd trusted him once, and there was no reason to think he had changed except that he had followed through on his promise of this weekend.

Her thoughts slipped back to last night and John Tucker on the landing outside her door. How he had refused to kiss her just as their lips were about to meet. She wondered to herself why what came so easily with Sam was so difficult with John.

"Hey, thanks, Mom!"

Angela took a step back from Sam as Hunter appeared in the doorway. But they were still holding hands and she could see in Hunter's eyes that the boy approved. "Is it what you wanted?" she asked.

"Oh yeah. It's great."

Then he was gone, back into his room, and she could hear him playing with the new toy.

"Nice going, Angie. Big hit."

She glanced up at Sam. His hand was so warm. "Thanks." As she gazed at him he brought his fingers to her face, looked deeply into her eyes for a few moments, then leaned forward. But at the last moment she turned her head to the side and he was forced to kiss her cheek. Just as John had done to her. But why? Why had John done that? Even now, with Jake Lawrence gone?

"Well," Sam said quietly, straightening up, "I was hoping for a little more than that."

"Is that why you brought Hunter here this weekend?" she asked quietly. "For that?"

"No. The visit is for real. I do believe he needs to see you more. I was just hoping you might believe that I need to see you more, too."

"I can't, Sam. Not while you're married."

He brought one of her hands to his lips and kissed it gently. "And if I weren't?"

"I suppose I might feel differently."

"How different?"

He still had that amazing hold over her. Even after all this time and all the terrible things he had done. "You know I've never been able to resist you."

"You just did."

She nodded. "Yes, I suppose I did, didn't I?"

"Hunter," Sam called. "Dad's got to get going. Come out and say good-bye." The boy appeared instantly, scampered to where Sam stood, hugged him tightly, then tore back to his room. "That was quick." Sam chuckled as he headed toward the door.

"Now you know how I feel," Angela pointed out.

"What do you mean?"

"That's how weekends with him are for me. I feel like I see him for a few seconds, then he's gone again."

Sam turned back when he reached the door. "I understand, and we're going to work on that."

"Thanks." She stood in front of him, hands clasped together. "You know I really appreciate it."

"Were you serious?" he asked.

"About what?"

"If I weren't married, would you consider renewing our relationship?"

"I thought we already had a relationship."

"You know what I mean," he said.

"I can't guarantee anything, Sam. Besides, your father would have a —"

"Screw my father, Angie. I'm not going to let him run my life again. I'm not going to let him tell me who I can be with and who I can't." He hesitated. "I can't get you out of my head. I want you back."

His strong arms slipped around her and then their bodies were pressed together. He sounded so sincere, and the words were words she had wanted to hear for so long. "You don't love Caroline?" she whispered.

"You mean the ice queen?"

Then Sam's lips were on her neck, and she could feel electricity race through her. But, just as quickly as it had come, it faded. Something that had never happened before. All she could think about was John Tucker, and why he had refused her twice. She had seen in his eyes that he wanted to kiss her, but for some reason he'd held back.

"Mom."

Angela pulled back, startled by the sound of Hunter's voice. "Yes, honey?"

"I'm kinda hungry. Do you have anything to eat?"

She slipped from Sam's arms. "How does a cheeseburger sound?"

"Yes!" Hunter pumped his fist several times.

Angela looked back at Sam, who had one foot out the door.

"I think I'd better get going," he said. "I'll be back Sunday at 7:00 to pick Hunter up." He glanced around. "Nice place you've got here." And then he was gone.

For several moments Angela gazed at the door, then she headed to the kitchen to put the burgers on. As she was taking out plates from the cupboard she heard a knock at the door, and she smiled to herself. Sam. It was the hopeless romantic in him coming out. He had been so certain that she was going to give him that kiss, and he couldn't leave without it. Well, he was going to be disappointed.

"Look, I —" Angela stopped short as she

opened the door. John Tucker stood on the landing.

"Hello, Angela."

"John." She checked back over her shoulder. Hunter was in his room. "Do you want to come in?"

"No. I just wanted to give you a piece of information I didn't think ought to be delivered over the phone."

Angela's ears perked up. "What?"

"William Colby had us all fooled last night."

"I don't understand."

"That wasn't Jake Lawrence in the helicopter. It was a decoy. Lawrence is alive." Tucker shook his head. "I don't like Bill much, but he knows what he's doing when it comes to protecting Lawrence."

Angela brought both hands to her mouth, a surge of adrenaline rushing through her body. "My God."

"Yes. And the message from Mr. Lawrence is that you are to keep pushing ahead." Tucker shrugged. "Whatever that means. I suppose it has something to do with Proxmire."

"Tell him that I will," she replied, still shocked by the news. "Are you sure you don't want to come in?"

"No, I can't," he said, turning away toward the steps. "I gotta go."

"John."

"Yeah?" He turned back, one hand on the railing. "What is it?"

"Given what you've told me, I'm going to need to go back up to northern Virginia on Monday afternoon to meet with Walter Fogel. I want you to go with me."

He smiled, then bowed. "At your service, Ms. Day."

"One more thing." She kept thinking about Liv's description of the person who had met her in the parking garage and passed on the incriminating information on Bob Dudley. The cowboy.

"Yes?"

"Do you know who Liv Jefferson is?"

"Nope," he answered. "Never heard of her."

"You sure?"

"Absolutely. Who is she?"

"A newspaper reporter here in Richmond. Short black woman who covers the business beat for the *Trib*."

"Like I said, never heard of her. I don't read the *Richmond Trib* real often, you know?"

"Right," she agreed slowly.

"Doesn't sound like you're convinced." Tucker winked. "Why are you looking at me like I'm KGB or something?"

"I'm not," she answered, her voice serious.

"That was a joke, Angela," Tucker said. "You were supposed to laugh."

"Uh-huh."

"Guess you aren't in a very good mood tonight. Kind of surprising too."

"Why?"

"You got your son in there."

350

"How did you know that?" she asked, moving out onto the landing.

"I saw your ex-husband walking up the stairs with the boy. I waited until he was gone so as not to disturb you. Be careful there, Angela," Tucker warned, descending the first step. "Never trust an ex."

"John!"

He turned around once more. "Yes?"

It was a question that had troubled her all day. Something she had remembered Tucker saying last night. "Last night you made a comment to me after I saved you."

"Yeah? What was that?"

"Something about a tattoo."

Tucker stared back at her intently. "So?" he asked after a few moments, as if he didn't even remember saying it.

Perhaps someone had been behind the mirror in her bathroom at the lodge. Perhaps that someone had gotten a very nice view of her. Someone like John Tucker. He had claimed that the lodge manager didn't let anybody up past the first floor. Perhaps that was a lie. "How did you know?"

"Know what?"

"That I have a tattoo there."

He smiled. "Lucky guess."

"John!"

Tucker rolled his eyes. "Look, when we went into that cave after whoever it was shot at us up on the mountain, we both bent down and leaned back against the wall. I happened to glance over and I saw the top of a little butterfly on your hip. Your jacket and shirt were riding up, and I guess those jeans we got you were a little big." He hesitated. "Satisfied?"

CHAPTER SIXTEEN

"So, where do we stand?" Angela asked.

It was early Monday morning. Hunter was back at Rosemary, and she and Walter Fogel were back in the Proxmire boardroom.

"Looks to me as if you and your board of directors met over the weekend," she continued when Fogel didn't answer right away. Two trash cans on one side of the room were stuffed with pizza boxes and Styrofoam cups, and the stack of legal pads in the middle of the long table was half as high as it had been when she and Fogel had met last week. "What did you decide?"

"We were here until 2:00 this morning, and four out of five of us voted to proceed with your offer," Fogel answered wearily.

Elation surged through Angela. One step closer. "Good. I assume, like most other boards, majority rules."

"Unfortunately not," Fogel informed her, rubbing his bloodshot eyes. "Not with respect to this decision anyway."

Angela's elation faded as quickly as it had jumped. "What do you mean?" Angela had confidently predicted to Tucker this morning that they would have a deal by noon.

"According to Proxmire's bylaws, a decision by the board of directors to sell the company must be unanimous. One member abstained last night. At this time, we can't move forward."

"Abstained?"

"Yes. He didn't vote *against* your offer, but he didn't vote *for* it either. And as long as he doesn't vote for the sale of the company, we cannot embrace the offer."

"Why did he abstain?"

"He wanted more information," Fogel explained, letting out a long, frustrated breath. "Translated, he wants more money than what you are offering."

"He won't get it, Walter," she assured him adamantly. "If you're playing good cop, bad cop with me, it won't work."

Fogel held up both hands. "That's not what's going on here, Angela, I promise."

She wasn't convinced. "I noticed in Proxmire's SEC filings that the lead bank in your $200 million revolving credit agreement is the First National Bank of North Carolina." She could smell a rat and she was going to quickly squash this attempt to squeeze more money out of Lawrence quickly. "I called a colleague of mine down there on Friday morning. She's a lending officer for First National in Charlotte, and I've known her for several years. She did some digging around and found out that the senior credit people at First are very nervous about Proxmire's ability to remain solvent," she said sternly. "They are close to putting Proxmire into default on the loan agreement for multiple covenant violations, and could force you into Chapter 11. Your board member would have egg all over his face at that point. Not to mention a lawsuit on his hands that would surely exceed the limits of your directors and officers' insurance policy," she added.

"Relax," Fogel pleaded. "I agree that what you are offering is fair. And believe me, I want my employment contract."

"Then let's call up your board member right now," Angela suggested, pointing at the speaker phone in the middle of the table. "He needs to do the right thing. I don't have time to screw around."

"You're quite a little pit bull, Ms. Day."

"I'll take that as a compliment, but let's cut the polite but useless chitchat and get on with the deal. Let's call this guy."

"I don't think calling him would do much good right now. He was dead set against the deal last night, despite the fact that we did our best to convince him to vote with us. We went back and forth for hours, but he wouldn't budge." Fogel paused. "You are exactly right about our cash situation, Ms. Day. We're almost out."

"Did you tell him that?"

"Several times. But he believes he can get a higher price. He said he was going to approach some people he thought might give us that better offer."

"Let me remind you, Walter, that if Jake Lawrence has to announce a hostile tender offer for Proxmire, you and your management team won't get contracts when he wins. You'll be out in the cold." Angela's anger was building. She'd been so sure that Proxmire was in the bag. Now Fogel was screwing up a smooth transaction. Screwing up Danny Ford's desire to talk, the woman's agreement to testify to her affair with Sam, and the judge's willingness to reopen the custody proceedings. "I'm warning you, Walter."

"Easy. I think I may have a solution."

"What?"

"You told me last week that you needed some time to perform your due diligence work, specifically at ESP."

"Yes."

"All right, then. Get started on it and let me deal with my board member. By the time you're done, I think I can have him in line. I've arranged for you to have full access to all the books and records at ESP as soon as you want to start. Hell, you can go out there straight from here, if you'd like. ESP is out in Chantilly, which is only a few miles west of here."

That sounded better. It would take several days of combing through ESP's records before she could tell Jake she was confident there were no skeletons in the closet. At least none that would get in the way of an initial public offering of ESP. "Which board member is giving me heartburn, Walter?" She had reviewed each board member's background — available in Proxmire's annual 10-K report to the SEC.

"A man named Dennis Wolfe. He's with an investment company called Sage Capital. We bought ESP from Sage," Fogel explained. "In addition to the Proxmire shares we gave Sage as consideration for ESP, we also gave them a seat on our board. Dennis is their representative."

"Sage Capital is based in downtown D.C., right?"

"Yes."

According to Proxmire's 10-K, Dennis Wolfe had been a managing director at Sumter Bank until six years ago. Until just before she'd taken her job at Sumter. "Sage owns almost 20 percent of Proxmire as a result of the shares you issued to purchase ESP."

"About that."

"Do you think Wolfe sincerely believes he can get a higher price for Proxmire, or does he have other motivations?"

A curious expression came to Fogel's face. "I'm not sure what you mean. What other motivation could he have?"

Angela's eyes narrowed. Wolfe's Sumter connection was too coincidental. "I don't know," she admitted, standing up. "I'll be going out to ESP now."

"Okay," Fogel agreed, standing as well.

"There's something I need you to do, Walter."

"What?"

"Keep my visit to ESP very quiet. Don't tell anyone other than staff people here at Proxmire and at ESP who absolutely have to know that I am going out there. Do you understand?"

"Yes."

Minutes later Angela was in the car with John Tucker. "Back to Richmond?" he asked, guiding the car toward the parking lot exit.

"No. Head west on the Dulles Toll Road. We're going to Chantilly."

"Okay." Tucker glanced over. "You seem upset. Everything okay?"

Angela grimaced. "I hope you didn't put your life savings into Proxmire stock."

"Why?" he asked nervously.

"I don't know if we have a deal or not," she explained, pulling her cell phone from her purse and turning it on. "And if there isn't a deal, Proxmire isn't going to be worth much."

"What happened?"

The cell phone beeped as the signal strengthened, indicating that Angela had a new voice mail message. She entered her code. "One of Proxmire's board members doesn't like the deal."

"That can't be good."

"It isn't," she agreed, listening to the message. It was from Liv, pleading with Angela to call her as soon as possible. Angela scrolled through her speed-dial numbers and selected Liv's office number. "It isn't good at all."

"Hello," came the quick reply at the other end of the line.

"Liv, it's Angela. You called."

"Yes," Liv said loudly, her voice intensifying when she realized it was Angela. "Thanks for calling me back."

"What's wrong?" Angela asked, glancing over at Tucker, who seemed to be trying too hard to convince her he wasn't listening.

"I found out this morning that the *Herald* is working on the Dudley story as well," Liv said excitedly. The *Herald* was Richmond's other daily newspaper. "I have a mole over there who told me in confidence that they are close to confirming that Bob Dudley approved a loan to a manufacturing company he secretly controls. The company is going belly-up because they dividended too much cash out to him. Dudley's really a bad guy, Angela."

"I understand," Angela said quietly, pressing the phone tightly to her ear so Tucker couldn't hear. "That's all good news."

"The hell it is! I want to break this story, Angela. I want to be the one who brings Bob Dudley down. Have you gotten any more information on him yet? I want to print something before the *Herald* beats me to it, but I can't until I confirm this stuff my contact gave me on Strategy Partners. My editor won't budge until I have another source. I've tried to figure out this stuff myself, but I can't get anywhere. Have you gotten anything?"

"I'm working on it. I'm close on a few things."

"What?"

"I can't say right now. Besides, what I have so far wouldn't be enough." To get what she needed, Angela had to go to Birmingham. She also had to hear back from a friend in Sumter's funds-transfer area who was trying to confirm the money wires Liv had referred to. The wires the bank had supposedly sent to Strategy Partners.

"When can you get it?" Liv pressed.

"I've got a lot going on right now. And what I need in terms of your information involves getting on a plane. I just don't know when I'll be able to get away."

"I know you hate flying, Angela, but you've *got* to do this for me. Please. I can't let the *Herald* break this story first. I just can't."

"All right, all right. I'll call you back later from a land line." Angela cut the connection without waiting for Liv's response. She'd call her back from a private office at ESP.

"Where do you have to go?" Tucker asked.

Angela looked up from the cell phone. She'd been dialing her office number to pick up her voice mails. "What do you mean?"

"I couldn't help overhearing you tell whoever it was you were talking to that you'd have to take a flight somewhere to get what they needed. Where do you need to go?"

Angela hesitated. "New York," she lied, a thought racing through her mind. The only reason Jake Lawrence would have had John Tucker anonymously contact Liv and have him provide damaging information on Bob Dudley was to put Dudley on the defensive — just as Lawrence announced to the world his intention to buy Sumter Bank. When the shareholders heard the damaging information regarding Dudley, they would run like lemmings to Lawrence's tender offer. A tender offer he had sworn several times to Angela he would not make. Suddenly, she didn't feel like she could believe anyone.

She turned in her seat toward Tucker. "You sure you've never heard of Liv Jefferson?"

"Only from you."

"She's a good friend."

"That's nice —"

"I'd like you to meet her."

He hesitated. "Okay."

"Maybe tonight for dinner."

Tucker smiled back thinly. "Maybe."

"Take a seat, Carter." Bob Dudley was in his large chair by the window overlooking the James River. He had moved the other wing chair to the opposite side of the window so they could face one another for this discussion. He motioned for Hill to sit in it. "Please."

Hill obeyed, not taking his eyes from Dudley. Dudley had called the meeting fifteen minutes ago, but hadn't explained what it was about.

"Carter, I have no shortage of enemies."

"Any man who's been as successful as you makes enemies. It's unavoidable."

"Cut the bullshit," blurted Dudley.

Hill looked down and cleared his throat, trying to control his resentment.

"I have friends too," Dudley said. "People who are intensely loyal to me. Thanks to one of them, I've become aware of some disturbing news."

Hill shifted uncomfortably in the chair. "Ah, what news?"

"Reporters are investigating rumors that I've been illegally funneling money out of Sumter Bank for myself." Dudley paused. "Do you know anything about this?"

"Of course not."

"You sure you want to stick to that story?"

Hill hesitated. "Yes."

Dudley glanced out the window at the building Albemarle Capital used as its head-quarters. At the two windows that looked into Chuck Reese's office. "I know how you feel about me, Carter. And I know what you want."

"Bob, I'm not —"

"Shut the hell up!" Dudley thundered. "I've known for a long time that you want to run this organization. That you feel I'm past my prime. That I'm more of a liability now than an asset. I'm also aware that one of the bank's board members conveyed to you my belief that you are not chairman material."

Hill gritted his teeth. He could feel himself about to explode, but he needed to maintain control. Dudley was still in charge. "I don't listen to idle talk, and as far as you being past your prime, just the other day I pointed out to someone that you have created a vast amount of wealth for the shareholders of this institution. That you are *still* creating wealth. That this bank is more secure under your leadership than Jake Lawrence's."

Dudley chuckled. "I should fire you right now, Carter, and be done with you."

Hill held his breath.

"But then you'd probably leak to the press the fact that for the last six months I've been having an affair with a hot little number half my age. I'm sure you know all about that."

Hill looked down into his lap.

"Of course," Dudley continued, "then I'd tell my contacts at the *Trib* and the *Herald* about that blonde you have stashed in an apartment complex over on the South Side."

Hill's eyes flashed to Dudley's. "That's a lie! You have no proof of any —"

"My people have plenty of proof." Dudley pursed his lips. "But what good would it do me to tell the papers that? Besides, if I fire you now in the face of the lies they're going to print about me, it wouldn't look good."

"So why did you call me here?" Hill asked.

"First, to ask you a question, then to give you some advice."

"What's the question?" Hill snapped.

"Are you working with Jake Lawrence?"

"I just told you that I think Sumter is more secure under you than Lawrence. What the hell would make you think that?"

"The comment Ms. Day made the last time we met with her. The one about Jake Lawrence asking her if you would make a good chairman."

"That's absurd. If Lawrence took over, he'd probably fire the both of us."

Dudley nodded, pointing a gnarled finger. "You anticipated my advice. He will fire you if he takes over this place. You can bet your bottom dollar on that. Even if he's telling you all the right things now."

Hill rose from his chair and headed for the door.

"Where are you going?" Dudley demanded. "I didn't dismiss you."

Angela leaned back in the chair and stretched, thinking about how she might need another cup of coffee to stay awake. Thinking about how she was supposed to be on a plane to Birmingham at 8:00 tomorrow morning. And here it was 10:00 at night and she was still immersed in piles of ESP due diligence in a conference room thirty miles west of Washington, D.C., and a hundred miles from Richmond. At this rate Tucker wouldn't have her back to her apartment in the Fan until three or four in the morning.

Perhaps she ought to just get a hotel room at Dulles Airport and change her plane ticket. But she hadn't brought another set of clothes. And she still had a lot more work to do here. Perhaps she should cancel Birmingham. She put her hand to her mouth to cover a yawn. Liv would be disappointed.

"You okay, champ?" Tucker sat at the end of the conference room, his boots up on the table as he read a copy of *Sports Illustrated*. "It's getting late."

"Too late to introduce you to Liv Jefferson tonight, I suppose."

"Yeah, I'd say."

"We'll do it another night."

"Fine." He smiled politely. "Want me to get you another cup of coffee?"

"No, thanks. I've had three cups since dinner. I couldn't handle any more caffeine. I'll be bouncing off the walls."

Tucker had spent the afternoon at a nearby mall, then brought Chinese food back for dinner around six. He'd stayed with her in the conference room after they'd finished eating, quietly reading the stack of magazines he'd purchased this afternoon. Most of the ESP employees had left the offices for the night, and she felt safer with him around.

"What exactly are you doing over there in between those paper mountains?" he asked, tossing the magazine onto the table.

Stacks of files and large, legal-sized envelopes surrounded Angela, piled high on the table and the floor around her chair. They'd been brought to her on request by a small group of ESP employees who Walter Fogel had ordered to help. "Due diligence."

"What does that mean, *due diligence?*"

"It means I'm studying everything I can about this company to figure out what it's worth. And to make certain there isn't something buried here that could cause big problems later on."

"Like what?"

"Like a lawsuit that the inside attorneys aren't telling anybody but senior management about. Sexual harassment or product liability. Or maybe inconsistencies in the numbers. Or the fact that a big customer is about to pull their account. The kind of stuff you might find in a stray memo or report."

"Smoking guns."

"And skeletons."

"That's a lot to try to go through."

"Especially when certain people at the company wouldn't want you to find what you're looking for if it were there. The chief financial officer certainly doesn't want me to uncover the fact that he's cooking the books, so sometimes I have to look very hard. You know, turn over all the rocks. No matter how small."

"How do you know where to find everything? How do you know where to look?"

"Experience."

Tucker glanced around, then pointed to a thick folder at one end of the table. "What's that?"

Angela squinted, trying to focus her tired eyes. "Customer reports, I think."

"Why do you have to go through those?"

"By checking out what ESP is billing individual customers, it helps me independently confirm what the accountants are reporting as ESP's consolidated revenue." She eyed the folder gloomily. Just another item on a long list. "I'm only interested in the bigger customers. I'll end up calling their accountants to confirm that they are actually paying ESP what ESP claims to be billing them."

"It's like herding cattle," Tucker observed. "You come at the figures from all different angles and head them where you want them to go so they can't slip anything by you. By actually calling the clients to confirm what they're paying ESP, you find out if ESP is telling you the truth about how much business they claim to be doing."

"Exactly." Angela glanced down at the detailed financial statement she had been reviewing.

"Let me help," Tucker volunteered.

Angela smiled despite the ache that was starting to throb in the corners of her eyes. "I don't know how you could."

Tucker thought for a moment. "How about if I go through those customer reports and flag the big ones? The file looks pretty thick. At least I could weed out the ones that you don't care about. The ones that are too small."

She hesitated. "Okay. Start by pulling the ones that ESP claims to be billing for more than fifty thousand dollars a year."

Tucker stood up and moved to the far end of the conference room table, happy to have something to do.

Angela watched him for a moment, then refocused on the numbers.

A few minutes later Tucker let out a low whistle.

Angela rubbed her eyes. "What is it?" she asked, checking out a small stack of papers he had pulled from the file. She assumed those papers represented customers doing over fifty thousand a year.

Tucker looked up from the sheet of paper he had been studying. "I think you might want to check this out," he said, sliding it down the length of the table.

"What did you find?" she demanded, scanning the small type.

"Look near the bottom."

Angela's eyes flashed down and her heart skipped a beat. "Sumter," she whispered. In a faint, handwritten scrawl in the left margin was a note to remember to include the Sumter "cloak account" in the "gross numbers." Beneath the words was a string of numbers. A code or perhaps the cloak account number buried somewhere in ESP's operating system.

"Cloak account?" Tucker asked. "What do you think that means?"

"Probably nothing," Angela replied quickly, gazing at the string of numbers, conscious of a strong sense of déjà vu. "Just an internal record-keeping code. Keep going through the file," she urged. "You'll probably find the Sumter account page."

Tucker shook his head. "I'm done. I've been through the entire file. There's no mention of Sumter other than what you see there," he explained, nodding at the paper in her hand.

Angela checked the paper again. "Did you find an account page in the file for a company called Cubbies?" she asked, still bothered by the eerie echo reverberating through her mind.

"Nope."

"Are you sure?"

"Yes."

That made no sense. Why would Jake Lawrence lie to her about Cubbies' licensing software from ESP Technologies? And if he was lying, how would he know how effective the ESP product was?

CHAPTER SEVENTEEN

Angela trotted up the jet way into the Birmingham airport, found a seat at a deserted gate, closed her eyes, folded her hands tightly in her lap, and murmured a quick prayer. The landing had been bad. The Delta Air Lines 737 jet had been battered constantly by turbulence from five thousand feet all the way to the ground, and she needed a few moments to gather herself. After a few deep breaths, she stood up and headed down the long corridor toward the rental car signs.

She had driven all the way back to Richmond with Tucker last night — getting to her apartment just after three this morning — then caught a few hours' sleep before driving to the Richmond Airport. Now it was a few minutes past ten. Her plan was to locate the main branch of the Birmingham library, then visit Strategy Partners — the firm Liv claimed Bob Dudley owned and was using to defraud Sumter. Then, depending on how her time at Strategy Partners went, there might have to be one more stop. After that, she'd board another Delta flight, this time headed for Dulles, where Tucker was to

370

meet her. She had a 6:00 appointment in northern Virginia with Ted Harmon, ESP's vice president of sales. Tucker was going to make certain she got to her meeting on time, then give her a ride back to Richmond when it was over.

Angela hadn't offered any specifics to the ESP vice president when she'd talked to him from the plane. At first he'd balked at her request to get together. But she'd quickly reminded him that Walter Fogel had given her free rein. She could interview anyone she wanted about anything she wanted. And he had relented. As she executed the rental car contract with initials and signatures on umpteen different lines, she wondered if the ESP executive had any idea what she wanted. If somehow he would anticipate that she wanted to know more about Sumter being an ESP client. And that she wanted to understand the "cloak account" notation scrawled in the margin of the neatly folded piece of paper in her briefcase.

She hadn't told Tucker where she was going today, just when and where to pick her up this afternoon. He had seemed uncomfortable about her going off on her own and pushed for more information. But she'd told him nothing more. For some reason, she wanted to make the trip to Birmingham on her own.

Angela picked up the keys to a Ford Taurus and hurried out to the rental car lot. Fortunately, on the way back to Richmond, Tucker hadn't asked her anything more about the "cloak account," or about what must have been a surprised expression on her face when he replied that he hadn't found a Cubbies account page. He hadn't asked her anything, perhaps thinking that she would sleep. But she hadn't slept in the car, or very much after he had dropped her off. There were too many things on her mind. Too many risks and returns to consider.

She slid in behind the Taurus's steering wheel, placing her briefcase down on the seat beside her. Perhaps her suspicions about Jake Lawrence lying to her were out of line. Perhaps the ESP executive would clear up the issue with Cubbies tonight. She grimaced. Perhaps there would be world peace someday, too. She'd found out that Lawrence had spent another hundred million on Sumter stock. Now he owned 12 percent of the bank. And, if she couldn't trust Lawrence, could she trust Tucker?

At two o'clock, after several hours of research at the Birmingham library, Angela walked briskly into the small lobby of Strategy Partners. The firm was located on the fourth and top floors of a refurbished brick building in a neighborhood bordering a run-down area of town.

The receptionist glanced up from her computer as Angela came through the door. "May I help you?"

Angela checked the receptionist's screen. She was in the middle of a game of solitaire.

"I'd like to talk to one of your professionals about a consulting job. That is what you do here, right?"

Behind the receptionist were just two office doors, both closed. These weren't the large, tastefully furnished offices she had expected a firm handling a $10 million assignment for Sumter Bank to occupy. Her friend in the funds-transfer area of Sumter had confirmed that a $10 million wire had been sent from the bank to Strategy Partners two weeks ago.

The receptionist reached for her phone. Before she could press the intercom button, one of the doors behind her desk opened, and a bearded man in a golf shirt, khakis, and Docksides appeared. "Can I help you?"

"I need to talk to someone about a consulting assignment." Angela noticed that the man wasn't wearing socks.

He gave the receptionist a quick glance, then smiled. "Sure, come on in." He moved quickly to his computer, flipped off the monitor, then extended his hand over the desk. "Jim Nelson."

"Veronica Williams." There was no doubt in her mind that this operation was a complete sham. That no real work was going on here. The questions now were, Who was keeping the doors open and why?

"What can I do for you, Veronica?" Nelson asked as he sat down in the spindly chair behind the old desk and gestured for her to sit as well.

"I own a small Internet firm here in town, and

I was hopeful that I could retain Strategy Partners to give me some advice."

"How did you hear about us?"

"Friend of a friend."

"What's your friend's name?"

"I don't think she dealt with this office."

"Really?"

"Yes."

"Well, that's strange."

"Oh?" Angela asked, trying to look puzzled. "Why?"

"This is our only office."

Angela smiled warmly at the elderly lady behind the front counter of the Alabama State Corporation Commission's administrative offices. The SCC offices were buried in the basement of Birmingham's public records building. "Good afternoon, ma'am."

"Hello, dear. How can I help you?"

Angela hesitated, holding back a sneeze. It was terribly musty down here. "That's a lovely brooch," she said when the sneeze had passed, pointing at the jewel-studded housecat pinned to the gray-haired lady's blouse.

"Oh, thank you. My oldest daughter made it for me last Christmas. She's quite talented. She actually sells a line of these pins through a couple of gift shops here in town."

"I'm not surprised. She certainly is talented."

The woman reached up and took the brooch in her fingers. Her head shook slightly as she looked down and admired it. "My cat that I'd had for fifteen years died around Thanksgiving, and she made this so I could remember him."

"That's so nice."

"Yes." The elderly woman admired the pin for a few more moments, then looked up, smiling broadly. "Now, what can I do for you?"

"I need to make certain my company has paid its annual registration dues. The president of my company, Bob Dudley, sent me down here to make certain we had. We've gotten several letters to the effect that you have no record of us sending in our hundred-dollar fee." Angela rolled her eyes and let out a sigh. "I'm just a secretary, so I get to come all the way down here to check it out."

The elderly lady patted Angela's hand. "Keep working hard, dear, and some day you'll get ahead."

"People in our accounting office swore to me that we paid the bill in January as soon as we received it, but someone in your office keeps sending us a letter demanding payment. I figured the best way to clear up the whole mess was to come down here and talk to a real person like you, not some computer-generated list of options over the telephone."

The elderly woman nodded. "You did the right thing. This happens all the time. And the issue would never get settled over the phone or with letters going back and forth. What did you say the name of the firm was again?"

"Strategy Partners," Angela responded.

The woman picked up her reading glasses and put them on. "You wait here. I'll be back as quick as I can."

She returned a few minutes later with a thin manila folder.

"Any luck?" Angela asked.

The woman placed the folder down on the counter, opened it, and leafed through several pages, then smiled triumphantly. "Here we are," she said, holding up a piece of paper. "Your company has definitely paid your annual dues. Here's a photocopy of the check."

"Could I get a copy of that so I can show the people in our accounting group? You know how they can be. Needing records and receipts and all."

"Of course, dear," the woman agreed, shuffling to a copier against a wall a few feet away. "It's so inconsiderate of them," she mumbled to herself as she positioned the paper on the glass surface, closed the copier's cover, and pressed a button. "Making you come all the way down here like this when they could have just looked through their checking account records."

"I suppose we have lots of different accounts."

"Isn't that always the way? Big corporations with so many different accounts the left hand doesn't know what the right hand is doing. My Lord. Well, here you are," she said, picking the paper up off the copier and handing it to Angela.

Angela took the paper from the elderly woman and scanned it quickly. Her eyes snapped to a stop at the beginning of her second sweep of the page. The check was written off of a Sage Capital account. The same company that had sold ESP Technologies to Proxmire. The same company whose representative to Proxmire's board of directors was trying to derail Jake Lawrence's takeover of Proxmire. Her eyes moved down. At the bottom left of the check was a notation: "Strat. Part. Bama dues."

"There's something else here you may want to clear up, dear."

Angela looked up, her pulse racing. "What's that?"

"Didn't you say your president's name was Dudley?"

"Yes. Bob Dudley."

The woman shook her head. "He isn't listed as the company's president. In fact, he isn't listed on here anywhere."

"What do you want to know?" Ted Harmon asked impatiently. "Why did you ask me to come here tonight, Ms. Day?"

Harmon was short and thin, with a face only a mother could love. She'd been expecting a Sam Reese look-alike. A man who could sell ice cubes to Eskimos with a quick smile and a handshake. But then the sale of ESP's software was almost certainly a very technical process, probably made most of the time to a chief technology officer who only cared how well the application worked, and not at all what the salesperson looked like.

"I have a few questions about your customers," she began.

"Uh-huh." Harmon glanced furtively around the crowded hotel lobby bar.

As if he were worried that somebody might be watching him, Angela realized, taking a sip of the hot tea she had ordered. She was standing at the bar, not sitting on a stool as Harmon was. She was concerned that if she sat in a comfortable seat she might actually doze off right in front of him. She'd slept all of three hours in the past two days, and it was catching up with her.

"Have you all —"

"The only reason I'm here is that Walter Fogel made it abundantly clear I *had* to be here," Harmon interrupted rudely. "I know you're representing a group that wants to buy Proxmire. Fogel didn't come right out and say that, but it wasn't hard to figure out."

He was very nervous, Angela noticed. "What are you frightened of, Ted?" she asked, intentionally trying to put him on the defensive right away.

"Nothing. Nothing at all." He took a quick sip of his Scotch and water. "Just ask me the questions and then let me get out of here. Come on."

"All right. How long have you been with ESP Technologies?"

"Three years."

"Then you were around when ESP was sold to Proxmire?"

"Yes."

"In your current position?" Angela wanted to make certain Harmon was intimately familiar with what had been going on since the merger.

"Head of global sales. Yes. Since before Proxmire acquired us."

She focused on his eyes, keenly interested in his reaction to her next question. "Has ESP ever had a client named Cubbies?"

Harmon thought for a moment, then shook his head. "No."

"Are you sure?"

"Yes."

"Absolutely positive?"

"Yes, dammit."

Why would Jake Lawrence lie about that? Perhaps he had just misspoken. But he had been specific about Cubbies being a chain of convenience stores, and they had talked about there being a Cubbies location near where she lived growing up. But then how could he have known so much about ESP? She took a deep breath. "Is Sumter Bank an ESP client?"

The little man glanced up over the rim of his glass, then his eyes narrowed. "Who?"

"Sumter Bank. It's a commercial bank headquartered in Richmond, Virginia. Is Sumter now, or has it ever been, a client of ESP's?"

He scoffed. "Did you see a Sumter reference on the client file folder my assistant gave you?"

He had spoken in a raised voice, like a prosecutor who always knew the answer before he asked the question.

"As a matter of fact, I did."

"What?" Harmon had just taken a large swallow of his drink and nearly choked on it. "I don't believe you."

The star witness had just rolled over. Angela could see it all over his face.

"That's not supposed to —" Harmon interrupted himself, gazing steadily into Angela's curious expression. "I mean there are so many clients. How would I —"

"The name Sumter was handwritten in the margin of one of the file's pages." It was Angela's turn to interrupt. She couldn't shake the feeling that there was something about that scrap of information she wasn't making full use of. Something about that brief note in the margin she wasn't connecting to something else stored deep in her memory. "Along with a scribbled notation about a cloak account. What's a cloak account?"

"I have no idea."

"Is Sumter an ESP client," she asked again, drilling hard, "and, if it is, what application is your software used for at Sumter?"

The little man placed his glass down on the marble bar. "I told you, I don't know anything about Sumter Bank or a cloak account."

"Ted, I'd hate to have to tell Walter that you were being completely uncooperative during this meeting."

"Go right ahead and tell him," Harmon said, encouraging her with a sweeping gesture and a wry chuckle. "Won't bother me at all, and I assure you, *he* won't be able to help you, either."

"I disagree. Walter has pledged to help me in any way he can. And these are such difficult economic times," Angela said, shaking her head sadly. "Terrible times to be out in the cold without a job, especially with a wife and three children to support." She knew the score. Harmon's personnel records had been made available to her by ESP's HR department. And her lack of sleep and Harmon's uncooperative attitude were putting her patience in short supply. She'd had enough of his evasiveness. She wanted answers. "I won't hesitate to tell Walter that you have chosen to stonewall me." She reached into her purse, pulled out her cell phone, and held it up so he could see it. "Understand?"

"Bitch," he muttered.

"What did you say?" she snapped, stuffing the phone back in her purse.

Harmon ground his teeth together and picked up his glass. There were only a few ice cubes left in it. "You don't know what you're getting involved in, Ms. Day. You don't understand how this could end up. For you and me. Leave it alone," he pleaded.

"Leave what alone?" she demanded.

He shook his head. "I'm warning you for your own good. Pack your bags and go home. Forget that you ever heard of ESP Technologies. Proxmire too."

Angela felt her adrenaline beginning to pulse. She'd stumbled on to something big here, and she wasn't going to let it go. "One way or the other, Ted, I will get to the bottom of this thing."

Harmon stood up and smiled his unfriendliest smile. "The only thing you'll get to the bottom of, Ms. Day, is the Atlantic Ocean. With a couple of cinder blocks chained to your ankles." With no warning he pivoted, cocked his arm, and hurled his glass at the huge mirror behind the bar.

The mirror shattered into hundreds of tiny pieces, and Angela ducked instinctively to protect her eyes from the flying shards of glass. When she looked up, Harmon was gone. She grabbed her purse and took off after him, sprinting out of the bar and into the crowded hotel lobby, dodging startled guests as she tried to catch sight of the small man. She scanned the large room frantically as she waded into the mass of people, but couldn't find him. Then she saw him hurrying through the revolving door at the far end of the lobby. She followed, running headlong into a huge man wearing a wool overcoat.

"Watch where you're going, lady!" the man yelled.

"Sorry," Angela muttered. She regained her balance, then darted past him toward the revolving door, aware that this would be her last chance to get anything out of Ted Harmon. He wouldn't be coming into the office tomorrow morning. Or ever again, for that matter.

She burst out of the hotel into the cold winter evening. Rows of parked vehicles stretched out before her beneath dim overhead streetlights. She searched the large lot, her breath rising up in front of her, but saw nothing. Then she heard a commotion to her left — a raised voice and a groan — and she sprinted toward the sounds of the struggle. Past a young couple walking toward the hotel entrance, looking back over their shoulders in the direction of the noises.

Between two SUVs Angela came upon the source of the commotion. Harmon lay sprawled on his stomach on the asphalt, beneath John Tucker's knee, which was firmly planted in the small of his back. "What are you doing?" she asked, amazed that Tucker had snagged Harmon.

"Just trying to be of help, ma'am," Tucker replied calmly, tipping his hat and smiling in the glow of a streetlight that was directly overhead.

"Let me go," Harmon gasped.

"Shut up." Tucker dug his knee deeper into Harmon's back.

"John, do you know who this is?" Angela asked.

After picking her up at Dulles Airport, Tucker had dropped her off in front of the hotel, located only ten minutes from the airport. As far as she knew, Tucker had never seen Harmon. She'd met Harmon in the bar.

"The guy you were meeting with."

"How do you know?"

"I walked inside after dropping you off and saw you talking to him," he explained, pointing down at the little man who had now stopped struggling. "Then I came back outside and hung out at the door. When I saw him come tearing out of the revolving door, I took a chance that it might make sense to stop him and find out why he was in such a rush." Tucker paused. "So, did I do good?"

Angela peered around the corner of the SUV at the hotel. The bartender who had served her and a uniformed hotel employee were scanning the parking lot from just outside the revolving door. "Where's the car, John?" she asked, making a snap decision.

"A few rows that way," he answered, pointing over his shoulder with one hand, the other at the back of Harmon's head, keeping his face pressed to the cold blacktop.

"Give me the keys."

Tucker reached into his jacket, dug the keys out, and tossed them to her.

"Stay here," she ordered. "I'll be right back."

Then she was off, bent over at the waist, moving stealthily between the cars until she found the Integra Tucker had picked her up in at the airport. She unlocked the driver's side door, slipped in behind the steering wheel, and started the engine, cringing at how loud it was as it roared to life.

Angela glanced at the hotel entrance again. The bartender and the other man were still there — maybe two hundred feet away — searching the parking lot. They had been joined by another uniformed hotel employee. Without turning on the headlights, she backed the car out of the spot, touching the brakes only long enough to shift from reverse into drive. Carefully, by the light of the overhead streetlights, she steered the car to the end of the row away from the hotel, then turned down the one where she knew Tucker was waiting. As she recognized the two SUVs parked side by side, she brought the Integra to a quick stop, popped the trunk, and jumped out.

"Come on, John!" She could hear sirens in the distance. If the police got Harmon, she'd never get a chance to find out what he knew. "Hurry!"

As Tucker lifted Harmon to his feet, the smaller man began shouting for help.

"Put him in here!" Angela ordered, racing to the back of the vehicle and lifting the trunk's lid. Over the roof of the car she could see the bartender sprinting toward them, followed by the two uniformed employees.

Tucker grabbed Harmon by the back of his shirt collar and his belt, and lifted him up, attempting to stuff him into the trunk. But Harmon grabbed the side of the car at the last moment, holding on for dear life.

Angela raced around Tucker and pried furiously at Harmon's fingers until finally he released his grip. With one last heave, Tucker shoved the small man into the well, and Angela slammed the trunk lid down on top of him. "Let's go!" she shouted, jumping in behind the steering wheel. She hesitated only long enough for Tucker to halfway make it onto the passenger seat before revving the engine, then slamming the car into gear.

"Whoa! Jesus, at least let me get the door closed!" Tucker shouted, reaching out and grabbing the door handle.

The hotel people were only a few steps away. She could hear Harmon beating wildly on the inside of the trunk, frantically trying to escape.

As Tucker pulled his door shut, the Integra leapt forward and the oncoming pursuers scattered, diving between parked cars as the car's tires screeched on the blacktop. In seconds the Integra had reached the end of the row. Angela steered around the last car and raced toward the parking lot exit. At the exit, she slowed slightly, saw flashing lights in the distance and headed right, then made a quick left past a strip mall onto a side street, before turning on the headlights. At the next stop sign she turned right again, drove a mile — with Harmon still beating crazily on the inside of the trunk lid — then turned into a darkened high school complex.

"Go behind the main building," Tucker directed, pointing at a road that led around toward the back where they couldn't be seen from the main road.

"No, I thought I'd stay out here where the cops can find me with a man in my trunk," Angela said. "Jesus."

"Hey, don't worry," Tucker said calmly. "We'll be all right." He glanced over at her as she guided the car around to the back of the large brick building. "Pretty good driving there, missy."

"I can handle myself," she said firmly, feeling her heart starting to settle down.

"Better turn the lights off," Tucker suggested.

"Right." She reached forward and extinguished the headlights, slowing to a crawl as they moved out of view of the main road.

"So what happened back there in the bar? Why was this guy running?" he asked, jerking his thumb over his shoulder in the direction of the trunk.

"Remember the notation you found in the margin of that page yesterday?" She was going to need Tucker's help with all of this. That was clear. So she'd have to level with him. "The one about Sumter Bank."

"Of course."

"The guy in the trunk is head of global sales for ESP. When I started asking him about Sumter and the cloak account reference, he denied knowing anything about either one. When I threatened to tell his CEO that he wasn't being helpful, he got defensive. Then he told me that if I was smart I'd get away from ESP, that I was stupid to be messing around in the whole thing. But he wouldn't tell me what the 'thing' was. Then all of a sudden he throws his drink at this mirror behind the bar and runs."

"Creating a distraction so he could get away."

"Yes. And it probably would have worked if you hadn't stopped him." She reached over and patted his hand gratefully as she brought the car to a stop between two school buses. "I appreciate it," she said quietly, wondering if she really wanted to know what Harmon had been referring to, sensing that there was more to all of this than a takeover and Bob Dudley's hatred of Jake Lawrence.

"Seems like you got more than you bargained for," Tucker observed.

"No doubt. But I'm in it now, and I have to finish."

"You want to find out why this guy was telling you to stay away from ESP? Or do you just want to let him go?"

Behind them, Harmon began yelling, begging to be set free.

She looked over at Tucker slowly. "I want to know what he was talking about."

"Are you willing to let me do what I need to do to make this guy talk?"

She hesitated, staring at Tucker for a long time, wondering if she should let this happen. Finally, she nodded slowly. She had to know what was going on. And it was clear that the only way Harmon would talk was if he knew he'd have his ass kicked if he didn't.

"Yes," she finally said.

Angela stepped out of the car and moved to the back of the vehicle.

"Let me outta here!" Harmon yelled, his voice muffled but loud. "I can't breathe."

"Shut up," Tucker hissed, kneeling down so his mouth was near the trunk's keyhole. "I'm going to open the trunk, pal, but you need to shut up. And if you try to run, so help me I'll kill you."

Harmon went silent.

"Now, after I open the trunk the lady is going to ask you some questions which you will answer. If you don't answer those questions to her satisfaction the first time she asks, I'll make certain you answer them the second time." Tucker glanced up at Angela through the dim light and winked. "Do I make myself clear, pal?" No answer. "What's this guy's name?" he asked Angela.

"Ted. Ted Harmon."

"Did you hear me, Teddie?"

"I heard you," came the muffled reply.

"But did you *understand* me, Teddie?" Again, no answer. "Teddie!"

"Yes, yes."

"Good." Tucker stood up and held out his hand. "Give me the keys, Angela."

She dropped them into his open palm.

"Teddie," Tucker called.

"What?"

389

"When I open the trunk, remember to stay right where you are. Don't move a muscle. If you do, so help me I'll break whatever moves. Got it?"

"Yes."

Tucker nodded for Angela to step back, then slid the key into the trunk and turned it. The latch popped and Tucker lifted the lid. Harmon lay on his back, gazing up at them under the light from the small bulb affixed to the underside of the trunk's lid. His clothes and hair were disheveled, and one hand was bleeding slightly. He made no move to escape.

"Ask away, Angela," Tucker said.

"Is Sumter Bank an ESP client?"

"Don't ask me that," Harmon pleaded. "Please."

Tucker cocked his right hand and reached down as if to grab Harmon by the throat, but Angela caught Tucker's hand. "No, John. He'll answer."

"I'll give him one more chance," Tucker growled. "But I don't think we ought to stick around here much longer, and you need to get your answers."

"Is Sumter a client?" she demanded again.

"Yes," Harmon whispered.

There. Some progress. "What's the application? What does ESP's software do for Sumter?"

Harmon closed his eyes and moaned softly as he shifted slightly on his back.

"Teddie!" Tucker barked.

Angela glanced over. Tucker seemed as interested as she was in hearing the answer.

Harmon grimaced. "It's a predictive software."

"What does Sumter use it to predict?"

Harmon shook his head. "It's used to analyze Sumter's on-line mortgage applications."

"Analyze them how?" Angela pushed.

"To screen people," Harmon answered evasively.

"Screen people *how?*"

Harmon gritted his teeth. "I won't —"

"Dammit!" Tucker shouted, reaching into the trunk and grabbing Harmon by his thin throat. "Talk, you little bastard!" he roared.

"All right, all right," Harmon whined, his eyes wide open. "To determine the race of the on-line applicants."

For a few moments it seemed to Angela that there were no other sights or sounds in the cold night except for the little man's eyes gazing back at hers and his hard breathing. "Why would Sumter want to determine the race of an on-line mortgage applicant?"

Harmon stared up at her, steam pouring from his mouth and nose. "Because they can't see the applicant when somebody tries to get a mortgage on-line."

"Jesus," Tucker muttered, relaxing his grip on the little man's throat.

"Let me get this straight," Angela said. "The ESP software can predict for Sumter the race of every on-line mortgage applicant."

391

"It can't go quite that far," Harmon admitted. "But with 99 percent accuracy it can predict whether or not the applicant is black, Hispanic, or any other minority."

"How?" Tucker demanded.

"For Sumter to process the mortgage request, the applicant must fill out the boxes on the application, giving name, current address, current telephone number, Social Security number, years of education, and all other personal debt, including credit cards." The words were spilling out now, as if Harmon wanted to talk. As if all of this information had been bottled up inside of him for too long, and now that he had the opportunity to reveal what he knew, he couldn't say enough. "The software crosses all the information from the application with reams of data bank information we purchase from third-party vendors to predict race. For instance, the current address information gets Sumter to about a 75 percent confidence level right away. The ZIP code and the telephone number tell the software three-quarters of what it needs to know. I mean, think about it: very few neighborhoods in our country are split fifty-fifty in terms of race. Then the software reviews what kind of items the applicant purchased on his or her credit cards, and where he or she went to high school or college. That kind of information further refines the confidence around the prediction until it spits out an answer with 99 percent accuracy. Actually the accuracy level is 99.4 percent," he added. "Minority or white. That's all the senior people at Sumter want to know."

"And of course the race box on the application is optional," Angela pointed out quietly. "The applicant doesn't have to fill out that information."

Harmon nodded. "Exactly. Now, if the application is submitted in person, the bank employee handling the application sees the applicant and can fill in the race information if the applicant doesn't when the applicant leaves the bank branch. But over the Internet, the applicant is anonymous. There's no way for the bank to know the applicant's race."

"Unless Sumter uses the ESP predictive software," Angela said.

Harmon sighed dejectedly. "That's right."

"My God," Tucker whispered, tightening his grip on Harmon's throat again. "I oughta —"

"John!" Angela reached down into the trunk and grabbed Tucker's hand. "Stop it."

Harmon gasped as Tucker released his grip. "You think this has been easy for me? Knowing all of this? Being a part of all of this?"

"Why would you have ever supported it if it's been so hard?" Angela demanded. "Why wouldn't you tell someone? Why wouldn't you have gone to the authorities?"

Harmon closed his eyes tightly. "I have a past," he said, tightening his mouth. "The senior people at ESP found out about it, and they used it against me. I'm sure our investment guy at Sage Capital was the one who told them."

"What kind of past?" Tucker demanded.

"What difference does it make?" Harmon shot back.

"It doesn't," Angela agreed. "But there is one more thing I need to understand."

"What?"

"How does Sumter use the information generated by the ESP predictive software? Does it simply deny all minorities a mortgage?" Angela shook her head. "I can't believe that would be the case. It would be too obvious. That information would come to light somewhere and the bank would be crucified in the Richmond press. In the *national* press for God's sake."

"Of course they would," Harmon agreed. "In fact, Sumter makes many loans to minority mortgage applicants."

"So what do they use the information for?" Angela asked impatiently.

"Obviously, the applicant must also fill out the box telling the bank where they intend to move. The address of the new home that the mortgage will be financing."

"Yes?"

"Sumter reviews that new address and, as long as it's in a neighborhood designated by Sumter's senior management as already 'heavy minority,' the application is approved. But if the new address is in an area designated 'heavy white,' the application is denied."

Angela glanced into Tucker's eyes.

394

He shook his head.

She nodded silently, then looked back down at Harmon. "Is this going on in just Richmond, or all over Virginia?" she asked.

Harmon shook his head. "From what I understand, the Sumter people apply the standard to every application that comes in, no matter the address." He hesitated. "And they aren't the only ones," he said ominously.

"One more question."

"What?"

"Does Fogel know anything about this?"

Harmon looked at his bloody hand in the light from the dim bulb. "No. He doesn't know anything."

"Thank you for coming so quickly," Carter Hill said, making eye contact with Booker, Thompson, and Abbott in turn as they all huddled around the side of his car. "We may have an issue."

"What is it?" Booker asked, glancing around the dark mall parking lot.

"Ted Harmon didn't come home tonight from ESP. And, at around nine o'clock this evening, his wife put their three children in the family station wagon and drove to her parents' house in Harrisburg, Pennsylvania. It took her several hours to get there from northern Virginia, but she didn't stop once. And our person informed me that she was doing no less than eighty the whole way." He paused. "Something's happened."

CHAPTER EIGHTEEN

"He shouldn't wake up till morning now," Angela whispered, turning back at the doorway to take one last look at Hunter. He was asleep in Liv's guest room, snug beneath the covers, his arms wrapped tightly around a frayed teddy bear with one missing eye. He hadn't stirred since falling asleep an hour ago on Angela's couch. Even on the ride over to Liv's, or as Angela had carried him into Liv's apartment from the car. "At least not before I get back."

"I don't know about this, Angela," Liv said anxiously. "What if he wakes up? What do I do then?"

"Just get him a drink of water and put him back into bed. Maybe read him a story."

"But he'll ask for you."

"I told him we were coming here before he fell asleep, and he was fine with that. Besides, he's known you for a long time. You're like his aunt."

"But he's never spent the night here alone, Angela. It's weird. I don't have any problem dealing with powerful people like Bob Dudley, but a six-year-old boy makes me really nervous."

"Relax. You'll be fine."

Liv leaned back into the room and began to pull the bedroom door closed.

"No, no," Angela advised, catching the door. "Leave it open a few inches. He likes the light. He's still got a problem with imaginary monsters under the bed."

"Oh."

When they had moved down the hall to the living room, Liv nodded back toward the bedroom. "By the way, Angela, why is he with you tonight? Didn't you just have him last weekend?"

"Hunter was asking for me. Sam said he was crying, so he decided it was best to bring him to me."

Liv shook her head. "It's sad for a child to be so unhappy. He should see you much more."

Angela nodded grimly. "Hunter was unhappy enough that Sam defied his father."

"I was going to say. This can't be making Chuck Reese very happy."

"I'm sure it isn't," Angela agreed, picking up her ski jacket from the couch. "I really appreciate your looking after him."

"How long will you be?"

"Not more than a few hours. I hope."

Liv hesitated. "What's this all about tonight, Angela?"

"Don't ask."

"Angela."

"Look, you're the one who wants to break the

Bob Dudley story before the *Herald*." She hadn't yet told Liv about her trip to Birmingham or what she'd found. There was one more thing she needed to do first. "Right?"

"Yes. But I don't want anything happening to you, either."

"I'll be fine."

"Not going to tell me any more than that?" Liv asked as they reached the apartment door.

"It's just something I need to do." Angela took Liv's hand for a moment. "Don't worry so much. Like I said, everything will be fine."

And then she was gone. Back to her car and headed toward the west side of town. As Angela was driving, she thought about trying Jake Lawrence on his cell phone one more time. She'd placed several calls over the past few days but hadn't been able to reach him since the night the helicopter had been shot down. John had explained that, according to Colby, the attack had been carried out by a right-wing terrorist group that had found out Lawrence was covertly assisting governments they were fighting. Somehow they'd found out about the chopper landing but been fooled by the decoy. Now Colby had Lawrence stashed in an undisclosed location, and had cut him off from all contact with the outside world. The incident on the mountain, a bombing in Tel Aviv, and now the attack on the helicopter had Colby taking no chances.

Angela was disappointed about not being able

to contact Jake. She desperately wanted to tell him what she had found at ESP, what she had uncovered in Birmingham, and what Ted Harmon had told her from the trunk of a rental car. She was certain Jake would shut down the Proxmire acquisition when he heard what she had to tell him. When what was going on at ESP and Sumter came to light, an ESP initial public offering would be off the table. For all she knew, the authorities might even shut it down.

So now she was in this thing to expose Bob Dudley and whoever else at Sumter was involved in the discriminatory practices being systematically carried out by the bank. She was in it for herself — and for Sally. Perhaps by destroying an animal like Bob Dudley she could dull the guilt that had plagued her every day of her life since Sally had fallen from the fraternity house window.

Angela took a deep breath and clenched the steering wheel. None of the fraternity members had suffered any punishment for what had happened. The Good Old Boy network had closed ranks around them and, despite Angela's testimony and her repeated pleas to school administrators and town officials, the local police had ruled Sally's death an "unfortunate accident." The young men who had kept her from getting to Sally had been right. They could do whatever they wanted. She gritted her teeth. To give up the fight against Dudley now would be cowardly. He might as well have been one of those young men who forced Sally out the window.

Angela recognized a Denny's on her left and swung her car into a strip mall parking lot just beyond the restaurant, then pulled to a quick stop in front of the Rite-Aid. She had noticed a pair of headlights behind her on the way from Liv's apartment, and, though the vehicle had passed by when she pulled into the strip mall lot, she was glad they had taken these precautions.

"May I help you?" A man behind the front counter called when she entered the store and headed toward the aisle stocked with shampoos.

"No, thanks."

Angela walked to the back of the store and the deserted prescription counter, which, according to the sign, had closed at 8:00 P.M. Then she moved through the swinging stainless steel gate separating it from the rest of the store and past several shelves of bottles and vials into the stockroom beyond.

"Hey, what are you doing in here?"

Angela froze, startled by a young woman taking inventory. "Oh, sorry," she said, spotting the back door. "Wrong number."

"What? Hey —"

Angela pushed through the store's back door and into the cold night air. John Tucker was waiting for her there, the engine of the Jeep running. He leaned over and opened her door as she reached the vehicle.

"Were you followed?" he asked as they sped away.

"I'm not sure," she answered over the noise of the engine, buckling her seat belt. "I think somebody tailed me out here, but they didn't follow me into the mall parking lot. They kept going."

"Odds are good they were following you. Probably waiting for you right now at the mall entrance or across the street. Well, they'll be waiting for a while, won't they?" He chuckled. "So what's the best way to get there?"

For an hour Angela guided Tucker toward a business park on Richmond's South Side — the opposite side of the river from downtown. Ted Harmon had given her the address. The address of a Sumter Bank location he and ESP dealt with on a daily basis. There they might confirm Harmon's allegation that Sumter was essentially engaging in housing segregation, not only in Richmond and across the state of Virginia, but in their entire market region — from just outside Washington, D.C., all the way down through the Southeast to Florida. It was one thing for Ted Harmon to accuse Sumter of such a despicable discriminatory practice. But if she had collaborating evidence from inside the bank, the allegation would be irrefutable.

"That was the entrance," said Angela, pointing at a sign as the Jeep raced past. "Turn around."

"We need to be careful approaching this place," Tucker replied. "Even at this time of night."

A half a mile past the business park entrance

the road snaked through a heavily wooded area. Tucker slowed the Jeep down, found a dirt road, and turned off onto it. A hundred feet into the woods, he pulled to a stop.

"Let's go."

"Wait a minute." Angela pulled out her cell phone and dialed Liv's apartment number.

"Hello," Liv answered softly.

"Everything okay?"

"Yes. He hasn't made a sound."

"Good. I'll call again in a little while."

"All right. Bye."

Angela slipped the phone back into her pocket. "Okay, let's go," she said, coming around to the driver's side. Tucker had his cell phone pressed to his ear. "Who are you talking to?" she asked suspiciously. There it was. That urge not to trust. But she hadn't paid attention to it in Wyoming and had almost been pushed from a five-hundred-foot cliff.

"Just checking messages. Bill Colby wants to know where I am every second these days." He glanced around the dark woods. "You ready?"

She nodded slowly, wondering if this was really a good idea — or maybe the worst mistake of her life. "Yes."

"Then let's do it. Whatever 'it' is."

"We have to get inside this Sumter location. We have to see what's there. Hopefully there'll be a file or a communication that confirms Harmon's story."

"Okay."

They moved through the woods to the edge of the business park, then kept to the shadows as much as possible as they tried to read street signs and building numbers. The commercial park was comprised of four long, two-story buildings containing everything from graphic design firms and computer repair shops to warehouses and light-manufacturing companies. Finally, they reached their target, identifiable only by its number on the building. There was nothing on the door or the front of this section of the building to indicate that it was a Sumter location.

"Okay, now we know which one it is," Tucker said, looking around. The long building stretched a hundred yards in both directions. "We need to mark it so we'll know which one it is."

"I've got an idea." Angela reached down, picked up a stone from a rock garden in front of the building, and trotted out into the empty parking lot. She placed the stone down beneath an overhead streetlight that was directly in front of the Sumter door fifty feet out into the lot.

"Good thinking," Tucker said when she returned. "Let's get to the back of the building."

They jogged to one end of the building, then around to the back and the delivery area, and located the first fire escape leading up the side of the building to the roof.

"What are you waiting for?" Angela asked, moving past Tucker as he gazed upward. She grabbed the first rung — four feet off the ground — pulled herself up to the third rung, managed to get her toe onto the first rung, then began climbing. She was glad it was dark so it wasn't as obvious to her that she was getting higher off the ground with each step. She could feel the ladder shaking. Tucker was climbing too. When she reached the top rung, she hauled herself up onto the roof and waited for him.

"Come on, cowboy. What's wrong? You look a little winded."

He winked at her. "I'm pacing myself, Angela."

They jogged across the long, flat roof toward the front of the building, carefully avoiding condensers, pipes, and other obstacles. When they reached the front, they turned right and kept going, staying within a few feet of the roof's edge, checking each parking lot streetlight until they reached the one with the stone lying beneath it.

"There it is," Angela said quietly.

"I see it."

"I hope your friend made it out here this afternoon."

"He did. He confirmed." Tucker moved carefully over the roof toward the center of the building. "Here we go." He dropped to his knees, grabbed a trapdoor handle, and pulled. "We're in," he said as the door came up.

Angela knelt down beside him. "How did he get in here?"

"Claimed he was a fire inspector and that he

needed to look around," Tucker replied, pulling out a small flashlight and shining it down into the darkness. "The people in charge here bought his act without a question. He left this open for us when he came down off the roof." Tucker leaned forward and pushed down a set of folding wooden stairs. They extended to the floor. "Let's go," he said, placing his foot on the top step and disappearing.

Angela followed, heart pounding. Now they were guilty of breaking and entering. But it was the only way.

The three men who had trailed Angela and Tucker to the back of the building each holstered a Glock 9 mm. They were hunters, skilled in the art of stealth — and killing.

"What now?" Tucker asked when they had both descended the wooden stairs and reached the floor.

Angela grabbed the flashlight from him. "Follow me." She led him out of a small hallway and on to an open floor furnished with several metal desks piled with papers. She moved quickly to the first desk and inspected the top folder. "Look at this," she whispered.

Tucker moved beside her. "What is it?"

She flashed the light over the pages inside the folder. "A mortgage application." She turned quickly to the third page. The Race/National Origin box entitled "black, not of Hispanic origin" had been checked. "Hold this," she said, handing him the flashlight. "Keep it on the file so I can see."

"Yes, ma'am."

Angela snatched a handwritten note paper-clipped to the front of the legal-sized manila folder and scanned it. "My God."

"What?"

"This note states that the application can be approved because the subject can service the debt and is moving to an 'acceptable zone.' "

" 'An acceptable zone'?"

"It must mean that this person isn't trying to move into a neighborhood that someone at Sumter has determined he shouldn't be moving to. He's staying put, not trying to break the neighborhood color barrier." She glanced up into Tucker's eyes. "It's incredible. There's probably enough evidence in this office to bring down the entire Sumter senior executive team." She caught her breath, thinking about the effect this information would have on the bank's share price. No doubt it would tumble if the press got hold of this information. If Liv Jefferson got hold of it. Then the value of Jake Lawrence's six hundred million investment would undoubtedly plummet.

"What do we do now?" Tucker asked.

"Keep looking."

"This isn't enough?" he asked, nodding at the file.

"I want more."

She had to talk to Jake and tell him what she'd found before she contacted federal bank examiners. She had to tell Jake to dump his shares, even if he had to take a discount for liquidating so large a position so fast. If she saved him from a huge loss, he would owe her and he'd come through on his promise to get Hunter back. Maybe. Of course, technically, she'd be guilty of insider trading for giving Jake the information, because insider trading worked both ways. Whether you gave someone a tip ahead of positive news, or saved them from taking a bath ahead of bad news. But she hadn't taken all these mammoth risks to fall short this close to her ultimate goal. And she wasn't going to cover up what she knew. She owed Sally that — and much more.

"Come on, John," she urged, grabbing the flashlight and heading for the stairs leading down to the first floor.

When the rays of the flashlight disappeared, the leader motioned silently over his shoulder for the other two to follow. The man and woman hadn't bothered pushing the folding wooden steps back up against the ceiling, so there would be no creaking sounds to worry about. He pulled out his pistol, then carefully began descending the stairs.

There were more desks on the first floor — as well as a closed door. Angela twisted the knob several times when she got to it, but the door didn't give.

"You want to get in there?" Tucker asked.

"If the door is locked, there must be something important behind it."

"Get back," he ordered. He grabbed the knob with both hands, then slammed his hip into it. It swung open, crashing against the wall behind it.

Angela moved into the room, which was filled with file cabinets arranged alphabetically. She moved quickly to the cabinet marked *J*, pulled open the drawer, and found Liv Jefferson's mortgage application. She caught her breath as she noticed that the Race/National Origin box had been altered from the "white, not of Hispanic origin" box Liv had checked to the "black, not of Hispanic origin" box. "Jesus," she said to herself quietly.

"What is it?" Tucker asked.

Angela shook her head. There was a memo attached to the file denying the mortgage request because the "applicant is black and is moving into a restricted zone." "More evidence," she said grimly, moving further into the room. Jake was going to have to move fast to dump his Sumter shares.

At the back of the long room was a cabinet marked "ZIP file." Angela opened it and inspected the contents. A cover memo at the front described the long list of five digit numbers as "restricted" ZIP codes.

"What do you think of this?" she asked, holding the cover memo out for Tucker to see.

He read the instructions and shook his head. "This is incredible."

"Let's see what else is here." Angela moved to the next row of cabinets. She pulled open the top drawer of one labeled "General Information," and whistled to herself as she rifled through the contents.

"What now?" asked Tucker.

"Memos back and forth between ExecCom and Carter Hill," she answered, her hands trembling as she held up the pages. This was the mother lode. "Memos describing a systematic plan by Sumter to deny mortgages to minorities based upon where they intend to move. It's all here," she said triumphantly. "How they review and update the list of restricted-zone ZIP codes once a month. How they use ESP Technologies to screen on-line applicants to determine race if the applicant chooses not to fill in the Race/National Origin box. How people who work at this location must be white and carefully screened to make certain they 'sympathize.' " Angela stared into Tucker's eyes. "The incredible thing is that Bob Dudley isn't mentioned anywhere in this information. At least, not that I can find. He's had Carter Hill do all his dirty work." She shook her head. "So, they're both involved."

"Don't move!"

Angela and Tucker froze as two men, dressed

in black, pistols drawn and leveled at their chests, burst inside and the room was suddenly bathed in light.

"Get down on the floor!" one of the men yelled. "Right now or you're dead."

As she knelt, Angela glanced up at Tucker. He was smiling at the men, making no move toward the floor.

"Hey, boys," he said calmly. "Doesn't sound like you're here selling Girl Scout cookies."

"Get down!" the man closest to Tucker roared. "Now."

"It's just that I've got this trick knee. An old high school football injury."

"John, get down," Angela pleaded.

"Nah."

The man moved directly in front of Tucker and pointed the barrel of his pistol at Tucker's forehead. "Down, asshole. Or I shoot."

Tucker shook his head and smiled. "You really don't want to do that."

The man brandishing the weapon smiled back smugly. "And why not?"

"Because if you do," Tucker answered, "those three men standing at the door will kill *you*."

Angela's eyes flashed to the doorway. Three more men were there, aiming Glocks at the two men holding Tucker and her. As she watched, they moved silently into the room, snatched the pistols from the two stunned men, then slammed their pistol handles into the back of each man's neck. Both collapsed to the floor. The entire series of events had taken only a few seconds.

The leader hurried to where Tucker stood as his two subordinates quickly cuffed the unconscious men on the floor. "The area is secure, sir," he announced, saluting Tucker.

"Good job, son."

"We followed you in, as requested. Over the roof and down." He nodded at the two men on the floor. "We observed these men entering the building through the front door a few moments ago, then moved. I apologize that they were able to threaten you."

"It's all right. You did well."

"Thank you, sir, but we need to get you out of here immediately. There could be more on the way."

Tucker looked over at Angela. "Give me a moment alone with Ms. Day. We'll be right out."

"Yes, sir."

The three men were gone a moment later, dragging the prisoners out by their feet.

Angela stood up slowly, mouth open. "That man just called you 'sir,' " she said, her voice hushed. "And he saluted you."

"So?"

Her mind reeled as the lightning bolt struck. The man standing before her was not who he claimed to be. He was not a ranch hand. The man standing before her was one of the most powerful men in the world. "It's you," she whispered. "It's been you all along."

Tucker grinned. "What are you talking about?"

Angela swallowed, barely able to speak. "You're Jake Lawrence."

"That's ridiculous."

"Is it?" She pointed at him. "The man who attacked me in the cave in Wyoming said that I was supposed to be with Jake Lawrence."

"And you had been."

Angela shook her head. "No. He made it clear that it was his understanding that I was supposed to be with Jake Lawrence at that moment." And then it hit her. "Oh, Lord."

"What?" Tucker asked, still grinning.

"The handwriting on that ESP file. The one with the comment in the margin about Sumter and cloak accounts."

"Yeah? What about it?"

"It was your handwriting."

"No, no."

"Oh, yes. It matched the handwriting of the note you gave me in the parking garage that day you surprised me. When I was on my way to Rosemary to pick up Hunter. The note with your cell phone number on it. I knew there was something I was missing all along. You led me to the connection between Sumter and ESP. You wrote that note in the margin of the file while we were sitting at the conference room table."

Tucker stared back, saying nothing.

"No wonder I didn't find a record of anyone

named Tucker at any U.S. military base in Alaska. That was a lie, designed to keep the illusion intact."

"Angela, I —"

"That's why the guy in the woods was asking you about the network after the helicopter was destroyed. That's why the Jake Lawrence I met with didn't know whether the Lawrence family was originally from Atlanta or Birmingham, why you ran down Ted Harmon in that parking lot, and," she hesitated, "how you know about my tattoo. You watched me that first night I was at the lodge. You were behind the bathroom mirror. I know you were."

Tucker continued staring back at Angela intensely for several moments, his expression grim. Then his smile returned, broader than before. "I had to make certain it was you," he admitted quietly.

"What?"

"As my decoy told you in the cabin that day, I have to be very careful at all times. I had to make certain you were the real Angela Day. Not some imposter sent by a group trying to kill me." He chuckled. "My information was that you had a small tattoo of a butterfly on your hip. When I saw that, I was confident I wasn't dealing with an imposter. I was confident that you were the real Angela Day." He laughed again. "That was my only motivation in doing that. I assure you."

She shook her head, the enormity of it all beginning to sink in. "Why? Why all of this?"

"I'll explain everything," he assured her. "But let's get out of here. There's someone you need to meet with."

Carter Hill had called another emergency ExecCom meeting. This time they were in the basement of the West End church.

"There's been a development," he informed the other three. "The location on the South Side has been penetrated."

"Holy Christ!" Booker shouted, slamming the bridge table with his fist. "Are you serious?"

Hill nodded nervously. "Yes, I received word an hour ago. We sent people out there, but we think they were neutralized."

"What does that mean?" Abbott demanded. " 'Neutralized'?"

"We sent a second crew out to the location, but the initial team was gone. We think they were —"

"We need to destroy everything at that location," Booker broke in. "Immediately."

"That's already in progress," Hill agreed. "The operation has been terminated. But there's still a problem."

"What?"

"Certain very damaging files are missing. Files that could break everything wide open."

"What in God's name are we going to do?" Thompson demanded.

Hill closed his eyes tightly. "We have only one option."

"What?"

"I am certain I know who was responsible. Or was at least involved in the break-in."

"Who?"

"Angela Day."

Booker leaned back in his chair. "Jesus Christ. How do you know?"

"I had people following her tonight. Unfortunately, they lost her, but her actions were very suspicious."

"So what's the damn option?" Abbott asked nervously, understanding that all of their lives hung in the balance. "What are we going to do?"

Hill gazed at Abbott, fighting desperately to stem the awful panic that was building inside him. How could he not have seen this coming?

CHAPTER NINETEEN

"Where are we going and why won't you explain what's going on?" Angela dialed Liv's cell number for the third time since she and the man she now believed was the real Jake Lawrence had hurried back to the Jeep through the woods and raced away from the business park.

"Relax. You'll get your answers. I promise."

Angela listened as the phone rang over and over. "Dammit." She ended the call, a wave of fear washing over her.

"What's wrong?"

"I left Hunter with Liv Jefferson tonight," she explained. "There's no answer at her apartment."

"Liv is the newspaper reporter?"

"Yes."

"Well, she probably just turned the ring down because she didn't want Hunter to be awakened if someone called."

That made sense. "I hope so." Angela checked the side mirror. The guards were behind them in a van. Also in the van were the two prisoners and several incriminating files she had directed the guards to take from the Sumter location. "I don't even know what to call you now," she murmured.

"Jake. It'll be refreshing to hear someone call me that again after so long. Especially you, Angela," he said quietly, slipping his hand into hers and squeezing.

She glanced over at him. She wanted to squeeze his hand back. She wanted to let him know how she felt, but her mind was still reeling after learning his true identity.

A few miles down the lonely road, Jake pulled to a stop at the entrance to a driveway. The driveway leading to the farmhouse the Lawrence camp was using as its base of operations near Richmond. Two armed men moved out of the shadows to intercept the Jeep, then waved them on when they saw Jake and he answered their query with the evening's password.

When they reached the house, Angela hopped out of the Jeep, trotting to keep up with Jake. He held open the farmhouse door, ushering her inside and directing her down a narrow hall and then into a quaint living room. As Angela rounded the corner into the living room, she stopped short and brought her hands to her mouth. Bob Dudley sat in a large chair near a fireplace, arms folded across his chest.

"Hello, Ms. Day," he said quietly.

Angela turned to run, but Jake caught her, immobilizing her. "How could you do this to me?" she shouted, struggling to break free.

"Easy, Angela," Jake urged. "It's okay. Bob's on our side."

She stopped struggling and looked up into his large brown eyes. "What?"

Dudley rose from the chair. "It's true, Angela. Carter Hill and the ExecCom members are responsible for what you found. I wasn't certain who was involved until you led Jake to that Sumter location." He took a deep breath. "Candidly, I wasn't really even sure what, if anything, was going on until tonight. But now I know. My bank has been engaging in some despicable practices," he admitted dejectedly. "It appears that the documents you obtained tonight prove that beyond a shadow of a doubt. I'll need to review the information but, as difficult as it is for me to find out how dreadfully we have treated people, I'm glad to know that it will continue no longer. I owe you a large debt of gratitude."

Angela's arms dropped slowly to her sides as Jake relaxed his grip. "You aren't involved?" she asked suspiciously, her eyes flickering back and forth between Jake and the Sumter chairman.

"No, I'm not," Dudley said firmly.

"I've been working with Bob for months trying to figure out what, if anything, was going on," Jake confirmed. "And, if something was, how to uncover it."

"But you're the chairman of the bank, Mr. Dudley," Angela pointed out. "Why didn't you just carry out your own investigation?"

He nodded. "First, as I said, I didn't really

know for sure anything actually *was* going on," he explained. "Six months ago I received an anonymous tip that Sumter Bank was engaging in discriminatory lending practices. And that a company named ESP Technologies was somehow involved. That was it. Though I still don't know for certain, I assumed the tip came from someone inside ESP. Or, based upon tonight's events, someone out at the South Side facility you and Jake penetrated."

Angela spread her arms wide. "But if you remotely suspected that something was wrong, even just on the basis of an anonymous tip, I still don't understand why you didn't carry out your own investigation."

"I didn't know whom to trust," Dudley replied. "I had already turned the bank's day-to-day operation over to Carter Hill, and I had never really been close to the ExecCom members: Booker, Abbott, Thompson. And there's something you need to understand about being the chairman of an entity as large as Sumter, Angela. You can't even use the men's room without the whole bank knowing. My every move is carefully monitored. My fear was that I would do as you suggested, commission my own investigation, and that the discriminatory practices, if they were really being employed, would be covered up by people I didn't know I couldn't trust. Or, that they would simply suspend those illegal operations until the storm blew over." Dudley's expression turned grim. "I also assumed that they would figure I had a deep throat, figure out who that deep throat was, and do something to that individual. As we now understand, these men are evil. For all I knew they would seek revenge on the whistle-blower. That was something I was not willing to take responsibility for." He gestured at Jake. "So, I contacted Jake Lawrence."

"That's how you knew I had gone to Wyoming in the first place," Angela whispered.

"Yes," Dudley admitted.

"But why would you think Jake Lawrence would, or *could,* help you?"

"Our families have known each other for a hundred and fifty years," Jake explained, before Dudley could answer. "Bob's one of my closest friends. However, because of the illusion my father created thirty years ago, we aren't able to communicate much. But Bob was one of the few individuals that my father confided in when he sent me underground."

Angela could barely believe what she was hearing. "Why did your father do that?"

"We were already very wealthy at the time. But my father realized early on that his computer investment with the Harvard nerd was going to take us to a wealth level usually attained only by oil sheikhs and dictators. I was the only child, and he wanted to make certain I lived." Jake raised one eyebrow. "As you now know, Jake Lawrence is a constant target. My decoy told me you were skeptical when he made that remark to you in the cabin, but it's true."

She nodded. "I do understand that now."

"My father and I decided when I was young that I wasn't going to sit around with all of his money and do nothing. We decided, for better or worse, that I was going to take sides. That I was going to get involved. I've pissed off an awful lot of people in the process, and supporters of mine have paid the ultimate price. But they knew what they were getting into, and I have no regrets. Behind the scenes we've made a difference in many corners of the world, and I'm proud of that. Sumter Bank is just the latest example. We're about to win an important battle in the war on racism. I'm not naive enough to think that we can ever wipe it out, but I need to do my part. We all do."

"This is incredible," she said, her voice hushed.

"I try to make a difference, Angela. I can't just sit idly by and let the bad things go on. I've been given the ability to help. I'm driven to do so. It's my passion."

"How rich are you?" she asked.

"Let's put it this way. When the world finds out what was going on at Sumter, the bank's stock price is going to take a hit. Probably a big hit. Even if it goes to zero and completely wipes out my investment, my financial advisors will barely notice."

"Be more specific," Angela pushed.

He smiled. "As you might imagine, my net

worth changes on a minute-by-minute basis. But, as near as I can tell, it's close to $500 billion."

Angela gazed at Jake, astounded. "My God."

He nodded. "A little intimidating, huh?"

"Yes."

Jake chuckled. "I just have to hope that the United States' budget deficit doesn't get too bad because they might send somebody to kill me."

"Why?"

His eyes got big. "Estate tax rates are more than 50 percent. Killing me would be a quick way for the Feds to get their hands on about two hundred and fifty billion."

Dudley chuckled as Jake explained.

Angela smiled when she understood. "But why did you need to buy such a huge stake in Sumter?"

"To make the illusion seem real," Dudley answered for Jake. "I suspected that Carter Hill would be involved if there was anything to the tip. So Carter couldn't think that Jake and I were working together."

"So I kept buying Sumter shares to convince Carter that Bob really did hate me," Jake added. "To convince Carter that I might actually be secretly trying to take over the bank, and to put Bob out of a job. And to convince you, as well. You couldn't suspect the Jake Lawrence connection to Bob, either," he said, his voice dropping. "You had to believe everything was as advertised. Which was also why I instructed my decoy to make a pass at you in the cabin on the mountain. I needed Carter to believe that you hated me. Otherwise, he'd suspect that *you* and Jake Lawrence were working together." Jake reached out and took Angela's hand. "I'm sorry about that."

She nodded, then shook her head, impressed. "That's one hell of a plan."

"Yes," Dudley piped up. "Right down to me getting into that public spat with your reporter friend Liv Jefferson at the Richmond University business forum. Carter, or whoever was responsible, had to believe that I wouldn't have cared what they were doing anyway. I made Carter believe that I wouldn't be looking for the operation. I knew that if the tip was accurate, someone would be watching me."

"But there was a memo."

"A memo?" Dudley prompted.

Angela nodded. "Yes. I found it behind a shredder in Ken Booker's office a few weeks ago. It alluded to the discriminatory practices." She pointed at Dudley. "It was from the chairman to Booker, Abbott, and Thompson. Carter Hill wasn't mentioned anywhere."

"I assure you," Dudley replied coldly, "that memo wasn't from me. Whoever used the term 'Chairman' was using my authority as a cover."

"Did you pass that memo on to Liv Jefferson?" Jake asked.

Angela nodded. "Yes." She glanced at Dudley

— his expression was serious but not unkind — then looked back at Jake. "You were telling me the truth about not being Liv's contact. You weren't the one in the parking garage the other night. The one who told her about Mr. Dudley being from Birmingham. About him owning a consulting firm named Strategy Partners in Birmingham?"

"No, I wasn't."

That person had also conveyed to Liv that Dudley was using Strategy Partners to defraud Sumter. And that Dudley was a Klansman. Now that she knew the extent of Jake's relationship with Dudley, it was clear to her that Jake hadn't been the contact. All of the information the contact had provided was intended to incriminate Dudley.

"Strategy Partners?" Dudley asked.

"Yes," Angela responded, still trying to figure out who Liv's contact had been. Or, at least, who they were representing. "The person met Liv in a downtown parking garage one night last week and told her you were using a firm by that name in Birmingham to defraud Sumter. That you owned it and that you were having Sumter pay the company significant sums of money for doing nothing. There were wire transfers. Ten million dollars' worth. I've confirmed that." She was certain now who was responsible for those wires. And, by extension, who Liv's contact was. "But now that I understand what's going on, I'd be willing to bet a year's salary that Carter Hill was responsible for those wires. That the whole thing was an effort to frame you."

"He would have been able to arrange that," Dudley confirmed. "And he certainly had the motive."

"He wanted to run the bank," Angela said. "He wanted you out. He confided that to me at one point."

"Yes. He knew I wasn't going to recommend him to become my replacement when I stepped down as Sumter's chairman. I had told another board member that, and it clearly got back to Hill."

"It's all beginning to come together," she said quietly. Then she frowned. "What about Cubbies, though?"

"What about it?" Jake asked.

"I went through the client records at ESP and Cubbies never licensed their software. But I did some research and found that one of your entities did buy the chain."

"My decoy threw you that one at dinner to whet your appetite. You're right. Cubbies was never a client."

Angela glanced at Dudley, then back at Jake. "But why me, Jake? Why was *I* involved?"

"I needed someone who knew the bank," Jake explained. "Someone who could move around it without creating a stir. Someone who had witnessed racism from a front row seat, too."

"Sally," Angela murmured.

"Yes. And I needed someone with incentive," he continued.

"Hunter."

Jake nodded. "You have my word that I will continue that battle. And that you will win it."

A thrill coursed through her. Jake was one of the most powerful men in the world. Sooner or later he would prevail.

Jake smiled. "Plus, you're damn smart and you don't take 'no' for an answer." He leaned down and kissed her hand. "Bob and I *both* owe you a debt of gratitude."

When Jake rose back up she stepped toward him and slipped her arms around his neck, hugging him tightly. "Thank you."

"No, thank you. You have an incredible resolve about you. It is inspiring."

She stepped back, looking up at him. "Does Bill Colby know who you really are?"

Jake shook his head. "No. As a matter of fact, I was getting worried that Colby was catching on to me a few months ago, so I used you to convince him I was a traitor, and not even close to the real Jake Lawrence."

"How did you do that?"

"Through connections of mine, I commissioned a former CIA officer to assassinate Jake Lawrence. He'd become a soldier of fortune and was willing to make the hit. I had this individual shadow you with orders to kill me when I showed up on your doorstep." Jake laughed. "But the pictures I gave him of the supposed

Jake Lawrence were fuzzy as hell and of no one even remotely related to our camp, so I doubt he could have actually identified anyone. Of course, you never know what those guys are going to do. Anyway, we apprehended this man on the lawn of the house across from your apartment and brought him here to be 'interrogated.' During that interrogation, and after, I'm fairly certain I convinced Colby that I was helping this man. And, in the process, that I wasn't the real Jake Lawrence."

"Where is Colby now?" Angela asked.

"Protecting my alpha decoy."

"But what about the men who showed up tonight at the Sumter location? Wouldn't Colby have had to know about them? Wouldn't he have given them the order to follow you?"

"I keep an elite five-member force outside of Colby's purview. Men who know what the real deal is," Jake explained. "They operate within Colby's regular group, and he believes they are no different from any of his other men. That they report to him. But, on a covert basis, they report directly to me. Actually, I think that he began to suspect that there was a group within a group, and *that* was what led him to believe that I might be the real Jake Lawrence. I had to shut down that suspicion immediately. So I created the incident on the lawn across the street from your apartment." He hesitated. "I call on those men when I need them. Three of them tailed us tonight just in case, and they're in charge of this location this evening."

The room fell silent for a few moments, then Angela grinned. "This is incredible."

Jake nodded. "Yes, and now I think it's time for us to go to the authorities." He took Angela's hand once more. "I'm going to ask you to take the lead on that. As you can imagine, I don't want the publicity. It will be as if I was never there tonight. Okay?"

She understood. Finally. "Yes."

"There is one thing that bothers me, Jake," Dudley spoke up.

"What's that?"

"Before you two arrived, I called the Sumter individual who is in charge of site maintenance in the Richmond metropolitan area. He's a low-level ops guy, and I was fairly certain he would not be involved in Hill's conspiracy. Anyway, I woke him up and asked him what he knew about that location on the South Side where you two went tonight." Dudley paused, glancing at both of them. "He told me that Sumter doesn't operate any site in that business park. Given that information, it's possible that the people who staffed the office weren't actually Sumter employees either."

"So what does that mean?" Angela asked.

"Carter Hill obviously makes a nice buck as Sumter Bank's president," Dudley answered, "but not enough to support an operation like the one you two discovered tonight. Neither he nor his wife are from a great deal of money."

"Then there has to be an outside money source," Angela reasoned. "More people involved."

"I believe that's right. Which, if true, has some fairly serious implications."

Angela's eyes narrowed. "We need to find out who pays the rent on the space in the business park."

Dudley nodded. "Excellent thought. One I had as well. I ordered the ops guy I called to find out exactly that and he was able to do so. Turns out the business park where you all were tonight is owned by a group called Sage Capital."

Angela's mouth fell slowly open. "Sage Capital?" she whispered.

"Does that mean something to you, Angela?" Jake demanded.

"Do you know a man named Dennis Wolfe?" she asked Dudley.

Dudley snorted. "Of course I know Dennis. He worked for me for several years. He was a man I trusted. Then he went to work for your former father-in-law at Albemarle six years ago."

"You don't —"

"Don't care for Chuck Reese?" Dudley asked, anticipating her question. "No. In fact, I'm probably the only person in Richmond who hates Chuck Reese as much as you do."

Angela turned toward Jake, her eyes wide. "Oh, my God, I think I —" But her cell phone

429

rang, cutting her off. It was Liv, she figured, pulling the phone from her pocket. "Hello."

"Angela."

The voice sounded familiar, but she couldn't place it right away. "Yes?"

"Do you know who this is?"

She struggled, trying desperately to identify the caller. Then she realized who it was. "This is —"

"Carter Hill."

"What do you —"

"I want my files back, Angela. The ones you took from me tonight. If you give me those files, I will give you back your son."

Angela was silent, the breath sucked from her lungs.

"That's right. Hunter is here with me, and he's fine." Hill's voice turned vicious. "For now."

Carter Hill stood before Angela, his thin smile barely visible in the moonlight. It was just after three o'clock in the morning and dawn was still two hours away. She had come to the swing set of this small park in the West End immediately after getting off the phone with Hill, as he had demanded. But he had made her wait. On the ground beside her was a cardboard box.

"I assume those are my files," Hill said, nodding down at the box. "The ones you stole from the South Side location."

"Yes," she said, shivering. She'd been standing here for an hour, waiting for Hill to appear.

"You've made a wise decision, Angela. Without all of that evidence, no one will believe your accusations. The South Side operation has already been shut down. Nothing there now but empty desks." His smile grew wider.

"I don't care about anyone believing me. I just want my son back."

Hill motioned over his shoulder and a man appeared out of the darkness. "Take that," Hill ordered, pointing at the box.

"Yes, sir." The man picked it up, then melted back into the shadows.

"Now give me my son," Angela said, her voice rising.

"Not so fast. My people will need time to review the files to make certain everything is there."

"What! You promised me —"

"Shut up!" Hill hissed. "Or your little boy will end up like Liv Jefferson."

Angela caught her breath. "What do you mean?"

Hill chuckled. "Let's just put it this way. Your little nigger friend won't be writing any more columns about discriminatory banking practices."

Her hands began to tremble. "You killed her?"

"You said it, not me."

"You —" But Angela couldn't get the words out. She could feel the tears coming to her eyes and a terrible pain tearing at her heart. One she'd felt before.

"That will be all for now," Hill said calmly. "I'll be in touch."

As he turned, Angela saw the three flashes over Hill's left shoulder. The signal that the area had been completely secured. "Stop right where you are," she ordered, smoothly drawing the pistol Jake had given her and pointing it directly at Hill's chest as he turned back around. "Don't move."

Hill spotted the glint of the gun in the moonlight. "What the hell do you think you're doing? You'll never see your son again."

He took a step toward her and she cocked the weapon, the metallic click stopping him dead in his tracks. She wouldn't hesitate to follow her father's advice this time. "Take one more step, Hill, and I'll kill you," she said coldly.

"You're making a grave —"

But Hill didn't finish. Two of Jake's men appeared like ghosts from the shadows, hitting Hill at exactly the same moment. One high, one low. And a second later his wrists were cuffed securely behind his back. Then they had him on his feet, a rag stuffed in his mouth, and they were hustling him away toward the waiting van.

Angela let out a long, heavy sigh, uncocked the pistol, and brought her hands down.

Jake moved behind her and placed a hand on her shoulder. "I hope you know what you're doing, sweetheart."

CHAPTER TWENTY

The sun's first rays were just beginning to break through a thick cloud cover as the *Boston Whaler* motored along the north shore of the James River. When they reached land, Angela jumped to the bank, then darted into the forest along with five of Jake's men. They'd come from downstream, hugging the wooded shoreline, and they were headed for Rosemary — the pool house specifically. They planned to enter the estate there, then scour the entire complex until they found Hunter. Angela was certain her son was with Chuck Reese.

These were the last pieces of the puzzle for Angela: Bob Dudley and Chuck Reese's mutual hatred; Dennis Wolfe's defection from Dudley's Sumter Bank to Reese's Albemarle Capital six years ago; the fact that Sage Capital was the lessor of the space in the South Side business park; and Dudley's observation that Carter Hill would have needed a financial backer to support that South Side operation. These were the last few pieces and Angela was certain she knew exactly how they fit together. She was sure that Chuck Reese was the money behind everything.

Certain that once the forensic accountants had a chance to scrutinize the Albemarle and Sage records, they would find that Sage Capital was ultimately controlled by Albemarle. And she was certain that Dennis Wolfe had set up Sage for Reese after spending time at Albemarle.

Sage Capital had originally controlled ESP Technologies, had paid Strategy Partners' Alabama State Corporation Commission dues, and were the lessors of the South Side facility housing Sumter's mortgage screening operation. It was obvious now why Dennis Wolfe had defied Walter Fogel at the Proxmire board meeting last Sunday evening. Wolfe would have figured out what was happening and reported it all back to Reese. But she and Jake had gotten to Ted Harmon and pierced the corporate veil anyway.

The Carter Hill–Chuck Reese partnership made perfect sense to Angela. Hill and Reese both hated Dudley, and they both knew that what he treasured most in the world was Sumter Bank. To wrest control of it away from him would hurt him more than anything else could. So they'd agreed on a plan to frame Dudley for fraud in order to have him removed as chairman, while at the same time pushing a mutual agenda of housing discrimination against minorities by setting up the South Side operation. Hill needed financial support, and Reese needed someone inside to arrange the Dudley frame. A man who was ideally motivated. A man who would ascend to the Sumter throne — albeit ultimately reporting to Reese — should Dudley be deposed. It was a perfect match.

Fifty yards from the pool house Angela knelt down behind a tall oak tree. She was joined by the leader of Jake's team. "That's it," she confirmed, gesturing at the outline of the huge structure barely visible through the trees and the murky light.

"You should stay here until it's over, Ms. Day," the team leader advised. "Mr. Lawrence ordered me to make certain that you were not involved in a dangerous situation."

She shook her head. "I believe my son is in there. I'll be going in with you."

"Mr. Lawrence was very clear."

Angela placed her fingers on the young man's shoulder. "You can't keep me away. It's my son. Besides, I'm safer with you than out here."

The young man grimaced. "You must stay very close to me. Do you understand?"

"Yes." She would, too. She saw no sense in being a dead hero.

The leader signaled silently to the team and they stole the last few yards across the forest floor through the gloom to the pool house. When they had checked the interior through one of the floor-to-ceiling windows and had seen no one, one of the men produced a glass cutter and quickly sliced out a piece of the window while two other men kept the piece from falling by holding it up with suction cups.

When the glass had been removed and laid carefully on the ground, the leader nodded to the others. They had to be ready for alarms to go off as they entered the building. But, as the leader stepped onto the pool deck, everything remained quiet.

Angela stepped into the pool house's humid air last and followed the men as they sprinted for the door at the far end of the space. Behind the door lay the staircase leading down to the underground corridor connecting the pool to the massive main house. She had briefed the team on the structure's layout as they'd headed up the James toward Rosemary in the *Boston Whaler*.

At the doorway, they huddled together. "Let me go first," Angela whispered to the leader.

"Please don't put me in this position, Ms. Day. Please stay back."

"I'll be fine," she said, pulling out the pistol Jake had given her. She opened the door and crept slowly down the stairs, aware of muffled voices ahead as she and the rest of the team reached the bottom step and the corridor.

She moved forward, gun drawn, her heart racing faster as the voices grew louder and the words discernible. She recognized Chuck Reese's deep baritone, Hunter's giggle, and then Caroline's high-pitched tone. Then a voice that sent shivers up her spine. It was exactly as she had surmised. That could be the only explanation for the voice she had just heard.

Angela and the men moved into position outside the playroom door, inside of which the Reese family was assembled. The leader tapped her on the shoulder, then pointed, indicating that two of his men would lead the assault. That there would be no argument this time, and she nodded.

The leader held up three fingers, then two, then one, then pointed at the doorway and waved. The first two men tumbled into the large playroom, Glocks drawn, followed by the team leader, the other two men, then Angela.

It was exactly as she had anticipated. Chuck Reese and Caroline were sitting in large easy chairs. Hunter was on the floor, playing. And Bill Colby was standing behind Reese. What she hadn't anticipated were the three armed guards against the far wall. Men of Colby's command who brought their rifles down and began firing as she hurled herself behind a wooden chair in a far corner of the room.

Serenity turned to chaos, the angry spray of automatic gunfire tearing apart walls and bodies. Colby's shouts. Caroline's shrieks. Hunter's screams.

Angela rose up from behind the chair just as one of Jake's men tumbled back against a wall, his body riddled with bullets. One of Colby's men was doubled over as well, clutching his stomach, a dark river pouring from his abdomen. Chuck Reese was scrambling across the floor toward Hunter and Hunter was crying hysterically. She fired at another of Colby's men who was aiming at one of Jake's men, and he went down, shouting in pain and grabbing his thigh. Then she turned her gun on Colby who was racing for the door, firing twice.

She barely felt the bullet pierce her arm. At first it seemed like nothing more than the sensation of hot grease hitting her elbow, a searing sensation that would pass after the initial pain. She swung her firearm in the direction she believed the bullet had come from, focused on the last of Colby's men who was standing, and tried to pull the trigger. But her fingers failed to respond, and she dropped the pistol and grabbed her arm, aware that the man she had been aiming at had dropped to his knees and collapsed. Suddenly it seemed like her arm was going to fall off.

She glanced down and saw crimson dripping through her fingers, and her head began to spin. She looked away and up into the eyes of the leader, trying to think of anything but the searing pain.

"You all right?" he shouted.

She nodded, not at all certain she was. But then he was shoving Hunter into her arms and the little boy's panic-stricken grip gave her strength.

"Mom!"

"It's all right, honey. Everything's all right," she said, tears streaming down her face, aware that the whine of bullets was gone. "Mommy's here. Mommy won't let anything happen to you."

The room had gone still except for the groans of the wounded and Caroline's sobs. Colby, his three men, and two of Jake's squad were down. The leader of the team had already secured Chuck Reese, and another of Jake's men was escorting Caroline out of the playroom, her anguished cries fading as the man led her away.

"I've got to get you and your boy out of here, Ms. Day!" The leader was tugging on her good elbow. "There could be more of Colby's people around!" he shouted.

"Okay," she agreed groggily. But as she staggered from the playroom, Hunter's tiny hand clasping hers, she heard shouting down the corridor toward the house. "What's going on?"

"There's a guy down the hall holding a black woman hostage!" the leader hollered, dragging her along.

"What?" She stopped, halting on the first step leading up to the pool. "What did you say?"

"Come on, Ms. Day! I can't have you hanging around here. I must get you out of the area. Let's go!"

"No!" The man down the corridor was Sam. And the woman was Liv. Carter Hill had lied. They hadn't killed her. They'd brought her here when they'd kidnapped Hunter. She nodded down at the boy. "Get him to the boat! I'm staying."

"Ms. Day!"

"Do it!" she screamed.

The leader gazed at her intently for several moments, then clutched Hunter and raced up the stairs.

Angela watched until they had disappeared, then staggered down the corridor toward the shouting voices.

"I'll kill her, I swear!"

Angela came around the corner of a doorway to another, smaller playroom a hundred feet down the corridor from the room where they had just recovered Hunter. Sam Reese stood with his back to the far wall with Liv directly in front of him, one hand clasping her neck, the other a revolver pointed at her head. He was wild-eyed, the hand holding the revolver shaking crazily. Liv's eyes were shut tightly, tears streaking her face. Her wrists were secured behind her back.

"Get out of here!" he yelled at Jake's man, who was aiming his weapon at Sam from the doorway. Then he saw Angela. "Tell him, Angie. Tell him I'll do it. You know I will."

"Get out of here, Ms. Day!"

But Angela ignored the order from Jake's man, stepping into the room, clasping her bleeding elbow. She watched as the gun shook wildly in Sam's hand, and as Liv's eyes flew open at the sound of Angela's name.

"Don't come any further, Angie!" Sam yelled.

She took several more steps.

"Ms. Day, get back!"

"You set me up, Sam," Angela said quietly, now just a few feet away from him. "All of that talk about us having a better relationship. Bringing Hunter to me because he needed me. Defying your father. All lies. You and your father were setting me up so Carter Hill could kidnap Hunter when he was with me. So it could look as if I were the bad person when he was taken from me. That was your out. What were you going to do? Kill Hill and install your own man at Sumter? Then *negotiate* Hunter's return."

Sam smiled but remained silent.

"But you left too many tracks leading back to Rosemary."

"You always were too smart for your own good," he hissed.

Angela took another step forward, and Liv moaned as Sam pressed the barrel of the revolver hard against her temple. "What are you going to do, Sam?" She noticed out of the corner of her eye that Jake's man had moved into the room, sliding along the wall next to the doorway so he could maintain a clear shot at Sam. "Kill me?"

"I will if you don't get out of here."

"I'm not leaving." She wouldn't either. She hadn't been able to save Sally, but she was going to save Liv. "Not without my friend."

Sam laughed harshly. "Then I'll kill you both."

"Let her go and take me."

"No."

They were only a few feet apart now. "Could you really shoot me, Sam?" she asked softly. "Could you really kill me?"

Sam gazed into her eyes, holding Liv's chin tightly. "Don't make me do it," he pleaded.

"Let her go. I'll help you. I promise."

He shook his head slowly. "No, you won't."

"I will," she said firmly.

His eyes took on a distant look. "How could you?" he asked, his voice barely audible. "After what I've done to you." He shut his eyes for a moment, and his chin dropped subtly.

Angela leapt forward, grabbing Sam's wrist and pointing the gun toward the ceiling. The revolver exploded twice, then she lost her hold on his arm and the gun came down. The shiny black steel disappeared behind Liv. Angela grabbed Liv's shoulder and pulled her violently to one side, but an arc of red burst from Liv's dress and she tumbled forward onto the ground. Then the barrel of the black revolver was pointing directly at Angela.

Instinctively, she put her hands to her face and turned, waiting for the searing pain.

Sally Chambers. 1971–1994. That was all the tombstone said. It should have said much more.

No, Angela thought to herself. It shouldn't say anything because it shouldn't be here. *Sally* shouldn't be here.

She stared at Sally's name for a long time, hollow sadness building inside until her lower lip began to quiver. Finally, she knelt down and placed flowers beside the stone, the memory of how close they'd been still strong. The emptiness unremitting. How could humans be so awful? Why couldn't they just get along?

"You okay?"

"Yes," she whispered, feeling his hand come to her shoulder.

"Let's take a walk."

As she stood, she gazed at Jake. He'd gotten a haircut and shaved, and he looked good in his dark suit. No more John Tucker. He was all Jake Lawrence now.

A gentle breeze blew strands of long dark hair across her face, and Jake moved them away, caressing her cheek. Then he gestured at the field beside the cemetery. "Come on."

They walked across the new clover until they reached the banks of a stream meandering toward Asheville.

When they stopped, Jake took a deep breath and put his head back, looking up into the cloudless April sky. "God, it's a beautiful day." He glanced over at her. "It's good to be alive, you know?"

"Mmm."

They were silent for a long time, each alone with their thoughts as they watched the water meander past.

"How did you know I was here in Asheville?" Angela finally asked.

She hadn't seen Jake since the night two months ago when they'd broken into Sumter's South Side operation. Since the raid on Rosemary all communication had been with his "people," not him. But, as she'd walked out of her hotel this morning, he'd been standing beside a limousine, looking very gallant. And for some reason, despite not understanding how he could shut her out so easily after what they'd been through, she'd granted his request and allowed him to join her on one of her most personal moments of every year. Her visit to Sally's grave.

"I've had you under constant surveillance for the last two months," he replied.

Angela rolled her eyes. "Of course."

"It's been for your own protection. We pissed off a lot of people. I wanted to make certain no one tried to take revenge."

"Thanks."

She wanted to be angry at him. Angry for not getting in touch with her for two months. Angry for having so much money and so much power. But that was impossible because he'd followed through on his promise. Hunter was hers. The custody judge had ruled that the Reese family could never again have contact with Hunter. And that had been that.

"Have you been following the aftermath?" Jake asked.

"In the newspapers. Just like everybody else."

Chuck Reese was in jail, facing a long list of criminal and civil charges. Albemarle Capital had been liquidated. And Rosemary had been sold at auction.

"How's Hunter?"

"Fine, thank you very much."

"And Liv Jefferson?"

"She still has pain, but she's improving every day." Angela hesitated. "But I'm sure that's not news to you. Seems an anonymous benefactor has been paying her medical bills. You wouldn't know anything about that, would you?"

"Maybe," he admitted.

She took a deep breath. "Well, thanks again. Seems like I'll never be able to stop thanking you." And she hadn't even gotten around to

445

thanking him for the money yet. For the fact that she'd never have to work another day in her life.

A week after the raid on Rosemary, Jake's accountants had "gifted" her $5 million, informing her that if she didn't accept the money, Jake Lawrence had instructed them to burn that amount of cash on the street in front of her apartment. She'd accepted it because she knew he was serious, and what good would allowing someone to burn $5 million do anyone? And maybe she did deserve it. He'd put her in terrible jeopardy.

"I heard about your courage in that room at Rosemary," he said. "My man told me you saved Liv's life. He said that if you hadn't come in there and approached Sam, the odds were good that Liv wouldn't have made it."

"How would he know? Maybe if I hadn't done that, both Liv and Sam would still be alive."

Sam had been killed by Jake's man after shooting Liv. A single bullet to the brain.

"Would you rather Sam be alive and Liv be dead?"

"No," she said quietly.

"There couldn't be another Sally Chambers, could there?"

Angela felt him take her hand. "No," she whispered. "There couldn't."

"How did you know Hunter was at the Reese compound?" he asked, changing the subject.

"The Sage connection to Albemarle," she answered, clearing her throat. "Dennis Wolfe and the hatred between Bob Dudley and Chuck Reese. Reese was Carter Hill's partner, and I knew Chuck would never let anything happen to Hunter. No matter what I think of him, I know he'd *never* let anything happen to Hunter. Sam's willingness to let me see Hunter more than usual suddenly made sense. I think I always knew that Sam would never go against his father. But I chose to ignore that so I could see Hunter."

"Now you can see Hunter all the time."

She squeezed Jake's hand. "Yes, and there's no way I can ever repay you for that."

"You already have, Angela. You risked your life for a cause I feel very strongly about. You pulled the curtain back on an organization and an executive team that was engaging in blatant racism. We won a great victory thanks to you." Jake hesitated. "Sally would have been proud of you."

She swallowed hard, the emotion so close to the surface. For some reason she didn't want Jake to see it. Didn't want him to see her weak. Then he might know how much she had missed him during the past two months.

"Whatever happened to Bill Colby?" she asked when she had regained control.

"He's still recovering from bullet wounds to one of his legs. Seems this hotshot markswoman hit him twice during the melee at Rosemary. But he's resting comfortably."

"Comfortably?"

Jake laughed harshly. "Sure, in a ten-by-ten-foot cell."

"He was the one who arranged for that guy on the mountain to attack us."

"Yes. Colby had come to suspect that I was Jake Lawrence, and he was going to do away with me for Chuck Reese right there. Chuck was smart enough to figure out that very bad things were on the horizon when I started buying Sumter shares. He might not have known exactly what those things were, but he knew having me involved was bad for him. He figured if he cut off the head, the body would go away. And it would have if he'd been successful."

"When did Colby start to work with Reese?"

"We're still trying to figure that out. Best guess, about six months ago."

"Which is why you had that guy follow me the night I had dinner with Liv. To make Colby believe you were working with him. To make Colby believe that you were in on the plot to kill Jake Lawrence."

"Exactly. Then I couldn't be Jake Lawrence. That's also why Colby had the assassin on the mountain pushed off the cliff."

"So he couldn't point the finger at Colby."

"Yes," Jake confirmed.

"There's still one thing I can't figure out about ESP Technologies," Angela said.

Jake let go of her hand, bent down, picked up a small stone, and lobbed it toward a wide pool in the stream. "What's that?"

The stone splashed into the stream, and Angela watched the circles expand slowly outward. "Why would Sage Capital have sold ESP to Proxmire? Why would Chuck Reese and Dennis Wolfe have given up control like that?"

"My forensic accountants tell me Sage Capital had a number of investors, not just Chuck Reese. Reese arranged the partnership that purchased Sage, but he used other people's money in addition to his own to fund the partnership. And apparently the other investors were getting impatient for a return." Jake chuckled. "It's one of the irrefutable laws of finance. Investors demand a return. So, Reese got Wolfe the board seat at Proxmire, thinking he had protected himself because Wolfe could veto any sale of Proxmire." Jake tossed another stone into the stream. "His mistake was that he didn't count on a woman like Angela Day."

"Or a man like Jake Lawrence to help her."

"Right." He turned slowly to face her, then placed a finger beneath her chin and gently lifted so that she had to stare back at him again. "I want you to come live with me, Angela."

She gasped. "You want me to —"

"You're the most incredible woman I've ever known. I've thought of little else but you for the last two months."

"But you haven't even called me."

"You needed that time with Hunter. It was critical that you and he have no distractions for the last two months."

So that was it. Jake had recognized that Hunter had needed all of her attention. And Jake had been right. Hunter had been traumatized by what he'd witnessed at Rosemary. Only now was he becoming himself again. "You are incredible."

He chuckled. "Yeah, well."

"I feel terrible."

"Why?"

"I thought you hadn't called because . . . well, I figured you were done with me."

"Were you disappointed?"

She hesitated. "Yes."

"So will you come with me, Angela?"

The emotions swirled inside her. It would be an incredible life, but of course she'd be the prisoner in the gilded cell. Always wondering if he would make it home every night. She now appreciated how many people were out to get him. But she cared so deeply about him. Which would make the pain of losing him so much greater. The anxiety when he went away so much more terrible. She'd started her risk return calculation. "I can't," she said. This was not going to be analytical. "Hunter still needs me."

"I understand," Jake said quietly.

"I still don't know what to call you," she said.

"Huh?"

"I like Tucker better than Lawrence."

"Oh?"

"But I like Jake better than John."

450

He laughed, taking a step back. "I have to go."

"Another cause?"

"Yes," he said, turning to walk back across the field.

"Jake," she called after him.

They were a few yards apart now. "Yes?"

"I don't much like the name Angela, either."

"No?"

"No. I like Angie."

Jake shook his head. "Sorry, but I won't call you that."

"Why not?"

"Someone else already has." He gazed at her in the afternoon sunlight. "Just in case we ever see each other again, I've already decided what I'm going to call you. I've thought about it a lot over the last two months."

"What?"

"Annie."

She gazed back at him, replaying the name over in her mind several times. In that confident voice of his. She loved the sound of it. "Yes. That would be nice."

"Just in case," he repeated.

"Right," she said, breaking into a smile that told him everything he needed to know. "Just in case."

ABOUT THE AUTHOR

Stephen Frey is a principal at a Northern Virginia private equity firm. He previously worked in mergers and acquisitions at J. P. Morgan and as a vice president of corporate finance at an international bank in Midtown Manhattan. Frey is also the bestselling author of *The Takeover*, *The Vulture Fund*, *The Inner Sanctum*, *The Legacy*, *The Insider*, *Trust Fund*, and *The Day Trader*.